Master vs. Temptress:
The Final Submission

EM BROWN

ISBN-13: 978-1-942822-09-7

A GENTLE WARNING

This novel contains BDSM elements, themes of submission and dominance, and many other forms of wicked wantonness.

OTHER WORKS BY EM BROWN

For more about these wickedly wanton stories,
visit www.EroticHistoricals.com

GOT HEAT?

"Ms. Brown has written a tantalizing tale full of hot sex…a very sexy and sometimes funny read that will definitely put a smile on your face."

– Coffee Time Romance review of
AN AMOROUS ACT

"Darcy's fierce, independent spirit and unconditional loyalty to her family will win readers over, and Broadmoor is a romantic hero to swoon for."

- RT Book Reviews on
FORCE MY HAND

"Sometimes you just pick up the right book that just hits you and makes you really love it. This was one of those books for me. I just got so into the story and never wanted it to end."

- Romancing the Book review of
SUBMITTING TO THE RAKE

"HOT AND FUN TO READ!!!!!!!!"

- Reader review of
ALL WRAPPED UP FOR CHRISTMAS

"This one made me go WOW! I read it in a few hours which technically I probably should have gotten more sleep, but for me it was that good that I deprived myself of sleep to finish this most awesome story!"

"…sex was intense…thrilling…."

"I loved this book. Clever dialogue that kept m[e] laughing, delightful characters and a wonderful story. I am not generally one who likes historical fiction but this book carried me along from page one."

Master vs. Temptress:
The Final Submission

Chapter 1

C harles gripped the arms of his chair with such intensity that, had the chair been made of weaker material, it would have snapped in twain. He did not desire the demonstration taking place in the center of the parlor but was powerless to stop it.

How quickly his reign as proprietor of the Inn of the Red Chrysanthemum had come to an end! Having seen her sister recover her health, Joan had returned and resumed command of the little den where men and women indulged their most wicked carnal cravings. Tonight she wished to provide instruction to some of the members, and had chosen Miss Terrell for a model. It was a risky choice, for Miss Terrell was still spoken for by the influential Sir Arthur, a man of questionable patience and temperament.

Though he wanted to leave the room, Charles found he could not. He had come under Miss Terrell's spell and sat mesmerized by her dark beauty. At first, he had not been partial to her darkness. Having recently concluded his travels in the Orient, where fairness was the mark of beauty, he had come to appreciate the contrast of ebony hair and pale complexions. But Miss Terrell had thrust herself upon him, smothering him with her allure till he had to surrender lest he suffocate.

Possessed of features that transcended her coloring—penetrating eyes fringed with long lashes, a smooth and unblemished countenance, and a form that enflamed a man's lust—Miss Terrell had no shortage of members interested in her favors.

Charles could not tear his gaze from her supple body reclined upon the sofa. Her breasts, slightly larger than he preferred, called for his hands to sink themselves into their flesh. Her hips flared almost as wide as her shoulders. The expanse of her belly, made provocatively perfect by the navel, never failed to cause his cods to boil. Then there was that triangle of black curls set between succulent thighs. The rest of her legs had shape, the proportion of thighs and calves all designed to entice.

He tried not to mind the equally naked fellow, Jones, beneath her, stroking her body with his large dark hands. As much as Charles dreaded the impending show, he knew he would witness it all.

"The man with the longer cock should take the rear position," Joan explained.

An uncomfortable current reverberated down Charles' legs, but there was no denying his cock had stiffened. Jones handled his impressive length. Miss Terrell spread her legs that the audience might see the penetration of cock into cunnie, moaning as the shaft disappeared inside her.

"Now the second," said Joan.

Master Troy, also naked, approached the sofa. A brawny man, Master Troy had a thick cock, which he pointed at Miss Terrell. She lifted her back leg, stretching the area between her thighs.

"Moisture is essential," Joan continued, "and I urge you to avail yourself of the many oils we have."

Having received an application of oil, Master Troy's cock gleamed. He positioned himself between the two pairs of legs, Terrell's and Jones', then slowly pressed his tip into her folds. Miss Terrell groaned, her eyelashes fluttering, at being stretched by the two men. Though this was not the first time her cunnie had swallowed two cocks, Charles wondered that a single cock—namely, his—could ever satisfy her hence. Never mind that she had never failed to spend with him before. The look of pleasure floating across her face made only the present matter. Master Troy had now sunk his entirety into her.

"As you might expect, it is easier for the cock on top to guide the action," Joan said.

Jones wrapped his arms about Miss Terrell to hold her in place as Master Troy began to move in and out of her. Her head fell back. Grasping the undersides of her thighs, she pulled her legs close to her chest to allow a better visual of the two cocks penetrating her.

Charles could not look away, a mix of emotions churning in him. There was something both provocative and emasculating in seeing Miss Terrell fucked by two men, one possessing the longest cock Charles had ever seen and the other possessing a stout one. Knowing that she drew delight from being filled to the brim and imagining how it must feel to rub against another man's erection inside her hot wetness, how tight the presence of a second cock must make her, added to the heady scintillation. It was all very wanton.

"Is it possible to add a cock to her bum?" asked a

man in the audience.

"It is possible," Joan replied, "and we may have Miss Terrell demonstrate that tomorrow evening."

Charles groaned inwardly. The thought of *three* cocks filling her lit a fire in his mind and his crotch. He ought not care, for he had shared a woman before, both in his time in the Orient and in his time at the Red Chrysanthemum. Why should Miss Terrell be any different? She was not his. To begin with, he had not wanted her. Yet he could not deny that jealousy tugged at his groin.

"We can add a third cock to her mouth," suggested another member.

"But how could the third man conveniently place himself?" asked a woman.

"He could stand on one leg and prop his other foot on the sofa, straddling them. It can be done."

"Let us see."

Joan turned to Miss Terrell. "Would you like another cock, *ma cheri?*"

"Always," the Negress sighed as Master Troy found a rhythm.

"And whose cock do you desire to taste?"

Terrell turned to the audience and stared at him. "Charles."

Joan raised her brows. "Whose?"

"Charles…Charles…"

Something poked him in the ribs, rousing him from his reverie. He pried open an eye to behold a beautiful woman with crystal-blue eyes that turned grey with concern.

"This is the best aria of the opera," she said.

Charles started, realizing he was not at the Red

Chrysanthemum but at a box in the King's Theatre at Haymarket. Instead of three naked bodies rutting before him, he beheld the singers for *La Clemenza di Tito.*

The woman who had prodded him in the ribs with her fan was his mother. He immediately straightened in his chair and conveniently allowed the playbill he held in his hand to drape over his crotch in the event that his Thomas be up. He shifted in his seat. It was bad enough that his body could not resist Miss Terrell when he was conscious. She had to seduce him in his dreams as well.

He turned his attention back to the stage several stories below, where Sesto sang of his decision to assassinate the emperor Tito at the urging of his lover, Vitellia.

"Parto, parto, ma tu, ben mio..."

Charles managed to sit through the rest of Act 1 without dozing off. Remembering how he had woken covered in his own seed the first time Miss Terrell had entered his dreams, he was determined to stay awake.

At the intermission, Mr. Jeffers, with whom they shared the box, said, "These librettos all bear the same story. Some poor fool of a man falling prey to a woman's wiles. Love makes fools of our sex, eh, Charles?"

Charles smiled graciously. "And we are better for it."

"Bah! Only a woman would request murder be committed out of jealousy."

"I hope you will not ascribe the qualities of Vitellia to all our sex," protested Mrs. Jeffers.

"No, just as I would not ascribe the qualities of Sesto to all men."

Mrs. Gallant blithely asked, "Do you mean to say you will not commit murder if your wife asked it of you?"

"I most certainly would not."

Mrs. Jeffers sighed. "His devotion does not run as deep as that of Sesto."

"Such fanciful devotion only exists in operas and Greek tragedies. No man of sound mind would commit a crime on behalf of a woman. Eh, Charles?"

Charles said nothing at first, but to keep the *tête-à-tête* lighthearted, he replied, "But you have noted that love makes fools of our sex; thus, we are not of sound mind when we act."

"I question the soundness of men, with or without the effect of love," Mrs. Jeffers quipped.

Mrs. Gallant chuckled. "And all's well that ends well, as we shall see in the next act. For myself, I am less concerned with the libretto than the music of Mozart. There is not a composition of his that does not enthrall me."

"Perhaps I would appreciate it all better with some refreshment," Mr. Jeffers declared. He and his wife stood. "Will you join us?"

"Perhaps in a moment."

When their friends had left, Mrs. Gallant turned her attention to her son. "I have never known you to fall asleep to Mozart. You enjoy his compositions more than I. Have you not been sleeping well?"

"Perhaps a few more hours would do me well," he admitted.

"Is Sir Canning working you too hard? Is he aware

of how much you have applied yourself to your election?"

"While my plate is full, it is not all the fault of Sir Canning."

She narrowed her eyes. "Then whose fault *is* it?"

Mrs. Gallant had always been an astute woman, but Charles was not prepared to divulge the most recent culprit of his sleeplessness. Instead, he said, "Joan was in need of a favor, and I agreed to assume supervision of the Red Chrysanthemum in her absence."

His mother raised her brows. "She would ask this of you when you are in the midst of an election?"

"Her sister is ill, and she found no other she could turn to."

The mother hen was not satisfied. "I think Joan takes advantage of your friendship with her."

"Worry not, my dear. It is only for a sennight."

She sighed. "At times, I regret I had discovered the Red Chrysanthemum to you."

Drawing upon a philosophy espoused by Miss Terrell, he replied, "Why mourn that which you cannot change?"

"I suspect that the Red Chrysanthemum is the reason you remain unmarried."

Charles drew in a long breath. He had been happy to escort his mother, who was staying in town with the Jefferses, to the opera but for the subject of matrimony, which he knew would arise in her company.

"You do not lament the state of bachelorhood of your older son," he answered.

"Because your brother is not here, and his

prospects at sea are next to nothing, and I *do* lament his lack of a wife. I fail to understand how I can have two sons, both of them handsome and with many qualities to recommend them, who have yet to secure a wife."

In their last conversation on the matter, Charles had considered, albeit fleetingly, the notion of seeking Miss Greta's hand, but it was clear she wanted little of him, her heart being still bound to Master Damien. It was just as well. The daughter of an apothecary, she was far beneath his station.

"The Dempseys are here tonight," Mrs. Gallant noted, peering out the box through her opera glasses. "How pretty Miss Dempsey looks!"

He kept his gaze upon his mother. "Miss Dempsey never fails to look pretty."

"But she is particularly fetching tonight, I believe. Look at her. Do you not agree?"

"I doubt I would."

She lowered her glasses and gave him a cross look. "You are intent on trying my nerves tonight."

"Your pardon, my dear, but do you, in all honesty, think Miss Dempsey would suit me for a wife? Aside from her beauty and her manners, what qualities recommend her to me?"

Mrs. Gallant relented. "I suppose Miss Pembroke, though a bit plain, would have a suitable temperament for you. Many consider her a bluestocking, but I suppose you might be rather pleased with someone who could converse well on all subjects. Her mother does send me quite the number of invitations, and I suspect it is not my company they truly seek."

"Both Miss Dempsey and Miss Pembroke hail from good families, wealthy families. They have known only a life of privilege."

"And you fault them for this?"

"What do they know of life outside a well-appointed drawing room or the grandeur of a dance hall?"

"The Pembrokes are quite active in their charity towards the poor."

"It is one thing to witness the impoverished conditions of another people from a place of privilege, quite another to face these conditions on a daily basis."

"Good gracious, what sort of woman are you seeking?"

"Struggle builds character."

"It would seem you consider wealth and privilege vices"

"They are not virtues."

"Then how do you consider yourself and your own family? Would you spurn me if I were an eligible young maiden?"

He took his mother's hand and kissed it. "My dear, I yearn to meet a woman of your likeness. I should have no qualms to fall on bended knee if I did."

"Your flattery is very pretty, but I am not convinced. You have found yourself a wench at the Red Chrysanthemum."

He started. How was it mothers could discern these things?

"That is the only explanation," she continued, "for your lack of interest in the many young women who have been partial to you."

Though many women of polite society would gladly have received a marriage proposal from him, the two women who would offer him no commitment came from the Red Chrysanthemum and were of significantly lower stations. Miss Terrell, a former slave, had yet to agree to forsake Sir Arthur for him.

"The women of the Red Chrysanthemum may satisfy your carnal desires, but can they satisfy your heart?" she inquired.

"Father found *you* at the Red Chrysanthemum, and I challenge any man to find better."

"I am not saying that I am such a thing, but your father could have done far better than me, and I am grateful that he cared not I was of the *bourgeoisie*, but I do think the quality of women there has declined since Joan became proprietor."

"I beg to differ, but worry not; I do not seek a wife at the Red Chrysanthemum."

At present, despite what he had avowed but days before, he only sought a submissive. No. Not a submissive. He sought Miss Terrell.

His mother nodded. "When it is the Season, and you have been elected MP, there will be women enough setting their caps at you. I should not be surprised if you received an invitation to the opening ball at Almack's even. Perhaps it is just as well you have no prospects at the moment. What that Whig paper printed of Mr. Chester's betrothed was beyond harsh."

Mrs. Gallant alluded to *The Independent*, which had investigated the intended of Mr. Chester a fellow candidate for the burgess of Porter's Hill, and found her claims to certain families of standing were greatly exaggerated.

Charles was reminded of yesterday, when he had stood outside a millinery shop where he had purchased a new bonnet for Miss Terrell, and had had a strange sensation that they were being watched. If *The Independent* should have seen him with a blackamoor, he did not doubt they would make mischief of it.

"You must take care," his mother advised, "with your involvement at the Red Chrysanthemum. I do hope Joan returns soon. If it should be discovered what the Red Chrysanthemum is about, it could ruin your career."

"Many an MP has weathered scandal. Even Sir Arthur."

"Yes, I do not recall the details of that, as your father was doing poorly at the time and I did not pay attention to the gossip of town. When does Sir Arthur return?"

"In no less than a sennight, I believe."

"You are assured victory if he and the Brentwoods support you. Well, Sir Arthur alone should be sufficient. But it would look quite admirable if you had both of them. If Sir Canning should become Prime Minister, you might be looked upon to succeed him as Foreign Secretary."

Sir Canning himself had said as much, and Charles would be delighted to assume the position if the opportunity arose, but first he had to succeed to Parliament. He could make the prospect a near certainty if he simply accepted the support of Sir Arthur, but the two did not see eye to eye, and, unlike Emperor Tito in Mozart's opera, Sir Arthur was not inclined toward clemency to his detractors.

"Surely the Brentwoods are aware of your promise," Mrs. Gallant said. "I know Mrs. Brentwood to have been away for some time, but now that they are returned to Porter's Hill, they are certain to make an endorsement. She can have nothing against you save that your mother came from the *bourgeoisie.* She considers herself high and mighty, but I think her rather old fashioned for putting so much stock in my background. Nevertheless, I am most sorry that you have to bear me for a burden."

"You are *not* a burden," he insisted. "I met with Mrs. Brentwood two days ago. She is inclined to support me, and the only pause to declaring her unequivocal endorsement is my commitment."

"Your commitment?"

"She wishes me to withhold support of the abolition of slavery till a more appropriate time."

"Oh." She knit her brows. "What does she consider a more appropriate time?"

"Ten years, mayhap more. Her brother is a plantation owner in the West Indies and dependent upon the economy of slavery."

"That is unfortunate, but ten years may pass easily. Or perhaps she will see fit to approve of abolition before then."

"Perhaps. But even ten days must seem an eternity to a slave."

"You have strong opinions on the matter?"

"You and I both believe slavery a wrong."

"Yes, but we cannot right all the wrongs in a day. These things take time."

"She made a reasonable case for the benefits of

proceeding cautiously and not implementing wholesale abolition throughout the empire without considering the devastation it would impose upon her colonies."

"The slaves might rise and, in vengeance, take arms against their former masters."

"They do so now in quest of their freedom."

His mother sighed. "You are your father's son."

The senior Gallant, who had thrice sought and thrice failed to secure the burgess of Porter's Hill, had refused to acquiesce to a similar stipulation of the Brentwoods for him to support the proposals of the Society for the Suppression of Vice.

"I have not yet rendered a pronouncement either way," he assured her.

"Well, with Sir Arthur's support, theirs becomes less critical."

It would be an easy matter to refuse Mrs. Brentwood if the support of Sir Arthur were not so important. Although most considered Mr. Chester, the other Tory seeking the burgess, a pretentious idiot, the man would undoubtedly prostrate himself for Sir Arthur's support.

"Oh!" his mother exclaimed as she peered over the balcony to another across the theater. "Is that not Regina? I did not know her to be in town."

Following her gaze, Charles saw a beauty of chestnut hair in restrained yet elegant dress. "It does look to be her. I ought pay my respects if she is in town. I was grieved to hear of Richard's passing."

"The earl passed some time ago. She is no longer in mourning. I thought you would have called upon her already. The two of you were good friends."

"She had little time to nurture our friendship once she became a countess."

"I thought her rather partial to you once."

"If she was, it was many, many years ago."

"I was rather surprised that she accepted the earl's proposal."

Charles had not been, for he knew Regina cared for the elevation that marriage to an earl would bring to her family. He could see his mother was prepared to launch into a recollection of the many qualifications of the countess when Mr. and Mrs. Jeffers returned.

"Tell me, does Vitellia see the consequences of her actions or must man bear the brunt of women's mischief?" Mr. Jeffers asked as he settled into his chair with his confections.

"You wish again to draw inferences of mankind from an opera?" Mrs. Gallant challenged.

"Do you think it mere coincidence that in almost all operas, the troubles of men begin with women?"

"That is because such stories are written by *men*," Mrs. Jeffers returned.

"Charles, do you not agree that women be the doom, the downfall, of our sex?"

Charles smiled. "If we could not possess their love another way, then we would have it all and gladly."

As the curtain rose on Annio telling Sesto that the emperor was still alive, Charles thought of Miss Terrell and had the odd sensation, though he could ascribe no reason for it, that she might very well spell his doom.

Chapter 2

I wonder who is the true sow," Sophia remarked to Lydia, "for see how she eats."

Sitting at the dinner table across from the flaxen-haired beauty, Terrell looked down at her plate to see that she had eaten it clean.

"I wonder that she will become as *fat* as a pig—no, *fatter*. What animal is more grossly corpulent than a pig?"

Terrell wanted to ignore Sophia, her least favorite member at the Red Chrysanthemum, but the words had an effect. Having come to England a thin and gawky creature, she liked the current suppleness of her body. The response she received from the other sex validated the appeal of her curves, but she had seen many a cartoon mocking Creoles. The drawings nearly always portrayed Creole women as fat and indulgent. Terrell had no desire to become one of those caricatures. She placed her last bite of bread upon her plate.

"But we have already seen what manner of animal these blackamoors can be," Sophia sniffed. "Little better than rabid beasts."

Terrell wanted to reach across the table and strangle the pretty swan-like throat of Miss Sophia, who was possessed of a most slender form but a buxom bosom. But her last reaction to Sophia's mischief had landed her a sound punishment from Master Gallant. Reminding herself to behave, Terrell bit back a rejoinder.

Sitting beside Terrell, Miss Sarah, with whom she shared a room, looked across at Sophia but said to Terrell, "She means to bait you. Do not mind her."

"Perhaps a good disciplining from a Master would improve her mood," Terrell could not resist, "if she had a man who would take her."

Sophia's eyes widened and her cheeks colored. Speaking through clenched teeth, she said, "I suppose if I had a mouth as large as yours for the swallowing of cock, I would not want for men eager to spill their seed down my throat."

"Miss Sophia," called the matronly cook from the other end of the table, "what are you grousing at? Apply yourself to your supper, for I intend to have the table cleared shortly."

Sophia paid no more attention to Terrell. Instead, they listened to the cook complain of Wang, a Chinaman who did not dine with the others, using her kitchen to cook his own meals with foul-smelling ingredients.

After supper, they had an hour before any of the members of the Red Chrysanthemum would arrive to satisfy their prurient appetites in wicked fashion. Terrell and Sarah watched George attempt to walk down the hall. Sarah's son, nearly a year and six months of age, had taken his first step with Terrell at St. James' Park but days before.

Terrell recalled the day with fondness. The wind had swept away her bonnet into the waters near Duck Island, and Master Gallant had walked her to a millinery shop and purchased her a new one. Though she, having been a courtesan to men of greater wealth, had once possessed far fancier hats, she prized her current bonnet with its tri-colored sash, because of the way he had looked at her when she wore it. His expression had not been one simply of lust, for when that urge rose in his sex, they could look upon most anything with desire; rather, his countenance had seemed to bear the sentiment of *affection*. How her spirits had soared then!

She ought not care quite so fervently of his reactions. Her carnal response to him, to his body and what he did to hers, did not alarm her as much as her response to him when they were not in the throes of passion. While she craved his touch like no other, counting the hours when he would arrive, impatient for his valet, Wang, to fetch her that he might prepare her for Master Gallant, she likened the yearning to that which a drunkard might possess for drink. But the enjoyment of the simple things, as when they had read from *Fanny Hill* last night, the emotions that had rushed through her when he had asked that she become his submissive, those concerned her, for they spoke to sentiments far more dangerous than lust.

From the beginning, she had wanted him for a Master. His dominance of Mistress Scarlet had enthralled her. But he had resisted, claiming he wanted no submissive, for his election occupied his time, and Mistress Scarlet his heart. Terrell knew not the depths of his feelings for the former Mistress, but she had not cared. She wanted only for him to wrap her in his wonderful rope bondage and for him to enjoy her as much as she would him.

He had asked her to be his and his alone. Their ensuing kiss had contained more depth, more passion than she had ever known. Of course she would be his, thrilled to be his submissive and have him as her Master.

But he had asked that she forsake Sir Arthur, still in Somerset for at least a sennight, mayhap more. She had not considered what she might do when Sir Arthur returned. Sir Arthur was one of the wealthiest men in all of England. If she could win his heart and become his courtesan, she could return to the grandeur she once commanded, a life that no slave would have dared dreamed possible. She had had a townhouse, servants, and gowns more splendid than those of her former mistress in Barbados. From field slave to a courtesan *extraordinaire*. She herself would never have thought it possible.

Lady Luck, however, was a fickle mistress, and Terrell had found herself back in poverty when the wife of her paramour demanded her ejection. Terrell had learned her lesson, however. She would save the money she earned while serving the members of the Red Chrysanthemum, find another paramour, and conserve her pin money this time that she might never have to worry of destitution and despair. Freedom tasted less divine when faced with hunger. Sir Arthur, wealthy, powerful, and of fair enough countenance, was the means to a much better life.

"You are quiet tonight," Sarah observed.

"I was merely thinking of Master Gallant," Terrell replied.

Sarah's eyes gleamed. "Of course."

Terrell hesitated. She wished to confide her

dilemma to Sarah, but Sarah was wary of Sir Arthur and his temper. For certain she would urge Terrell to renounce his patronage.

"Do you think you will enjoy another night's reprieve?" Terrell asked.

"I hope to. Madame Devereux had thought I, being formerly a lady of gentle society, might offer an experience different from..."

"From the likes of I, Sophia, Lydia."

"Yes, well, it would seem I am not as desirable as Madame believed. Of course I would prefer to spend every night with Georgie if I could, but Madame is prudent. If the cost to provide my room and board should exceed what I am able to attract, I wonder where Georgie and I could turn to next?"

In that moment, Terrell reconsidered her desire to return to that *gentle* society that would so easily turn its back on its own. Even Sarah's own family had refused to have anything to do with the condemned adulteress. Sarah herself had made it difficult for any friend to extend her a helping hand when she had stolen away Georgie, rightfully the property of her husband.

"Perhaps you could find yourself a man willing to keep you and Georgie in secret," Terrell suggested.

"No man would undertake such an effort for me lest he was smitten, and I hardly think the Red Chrysanthemum a place where love might spring."

"If I could become the courtesan of the likes of Sir Arthur, I would help you and Georgie where I could."

Sarah came as near to a friend to Terrell as anyone. Perhaps the only one. In England, those who Terrell had thought to be friends had revealed themselves less than true when the wine no longer flowed and the music and parties ceased.

"Is it wise to fancy the likes of Sir Arthur?"

Terrell silently sighed, for she had not wanted to provide Sarah an opening to air her misgivings of the man. Believing herself to possess a stronger constitution than Sir Arthur's deceased wife, Terrell was confident she could handle the man, even if he did cause her unease.

"It is only important that he fancies me," Terrell stated.

"What of Master Gallant?"

"What of him?"

"He is partial to you, and you cannot deny that you are partial to him."

"And when Madame returns, he will be done with me. You yourself have wondered that he has not taken a wife. There must be dozens of women vying for his attentions. I imagine he only waits till the election is over, then he can properly attend to the business of matrimony."

Sarah made no protest. She was no simple schoolroom chit and knew all too well the expectations that a gentleman like Charles Gallant must satisfy.

While his proposition to Terrell suggested that he might wish to continue his dalliance with her past the time when Madame and Sir Arthur would both return, the day would come when they would part ways. The man had too much integrity to betray his inevitable matrimony or do so without great pain and strife to himself. Thus, Sir Arthur was the safer option. Possessed of an heir, Sir Arthur had no need to marry again. His standing assured, he could take whomever he pleased for a courtesan with barely a repercussion.

"But I do intend to make the most of my time with Master Gallant," Terrell said with a wicked smile.

Sarah returned her smile, then looked past her. "Speaking of whom…"

Terrell turned to see Wang, Gallant's Oriental valet. She had not heard his approach. The man had the lightest foot tread. While only a little taller than the women, he was not so small that he ought not go unnoticed. She suspected a sinewy build beneath his garments and found herself wondering what he might look like naked.

Wang said nothing, but she knew his purpose. He had come to prepare her for Master Gallant, and her pulse quickened at the prospect.

"Georgie and I will expect to have the room to ourselves tonight, then?" Sarah whispered before going to fetch Georgie, who had made it a third of the way down the hall.

Terrell hoped so. Without word, she followed Wang up the stairs to Madame's chambers, which Gallant now occupied. In the bedroom, she saw that he had the customary tray of tea, most likely of the Chinese green variety that she was less fond of, set in the sitting area. She settled herself in one of the chairs, reclining with her legs thrown over an arm, as he poured her a cup.

"And where is Master Gallant this evening?" she asked, though she knew that the chance of the taciturn valet answering was low.

He gave her a blank stare, which she took to mean

that she should have known better than to ask. After handing her the cup of tea, he went to the bed, where he had laid out a roll of black fabric, long and narrow, like bandages. He waited patiently for her to finish.

Having learned her lesson not to drink too much of the tea, Terrell finished the one cup and sprang to her feet. "What have we in store for Master Gallant tonight?"

With a simple sweep of his eyes, he indicated she should undress. In a short period of time, she had learned the language of few words with Wang.

"To the buff?" she inquired. "Or, rather, to the black?"

He did not refute her assumption, so she deduced the answer to be an affirmative.

"A little assistance then, if you please," she said, turning around that he might access the pins in her gown.

He removed the pins with the thoroughness of a dressing maid, and she wondered if there was any task that he could not master. While he placed the dress over the back of a chair, she undid her petticoats and unlaced the ribbon in the front of her stays.

"No need to treat them so gently," she said when the placed the petticoats with equal care. "My garments aren't so fancy."

She had once had gowns of such delicate weaves that she hardly trusted her maids with them. If she were the courtesan of Sir Arthur, she would have such fine gowns once more, perhaps finer.

As she undid a garter and stocking, she noticed a slight tenting at Wang's crotch. It called to her own arousal. She recalled the first time he had seen her naked, how he had pressed two metal balls into her cunnie, delighting her with their vibrations whenever they moved inside of her. She had never lain with an Oriental before.

"Has Master Gallant granted you membership here?" she asked.

Retrieving the black fabric from the bed, he said nothing.

She lowered her gaze to his groin. "Do you suppose he would allow me to provide you a bit of relief? Perhaps you ought suggest it to him as a reward for services rendered?"

This time Wang hesitated. It was the first time she had unsettled the stoic valet.

"It must be rather difficult to perform your tasks without arousing any tension," she said, slipping the final stocking from her leg and standing without a shred of clothing before him.

He did not ogle her as many others of his sex would, but she suspected he took in the sight of her body nevertheless.

"What do you do?" she asked when he pressed one end of the long narrow fabric to her head. She trusted Master Gallant, and thus trusted Wang, but hoped he would answer her.

He did not.

Reminding herself that a good submissive would accept her Master's bidding without question, she remained still and ceased to pester the valet with further questions. Shortly, her ability to question him, even had she desired to do so, was cut off, for he had encased the whole of her head with the black silk bandages. He had swathed the top of her head, covering her eyes, across her nose, though he left the nostrils free, and around her mouth. The wrapping took sight and speech from her. He continued down her body, binding her arms to her sides as he wound the fabric around her, past her derriere and down her legs. He lifted her with ease and placed her upon the bed to finish wrapping her feet. When he was done, she was completely encased from the top of her head to the tips of her toes.

She tested the tightness of the bindings and found she could not even move her fingers more than half an inch to the sides. Rendered immobile, unable to speak or see, she could do nothing but lay upon the bed. She thought she heard Wang leave, but she could not be certain. Alone in her cocoon, she was confident of only her breath. She listened to her breathing, felt the air through her nose and the rise and fall of her chest. Boredom set in quick. She wondered what Master Gallant would do to her. What could he do if she was swaddled as thoroughly as a mummy? How would he be able to fuck her?

With these thoughts, she passed the time and became aware of a slow heat building within her. She wanted to touch herself and wriggled in her frustration, but the effort only made her bindings feel tighter. Relenting, she lay still. The tension in her loins called, wanting attention, craving touch, but she was utterly helpless. If anyone should come upon her, they could do anything with her, and she would be powerless to stop them. A brief panic overcame her. Though no one at the Red Chrysanthemum, save Sophia, had ever attempted anything untoward against her, she trusted no one save Sarah and Master Gallant.

Surely no one would dare come into Madame's chambers, though the proprietress was not expected to return for several days. Terrell took in a deep breath. But how long would she have to wait before Wang or Master Gallant returned?

Her attention turned once more to the stirring in her groin, the yearning between her legs. She flexed her cunnie. She could make herself spend, but she needed Gallant's permission first. And he would know if she had. Even if she lied, he would see the truth in her eyes. And she had no wish to lie to him. She had vowed she could be the perfect submissive, the best he ever had, and she would keep her promise.

Chapter 3

Though fatigue had overcome him during the performance of Mozart's *La Clemenza di Tito*, Charles stepped across the threshold of the Red Chrysanthemum with vigor. He knew that Miss Terrell played a significant part of his renewed wakefulness. She would be in his bed now, wrapped in black silk, with only her thoughts and her breath to occupy her.

But first, he had the business of the inn to tend to. Though he had been reluctant to assume his post, he felt quite at home in overseeing the establishment. He settled himself into Joan's study upon the first floor. Wang awaited him, with a tray of tea in hand.

"*Xie xie*," Charles said, "I could not get on without you, Wang."

Wang said nothing. Even in his homeland, Wang said little, but Charles required no conversation from the man. It was enough that he had risked his life aiding a foreigner outside the walls of the Canton factory.

"Was Miss Terrell well behaved?" Charles asked as he took a seat at the writing table after accepting a cup of tea.

The pause was slight, but Charles caught it before Wang answered in the affirmative with a nod.

"What happened?" Charles asked.

Wang answered blandly, "She submitted to the wrapping."

"Did she protest at first?"

"No."

"Talk too much?"

"No."

Charles eyed a letter requesting membership to the Red Chrysanthemum. "Miss Terrell has a defiant bent to her and is unafraid of mischief. I should not be at all surprised if she was not perfectly behaved."

Wang said nothing. In their time together, Charles had never known the man to hide anything from him, and he was tempted to let it pass.

"But, lest you dispute my conclusion, I gather I should be completely pleased with how Miss Terrell conducted herself?" he tried one last time as he took another sip of tea.

"You ought be pleased."

Charles took another sip. "But not *completely* pleased?"

"You do not forbid her to talk."

"I do not. Some dominants demand silence from their submissive charges, but I do not require it at all times."

"Then you ought not be cross that she suggested she be allowed to satisfy me as a reward for my services."

Charles began coughing on the tea. *The naughty vixen.* Perhaps he *should* command her complete silence. He stared at his unflinching valet. Of course he would grant Wang anything the man wished. Almost anything. And though the man was possessed of as much forbearance as a Buddhist monk, Charles doubted Wang could be unaffected by his tasks or the mere sight of Miss Terrell naked.

"Do you, er, wish satisfaction?" he asked.

"Miss Terrell is not the only source of satisfaction available."

Charles felt a small sense of relief. Recalling the jealousy from his dream, he was not quite prepared to share Miss Terrell yet, even with Wang. Nonetheless, he owed it to his valet to say, "You have but to ask. There are many here at the Red Chrysanthemum who could fulfill your needs."

Wang made no reply. Charles was half-tempted to assign a woman to Wang. In Wang's time in England, Charles knew not how the man tended to his urges. He knew Wang must prefer the features of women of his own kind and wondered if he ought to inquire where such women could be found in London. But Wang would receive such assistance from Charles as presumptuous, and Charles knew no one more resourceful than Wang. It was possible the man already had female companionship.

"Enter," Charles responded to a knock upon the door.

It was Miss Sarah with her son. Charles stood as Wang withdrew.

"Miss Sarah," Charles greeted. He smiled at the boy. "I see that your son grows bold in his steps. Pray, have a seat."

She set George down beside the sofa, where he promptly demonstrated his newfound ability.

"Bravo," Charles said. George took three steps before sitting down with a grin. "He appears quite delighted with himself, as he should be."

"I thought he might not walk till he was nearer two years in age, for his father had not walked until then."

Charles did not know the details of her trial, only that she had protested her innocence and that the jury had found her guilty of criminal congress and awarded her husband, Sir Rowan, five thousand pounds, an amount her accused paramour could ill afford. Charles knew little of Sir Rowan but deemed Miss Sarah a woman of good heart. With alabaster skin, bright blue eyes and dark full hair, she was as lovely as she was dignified. She possessed far too much grace for a place like the Red Chrysanthemum.

"What may I do for you, Miss Sarah?" he asked.

"I hesitate to ask, but I have waited a month, and Georgie grows at such a pace that I am compelled to speak. I wish for a loan—in a small amount—to purchase a new gown for Georgie."

They watched as George pushed himself back onto his feet. Charles saw that the hem of the gown nearly reached the boy's knees.

"And a pair of shoes," she added. "I had thought to request a loan from Captain Gracechurch but am uncertain when he will return. I will repay the loan to Madame as soon as I am unable. Perhaps there will be a member tonight in want of my company? I know I am not as young as Miss Sophia or as pretty, but—"

"You need not worry of tonight, and will spend it in the delightful company of your son. As for the loan, it is yours."

Her whole countenance brightened. "Master Gallant, I cannot thank you enough. I hope your decision will not vex Madame, though I admit your presence prompted me to make my request sooner."

"The loan is a personal one, Miss Sarah, and you may repay it at your convenience."

"That is more than generous of you. Would I offend you if I offered to pay interest on the loan? My husband said only J—"

"It would offend me. A gentleman would never request interest on a personal loan."

"Thank you. I am most indebted to you, Master Gallant."

He smiled. "For the cost of a child's gown and shoes, hardly."

At a knock upon the door, Miss Sarah rose and picked up George. Charles walked them to the door.

"Thank you, Master Gallant," she said once more.

He bowed and opened the door. Upon the threshold stood Miss Sophia. She colored upon seeing Miss Sarah, no doubt recalling that she had, by spilling red wine, ruined the lovely shawl of the woman. Charles had arranged a payment plan for Miss Sophia to compensate Miss Sarah for the loss and knew it would be some time before the young maiden would be able to repay Miss Sarah in full, though the golden locks of Miss Sophia had paid a price already in her brawl with Miss Terrell. Miss Sophia wore a turban over her flaxen curls and appeared quite fetching in the headdress.

"You wished to see me, sir?" she inquired as he closed the door after Miss Sarah.

"Have a seat, Miss Sophia."

On her way to the sofa, her fan dropped. They both bent to retrieve it, and he found himself looking straight at her bosom.

"Your pardon," she murmured, rising and allowing him to pick up the fan.

He presented her the fan and guided her to the sofa before she dropped anything else.

After sitting down, she took in a deep breath, causing her bosom to swell. Her lashes fluttered over crystal eyes. "What do you wish of me, Master Gallant?"

He leaned against the front of the writing table before her. "Forgive the bluntness of the query, but how familiar is your derriere with penetration?"

Her lips pursed into a grin. "Quite familiar."

"You are comfortable with it?"

"Indeed. I can be quite fond of it, sir."

She passed a hand over the top of her bosom and played with the lace edging of her décolletage, but he kept his gaze at her face.

"What do you know of Mr. Carmichael?"

Her coy smile began to fade. "That he is one of the older men."

"Mr. Carmichael is a valued member of the Red Chrysanthemum. He knew Madame Devereux before she became proprietress here. He is in search of a new partner for the evening."

She frowned. "Indeed."

"As a member with seniority, he has first choice among available members but, as he has been absent for the past year, he is not familiar with the more current ladies here. I would like to recommend him to you. His only requirement is a woman who can accept anal congress."

Miss Sophia was not pleased. "Surely there are others? What of Miss Terrell? I'd wager she has had far more cocks up her bum than I."

"Joan would wish to please Carmichael, as he is a very good friend of hers, and the Red Chrysanthemum would compensate you for satisfying him. You could then afford to cover a quarter of what you owe Miss Sarah."

Miss Sophia huffed and looked away. Charles waited as she weighed the opportunity.

"Joan and I would be much obliged if you gave him your company," he said. In truth, he could simply demand it of her. She had agreed to offer her services wherever needed in exchange for room, board, and perquisites.

"Very well," she relented with a pout.

"Carmichael is a good man. He will treat you well."

For several seconds, she merely frowned, then brightened as she looked at Charles. "I hope you will consider me favorably after this? I am not accustomed to entertaining old men."

"Mr. Carmichael is fifty years of age. Is he so very old?"

"Old enough to be my grandfather."

Charles did not dispute that this was possible, though unlikely. "You will find his manners far more agreeable than many a young buck."

He stood, indicating their meeting was at an end. He escorted her to the door. On the way, her fan dropped once more. This time he remained standing and caught her by the elbow before she bent down.

"Allow me," he said. He retrieved her fan and placed it in her hand.

"Thank you, sir." She paused before crossing the threshold. "Are you certain Mr. Carmichael would not prefer Miss Terrell?"

"Miss Terrell is occupied."

"I see. I suppose it is just as well, for her sake. I understand Sir Arthur to be the jealous sort."

Charles stiffened.

"Good evening, Master Gallant," she said before drifting past him, fan in hand.

He looked to the longcase clock in the corner, impatient now to head upstairs where Miss Terrell awaited him. He dispensed of his other duties as quickly as possible, including a dialogue with a member unable to pay his dues, listening to the cook complain of her allowance for food, and addressing a marchioness who wished to replace Tippy, the dressing maid, with her own servant. After seeing to the arrival of the members, he was finally finished with the bulk of his responsibilities for the Red Chrysanthemum.

At last, he could turn his attentions to Miss Terrell.

Chapter 4

His cock perked at the sight of her, wrapped from head to toe in black silk. It never took much for Miss Terrell to arouse him; the response moved faster than the speed of reason. The more Charles became acquainted with her, the more he desired her. Though he had been unfamiliar with the features of Negresses, from the beginning, hers had called to him at a visceral level. He had found her brazen attempts to seduce him both off-putting and enlivening. Perhaps it was her confidence and unabashed wantonness that impressed him even while she unsettled him. He knew no woman like her and would hazard that even men with no given partiality to blackamoors—like the Viscount Wendlesson—could not resist her qualities.

She stirred upon the bed, her movements restricted to that of an inchworm. He watched her, taking in the shape of her body: the swell of her breasts, the flare of her hips and thighs, and the length of her legs—all proportioned to entice. He adjusted his crotch, then sauntered to the side of the bed nearest where she lay. As his gaze continued to feast upon her, he wondered how she had passed the time. Did she find peace or frustration in the seclusion provided by the binding?

"Good evening, Miss Terrell," he greeted.

She instantly stilled. Her nostrils flared. She made a muffled reply.

Wang had assisted him from his coat earlier, and Charles, feeling warmth building inside him, proceeded to unbutton his waistcoat. After setting aside the garment, his cravat, and collar, he grazed his knuckles up her torso. She inhaled audibly. He cupped a breast and heard her grunt. He pinched at the nipple through the fabric. She gasped.

"Will I find you quite wet, Miss Terrell?"

She responded with what sounded like a "yes." Given her nature, he suspected she had spent a good part of her time in impatience. Her marked reactions to his simple touches indicated her level of arousal. She was poised for pleasure and at his complete mercy. Her every sensation was his to command. To ease some of her tension, he rubbed her shoulders, neck, arms, and legs till he felt her relax.

He retrieved a thin rod, a pair of scissors, and two small clamps. The latter items he set upon the table beside the bed. He tapped the rod lightly over her, leisurely awakening her flesh before bringing it down harder upon a thigh. She yelped. He whipped the rod against the other thigh and the sides of her breasts, then flicked the tip at her belly and nipples. A number of strikes elicited her cries, which, trapped, reverberated in her throat. He turned her over.

With the rod, he warmed her backside and the back of her legs. By her quickened breath, he could tell she was ready for more. He returned her onto her back. He replaced the rod with the scissors. Wang had wrapped her well and tight with several layers of the silk bandage. Charles cut an opening about her breasts, freeing the dark brown mounds, and tucked the cut ends of the fabric so that the bindings remained secure over the rest of her. He looked at her, reduced to her breasts—but such lovely breasts they were!

He rolled a hardened nipple between thumb and forefinger, then captured it in his mouth. Miss Terrell gave a long moan. For several minutes, he played with the bud, licking, nipping, suckling, till her hips began to move up and down, indicating the craving between her legs. Picking up a clamp, he affixed it to the nipple, swollen from his attentions. He applied his mouth to the neglected nipple, caressing it while its twin suffered the pinch of the clamp. Making all manner of sounds, Miss Terrell arched and retracted her back as if undecided as to whether she wanted the stimulation, the contrast of pain and pleasure tugging at her mind.

Leaving her breasts, he cut another opening at her pelvis to the middle of her thighs. The scent of her desire made the blood throb to his groin. Setting aside the scissors, he fit a hand between her legs and, to no surprise, found her wet. He stroked her till she panted. He mauled a breast with his other hand, pinching and pulling at the nipple without the clamp. She writhed and grunted. She began pleading, but he could not discern her words. With any other submissive, he would have provided a gesture so they could call a stop to what he did. But Miss Terrell had decried the need for a safety word. He was not yet done teaching her the imprudence of such a declaration.

Knowing she was not to spend till he had granted

her permission, she began to tremble as the need for release pressed down upon her. He eased her from the edge, lightly caressing the lips and avoiding her swollen clit. She sighed in some relief. Of course her body would have preferred to spend, especially after having waited for him. Perhaps one of these days he would take her without ceremony and not deny his own lust raging inside of him. He would fuck her, ready or not.

But first she would have to forsake Sir Arthur.

At the thought of the man, he flipped her over, pulled up her hips and delved two fingers into her quim. Crooking his fingers, he found the spot that made her legs tremble. Still near the precipice, she squirmed, her incoherent murmurs quick and high-pitched. Over and over, he plunged his fingers ruthlessly into her, throwing her over the edge into the sea of ecstasy. As he watched her body spasm and felt her cunnie convulse about his fingers, his cock stretched painfully against his trousers, for it knew where it longed to be. Unable to maintain her position on her knees, she had slid onto her side. Shudders racked her body long after the pleasure had peaked.

Can Sir Arthur bring you to such heights? he wanted to ask. Instead, he remarked, "Spending without permission is no small transgression, Miss Terrell."

Chapter 5

Terrell moaned. Master Gallant sounded cross with her, and not merely for spending without permission. But what mortal would not have spent after waiting what felt like an eternity, and after being deprived of all sensations but for his touch? With her body wrapped save for the most titillating aspects, the intensity of the stimulation to the exposed parts were magnified. The area between her legs had become all of her. She had withheld for as long as she could. He could have kept her from going over the edge, as he seemed to always know just when to cease to exploit the greatest possible aggravation. Although the climaxes were often grander afterwards, until then, the denial of that most rapturous end was agony. Perhaps it was better to spend without permission.

Perhaps. It would depend upon her punishment.

"Well, Miss Terrell," Gallant drawled. "I was going to remove your bindings, but since you have spent without permission, you will have to endure them a while longer."

She swallowed a moan and instead mumbled, "Thank you, Master."

He seemed to understand her and gave her rump a pat. She felt the clamp at her nipple torn from her and cried out. He rolled her onto her back. She wished she could see him, his handsome features and especially the blaze of lust in his shimmering blue eyes as he looked upon her. Did he stand clothed or might he have taken off his shirt and trousers? She hoped the latter, so that when he did remove the silk bindings, she could see his cock, long and hard for her.

A warm hand covered her breast. She sighed. His every touch, even those that brought pain, delighted her. He groped and rolled the flesh, and though she had spent wondrously but moments ago, desire warmed her loins once more. Though she was at his complete mercy, unable to defend herself against his caresses, anticipation weighed more than fear at the moment. At times, while she had waited for his arrival, she had found serenity inside her cocoon. Inevitably, however, her thoughts drifted to Gallant and what he might do. Once lust settled in, the bindings no longer brought her peace. They stifled and frustrated. She wanted sight, a connection to the world about her. Accustomed to years of constant movement toiling in the sugar fields, when rest was always joined to exhaustion, she wanted mobility.

She inhaled sharply when his mouth encased her already tortured nipple. The sensation upon her aching bud was too much. She tried to remain still but whimpered at the licking, biting and sucking. She had once dreamed of thrusting her breast into his face, of his ravenous feasting upon its tip, but the removal of the clamp had caused the blood to rush into the nipple, making it particularly sensitive. And he was not as gentle as he often was. He pulled at the nipple with his teeth, swirled his tongue over it for a momentary respite, then bit down hard enough to make her scream. The poor nipple would be sore into the morrow.

Still, he did not relent but offered up another source of relief by insinuating a hand between her thighs, stroking her.

Lord.

Overwhelmed by the contrasting touches, one pleasurable, the other vexing, she writhed beneath the dual assault. How could his caresses wreak such havoc upon her? It was hardly fair. Yet, she knew this, knew his power, for she had witnessed its domination over the formerly impervious Mistress Scarlet and had wanted him from that moment. A man who could take her body to the boundaries of madness.

"You do not desire to spend a second time without permission," he reminded her.

She groaned, for his fondling had once again brought her within sight of the edge. She focused on the tenderness of her nipple, now relishing the distraction of discomfort. But her body betrayed her. The pain in one place began working in tandem with the pleasure in the other. Pain fueled pleasure, or perhaps the latter merely diminished the former. Either way, her body was being coaxed where she had to resist. She had boasted she could be a perfect submissive. He had already proven her wrong, but she did not wish to further corroborate his findings. She could still learn to be the best submissive he had ever had.

Her teeth would chatter if they could. Though she could see nothing, she squeezed her eyes shut and tried to transport her body, through thought, away from that tempting cliff, away from his caresses. She tried shorts breaths, she tried long breaths. She tensed, she squirmed. But there was no escape. His fingers were inside of her. She could not win this battle, but she would go down fighting.

Suddenly, he withdrew. She nearly sobbed in relief, though her body wailed at being left to hang upon the precipice.

"On your knees," he directed.

She positioned herself with her arse once more in the air, the rest of her weight pressing her shoulders into the bed. She felt his hand at her mound, then something pinched her clitoris. He removed his hand, and she felt a small weight brush against her thigh, pulling her clitoris down. A rigid object caressed her folds next. She did not know its identity till he pushed it inside of her. It was a dildo. Her cunnie clenched it greedily. She sighed at the satisfying fullness.

She jumped when another object touched her anus, then settled in glee when she realized he meant to fill her there, too. The second dildo was much smaller but stretched her all the same. The effect of being filled in two places was heavenly.

"How fares my naughty little whore?" he asked.

Her ears burned in delight. There was no denying that a part of her enjoyed misbehaving at his hands. She could never aspire to his goodness. Why not be his opposite?

"Thank you, Master," she mumbled into the fabric.

She felt him caress the curve of her rump. He then left her to the dildos. She heard the rustle of clothes and assumed he was undressing. That boded well. She wanted to be fucked by him. Desperately. She flexed her cunnie and felt both cocks inside of her. She shivered and wondered which dildo he would replace with his own cock.

He did neither at present. Instead, she received a sharp sting upon one buttock. She nearly lost her balance. He had struck her with a crop. She yelped at the second smack against her derriere. He rained down several more blows till her whole arse was on fire. Wetness brimmed her eyes, and she trembled. Staying in her position required effort. Her shoulders were sore. Her arse smarted. Her cunnie throbbed. The bindings had become oppressive. But most grueling of all was her desire to be fucked, fucked into an oblivion that would wash away all the discomfort.

A plume replaced the crop, its feathery lightness brushing where the latter had stung, occasionally grazing her folds below. With a sigh, she marveled at the conflicting sensations he imposed upon her body. She both wanted relief from the silk encasing her, wanted freedom of movement, yet felt secure in the bindings and relished how it compelled her attention to her loins, which Gallant tortured with the greatest pleasure. Or pleasured with the greatest torture.

Both dildos were gently withdrawn from her. She moaned for their absence and hoped he would replace one of the cavities with his own length. He caressed the area of her clitoris, nudging the clip, making her cunnie clench in response. And then he fulfilled her wish, pressing his hardness into her cunnie. It was, without doubt, her favorite sensation. She would never tire of it, of being filled by him. He thrust with slow deliberation, making her shiver in delight. She could not request his permission to spend and hoped he would remember to grant it.

He pulled out of her, and her breath skipped when she felt his tip press against her derriere. He would fill her *there*. But first he replaced one of the dildos into her cunnie. She could barely contain her excitement. She heard the uncorking of a bottle or vial, then felt an oil drip into her nether hole. Then the head of his rod was at the entry once more.

"Relax," he urged, rubbing a buttock.

She had not realized she had tensed. When she eased the muscles of her sphincter, he pressed the crown inside. She gasped when the flare lodged inside her tightness. She had had cock in her bum before but thrilled to the fact that it was Gallant filling her where nature had not intended. But then, if nature had not intended it, why did it feel so wondrous? There seemed to exist far more nerves there than anywhere.

Having had the dildo, she did not require long to adjust to the new intruder. Slowly, Gallant pressed himself deeper. She savored every inch of him, stretching her far more than the dildo had done. The presence of his cock amplified the fullness of the dildo in her cunnie, and she could hardly wait for him to begin his thrusting. He buried himself fully in her, his cods resting against her.

Divine. Heavenly. There were not words enough to describe how exquisite she felt, filled to the brim. When he began moving, she almost sobbed at the bliss. Her body had never known such rapture. It was too much. She had nothing to grasp, to diffuse the concentration of stimulation. She could not even dig her fingers into her palms. Thus, the intensity only folded into itself, growing a tide that would surely drown her.

He kept his motions long but quickened them. She could not refrain from cursing, albeit incoherently. Her body was awash in a rapture that thrilled even as she prayed for it to come to an end. As he ground himself more forcefully into her, she became desperate, frantic for the end. She could not tolerate such staggering rhapsody for much longer.

"Please, Master," she mumbled between her cries and oaths.

Her body wanted to fall away from the assault, but he gripped her hips and held her in place as he slammed himself into her, his loins smacking her arse.

"You wish to spend, Miss Terrell?"

"Yes, yes, yes," she sobbed, though she knew not if she sounded intelligible.

"Then spend."

The tide crushed her, shattering her into pieces, for the ecstasy was far too great in size for her poor tortured body to contain. She convulsed as bliss raged inside her, a brutal tempest that wrung every nerve. She was tossed into the heavens, made to fall through the air with nothing to catch her.

When the storm finally began to abate, when she realized her body was still whole, with him pulsing inside of her, she wondered that she would ever again have the use of her limbs. After he slid his length from her and released his hold, she crumpled to the bed. Her heart beat in her ears. She took in the cool air through her nose but needed more.

"Hold still," he said.

She felt a blade against her cheek, and the fabric was cut from her head, then the rest of her upper body. She gulped in the air. Perspiration had matted her hair to her head. He cut the remaining bindings from her legs. Turning her onto her back, he removed the clip between her thighs, extracted the dildo, then rubbed the numbness from her arms and legs.

"Thank you, Master," she murmured, exhausted, her body not yet recovered.

He brushed a tendril from her temple and, scooping her into his arms, lay with her. She melted into his embrace. Indeed, she could do little else. Her arse was a little sore, both from the crop and from his penetration, but all was well. She had survived a euphoria of amazing proportions. She lay for some time cradled in his arms as he planted light kisses along the side of her neck. At the moment, she wanted nothing more from the world. Yes, all was well.

If only it could last.

Chapter 6

Charles swept his gaze downward, over her dark body nestled against his. She was most beautiful after she had spent. Her skin glistened with perspiration. The crimson in her arse where the crop had landed had already begun to fade, but the blush in her cheeks remained. He brushed the tight curls from the nape of her neck and kissed her. Her hair had not the softness of Miss Lily's or Miss Greta's, but he was fast becoming accustomed to its quality.

This, too, satiated—the holding of her in his arms, the peace after the torrent. He enjoyed pushing her body to the brink. She possessed a strength that allowed him to hold nothing back. And yet, when she lay in his embrace when all was done, the fierce panther seemed to settle into a gentle fawn. He stifled the temptation to contend that Sir Arthur surely did not deliver her such carnal bliss. She had yet to proclaim that she would forsake Sir Arthur, but surely she had no reason to remain with the man save for his coin.

Charles had not Sir Arthur's wealth and knew few, including other nabobs, who had that man's affluence. But Charles had a gentleman's income and wagered what he could offer Terrell to be decent, even in Joan's estimation. Joan might not be pleased at first, but she owed him a favor for looking after the Red Chrysanthemum in her absence. His only concern lay in the consequences to his election. He doubted Sir Arthur would draw a distinction between what occurred in the inn and other affairs, but it was possible the man would only be mildly disappointed if he was not overly fond of Miss Terrell.

And yet Charles found this thought unlikely. His own attachment to her had caught him unawares. He had spoken rather impulsively when he had proposed she forsake Arthur. He had told her that he sought no submissive at present, for he would be too occupied by his election, yet he now felt a strong desire to possess her with some urgency. Perhaps, if he had asserted himself more quickly, he might have secured Miss Greta.

Miss Terrell's even breathing indicated she was asleep, and he was reminded of his own fatigue. He reached for the bedclothes and drew it over them. She turned and settled into the crook of his arm. He drifted to sleep with her breath upon his chest.

In the morning, he awoke with a stiff cock wrapped in warmth and wetness. He pried open his eyes. Miss Terrell no longer lay beside him. She was under the bedclothes and between his legs, her mouth gliding up and down his shaft. He groaned. There could be no finer way to greet the morning.

She had recovered from the prior evening far faster than he expected. He gently lifted his hips, pressing himself deeper into her orifice, grunting when she took all of him. Her hand cupped his sac, clasping his cods hard enough to create more than a weak discomfort, but it was offset by the pleasure rippling from his erection. She came off his cock and took his scrotum into her mouth, tugging and sucking, as she rubbed his perineum. Pleasure vibrated from his groin down his legs, thrusting his body to the edge. Though his cock remained untouched, he was near to spending. He wove his hand through her hair.

With one hand, she continued to fondle that small area between scrotum and anus. With the other, she rolled and squeezed his cods till he roared at the pain. At last, her mouth returned to his cock. The assault overwhelmed and within minutes he shot his seed into her. He tried to keep his hips from bucking too harshly, though it was no easy task when spasms overtook his body as if trying to wring every last nerve from him. She kept with him, sucking and licking him till he had to push her off.

"Mmm," she purred as she hovered over him, "you make a mighty fine breakfast, Master."

A final shudder went through him from head to toe. He stared till her smile came into focus. He pulled her to him and crushed her mouth atop his. He could taste the tang of his own mettle in her mouth. He flipped her onto her back and reached a hand between her thighs. New moisture mixed with the viscousness from last night. He fondled her till she gasped and writhed. He had intended to frig her by hand till she spent, but his cock showed signs of life. Straddling her, he rubbed his length along her folds till he hardened sufficiently. He sank himself into her. She grasped at him.

Yesterday, he had fucked her, pounded into her tight and delightful arse. This morning would see more lovemaking than fucking. He claimed her mouth once more as he rolled his hips at her. She met his rhythm with her own motions and wrapped her arms about him. They worked together for that divine climax. He stopped kissing her to view the tension in her countenance. The sight of her about to spend caused the heat to flare in his loins. She gazed at him, her eyes bright and glossy.

"M-May I?" she remembered.

"You may."

He thrust deep into her, and she fell into her paroxysm. Her cunnie convulsed about him, and he allowed himself to follow her into ecstasy, emptying the very last remains of his cods into her. For a brief moment he wondered that she might not be as barren as she claimed, but given the number of men she had lain with, if she had not yet conceived, she was not likely to. Oddly, the thought of her impregnation titillated.

Perhaps his mother was right and he needed to find himself a wife.

"If you wish, I will dine upon your cockmeat every morning," Miss Terrell said after he had disengaged his body from hers.

"I might accept such an offer," he replied, pulling her into his arms as he lay beside her.

"Why would you not?"

"Do you intend to return to Sir Arthur?"

She lay with her head upon his chest, her face turned from him. "He owns half the borough you seek to represent."

"Nearly half. It is possible to win without his endorsement."

"Possible but not likely."

"And when have you become versed in Parliamentary elections?"

"Sir Arthur is not the only MP I have lain with."

He had forgotten that. She had had an entirely different life before the Red Chrysanthemum.

"My election is not the subject at hand."

"It might bear the consequences. Do you not wish to win?"

Of course he did. He had known since he was little that he would follow in his father's footsteps and stand for Parliament. He had expected one day to succeed to his father's seat and had been crushed when his father failed to win in his first effort. While in China, Charles had thought often of how he might win where his father had lost. He had not expected the occasion to manifest as quickly as it had. After returning from China and assuming a position for Sir Canning, the Secretary of State for Foreign Affairs, he discovered that one of the MPs for Porter's Hill had passed away unexpectedly. He could not forgo the opportunity.

"Do you not wish for me to claim you as my submissive?"

Her breath seemed to catch.

"I do," she said, her voice husky. "But Sir Arthur will not be pleased. He seems a man accustomed to having his every wish granted."

"He will be disappointed, but he is a grown man, and you are not his to own."

"He might blame you and withhold his support. Are you certain you wish to risk his ire?"

"I can win without his support."

Why was she arguing with him? *She* was the one who had approached him, attempted to seduce him at every turn. Now that she had succeeded, she would refuse him?

"What will Madame say?"

"Do you not wish me for a Master?" he countered.

She stiffened,her eyes blazing. "I do. I've not wanted a man as much as I have wanted you."

Warmed by the earnestness in her tone, he kissed her forehead, her nose, and then her mouth. She pulled him closer to her and returned the kiss fervently, impressing upon him her desire.

"I am yours, Master Gallant," she spoke into his lips, "yours, ever truly yours."

She bit and sucked at his mouth. He lost himself in the kiss, locking lips to lips, claiming her as she claimed him.

He would have preferred her verbal avowal and words specific to Sir Arthur, but he was satisfied by the ring of commitment in her tone. He vowed to himself that when he was done with her, she would surrender to his wishes, and surrender willingly.

Chapter 7

At times, Providence seemed to conspire to put in his path a relation to that whichoccupied his mind. For as Charles walked the street on his return to Whitehall from the residence of a supporter who wished to address Parliament's next appropriations bill, he came across an elderly gentleman standing before a neighboring townhome. The man looked to his left, blinked several times, then to his right. His brow furrowed.

Guessing the man to be lost, Charles approached. "Are you in need of assistance, sir?"

The man glanced down at the books and papers he held. One of the papers appeared to have the words "*Society for the Conversion of Jews* presented by Granville Sharp."

"Do you seek a meeting with this Society?" Charles asked.

His puzzlement dissipated, the man replied in a rich bass, "No, no. I came from the meeting. I mean to return now to Fulham but had momentarily forgotten where I was."

Charles studied the man of sixty or seventy years. He had a sloping brow, thinning hair, and prominent cheekbones. But they were distinguished features. The corners of his mouth turned downward, giving him the appearance of always being in serious thought.

"Are you Mr. Sharp?" Charles ventured.

The man returned Charles' study. "I am."

"I recall my mother once talking of the concerts your family performed upon the river. She enjoyed them greatly."

"Ah, yes," Mr. Sharp recalled with fondness. "That was many, many years ago. Before you were born, I would wager. Do I know your mother?"

"I think not, but music is a passion of hers, and she hardly forgets a performance. I am Charles Gallant, at your service."

The man weighed the name. "Gallant. That name is not unfamiliar to me, but I do not believe we have met. Have we?"

"No, but you are known to me. I recently read a letter you wrote to my employer, Sir Canning, urging the use of frankpledge as a means of combating the Hindu caste system. Though your deeds in other areas precede your name."

"You are with the Ministry of All Talents?"

"I am."

"You are the Gallant of Porter's Hill?"

"Indeed."

"I read you are standing for Parliament. That is an invitation to someone like me to take your time."

"I would be honored to have yours."

The two agreed to walk to the nearest coffeehouse.

"I was in the Orient when Parliament passed the bill to abolish the slave trade," Charles said after they had been served their coffee. "Your committee made such a triumph possible."

"I would not call it *my* committee."

"Were you not the chair?"

Mr. Sharp leaned in conspiratorially. "I often contrived to be late to eschew having to take the meetings."

"You are modest, but you must exalt in the abolition of the slave trade."

"I did fall upon my knees when word of the bill's passage came."

"I believe the Duke of Norfolk declared it the most humane and merciful act which was ever passed by any legislature in the world."

"It will be such when all of slavery is abolished. I had proposed that slavery's complete abolition from the empire be the goal of the committee, but I think the others were wise to confine our target to the slave trade. Even the United States have followed suit in banning the trade, though I wish they would choose to enforce it. It is my hope that we can dedicate more of our Navy to the cause. On this, I believe we are aligned with the West Indies' interest."

"Yes," Charles affirmed of the irony. Having fought abolition for the past two decades, the West Indies planters now lobbied for greater enforcement—in order to deny their competitors the supply of slaves they no longer had legal access to.

"Britannia will have a new role: from chief poacher to chief gamekeeper."

"Will your committee now pursue the abolition of slavery itself?"

"There is much work to be done. The Duke of Clarence remains a fierce proponent of slavery, and, as we all know, he might well ascend the throne."

"The Regent does not favor abolition, but that has not stopped you or the committee."

"True, but a number of my fellow committee members believe that full emancipation will spring from the abolition of the slave trade."

"And what think you?"

"I pray it may be so, but I would not be surprised if we were called to task once more."

"You waged a long and arduous campaign to abolish the slave trade. It would weary any man."

Even as he spoke, Charles doubted fatigue or even old age would stay a man like Granville Sharp.

"Slavery is an institution that ought not be tolerated in any part of Britannia," Sharp replied.

Recalling the reason Miss Terrell had provided for why she consumed her meals with swiftness, Charles said, "I had heard that some slaves are barely fed. It is hard to believe this to be common practice among all the plantations. What is the advantage in starving one's labor force?"

"Sugar does not command the prices it once did. The plantation owners must think it necessary to minimize the cost of maintaining their slaves, though these sugar kings do so even while they live in opulence. Negro slaves are treated worse than livestock, considered dispensable goods that one can toss into the sea as if discarding dirty linen."

No doubt Sharp alluded to the case of the *Zong,* a slave ship from which over a hundred slaves had been tossed overboard, so that the ship owners could collect on the insurance. Sharp had attempted, unsuccessfully, to see the crew tried for murder.

"Women and children are treated no better."

Confirming Charles' supposition, Sharp said, "Women and children were the first to be tossed into the sea from the *Zong*. On the first day of that dreadful massacre, fifty-four women and children were jettisoned. You were perhaps too young at the time to recall the case of Captain Kimber, accused of whipping a young slave girl to death aboard his ship because she would not dance for him. And these are but the incidents that have come to light. Many more horrors go unnoticed."

In his mind, Charles could see Miss Terrell's ravaged back, the scars and ridges from the heavy lashing she had sustained.

"And it would be impossible to seek out all abuse and bring the offenders to justice," he sighed.

"Our courts would be inundated. It is impossible to legislate compassion. Slavery, at its core, is incompatible with English principles of freedom and the teachings of Christ. We should not have to draw upon its horrors to argue that slavery is, simply put, wrong."

"But you, your committee, Mr. Clarkson are not now actively pursuing slavery's abolition."

"I have learned to be patient, Mr. Gallant. The Society for Effecting the Abolition of the Slave Trade was formed in 1787. The slave trade was abolished last year, a full twenty years later."

"I am in awe of what twelve men have been able to accomplish."

"I am humbled that my Quaker friends invited me to join their effort. The Quakers were the first to petition Parliament to end the slave trade."

"I know many an upstanding Quaker. It is

unfortunate they cannot stand for Parliament."

"You and I, as Anglicans, bear the torch, but we stand upon the shoulders of others. Ours is a responsibility that makes it more incumbent upon us to do what is right."

A longcase clock in the corner chimed the hour.

"I have taken a sufficient amount of your time, I think," Charles said.

"It was my pleasure, young man. I should like to be better acquainted."

"I would be honored."

"No need for that. I am but a humble servant doing God's work."

"If not for your efforts in Somerset's case, slavery might still prevail in England."

"It is uplifting to meet a young man with such a keen interest in the matter."

"To be honest, Mr. Sharp, my interest was only recently spurred by an acquaintance. While I supported Sir Wilberforce and all the efforts to abolish the slave trade, the majority of my attention was directed elsewhere."

"It is never too late. You perhaps know of John Newton?"

Charles nodded. He had heard of the former slave trader turned priest. "My mother is partial to one of his hymns. 'Amazing grace, how sweet the sound! That sav'd a wretch like me.'"

"'I once was lost, but now am found, was blind, but now I see.' We have all been blind at some part of our lives."

Sharp pulled a pamphlet from his stack of papers and books. "I wrote this a few years ago. Perhaps you would indulge an old man and give it some of your time."

Charles accepted the pamphlet, entitled *Serious Reflections on the Slave Trade and Slavery Addressed to the Peers of Great Britain*.

After Sharp bid him good day, Charles remained, reflecting upon his options. Mathilda Brentwood had been unwavering in her position: her support of his candidacy was contingent upon his agreement not to support slavery's abolition for at least ten years. Sir Arthur had no opinion on the matter that Charles could discern, provided Parliament did not attempt to address slavery's form in India. Arthur had no ties to the West Indian interest in slavery and had been at odds with them when the East India Company contemplated expanding sugar production in its territories. Sir Arthur might not concern himself with how Charles voted on potential legislation to abolish slavery, but he would demand Charles' compliance in other areas.

Winning election without the support of either the Brentwoods or Sir Arthur was unlikely. Charles would have to choose.

Feeling the gaze of another upon him, Charles looked up and saw Mr. Phillips, a reporter for *The Independent*, an oppositionist paper. Remembering that he had the sensation of being watched outside the millinery shop where he had purchased a bonnet for Miss Terrell, Charles wondered if it had been Mr. Phillips.

"Pray tell, you have not been following me, Mr. Phillips?"

Mr. Phillips rose from the table where he sat and

took the chair vacated by Mr. Sharp. "Good day to you, Mr. Gallant. It would seem we favor the same coffee shops."

"And at the same times," Charles replied, sitting back in his chair. "Rather convenient, I should say."

"Yes, quite convenient. It would seem you are acquainted with Mr. Sharp?"

"I am now. He is a man worth being acquainted with."

"Indeed, he is. My father was a journalist and chronicled Somerset's case. Mr. Sharp was no attorney, but he was as versed in the law as any jurist. Better, I would wager."

Phillips spoke with apparent admiration. He looked at the pamphlet before Charles.

"You have an interest in the matter of slavery, Mr. Gallant?"

Knowing *The Independent* to be a supporter of Fox, Charles said, "Mr. Fox was a passionate advocate for the abolition of the slave trade."

"That he was! He would have led the campaign to abolish the slave trade if Mr. Wilberforce had not taken the lead. Mr. Fox gave such an eloquent and impassioned speech in the House of Commons on behalf of the bill to abolish the slave trade. It is sad he did not live to see its passage."

"The bill passed with a large majority. The harder consideration is the abolition of slavery throughout the empire."

"Mr. Fox believed in the liberty of men. He did not believe the slave trade could be regulated. Instead, he called for its destruction. I believe the same argument can be made for all of slavery."

"It is a much harder war to wage."

"But one that needs waging, sir, if good men will take arms against it."

"Good men like Mr. Laurel?"

Mr. Phillips faltered at the mention of the only Whig candidate in the race. "Well, I do not know precisely where Mr. Laurel stands on the issue. I suspect he would favor its passage were such a bill to come before Parliament. Would you, Mr. Gallant?"

"I believe as Mr. Sharp does: that slavery has no place in a society that believes in the freedom of man, that believes men are endowed with natural rights no government ought take away."

"Well said, sir."

Charles let out a breath and looked into his near empty cup of coffee. "Whether or not I can vote my conscience…"

He had not intended to make such a confession, and before Mr. Phillips of all people, but the subject had weighed upon him for some time.

"Ah, of course. You must fall in line with the wishes of Sir Arthur."

Charles glanced sharply at the man. "I know not how Sir Arthur views abolition, and I am not assured his support at present."

"Still?"

"He is in Somerset present."

"But when he returns, it is expected you will have his endorsement."

"I take nothing for granted."

Mr. Phillips looked once more at the pamphlet. "If I may, you speak with some passion with regards to slavery."

"What man who has heard of the horrors of the institution would not condemn its practice?"

"But there is more ardor in your speech. Perhaps you have a personal connection to the matter?"

Charles leaned in toward Mr. Phillips. "And why would you suggest such a thing?"

"I happened to see you with a young Negress the other day."

"Another convenient circumstance. How is it our paths have crossed thrice in the past few days?"

Mr. Phillips flushed.

"Permit me, Mr. Phillips, since you appear to have a dose of shame such that the admittance of truth proves uncomfortable. I know your paper seeks to print some scandal to discredit my name. Never mind that your exalted Mr. Fox was deemed a profligate, a dandy, rake and debtor. Despite that, I do believe his legacy should be that of a great and noble statesman, a defender of civil liberties, and an eloquent orator. Shall I save you the trouble of shadowing me from afar by sharing my day's schedule with you?"

Such a challenge was risky, for Charles did not know how much Mr. Phillips had seen. Had the reporter followed him all the way to the Red Chrysanthemum?

Mr. Phillips blushed to the roots of his widow's peak. "I—I am not partial to this aspect of my occupation."

"Perhaps you would agree that a debate of a man's qualifications to serve in Parliament would be more apropos than what he might do in his private time?"

"Indeed."

"It would seem we both have considerations

beyond our conscience, Mr. Phillips."

Mr. Phillips could not meet his gaze.

Charles rose and replaced his hat. "I think, Mr. Phillips, in other circumstances, we might be friends. Good day, sir."

Taking Sharp's pamphlet, he took his leave. He was satisfied to see Mr. Phillips' unease regarding his less savory responsibilities, but he worried of what the man knew. He could not probe too deeply, for fear of drawing attention to that which he wished concealed. That he was venturing nightly to the Red Chrysanthemum did not aide his cause. If *The Independent* were to expose his involvement there, it might well spell the doom of his election. Mrs. Brentwood might overlook the occasional dalliance or the opera dancer as mistress, but she would not be able to stomach the true nature of the Red Chrysanthemum.

If he were not responsible for the inn in Joan's absence, he would refrain from visiting there this evening.

Or would he? Miss Terrell was quite the enticement.

"Behave yourself today," he had told her in the morning before taking his leave.

"Yes, Master," she had replied with eyes downcast.

He had lifted her chin that she could meet his gaze. "And if Miss Sophia should trouble you, what are you *not* to do?"

"Tear out her hair no matter how much she might deserve it."

He had given her a warning look.

"Engage with her," she rephrased.

"If she causes mischief, you are to approach me."

"Yes, Master."

He had brushed his lips over hers but did not linger. If he had, he would have been late to his morning engagements.

He wanted another taste of her and remembered how he had thought her as addicting as opium. He wondered if she had behaved herself? The danger was that he would enjoy her either way.

Chapter 8

P ain exploded her backside. The area beneath her shoulder blades burned with an icy flame. If only she could shed that part of her body, smarting as if pierced by a thousand bees. But she could barely move, barely breathe through the agony. A male slave on either side of her held her arms. There was no relief available to her. The air itself seemed to sting. She could only hope that Mr. Tremayne, the overseer, would not later add lemon juice or salt to her wounds, as he had done before to other slaves who had earned his ire.

The flogger landed another burst of pain. It did not matter now if she relented, if she divulged the whereabouts of her half-sister to Tremayne, if she begged his forgiveness. He seemed to delight in her screams, her sobs. Though perhaps she only heard them in her head, for she doubted her body capable of anything at the moment. She wondered if she might meet her death, then realized there was a source of relief for her after all...

Terrell woke, gasping for breath as if she had been drowning. Perspiration clung to her. Looking out the window, she saw it was night. She was in her room at the Inn of the Red Chrysanthemum. In London, England. Not Barbados.

Taking in a deep breath, she sat up in her bed. Her

heart continued to race. When awake, she did not allow herself to venture into the past. But in sleep, she could not prevent the undesired voyage. She crossed her arms over her belly and pressed her forehead to her bent knees. Her back seemed to throb and she sensed the unevenness there.

Her memory would not allow her to recall the full intensity of the pain, of the excruciating days of anguish that followed as she lay upon her stomach. She was fortunate that Miss Ruth, with the help of the slaves who had held her while Mr. Tremayne administered the flogging, had her taken to the Great House and installed her in the servants' quarters. Miss Ruth had nursed her with the care of a sister or a mother, using all manner of pomades and ointments to guard against infection, though Terrell had often protested that surely the cure was worse than any possible infection.

She had cried often, long past when the tears had dried.

"Quit your fussin'," Miss Ruth had said. "Do you know how fortunate you be?"

Fortunate? How the bloody hell was she fortunate? she had wanted to scream to the woman who had mentored her in the ways of pleasing a man.

"Remember how Massie died? You not be dead. Mr. Tremayne let you live."

So he could fuck me, Terrell had thought, bitter and rueful. But perhaps Miss Ruth was right. As unbearable as her flogging had felt, she could not imagine the pain Massie must have suffered when, sick with dysentery, Mr. Tremayne had stuck a corn cob up her arsehole.

"You be grateful for that," Miss Ruth had continued. "And don't never lie to him again."

Miss Ruth had known the reason why Terrell had not been forthcoming to Mr. Tremayne, but on the plantation, not doing right by the white man could lead to Death, which might be the better prospect.

"Be grateful he left you your beauty. He didn't touch your face, your bosom. No part of you that they care for."

In the weeks that followed her flogging, Terrell had found it hard to be grateful for anything. But when her back finally, slowly, painfully, began to heal, she came round to what Miss Ruth said. Certainly now, as a free woman in England, waiting the arrival of the most desirable man of the Red Chrysanthemum, she had much to be grateful for.

Feeling as if she could not shake her dream till she left her room, Terrell made her way downstairs to the ground floor, where she came across the Viscountess Wendlesson, a recent bride who had unknowingly facilitated Terrell's seduction of Master Gallant.

"Your ladyship," Terrell greeted the young woman who had passed by Baxter, the doorman for the Red Chrysanthemum.

The viscountess blushed, her cheeks red as apples against the pale of her skin. Slight of frame and with eyes that sparkled with childlike innocence, Miss Katherine appeared a delicate violet amidst the thorns of the Red Chrysanthemum. But, under the gentle guidance of Master Gallant, she had taken to the wicked practices with surprising swiftness.

"Shall I call for Tippy?" asked Baxter.

"I should be pleased to assist the viscountess," Terrell offered. She had interposed herself in just such a fashion, insinuating herself into the lessons between Gallant and Miss Katherine. In the course of the instruction, Terrell had taken an interest in the viscountess and saw her as her own student. Without Miss Katherine, Terrell would not have been awarded better quarters for her assistance in successfully initiating the viscountess into the ways of the Red Chrysanthemum, to the great satisfaction of the viscount. Without Miss Katherine, Terrell would not have had prolonged access to Master Gallant. Against his own wishes, he had permitted her involvement, though he had made her pay for her interference.

"You are here early," Terrell remarked as the two women made their way to the dressing chambers. The evening festivities would not begin for another hour, and she knew Miss Katherine tended to her husband's ailing mother.

"My sister-in-law is in town and sees to the dowager," Miss Katherine replied.

Terrell took Miss Katherine's gloves and bonnet as the viscountess took a seat before a vanity. "And where is his lordship?"

"He will come in an hour's time. I have displeased him and he wishes me to contemplate my error."

Terrell smiled in mischief. "How delightful!"

"Oh no—it was quite the terrible mistake. I had neglected to invite his cousins, the Brentwoods, to a dinner we were hosting. They had been out of town some time, and I was unaware that they had returned."

"Brentwood," Terrell murmured to herself.

Charles—er, Master Gallant had talked of the Brentwoods. Unless he secured the endorsement of Sir Arthur, he needed the support of the Brentwoods to win his election.

"They reside in Porter's Hill, do they not?" Terrell asked as she unpinned Miss Katherine's long straight hair.

"You know of them?"

"I only heard Master Gallant mention them. By accident, I had come across a letter of theirs."

It was true that she had come into possession of a letter addressed to the Brentwoods. The letter had lain beneath the package containing the shirt Gallant had gifted her. She remembered how she had considered—briefly—forcing Gallant's hand in exchange for the letter. At the time, he still resisted the notion of becoming her dominant one. But she had wanted to prove, through good behavior, that she could be the submissive of his dreams.

To no surprise, upon discovering the letter's absence, he had thought the worst of her intentions. Perhaps he would not have if she had not toyed with him, stalling for fear that if she gave him the letter too early, he would take his leave. She had been on the verge of telling him where he could find his letter when he had swept her into a dark room, pressed her into the back of the door, and growled, "You wish for me to dominate you, do you?"

She remembered the fire in his eyes, of anger mixed with lust. She did not fear what he might do to her. Well, a little. Though knowing it, like gambling or drink, to be wrong for her, she desired it nevertheless. Deep within her, she wondered if indulging in the moment might lead to misery for her, but the temptation of him was far too great. She had never met a man like Gallant before, a man of consideration and integrity who could wield such carnal wickedness.

Thus, she had allowed him to believe her guilty of extortion and hoped he would have his way with her.

Terrell shivered in memory of how he had pinioned her arms with the shirt he had gifted her, affixed clamps to her nipples and made her take the chain that joined them between her lips, bent her over the back of a chair, and spanked her with a crop. She had enjoyed every moment of her punishment, his delightful caresses made the pain more than worth it. Although, she did have her doubts that long, rapturous night. Lying shackled to the bed and watching him depart the room, leaving her body tense with unrelieved desire, she was reminded of how he had once left her tied to the rafters for half an hour before Tippy, the dressing maid, arrived to assist her from her bonds.

But he had returned after learning the truth, and her reward for his misapprehension was the greatest ecstasy a body could know. She had spent at his hands, at his cock. She thought she might not recover to spend ever again. However, she discovered she had an insatiable appetite for Master Gallant. He had only to stand near for the heat in her loins to start churning.

"My husband wrote a letter of introduction for Master Gallant," Miss Katherine said. "I believe the Brentwoods are inclined to support him. I do hope he wins. Master Gallant would make an exceptional

Member of Parliament."

Having lain with a few in her time in England, Terrell would venture to say that Gallant would make the *best* MP.

"What of your husband? Does he support Gallant's bid for Parliament?"

"My husband does not like to engage in politics."

"Does he not sit in the House of the Lords?"

"He never attends."

Remembering that Gallant had said the support of the Brentwoods was contingent upon his guarantee that he not vote in favor of any measure to abolish slavery within the next decade, Terrell inquired, "The Brentwoods must regard his lordship highly."

"They do, and I have seen Mr. Brentwood most effusive in his praise of his cousin, but I believe it Mrs. Brentwood who is most active in the elections. In any case, I understand that the support Master Gallant most requires is that of Sir Arthur." Miss Katherine lowered her voice. "And I think I have seen Sir Arthur *here.* Can you imagine? A man such as that? Here?"

"The Red Chrysanthemum attracts all manner of men and women," Terrell replied, setting aside the brush and admiring the shine in Miss Katherine's smooth locks.

"I suppose. I never thought I could take to a place such as this. You recall how terrified I was? I must admit this place scares me still."

"Then you are truly brave."

"I wanted to please my husband. You cannot know how wretched it feels to think you are inadequate as a wife. That did not sound—I did not mean to imply you will never marry. You seem quite young, and as you are *here*, I presume you were not, or are not, married. That is, if blackamoors engage in the practice of marriage."

Terrell paused. She had not given matrimony much thought. "Some of us do, if given the opportunity."

"I saw there is a Negro man who works here. He is quite the strapping fellow and quite frightening."

"Yes, Madame employs Jones to keep the order."

"Perhaps you and he might—"

"I do not seek marriage," Terrell replied. She had lifted her skirts to Jones a few times. The man had a monstrously long cock, and he wielded it well. But Jones had no aspirations beyond working for Madame Devereux. And Terrell required more if she was to support herself in the manner she intended. A part of her wanted to return to her former glory, when she had been the mistress of a wealthy baronet, a friend of Sir Arthur's. She wanted the beautiful gowns and the lavish apartment with servants at her command. At a minimum, she wanted an allowance that would enable her to save enough to survive on when youth and beauty would no longer serve her. A woman of her situation could rely on nothing and no one. Marriage was both fanciful and unnecessary.

"No? If you married, you would not need to work here."

"Jones is paid in room and board. His wages beyond that are minimal."

"Oh, well, surely there are other Negroes who earn more."

"Most of the blacks I know earn nothing at all."

"Nothing? Then what do they do with themselves

if they are not employed?"

"They are slaves. They work at the bidding of others."

"Oh."

Terrell did not often revisit the life she once led as a slave in Barbados. Gallant was one of the few she had talked to at length of her past. Not for pity or sympathy. Rather, she had hoped to impress upon him the abomination of slavery. As a Member of Parliament, he could propose measures to abolish the institution. But she saw that he was hesitant on the matter because of the Brentwoods.

"How does the viscount wish you to dress for tonight?" Terrell asked, turning to an armoire filled with garments.

Miss Katherine turned around in her chair. "Perhaps I could convince my husband to hire Jones as a footman. He might then earn a decent wage and even have opportunities for promotion."

"I do not think Jones partial to me. He is a little enamored with Mistress Primrose," Terrell said, wishing to put an end to the subject. She pulled out a diaphanous garment. "Shall we dress you as a Grecian goddess?"

"Or nymph, rather," giggled Miss Katherine. She rose to inspect the other available attire in the armoire. "I could have Wendlesson find another Negro to hire."

"You have some stake in seeing me married?"

"No—I—I merely wish you happiness. Surely you do not wish to become a spinster?"

"I do not fear spinsterhood. It would be preferable to being married to an overbearing husband."

"Oh, no. To have a husband is much better than none at all. You cannot work here all your years. And if you should marry a man whom you love, then marriage is the greatest happiness a woman can know."

Her eyes sparkled, and Terrell suddenly felt a little envious.

"Love? Love is no easy matter for anyone, let alone a blackamoor, to attain."

"Because many do not seek it. Love is quite a *simple* matter."

Terrell refrained from responding that love may be simple for Miss Katherine but few others. And what was this love that her ladyship spoke so highly of? A schoolgirl's fancy. Did it ensure happiness or fortune? If not, why should one seek it?

"My simple hope is to become a courtesan of a wealthy man," Terrell replied.

Miss Katherine looked surprised. "Are there wealthy Negroes?"

"None that I know of, but there are many other men who are." Terrell wondered if Miss Katherine thought she only serviced Negro patrons. Terrell was not surprised the Red Chrysanthemum saw no black members aside from herself. She herself had originally sought the position of dressing maid at the inn, but the proprietress had convinced her that she could earn far more as a member. And Madame had proved right. Terrell remembered the first time a member had taken a flogger to her; she had thought her past would descend upon her and suffocate her. Fortunately, she had been under the tutelage of Mistress Brownwen, who was as patient as she was forceful. But Terrell would not expect another black person would submit themselves to being flogged or acquiesce to flogging another, even if it was done for lascivious purposes and not to subjugate his fellow man.

And she had always thought herself to be made of different matter. She had learned at an early age that she could use venereal pursuits to her advantage, that men could be slaves to their cocks, weak when overcome with lust. They could also be dangerous, but if she offered herself before they took her by force, then she was not the victim. By making herself available to them without resistance, by providing them quick and easy pleasures, she garnered their appreciation and could put forth requests of her own. There were slaves who accused her of living a fantasy and of being some manner of traitor for accepting white cock without complaint. But these slaves toiled in the fields from dawn till dusk while she served as a housemaid in the Great House. Until the Mistress, suspecting her husband of partaking of black flesh, sent Terrell back into the fields before eventually selling her to another.

"Other men?" Miss Katherine repeated, puzzled.

"I was once a mistress of Sir Fairchild."

Her eyes widened. "Indeed?"

Miss Katherine clearly had not contemplated the possibility a white man would take a blackamoor for a mistress, though she herself had not balked terribly when Miss Terrell had crawled between her legs and applied her mouth to her.

"Do you service his kind here?"

Terrell paused. She had once serviced the

Viscount Wendlesson. Frustrated that he had not spent with his wife, and after Miss Katherine had left, Wendlesson had turned to Terrell and agreed to a guinea for her cunnie. She doubted Wendlesson had confided his infidelity to Miss Katherine.

"I have. You see, I have not your fortune. I cannot aspire to such happiness as marriage and love. My sights must be set lower."

And more practically, she added silently.

"You must not despair," Miss Katherine cried. "You are young yet and, I daresay, quite lovely for your sort."

Terrell smiled. She could not expect Miss Katherine to understand her circumstances. She had no use for marriage and, even less so, love.

Chapter 9

Looking at the older man behind the counter, Charles felt as if he were looking into *her* eyes. And though the apothecary's hair had turned grey, there were streaks of the same red hair that the daughter possessed. With her flaming locks and the garments of similar hue, she had aptly named herself Mistress Scarlet. But she was and would always be Miss Greta to him.

"I am much obliged to you, Mr. Gallant, for calling," said Mr. Barlow.

Charles looked over the many vials lining the shelves behind the man.

"I wondered if you had more of that Chinese ginger?" Mr. Barlow asked.

"The *ginseng.*"

"Yes. I had recommended it to a patron of mine, and he is convinced of its properties and abilities to keep the influenza at bay. All in his family have been ill save him. I myself continue to partake of it from time to time."

"I have a small supply left but can arrange for more to be shipped."

"I will pay what price you name."

"I seek no profit. The cost and its shipping will do."

"Sir! You are too generous."

Charles would not have made such an offer were

the man not Greta's father.

The man must have sensed his thoughts, for he cleared his throat. "My daughter would have found the root most curious."

A silent pause ensued before Charles asked, "I hope your daughter is well. She remains in Liverpool, I take it?"

"For a little while longer. I imagine she must desire to return to London, and my sister must not always require her help."

Charles heard this to mean Greta had provided no indication that she would return to London at a time soon but that Mr. Barlow wished to provide no discouragement.

"My regards to your whole family," Charles replied and prepared to take his leave. "I hope you all remain in good health."

Perhaps because he realized he could not make Charles stay, Mr. Barlow appeared wistful and resigned. "And you as well, good sir."

After stepping out of the apothecary shop, Charles heaved his own sigh. He had had a small amount of time to mourn Greta's sudden departure from town and felt himself responsible for it. Wanting to satisfy his own desires for her, he had challenged Mistress Scarlet and compelled her to unearth the submissive she once was. Perhaps it had been selfish and erroneous of him to have done so, but he had not anticipated the return of Master Damien. Confident that he was on the verge of commanding Greta's complete submission, he had underestimated the influence Master Damien still had upon her or the feelings she must still have harbored for the man.

Charles had allowed her to choose between them.

She chose neither.

A devoted and senior member of the Red Chrysanthemum, she had left no word to Joan as to her intentions. Charles had learned from Mr. Barlow that Greta had left to stay with and assist her aunt, who had seven children. Charles had been tempted to make the journey to Liverpool. He wanted to understand why she had fled, why she did not choose a winner.

But the election prevented him from making such a long trip. And there was his commitment to Joan from having lost a wager. He had bet his servitude that Mistress Scarlet would choose him over Master Damien. And though Joan had seen fit to relieve him from his pledge as an enticement for him to accept the role of instructor to the Viscountess Wendlesson, he had then come across another distraction.

Miss Terrell.

With Miss Terrell, he had little time to nurse his wounds, though a part of his heart ached still when he thought of Greta. Upon his return from the Orient, he had been thrilled to hear she was still a member at the Red Chrysanthemum and no longer attached to Master Damien. He had been more than surprised to learn that she had become Mistress Scarlet, for he had seen her with Master Damien, seen how she gave all of herself, how enthralled she was in the embrace of submission. He had believed submission her true nature, had found her vulnerability more than alluring.

Miss Terrell was not a true submissive. She played the part for lascivious purposes. It mattered not. All that she did aroused him. He had not expected to have such a strong response to her, but from the beginning, he had been intrigued even whilst he was incensed, disconcerted, and appalled by her behaviors. She was dangerous, and that only fueled his lust.

Despite her waywardness, she had remarkable qualities, a strength of spirit that he suspected exceeded his own and that he saw in few others, save perhaps Wang.

Arriving at the Red Chrysanthemum, Charles dismounted from his horse and gave the reins to the stable boy. With anticipation and with Miss Terrell upon his mind, Charles took the steps two at a time to the entry of the modest four-storied inn. He was greeted at the door by Baxter.

"I fear there is a disturbance, Master Gallant," Baxter informed.

Charles immediately recalled the time he had arrived at the inn to find Miss Terrell and Miss Sophia in near fisticuffs. Miss Terrell had managed to extract a handful of hair from Miss Sophia, whom Terrell had believed guilty of ruining Miss Sarah's shawl.

But the discontented voices he heard from one of the small drawing rooms were that of a man and a woman.

Baxter supplied their names. "Mistress Primrose and Mr. Nicholas."

"Have you called for Jones?"

Baxter nodded. Charles then proceeded in the direction of the drawing room. Mistress Primrose was a more recent member of the Red Chrysanthemum, but, aside from Miss Terrell, one of

Joan's prized damsels. Mistress Primrose, a young woman with some amount of breeding, commanded two submissives: Nicholas and William Edelton, cousins from a distinguished and titled family. Nicholas' brother was the Marquess of Carey. From what Charles had once witnessed, the two young men were quite devoted to Mistress Primrose.

Outside the drawing room stood Mr. Fields, a modestly dressed gentleman who seemed to blend in with his environment. His ear was pressed to the door, but upon seeing Charles, he straightened. Joan dubbed the man her *voyeur*, for he merely observed and never participated in the doings of the inn, but Charles had discovered the man to be a former Bow Street Runner hired by the Edelton family to follow Mr. Nicholas.

"Mr. Gallant." Mr. Fields greeted with a bow. "I have some news for you."

"I should like to hear it," Charles said, "but first I think I might have to intervene."

He had no need to press his ear to the door, for the voices could be heard clearly.

"But, Mistress Primrose, I implore, if I have not done wrong—indeed, I would never knowingly, willingly upset you—why will you not keep me?"

"I have told you in words both written and verbal that I *tire* of you," Mistress Primrose replied.

"But I have done all that you have ever asked. Is it the money? I am certain my brother will grant me the sum."

"You said he had refused your request."

"I have other friends who would loan me the money."

"No, no. I am done. It is not the money. Lest you can move heaven and earth or bring to life the dead, there is nothing you can do that will alter my mind."

Charles paused. She had chosen an odd set of words. He would have thought their dispute a lovers' quarrel, which he would not have wished to interfere with, but for the mention of money.

"Mistress Primrose, I beg of you to reconsider!"

"Stop! Do not *dare* to touch me."

"Mistress Primrose, please!"

"Leave me be!"

The sounds of a struggle could be heard. At that, Charles had no choice. He opened the door. Mr. Nicholas, a handsome young man dressed in fine fashion, knelt before a lovely young woman, grasping at her skirts and legs. Disdain and disgust seethed from her countenance.

"Mistress Primrose, are you in need of assistance?" Charles asked.

Her mixed heritage reminded him a little of Miss Terrell, though her complexion was not nearly as dark. She tore herself away from Nicholas and strode to where Charles stood.

"Thank you, but Mr. Nicholas and I are done," she declared. "I was impressing upon him this fact."

Nicholas hung his head.

Stepping aside, Charles allowed her to sweep out of the room. Her cold tone suggested she had not been touched in the slightest by Mr. Nicholas' impassioned pleas. Charles remembered the flare of anger in her eyes that day he had witnessed her parading Nicholas and William as her pets before the other members. She had made them wear tails in their arses and derided them with such vitriol that Charles wondered if she might hate the men. But that had made little sense. Perhaps she was simply an angry woman. It was not Charles' business to sort it all out, but it was his responsibility to keep the Red Chrysanthemum in order.

"Mr. Nicholas, may I have a word with you?" Charles asked.

Glumly, Nicholas stood. With shoulders bowed, he followed Charles out of the room. Mr. Fields had disappeared. Charles was disappointed, for he had wanted to learn what news the man had for him, but Nicholas was the more pressing matter. Charles led the young man to a room that served as Joan's office. Nicholas stumbled at the threshold, and Charles had to steady him. Charles caught the faint smell of brandy.

"Have a seat, Mr. Nicholas."

The young man flopped into the nearest chair and buried his head in his hands. "She cannot mean it. She cannot."

Charles had just closed the door behind him when a knock followed. He opened the door to Jones, a tall and strapping blackamoor. Charles stiffened, for the role Jones had played in Miss Terrell's mischief had not faded enough. But Jones had been misled or seduced or both by Miss Terrell and had been quite repentant over the affair.

"You sent for me, Master Gallant?" Jones asked.

"Have the page fetch Mr. Nicholas a cup of coffee, and I will have you stand near upon your return," Charles answered.

"I will secure the funds," Nicholas murmured,

rising to his feet. "She cannot refuse me then."

After closing the door a second time, Charles pressed Nicholas back into the chair. He drew another chair and sat facing the man.

"Mr. Nicholas, it is against the rules to come here in a state of inebriation."

Nicholas met his gaze, and Charles was struck by the bright blue hue of his eyes.

"I am hardly inebriated, sir. A glass of brandy was all I had before I came."

Charles said nothing. Though Nicholas could not have been greatly younger, Charles looked at him much as a knowing father might his fibbing son. After a moment, Nicholas hung his head.

"Mistress Primrose is a captivating creature," Charles said more gently, "with a masterful hand. Many here are taken with her."

Nicholas looked up. "She is a most remarkable woman."

"I know how it is to be drawn into the spell of such a woman. The days are not complete without her presence."

"Yes! She is the very air that I breathe, but she spurns me now, and I cannot understand why."

Nicholas looked ready to cry. The page arrived with the coffee. Charles presented the coffee to Mr. Nicholas, then took his seat again. He took in a deep breath.

"Madame warns us all not to engage with the heart at the Red Chrysanthemum. Our pursuits here are purely prurient. I knew this, yet I could not help myself. I was taken by a member here, but she belonged to another. Nevertheless, it seemed she occupied my every thought, and I went as far as China to free myself from her captivation."

"My uncle wishes to take me to Brussels or some such place, but he does not understand what ails me. Only Mistress Primrose can fill the hollow in my soul."

"I will not claim that the suffering dissipates easily, but the distraction of a foreign land did inspire me."

Nicholas shook his head. "I am devoted to Mistress Primrose. Nothing can dissuade me."

"Your passion is understandable, but I would not dismiss your uncle's offer so readily. For certain, your continued persistence here will not aid your cause."

"I cannot live without her!"

Tears glistened in the man's eyes. Charles drew in a long breath. The poor fellow was smitten, and it was not merely the brandy that spoke.

"You can survive one day without her," Charles said. "This I know. I bid you not return tomorrow night."

"No, no! I plan to secure the money she requires. I will seek Jewish money if I must! That will prove to her the lengths to which I will go for her."

"What sum is required?"

"Ten thousand pounds." Nicholas straightened. "Do you think Madame Devereux would part with such an amount? It is only a portion of what I have paid to her thus far."

Charles was stunned. Ten thousand pounds was a grand sum, even for a gentleman like Nicholas. If Nicholas had already parted with such funds, or more, Charles began to understand why Mistress

Primrose tolerated Nicholas, then cast him aside.

"I cannot speak for Joan," Charles replied, wondering how much Joan knew of what transpired between Mistress Primrose and Mr. Nicholas, but suspecting Joan to be party to the arrangement. "Mr. Nicholas, I would advise you to take great caution before seeking such monies. Ten thousand pounds can sustain a man for many, many years. Surely Mistress Primrose jests."

"You do not understand her situation. She has a family to support, and such a sum is required if she is to be free from the Red Chrysanthemum, free to marry whom she pleases."

Charles stared in surprise. "You wish to marry Mistress Primrose?"

"If she would deign to have me."

Deign to have him? Charles could hardly believe Nicholas but for the desperation with which the latter spoke. While Charles could tell from her speech and carriage that Mistress Primrose had some breeding, she was far below the station of an Edelton.

"And she has made mention of marriage?" Charles asked.

"She has not, but I would provide for her as no other man could. I have commissioned a ring of diamonds and rubies for her. When she sees its beauty—it is but a small symbol of my affection."

"Finish your coffee, Mr. Nicholas."

Charles rose to his feet. It must be the brandy talking. He shook his head. The whole affair was quite troublesome, but his responsibility was keeping the members of the Red Chrysanthemum safe.

"Mr. Nicholas, I urge you, in the light of day, to

discuss the matter with your family. Have you told them of Mistress Primrose?"

"Indeed not! They would neither understand, nor approve. But it does not matter. I can get myself to Gretna Green."

"There must be someone whose counsel you may seek."

"My cousin, William, understands. He would lend me the money I seek, but he has already given his allowance to Mistress Primrose."

Mistress Primrose was fleecing the cousin as well? Charles wondered. He would have to speak with Mistress Primrose. She could not use the Red Chrysanthemum for extortion.

"Mr. Nicholas, I have a duty to protect those who depend upon the Red Chrysanthemum for their livelihood. If Mistress Primrose says she will not see you, I cannot support your return. Pray, take a respite for a few days. You may feel differently—"

Nicholas jumped to his feet. "I will not! If you understood, you would not dare suggest such a thing! I think your affection for the member you spoke of is not half mine or you would be assured of its constancy. She does not understand the depths of my esteem, but she will!"

"Mr. Nicholas, you will not return tomorrow evening."

"And who, sir, are you to deny me? Where is Madame Devereux?"

"I govern the inn in her absence. Upon her return, I can have word sent to you, and you may appeal your case to her—"

"I cannot wait. I *will* not wait. Mistress Primrose

will hear from me. Perhaps if I proposed—I had hoped to do so when the ring was ready—but if she knew—yes, I will propose this night."

"Mr. Nicholas, the brandy influences you. I bid you return home and let its effects withdraw."

"I will speak to Mistress Primrose first." Nicholas turned for the door.

"Jones!"

Jones entered. Nicholas balked.

"Jones, please see that Mr. Nicholas finds a sedan if he did not come by horse or carriage."

"I will speak to Mistress Primrose," Nicholas insisted.

"You will not. You will go home, sleep, and think long and hard upon the wisdom of your proposal. Your passions rule you now, but reason must prevail in the end."

"Mr. Nicholas, if you please," Jones said in a deep baritone.

Nicholas hesitated but had not the courage to defy the imposing Negro.

"Tomorrow," Nicholas mumbled. "I will return tomorrow. With the funds secured."

Charles watched Jones and Nicholas depart. What the devil transpired between the Edeltons and Mistress Primrose? Though he had credited the brandy for Nicholas' fervor, Charles would not be surprised if the young man returned sober but as ardent as ever. Did Nicholas conceive the uproar he would throw his family into? Even were she not a member of the Red Chrysanthemum, Mistress Primrose had not the qualities to marry into the Edelton family. Or any gentleman's family.

Charles thought of his own situation, and if he would put his own family into such a predicament by marrying beneath himself. He doubted he would, though he had briefly entertained the notion with Miss Greta.

"You're late," Charles remarked when Wang appeared with the tray of green tea. His valet seemed always to anticipate his arrival and had the tea ready and waiting for him.

The jest fell flat with the stoic Chinaman, who replied in a monotone, "Your pardon. I was tending to Miss Terrell."

"Wang, I was not being critical. Indeed, I meant it as praise for your assiduousness, though I own it was poorly done. How is Miss Terrell?"

"Ready and awaiting your orders."

Charles felt warmth began to swirl in his groin. He sat down with a cup of tea. "My directions for this evening were not complicated, yet you were delayed."

Wang stiffened.

"Have no fears, my good man," Charles said between sips of the hot beverage. "Miss Terrell can be quite the distraction. The fact that we are mortal men could not be more obvious than in her presence. Was she well-behaved?"

"She did all that was required."

Charles pondered the response. A simple "yes" was the more expected answer from the taciturn Wang, but he did not press his valet further. Instead, he asked, "Have you seen a fellow dressed in dull brown clothing? Mr. Fields is his name."

"A man such as he followed shortly after the Negro

and a young gentleman of flaxen hair."

Charles cursed silently. If Nicholas did not return tomorrow, then Mr. Fields was unlikely to as well. Suspicious of the man at first, Charles had been tempted to terminate his membership. After Mr. Fields had divulged his true reason for frequenting the inn, following Mr. Nicholas at the behest of the family, Charles had allowed him to continue on one condition: that Mr. Fields offer his services to Charles.

Sir Arthur had a dubious past. The death of his wife had not been without mystery, but though the Justice of the Peace had concluded the matter a sad tragedy, Charles was not as readily assured. He had tasked Mr. Fields with discovering the truth.

Having decided he could not wait for Joan's return to deal with the Edelton-Primrose matter, Charles bade Wang have the page bring Mistress Primrose to him.

"Then see that Miss Terrell is comfortable," Charles said, "but do not tarry."

As he awaited Mistress Primrose, Charles recalled how, in a brothel outside the Canton factory, he had been transfixed by the sight of Wang with one of the pale, young Oriental women. The positions Wang sustained with the maiden had astounded Charles. One required the young woman to press herself up off the floor. Wang, holding her legs about his hips, penetrated her while standing. Their bodies reminded Charles of a wheelbarrow. As with many Oriental women, the woman had a slight build, but Charles could tell that Wang held most of her weight aloft or she could have crumbled to the ground when her arms gave way.

Part of Charles would have granted Wang access to Miss Terrell. The other part of him had no wish to share Miss Terrell. Though her cunnie had not been made worse from wear. Charles stopped himself from wondering just how many cocks she might have taken and dwelt instead on how marvelously tight she still felt. As tight as that of a virgin.

His cock stretched.

"Mistress Primrose," the page announced.

Sitting up, Charles crossed his legs. "Have her come in."

For someone who might have extracted pounds in the thousands, Mistress Primrose showed no evidence of it. The gown she wore was even plainer than the one Miss Terrell had worn, but Mistress Primrose carried herself with the poise of a lady. Her features were uncommon but striking. The blend of her characteristics contrived to give her an appreciable beauty. Only her exceedingly curly hair leaned more toward the likes of Miss Terrell. She was, otherwise, a perfect balance of light and dark. Joan had dubbed Mistress Primrose her Cleopatra.

"Would you care for tea?" he asked, diverting her attention to the tray upon the nearby table.

She inhaled the fragrance, wrinkled her nose, and declined.

"As you may know, Joan left the Red Chrysanthemum in my charge," he began.

"I am aware of this, Master Gallant."

"My first priority is seeing to the safety of its members. Your situation with Mr. Nicholas concerns me, as he is quite taken by you."

"I am done with Mr. Nicholas and Mr. William,"

she affirmed.

"Are you certain?"

Her dark brown eyes flashed. "I have no wish to set eyes on them ever again."

"Mr. Nicholas is convinced he can secure the funds you need."

She narrowed her eyes a little. "I do not care for his money."

"Because you have enough of it already?"

She bristled.

"While it is understood that some members make a living here, the amount Mr. Nicholas mentioned speaks to extortion."

"And I am to blame if the Edeltons wish to be reckless with their funds? I do not force their hand, Master Gallant."

"No? It is one thing for a lovesick pup to lavish extravagant gifts upon his mistress, but Mr. Nicholas spoke of ten thousand pounds."

"An income his family can easily part with."

"Perhaps, but I think not willingly, especially if they knew the recipient."

Unconcerned, she merely stared at him.

"Mistress Primrose, the Edeltons are not to be trifled with. Your actions could bring their scrutiny upon the Red Chrysanthemum."

"Madame Devereux has already weighed the risks to the Red Chrysanthemum and approved the sum. I bid you have this *tête-à-tête* with her."

She turned to leave.

"I did not dismiss you yet, Miss Primrose."

Her back arched farther at his purposeful address to her, but she turned to face him. "My affairs with the Edeltons do not concern you."

"They concern the Red Chrysanthemum. My hand is forced."

"As I have said, I am done with them. In fact, I wish to take a leave of absence from the Red Chrysanthemum and prepare to return home to Liverpool within a fortnight."

"You hail from Liverpool?"

"Yes. My neph— I have family there."

"I plan to discuss the matter with Joan upon her return. In the meantime, regardless of whether you are done with Mr. Nicholas, he is not done with you. I forbid his return tomorrow night, but he is eager to speak to you. The man was a little intoxicated tonight and talked of offering for your hand."

She seemed mildly surprised, but her disdain reappeared. It was clear she would never consider marrying the man. Charles could not quite understand why. Mistress Primrose could not do better than an Edelton, and Mr. Nicholas was more devoted to her than any man she could possibly consider. Charles could only guess that perhaps Nicholas was too much a fool for her.

"If Mr. Nicholas presents a problem, I urge you to seek my assistance," Charles told her. "Know that I may be more averse to risk than Joan when it comes to the Red Chrysanthemum. I will not tolerate activities that place our membership, or your person, in jeopardy."

"I applaud your guardianship, Master Gallant, and assure you that, as I owe much to the Red Chrysanthemum, I will not see it harmed either. Have no fear. The Edeltons will tire of me and move on to a new conquest. They can sustain no emotion of redeeming quality. They are a ruthless lot."

Charles raised his brows at such a sweeping assessment. He did not understand her resentment toward the men who had apparently given her copious amounts of money. Why had she taken them as her submissives if she detested them so? He considered telling her about Mr. Fields but hesitated to reveal the man.

"All the more reason to proceed with caution then, Mistress Primrose," Charles said.

She lowered her lashes in thought, then lifted her chin in defiance. "Your concern is much appreciated, but I can handle the Edeltons."

"I hope that to be true."

Charles did not know the Edelton family well, but he could not help a sense of dread that Mistress Primrose was wrong.

Chapter 10

Terrell gazed into the looking glass across from the bed. She had never known the proprietress of the Red Chrysanthemum to engage as a participant herself. It was not even known if Madame Devereux would take the dominant or submissive role, if she favored men or the fair sex, but why then, would she have had the looking glass placed where it was? Why did she have implements at the ready in her chambers? And a cage? Terrell could not envision Madame Devereux submitting to the enclosure.

Remembering how Master Gallant had confined her to the cage, Terrell pursed her lips. She had both liked and disliked the experience. He had made her wait inside the bars whilst he'd conducted an interview of a young molly applying for membership and forbidden her to pleasure herself though her body had been tense with lust. But the naughtiness of it, the wickedness of it, had ultimately aroused her.

Given that she valued her freedom, when she had spent most of her life without it, one would think a cage reprehensible to her sensibilities. Yet, she had found an odd relief inside its confines. Perhaps it was akin to the security a babe found in being tightly swaddled. Or perhaps it owed to the comfort she felt with Master Gallant. There was a *tranquility* to placing herself in his hands. Now that she had him, she did not have to ponder, maneuver, manipulate, anticipate, or initiate. In surrendering herself to him, she found a different sort of freedom.

His instructions to her tonight had been simple. She was to wear the shirt he had gifted her. The linen was much finer than that of the one she had previously owned. As it was cut for a man, it fight tight about the bosom, and the outline of her nipples could be seen through the material. She crossed one bare leg over the other and admired her own figure. If only her back were not marred, then there would not be a part of herself that she did not like.

She recalled well the look of horror upon Gallant's face when he had unknowingly exposed her back after ripping her shirt. She had always hidden her ugliness because she had thought she could not bear such a reaction. On the plantation, she had been the beautiful one, the one all the men wanted and the women envied. As long as she covered herself, she could still present herself as beautiful.

She preferred still to conceal her back, though Gallant had already laid eyes on her hideousness, though his guilt over the matter had led to their reconciliation. He had been furious with her for tying him to a chair and forcing herself upon him. Her mouth upon his cock proving too pleasurable, he had succumbed and consented to her attentions. Spending, however, had merely stalled, not alleviated, his anger. He had seemed intent upon repaying her in kind.

Till he saw her back.

After sending him away—for, in that moment, she

wanted only a hole in which she might burrow and never emerge—she had followed him and begged his forgiveness. Sure that he would want nothing further of her, she had been stunned when he'd swept her against the wall of the dark alley and kissed her.

She relived all her moments with Gallant, but that one she recalled more often than others. The cool night air around them contrasting with the heat between them, their bodies finding each other despite the darkness, his hard length filling her, his ardent thrusts and palpable desire for her despite her unsightliness. He had desired her nonetheless. Desired her still.

Heat simmered in her loins as she waited for Gallant. Restless, she picked up the novel of Fanny Hill. She opened the book and looked at the words. She liked the character of Fanny, a young woman who takes to whoring to provide for herself. She is introduced to the pleasures of the flesh by Phoebe, who shares her bed.

Terrell had had her Phoebe in the form of Miss Ruth, a house slave. If not for Miss Ruth, Terrell might have perceived the carnal in an entirely different light. She recalled hearing the quiet sobs of a field slave ravished for the first time by one of Mr. Tremayne's secondaries. Had she not been introduced to the insights of Miss Ruth, she would have feared for herself. Men had started staring at her when she was about ten years of age.

"I not be the prettiest," Miss Ruth had said with pride, "but I got m'self into the Great House."

Seeing the superior clothes Miss Ruth wore, Terrell had been determined to make her way into the Great House as well. She had been raised there, for her mother had been a house slave till she had fallen out of favor and had been sent back into the fields. For reasons Terrell never questioned, Miss Ruth had taken her under her wing and taught her how to pleasure the opposite sex.

"You being pretty, they is going to fuck you, like it or no," Miss Ruth had told her. "You can cry like a babe 'bout it, or you can please 'em and be rewarded."

It had seemed an obvious choice to Terrell.

A crack from the fire drew Terrell from her thoughts. She glanced at the small clock above the mantle of the fireplace. Master Gallant might be a while longer, depending upon how many members arrived. She could not recall ever taking such satisfaction from pleasuring a man. Aside from the rugged field slave whom she had pottered with, Gallant was the only man whom she pleasured without regards to a reward, whose pleasure *pleasured* her. She smiled as she considered all the ways she could delight his body. It would behoove him to allow her the freedom to show him.

As if materializing from her thoughts, Master Gallant stood at the threshold. She took in his handsome form, his soft and slightly tousled hair, the glimmer of his crystalline eyes, the set of his jaw. His clothes always fit him well but bore none of the ostentation that others of his means might have preferred. She liked how his blue coat paired with the light sapphire of his irises, but her favorite was how closely his trousers encased his legs.

Remembering herself, she went to her knees upon

the floor, clasped her hands before her, and lowered her gaze. "Good evening, Master Gallant."

Crossing to her in long strides, he cupped her beneath her chin and drew her to her feet. She had expected him to inquire as to whether or not she had behaved this day. Instead, his mouth clamped over hers. In the dizzying kiss that ensued, he plumbed the depths of her mouth, his lips moving forcefully over hers, his breath hot and heavy upon her. Desire surged within her. Her hands had grasped his arms in surprise and a need to keep herself upright against the assault. He kissed her deep and long.

She let him work her mouth, then began to increase her participation little by little. Her tongue teased and flirted with his. He released her chin and, grabbing a buttock, crushed her body to his. She thrilled to his erection pressing against her and hoped it would not be long before he buried his hardness inside of her. She came farther onto the tips of her toes and wrapped her arms about his neck, pulling him to her that she could more fully drown in his kiss.

She gasped when his hands roamed her back. His touch did not hurt, but she wondered that she would ever be comfortable.

"I'm sorry," he whispered.

Not wanting him to be sorry, she wrapped a leg around his and pushed her pelvis at him. He hoisted her up by the back of her thighs. She licked and kissed at his throat. He grunted when she plunged her tongue into an ear. She sucked upon his neck with the desperation of a starving babe. He sat down upon the bed. She straddled his legs, and they continued to kiss as her hands fumbled for his cravat. In an instant, he had a hand in her hair.

Yanking her head back, he reminded her, "Ask permission, Miss Terrell."

"May I undress and pleasure you?"

"Have you been good?"

"I have, Master, I have."

"Then you may."

Gleefully, she undid his neckcloth and collar, kissing the small amount of skin exposed about the throat. She unbuttoned his waistcoat next. She wanted to rip the buttons apart, for she would have him naked, but she did not wish to part her body from his yet. He cupped her breasts and kneaded the flesh. When he passed his thumbs over her erect nipples, she shivered. He rolled the buds through the shirt.

"Wang was tardy with my tea," he remarked.

She moaned as she pressed her breasts at his hands. Her cunnie pulsed with need, and she ground herself atop his thighs.

"I had given him simple orders for tonight. Were you the cause of his delay?"

"I did only as he bid," she answered.

"And nothing more?"

"Your Chinaman is made of stone. I doubt anything could move him."

She did not think her statement entirely true. She had seen hints of a reaction from Wang at different moments.

"Because you have tried without success."

She looked into Gallant's eyes. Was he possibly jealous of his own valet?

"I have attempted nothing with Wang," she said.

He began twisting a nipple.

She yelped. "Perhaps I teased him a little. I asked if he had ever tasted black flesh?"

"And what was his reply?"

"He made no reply."

"Have you ever had yellow cock?"

"I have not."

"Would you wish to?"

"If my master wishes it. I would gladly take any cock he commands, but I do desire one above all others." She fixed a smoldering stare at him. "Yours."

Satisfied, he threw up her shirt, lowered his head, and devoured her breasts. She gasped and moaned with quivering breath. Her body squirmed at the delicious agony.

"Master, may I have your cock?" she asked when she did not think she could bear the agitation in her loins any longer. "I have hungered for it all day. Let me pleasure it and worship its greatness."

He pulled back. She took this gesture as an assent. Lifting herself off his thighs, she assisted him from his coat and waistcoat. She undid his braces next, then pushed him down to the bed. Pulling the hem of his shirt from his trousers, she pushed it up his chest and attended to his nipples with as much ferocity as he had tended to hers. She then kissed her way down to his fall. She caressed the hardness there before unbuttoning his trousers.

His beautiful cock sprang forth. How she adored his length, the wide flare of the crown, the slight curvature of the stalk, the lovely veins providing the perfect hint of texture. She licked just beneath the head and heard his shortened breath. Holding him in hand, she wrapped her mouth over the top. Her lashes fluttered as she savored the taste of him, the hardness. How such soft, pliant flesh could take on the stiffness of metal was a wonder of nature. She sucked as her mouth slid up his shaft. But for her own desires, she would have happily coaxed him to spend with her mouth.

She straddled his hips and squatted over his cock. As she sat down, her cunnie swallowed his length. She wiggled a little and felt his cock touch all the right spots inside of her. With her legs spread, he had easy access to her clitoris, which he fondled with his thumb till she quaked. Resisting the desire to spend because he had not granted her permission yet, she put her hands on his chest for support and began pumping her body up and down his cock.

From her position, she could look into his eyes, and the lust she saw there fueled her own. He held her under arse and thigh to aide her motions, lifting her before letting her fall back down his length. He met her descent with a thrust, and flesh slapped flesh with steady occurrence. Her legs began to burn with the exertion and she paused to pull off her shirt. His eyes gleamed as her breasts bounced before him. While one hand continued to support her beneath a thigh, his other caressed a breast and toyed with the nipple. Perspiration dotted her bosom and brow, her heart hammered, but she continued to ride his cock, wanting to see him grimace with the intensity of pleasure.

Seeing she might need a reprieve, he pulled her ankles toward him to straighten her legs and rolled her onto her side, away from him. He positioned himself behind her such that their head and feet were at opposite ends. He angled his cock down and slid it between her thighs. She felt him glide over her moist folds. She softly moaned, but while she enjoyed the sweet sensation, she wanted more and tried to bear down on his hardness.

He pulled his cock from between her legs. She felt it next at her arse. Her breath caught. And then she felt him, pressing into the smaller opening. When the flare of his shaft popped into her orifice, she thought she might spend in seconds. She took long, deep breaths to still the quake from erupting. Slowly, he slid more of his cock into her. The angle of penetration, pressing upon new places within her, made her feel as if she had never taken a cock in her arse before. The rapture threatened to overwhelm her.

"Will you spend, Master?" she whispered, hoping he would so that she might soon follow.

He took her nearest hand and guided it to her mons. With a difficult exhale, she wriggled her fingers against herself. Resisting the onslaught of pleasure, she could not speak to ask his permission to spend. He placed his hands upon her thighs and began a gentle thrust.

"Master…" she whined.

Her hand slipped away, but he replaced it. "Fondle yourself."

"But—"

At her hesitation, he rubbed her himself.

"No! I—Lord—"

Holding her climax at bay had never required such

strenuous effort. With shaky fingers, she petted herself.

Holding her thighs, he resumed his thrusts.

"P-Please..." she cried. She would have preferred he cane her arse then require her to withhold the tempest inside her body.

He thrust harder, slamming his groin at her buttocks. If she had not been so highly aroused, she might have found the penetration uncomfortable, painful even. The bed trembled from their motions. The sound of flesh slapping upon flesh filled the air. She gripped the bedclothes below with her free hand till her knuckles whitened. Eyes squeezed shut, brow furrowed, she would have sobbed if she could spare enough attention to do so.

Then through the haze, came his command. "Spend!"

She allowed her body to uncoil. Tension sprang free to the tips of her fingers, the tips of her toes. Her body fell into a violet paroxysm and bucked against him. Fluid streamed from her. Her anus spasmed about his cock, causing him to spend. She heard his roar amidst her wails of devastation and relief. She collapsed farther into the bed, drenched in perspiration and bodily fluids.

The tremors persisted long afterward. Repositioning himself, he scooped her into his arms. She shuddered, then sighed.

"Thank you, Master."

He kissed the back of her head and pulled her closer. She could hear the fast beating of his heart and realized there was no place she wanted to be more than in his embrace.

Chapter 11

Here I laved and wantoned with the water, or sportively played with my companion, leaving Emily to deal with hers at discretion. Mine, at length, not content with making me take the plunge over head and ears, kept splashing me, and provoking me with all the little playful tricks he could devise, and which I strove not to remain in his debt for. We gave, in short, a loose to mirth; and now, nothing would serve him but giving his hand the regale of going over every part of me, neck, breast, belly, thighs, and all the et cetera, so dear to the imagination, under the pretext of washing and rubbing them; as we both stood in the water, no higher now than the pit of our stomachs, and which did not hinder him from feeling, and toying with that leak that distinguishes our sex, and it so wonderfully water-tight: for his fingers, in vain dilating and opening it, only let more flame than water into it, be it said without a figure. At the same time he made me feel his own engine, which was so well wound up, as to stand even the working in water, and he accordingly threw one arm round my neck, and was endeavouring to get the better of that harsher construction bred by the surrounding fluid; and had in effect one hiway so far as to make me sensible of the pleasing stretch of those nether lips, from the in-driving machine; when, independent of my not liking that awkward mode of enjoyment, I could not help interrupting him, in order to become joint spectators of a plan of joy, in hot operation between Emily and her partner; who impatient of the fooleries and dalliance of the bath, had led his nymph to one of the benches on the green bank, where he was very cordially proceeding to teach her the difference betwixt jest and earnest.

"'There, setting her on his knee, and gliding one hand over the surface of that smooth polished snow-white skin of hers, which now doubly shone with a dew-bright lustre, and presented to the touch something like what one would imagine of animated ivory, especially in those ruby-nippled globes, which the touch is so fond of and delights to make love to, with the other hand lusciously exploring the sweet secret of nature, in order to make room for a stately piece of machinery, that stood up-reared, between her thighs, as she continued siting on his lap, and pressed hard for instant intromission, which the tender Emily, in a fit of humour deliciously protracted, affected to decline, and elude the very pleasure she sighed for, but in a style of waywardness, so prettily put on, and managed, as to render it ten times more poignant; then her eyes, all amidst the softest dying languishment, expressed, at once a mock denial and extreme desire, whilst her sweetness was zested with a coyness so pleasingly provoking, her moods of keeping him off were so attractive, that they redoubled the impetuous rage with, which, he covered her with kisses: and kisses that, whilst she seemed to shy from or scuffle for, the cunning wanton contrived such sly returns, of, as were, doubtless the sweeter for the gust she gave them, of being stolen ravished.'"

Her breath grew uneven, but Miss Terrell remained where she sat on the bed beside him, nestled in the crook of his arm.

In the light of morning, Charles continued to read from John Cleland's *Memoirs of a Woman of Pleasure.*

"'Thus Emily, who knew no art but that which nature itself, in favour of her principal end, pleasure, had inspired her with, the art of yielding, coyed it indeed, but coyed it to the purpose; for with all her straining, her wrestling, and striving to break from the clasp of his arms, she was so far wiser yet than to mean it, that in her struggles, it was visible she aimed at nothing more than multiplying points of touch with him, and drawing yet closer the folds that held them every where entwined, like two tendrils of a vine intercurling together, so that the same effect, as when Louisa strove in good earnest to disengage from the idiot, was-now produced by different motives.

"'Mean while, their emersion out of the cold water had caused a general glow, a tender suffusion of heightened carnation over their bodies; both equally white and smoothskinned; so that as their limbs were-thus amorously interwoven, in sweet confusion, it was scarce possible to distinguish who they respectively belonged to, but for the brawnier, bolder muscles of the stronger sex.'"

She took in a sharp breath. A blush tinted her cheeks, and his responding heat was immediate.

"How skillfully he casts the scene in our heads,"

she exclaimed.

"With words as his paint," he agreed.

She shook her head and looked at the words on the page with marvel.

"Shall I continue?" he asked.

"Oh, yes!"

"'In a little time, however, the champion was fairly in with her, and had tied at all points the true lovers' knot; when now, adieu all the little refinements of a finessed reluctance; adieu the friendly feint! She was presently driven forcibly out of the power of using any art; and indeed, what art must not give way, when nature, corresponding with her assailant, invaded in the heart of her capital and carried by storm, lay at the mercy of the proud conqueror, who had made his entry triumphantly and completely? Soon, however, to become a tributary: for the engagement growing hotter and hotter, at close quarters, she presently brought him to the pass of paying down the dear debt to nature; which she had no sooner collected in, but, like a duelist who has laid his antagonist at his feet, when he has himself received a mortal wound, Emily had scarce time to plume herself upon her victory, but, shot with the same discharge, she, in a loud expiring sigh, in the closure of her eyes, the stretch-out of her limbs, and a remission of her whole frame, gave manifest signs that all was as it should be.'"

Terrell gave her own sigh. "I wonder how much of his own life might have inspired these passages?"

Charles closed the book. "I think Mr. Cleland a man of immense imagination. If he were as active as the characters he invents, he would have had no time to write such a novel."

"No? You could write such a novel, I think. Your experiences here at the Red Chrysanthemum could easily rival those of Fanny."

He set aside the book and drew the bedclothes off them. Her dark, naked body contrasted with the light-colored linen. He drank in her curves, formed, it seemed, with the sole intent of arousing desire in the opposite sex.

"I've not Cleland's gift for color," he murmured, straddling her hips.

Her eyes shone. "But you have other skills."

He leaned down to kiss her neck, inhaling her scent. The musk of last night's exertions still clung to her, making his blood course thick and strong within him. She grasped his hand and brought him to her mouth. Their lips locked. He could have feasted upon her soft, plump lips for hours if another part of him did not call so fiercely. Fortunately, Miss Terrell required little. Her arousal was swift, her impatience sizable. She writhed beneath him and, like Emily, seemed to want to touch as many parts of her body to his as possible.

He disengaged from her mouth to attend her breasts. She gasped and squealed as he nibbled upon a nipple, biting and tugging. But unlike the playfully squirming Emily, Miss Terrell took quick aim at her target and reached for his cock. Her carnal appetite was fearless. He wondered if teaching her her place would always prove a struggle? Then wondered if he truly wanted to tame her into submission? Her boldness often invigorated him.

He sat up and angled his cock at her mound. With

his knees on either side of her hips, she could not part her legs far. He pushed the tip between her thighs and grazed the ready wetness there. The poor laundry maid would have her hands full with the bed linen. He fondled her clitoris with his cock. Pinned beneath him, she had limited movement, but her hands roamed freely. She touched herself, winding fingers through her hair, cupping her breasts and pinching her nipples.

His hardness stretched at the sight, and he could wait no longer. He had to possess such voluptuousness. He slid into her. The penetration was shallow from this position, but the tightness of her opening more than compensated. Bracing himself on his own ankles, he started to thrust, joining the golden curls at his groin to her black moss. Her mouth parted and her eyes widened. He could see from the look in her eyes that she hoped he would be more merciful and allow her to spend earlier this time.

"You may," he granted.

She flexed her cunnie in appreciation. He shivered at the pleasure that shot through his groin. Their bodies found an easy rhythm. Before long, she was panting and straining, her back arching, her brow furrowing. Nothing could be more arousing than the sight of a woman on the verge of spending.

"Spend," he urged.

With a cry, she did. Her thighs bumped against his buttocks, and her arms flailed. Her head was thrown back, her body jerked, and her breasts quivered. The throbbing of her cunnie would have compelled him to spend with her, but he was momentarily mesmerized.

When the tide had passed through her body, she gazed at him with glimmering eyes, and he was once again struck by the contrast between her dark irises and the bright whites of her eyes. Her cheeks flushed. Her whole countenance glowed with contentment till she realized he was still hard inside of her.

"Spill your seed upon me," she said. Her eyes flared with lust.

How could he resist this woman when she spoke in such fashion? Withdrawing from her wet heat, he took his cock in hand. He stroked himself as she watched intently, her tongue passing over her bottom lip. That devilish tongue. How it had undone him! He pulled harder upon his cock. He could feel the tension coiling in his groin.

"Yes, yes!" she panted. She cupped his cods and tugged.

The discomfort only fueled his ardor. After several thrusts, his cock poured forth its effusion. His body jerked as the last of the thick white liquid sprayed over her belly, a few drops landing at her breasts. He stared as she skimmed a finger atop her belly then sucked the digit clean. He shuddered. She took another dollop of his seed into her mouth and seemed to relish the taste. Her hand drifted down past her mons. He watched her rub herself, impressed by her lack of timidity. He joined his hand to hers. Together, they fondled her till her head fell back once more and the moaning returned. With her other hand, she spread his mettle over her nakedness. His head swam from the vision, from a primal satisfaction at seeing her marked and coated with his seed. He inserted a finger, then two into her sodden furnace. She cooed and continued to ply her clitoris. He pushed in a third finger. His pulse pounded with the memory of having his whole hand inside her. Withdrawing, he passed his hand over her belly, coating his palm and knuckles. She lifted her hips, wanting his return. Gently, he pressed three fingers into her.

"Thank you, Master," she murmured.

He added a fourth. When he sensed she was relaxed enough, he tucked his thumb and slowly pushed his hand in. Her breath quickened when his knuckles approached her entry. He paused.

"Please, Master, please."

He pressed the widest part of his hand into her. Her cunnie clenched upon his hand and drew him in to the wrist. His fingers curled naturally into a fist. She was still but for her wildly fluttering lashes. He remained still, amazed that she had engulfed his entire hand, that he could touch her most intimate parts in such fashion.

"Master..."

"Do you require your safety word?" he asked, worried the thickness was too much for her.

"...fuck me."

She resumed fondling her clit. Her other hand grabbed the headboard behind her. With small motions, he thrust his hand in with minor rotations.

Within minutes, she groaned, "May I?"

"You may."

Her cunnie convulsed. Her body quaked. Fluid drenched his arm. He held her down with his free hand to keep her body from bucking too violently. She let out several cries that reverberated in his ears.

A most gratifying sound. Her breath trembled even as her body gradually fell into repose. On occasion, a tremor would shoot through her. He waited till she could be still before he gently withdrew. She lay as if in a trance, her eyelids drawn halfway down, her bosom rising and falling with more even breaths. Crawling over her, he joined his mouth to hers. His kiss was light and tender. When he pulled away, she looked at him with in a soft, heartfelt gaze.

"Thank you," she said.

"Your servant," he replied with a smile before he realized how incongruous the words sounded. It was a response of politesse, a natural outcome of his upbringing as a gentleman, but her eyes widened a little in surprise.

"*Mademoiselle*," he added as he took her hand and kissed it, as if they were being introduced at court and not lying naked upon a bed, each adorned with the other's essence.

She grinned. "An enticing thought if not merely a manner of speech."

He cut her line of thought before she proceeded too far down that path. "You have had your fun already, Miss Terrell."

She retreated. "Yes, well, I speak only if you were ever inclined in that other direction, if you were curious or the sort of Master who shifts..."

"I am not." The hardness had returned to his cock at seeing her spend, and he would have considered taking her a second time but for the hour. He offered his hand to assist her from the bed. "Come. I will cleanse you."

"Are you so very certain? It may be more

enjoyable than you think."

"When I first started here, I assumed the submissive position. One cannot be an accomplished dominant without knowledge and appreciation of the other party, and I did enjoy my instruction under Mistress Brownwen."

"But you've no interest in revisiting, even briefly, that role?"

He found linen and dipped it into a washbasin filled with water. "I would not say it were impossible for me to reconsider, but at present I am quite content with the part of the dominant one."

He passed the linen over her belly and wiped his drying seed from her. She shivered at the coldness of the damp cloth.

"And I have no complaints of that." She lowered her lashes. "I do not think I would allow any other to do as you have done, fitting your fist inside of me. You must have done it before?"

"With Mistress Brownwen. But no other woman has granted the entry of my hand. The girth presents too much pain."

"If they knew the wonder that awaits upon the other side," she murmured, "they would not hesitate."

He cleansed the rest of her, then wrapped her in his banyan. After finding another robe for himself, he went to ring for Wang. Within seconds, a knock at the door announced Wang's arrival. Charles shook his head. The man possessed a mysterious power with his timing.

Wang placed a tray of tea, coffee, toast, ham and eggs upon the sideboard. Terrell did not wait for Wang to leave before falling upon the food. Charles remembered that the alacrity with which she ate was out of habit from her days as a slave in Barbados, where food was scarce and often stolen if not consumed. While she helped herself to two slices of ham and smothered a slice of toast in butter, Wang assisted him with his shave and then his attire.

"I will send for the laundry maid," Wang anticipated after Charles was dressed in buff-colored trousers, striped waistcoat, and coat of burgundy with brass buttons.

"*Xie xie*," Charles replied.

"Was that Chinese you spoke?" Terrell asked after Wang had departed. She sat with her legs draped over the side of her chair, the last slice of toast in hand.

"Yes." Crossing to her, he captured her hand so that he could take a bite of her toast. He had conjured an appetite after their morning activities.

"I suppose I should have saved the last toast for you," she said, offering the remainder of what she had.

"Keep it." He took a boiled egg for himself. "How else are you to keep your supple figure?"

"They would consider me fat in Barbados."

He imagined the island full of emaciated slaves everywhere one turned. "Thankfully, we are not in Barbados."

"When I was the mistress of Sir Fairchild, I had meat pie, eggs, cheese, and bread every morning. I would I could start every morning with such a feast!"

Finishing her toast, she reached for the last egg, then reconsidered. "I think I have eaten twice as much as you."

"I became accustomed to a light breakfast in my time in the Orient," he replied. "We often started with a sort of rice porridge that was nothing more than water and cooked rice. For flavor, I would add pickles and small slices of dried meat."

"It sounds rather plain, but I would have it over breadfruit. I should be happy never to have to eat breadfruit again."

Breadfruit, he understood, was a cheap food for the slaves. He handed her the last egg.

"What else did you have to eat while in the Orient? Did you find any of their foods pleasing?"

He recalled how much Miss Greta had enjoyed the pears he had brought back from China.

"Quite a lot. My father had not taken to their fare much. He found their vegetables could be bitter. But they have all manner of fruits. And they make use of rice in most fascinating ways, as desserts and noodles."

"And you spoke their language when you were there?"

He went to where Wang had laid out her articles of clothing. After finishing her egg, she went to him to be dressed. She let the banyan fall from her. He admired the many curves of her body, from her breasts to her hips. His gaze settled at the patch of curls above her thighs, and warmth spread through his loins. But he could not tarry. He was to meet with Sir Canning later in the morning.

"I could speak one dialect of Chinese with some fluency," he said as he assisted her into her shift. "Like young Thomas Staunton, I studied Chinese at an early age. But the speech differs from region to region. Even Wang is familiar with only three."

"Is it difficult to learn? Much harder than French?"

"Much harder. There are sounds that I can hear but cannot make manifest with my tongue."

"I had a wish to learn French. All the proper folks of polite society know French. Women who talked of me but did not wish me to understand them would fall into French. I will take up French after I have learned to read."

"You speak with surety, your ambition commendable."

"For certain, I do not plan to remain here. I was once a coveted courtesan to esteemed gentlemen and have every intention of returning to my prior situation."

He tied a petticoat in place. He had not considered what aspirations she might have beyond the Red Chrysanthemum and felt unsettled by her declaration. It reminded him of Sir Arthur.

"Though I would remain for as long as you wished to be my Master," she hastened to add.

"Or until Sir Arthur returns," he said, then pressed his lips into a grim line. He took up her stays next. "You will not forsake him."

She hesitated. "I did not say I would not."

"Your want of an answer is itself an answer."

"I protest. I cannot answer till I know what Madame Devereux might wish. I cannot vex her."

Charles had to acknowledge the sensibility of her consideration but found no comfort in it. Joan would not wish for Terrell to relinquish Sir Arthur. "Madame Devereux will be unhappy to part with you. Of that I am fairly certain."

"Yes, but she cannot expect I will always be here. Oh!"

He had pulled upon the ribbons harder than he'd intended. "You wish to be Sir Arthur's mistress then?"

"I doubt a man of his standing would take a blackamoor for a mistress."

"But if he did? He seems quite taken with you."

"The novelty for him will fade. It often does."

"Did it fade with Sir Fairchild? With Mr. Worthington?"

"Mr. Worthington is a West Indies man. He is accustomed to black flesh. As for Sir Fairchild, if his wife had not forced his hand, he would have let me go eventually."

Somehow Charles doubted her conclusion. She had a way of increasing a man's appetite even as he sated his desire of her.

"*You* will tire of me, Master Gallant," she said.

He wondered if her accusation was a diversion from the fact that she had yet to answer his question regarding Sir Arthur.

"I think you will tire of me first," he replied, tying the laces. Tight.

She grunted. An uncomfortable silence settled between them.

"I think not, but our hands may be forced," she said at last, turning to face him. Her eyes brimmed with more emotion than he expected.

How had he arrived here? From not wanting her attentions, he now had no desire to see her with anyone else. But there was truth in her statement. And pragmatism.

"You are a woman of sense," he acknowledged and

assisted her into her gown, "a quality that has stood you in great stead. That and your ability to overcome tribulations through gratitude. How you can speak of your past without bitterness is impressive."

"I am not without resentment, but I cannot reflect on my prior life without immense *relief* for my current fortune."

He knew few women who would describe her situation as one of fortune. Terrell was an intriguing mix of humbleness and arrogance. Without doubt, this combination allowed her to preserve a state of mind that enabled her to forge through hardship and aim for more and better for herself.

"When you have learned to read and to write, you could attempt your own memoirs," he mused aloud.

"You mean like Fanny?"

"I was thinking of Mr. Equiano."

"I am but a naughty wench. Like Fanny, I can recount the many sorts of men I have encountered for your amusement."

Charles was tempted to respond he was unlikely to find any amusement in her paramours, but said instead, "Your journey from slavery is not unlike Equiano's. You may not have endured the passage from Africa as he had, but you have both endured and survived a life of bondage."

"I met a Negress, a servant more learned than I. She had read the writings of Mr. Equiano and described them to be filled with arguments of philosophy, the disadvantages of slavery, and the advantages of ending the institution. Such matters require a wisdom greater than what I possess."

"You have but to tell your story. One cannot

receive it without being stirred to the injustices of slavery."

"But not enough to vote for its abolition?"

It was his turn to hesitate. She reached for his hand.

"I know no man of greater integrity than you, Master Gallant."

"Forgive my impertinence, but I question the quality of men you have known."

"Nevertheless, I know you will do what you esteem right and honorable."

"And that would be to support abolition and not its delay."

To his surprise, she replied, "That is for you to decide. Your truth may differ from mine, but you are not the lesser for it."

She covered his hand with her other hand, and he felt the warmth of her compassion.

"I could do much more if elected to Parliament than not," he said. "I know Mr. Chester does not favor abolition."

"A man with your noble qualities ought to serve in Parliament."

"Even if I were to support the deferment of abolition?"

"Yes. I may not have thought it at first, but as you say, you can do more within Parliament than without. Your first consideration is to win the burgess and to do what is necessary for victory."

"At whose expense? Save for my conscience, I am not the one who must suffer for my decision. My freedom is not at stake."

"If you cannot win your election, you will not have

the chance to improve matters for anyone."

He pulled his hand toward himself, drawing her to him. He kissed her hands. "You underestimate your wisdom, Miss Terrell."

"May I ask how I am to prepare myself this evening? Perhaps I could save Wang the trouble."

"Name your pleasure."

She inhaled sharply. "I must deliberate upon such a privilege."

"I await your answer upon my return then."

He smiled at the delight radiating from her. Cupping her face, he kissed her with a new depth of emotion, which, were he not in a good disposition, might have troubled him. Especially as she had not answered his question regarding Sir Arthur.

Chapter 12

What have you discovered?" Charles took a seat opposite Mr. Fields in Joan's study.

The man had returned to the inn just as Charles was headed out. Though Charles had hoped to review what letters might have arrived at Whitehall before his meeting with Sir Canning, he could not pass up the opportunity to speak with Mr. Fields.

"I have found the former maid to the Arthur household," Mr. Fields said. "She is employed by an Italian woman married to a merchant in Norwich. The maid's name is Jenny Adams."

"Well done, Mr. Fields. You truly are skilled at what you do," Charles commended.

"The name was easy to come by. It was in the records taken by the Justice of the Peace. He had, however, retired, but the family of the late Lady Arthur had requested to keep the records. They would not grant me access at first, but I convinced them that I had been hired by a woman very interested in employing Miss Adams, who reminded her of her own daughter, whose life had been cut short by the fever, but this woman was confused as to why Miss Adams had no reference from her previous employer. I was told in no uncertain terms by Lady Arthur's mother that a more dedicated maidservant could not be had. And courageous. I remarked that that was uncommon praise for a servant. She explained that Miss Adams had been brave enough to speak the truth of what happened in the tragedy that took Lady Arthur's life."

Charles sat at the edge of his seat. "Lady Arthur fell down the stairs."

Mr. Fields nodded. "She had been with child and in her ninth month. Sir Arthur had told the Justice of the Peace that she had been unstable, that she could not move about without the greatest discomfort. But Miss Adams attests that her ladyship and Sir Arthur had been engaged in a quarrel, after which Sir Arthur *pushed* his wife down the stairs. The fall broke her neck."

A chill went through Charles, though he had half-suspected such a thing.

"According to the testimony of Sir Arthur, the maid went into hysterics," Mr. Fields continued. "The doctor happened to be in the house and extracted the unborn babe. That it survived is rather a miracle."

"Miss Adams had witnessed their quarrel then?"

"She said she could hear them from the library and thought to intrude into the hallway where they were, to spare her ladyship the wrath of Sir Arthur, who was accusing his wife of being unfaithful. But Sir Arthur maintains that Miss Adams was not in the hallway until after her ladyship had fallen. From where he stood at the top of the stairs, he had a full view of the hallway. The Justice of the Peace determined this was indeed so."

"And even were it not, who would take the word of a young servant girl over that of an esteemed

Member of Parliament?" Charles wondered aloud.

"Sir Arthur had motive," Mr. Fields acknowledged. "Miss Adams had confessed Lady Arthur indeed had a lover."

"But it was concluded that no foul play was present."

"After much questioning, Miss Adams admitted that she had not clearly seen Sir Arthur push his wife. She saw a struggle at the top of the stairs. The bannister interrupted her sight. She inferred that Sir Arthur had pushed Lady Arthur, but Sir Arthur had said he was trying to prevent his wife from going downstairs, that he bid her remain in her bed, given her fragile state with child. Miss Adams acknowledged, in the end, that this was possible and she might have mistaken what she had seen."

"She changed her story?"

"From what I am able to gather from reading the accounts of the investigation, after much interrogation of the maid, she was certain only of her name."

"I wonder how accurate her initial intuition of the situation to have been?"

"Would you like me to further my inquiry?"

"Discreetly."

"Of course."

"It is not my intention to renew the investigation, but I would have a better understanding of what transpired. Were there no other witnesses to Lady Arthur's fall?"

"None that the records mention, though I did, when talking to one of the current Arthur servants, discover that the housekeeper, Mrs. Franklin, had left her employment shortly after the death of her ladyship, though Mrs. Franklin had been with the Arthur family nigh on thirty years. It may be mere coincidence, but if you wish, I could look into her as well."

Charles nodded. "Unearth as much as you can."

"I will do so as expeditiously as I can, but I must remind you that I have also my other assignment."

"Yes. I have barred Nicholas from returning tonight. I think he requires time and space to cool his ardor. If you could see that he—"

"Mr. Nicholas knows not I follow him, and it is not my duty to intervene, merely to observe."

Charles wondered if Mr. Fields was aware of the monies Nicholas had given to or promised to provide Miss Primrose. "It concerns me that his family has knowledge of the Red Chrysanthemum."

"My employer is aware of the need for discretion and a man of his word. He forfeits a tidy sum if he breeches the confidence."

Charles shook his head. Joan had relaxed her standards since his return. "I take it your employer can afford to forfeit his tidy sum."

"That is true."

There was little Charles could do, as Joan had already granted Mr. Fields entry. He leaned back into his chair.

"And what think you of this humble establishment?"

The man colored. "I am not tasked with forming an opinion."

"But you must have one. I would hear it, and spare no words. Your horror could be no worse than mine when I first set foot in the inn."

"I was surprised, sir."

"That would be putting it mildly, Mr. Fields."

His flush deepened. "Yes, well, if you desire my honesty, then I fail to understand the appeal of these activities, but the women here are pretty. Miss Sophia in particular."

Charles suppressed a smile, half wondering what Mr. Fields would agree to if in a room alone with Miss Sophia. "Mr. Fields, the women here are *very* pretty, their natures exceptional and beyond what you will find in ordinary women."

Mr. Fields gave a slow nod.

Charles rose to his feet. "I thank you for your service, sir, and hope I will not see you here tonight. Lest you think you might wish to have Miss Sophia's company. I could make arrangements."

The man's eyes widened. "Oh, well, perhaps—no. I will take your offer under advisement."

Charles smiled. "Please do."

Chapter 13

And what will you do when Sir Arthur returns?" Sarah asked, pushing the pram with George in it as she and Terrell strolled by the docks along the River Thames.

In the distance, Terrell could see the Tower of London. Recalling how massive the structure had appeared to her when first she had laid eyes upon it, she remarked, "When I first came to London, I was in much awe of everything I saw. Mr. Terrell took great pride in showing me the magnificence of Westminster Abbey, Hampton Court, and the other palaces. There is nothing of such things in Barbados."

"Perhaps because I have lived here for many years, I have come to prefer the country," Sarah said. "The air can be insufferable in town and winters hard to bear, though, as a child, I once attended a frost fair with puppet shows, music, ox-roasting and mutton pies. It was quite the sight to see the river frozen enough for people to walk upon."

"I think that I shall never like winter. When it is cold, I want nothing more than to sit by a lively fire and burrow beneath pelts of heavy fur. I have no wish to spend winter at the Red Chrysanthemum."

"Winter will be here all too soon."

Which brought the conversation back to Sir Arthur. Terrell wondered how far she could ingratiate herself into his good graces. Would he take her for a mistress and provide her an apartment before the winter?

But then the welcome image of curling before the hearth beside Master Gallant cut into her thoughts.

"You have the ear of Master Gallant," Sarah said. "You could appeal to him if Madame does not grant us enough firewood or thicker blankets."

Terrell thought of the money she had saved. She could purchase firewood and bedclothes, though she preferred not to have to use her funds till she had exhausted all other avenues.

"In truth, I had thought to occupy my own apartment by now. I had intended to ask Mr. Worthington to rent a place. Alas, I should have broached him sooner, but I did not anticipate that he would have to return to Antigua so soon."

But, luckily, she had a new prospect in Sir Arthur, and she would not lose her opportunity again.

"What of Master Gallant?" Sarah inquired. Seeing that George moved restlessly in the pram, she took the boy into her arms, leaving Terrell to push the empty pram.

"What of him?"

"Does he not wish you to be his?"

"His submissive, yes, but I doubt he would take me away from the Red Chrysanthemum."

"Is that not a start? He seems rather fond of you."

"But then I would have to forsake Sir Arthur. Madame would not be pleased."

"Madame does not own you. You are free to please and displease her."

Terrell drew in a breath. Yes, she was free. And

though she had not her freedom before, she had always had choices, even as a slave.

"I do not think Madame would keep me merely for Master Gallant. I would not be of sufficient service to her."

"But she owes Master Gallant. It is no small favor he undertook for her in the midst of his election."

Feeling her hopes brighten at the thought that Master Gallant would desire her enough to request her, she quickly called upon pragmatism. "What will become of me when he takes a wife?"

Sarah had no reply.

"My chances with Sir Arthur are better," Terrell continued. "He does not require a wife, nor does he appear to seek remarriage. He can take a Negress for a mistress and society will look the other way."

"He is not impervious to criticism."

"But the damage to him will be small in comparison. With Sir Arthur, I am at liberty to be as selfish as I please. It is different with Cha— Gallant."

"Because you love him."

Terrell stopped, then replied, "What a frivolous thought, Lady Sarah!"

Sarah took some offense. "How is it frivolous?"

"For what purpose would I, a *blackamoor*, wish to fall in love with a *gentleman*?"

"There is no purpose behind love. It happens as *it* wishes, not as *we* wish."

"Love is a choice."

"I think not. It is a matter of the heart, not the mind."

"You can assign it to whichever part of the body you wish. It is a useless sentiment."

"You may deride it, but love has a way of settling in your heart like an unwanted guest or like—like lice in one's hair!"

The ensuing laughter lightened their disagreement. They both breathed in a sigh of relief.

"Love would only be a curse for me," Terrell mused.

"I suppose it has brought me no benefit. I thought I loved my husband, but being married was not what I expected. I often felt more alone as a married woman than I ever did unmarried."

"Perhaps you mistook affection, or even carnal desire, for love."

"Perhaps."

"Perhaps this thing called love is merely intense affection or a manifestation of lust."

"No, it is stronger than all of those. Words cannot do it justice, but you will know it when you feel it, as I feel it for George."

"The bond between mother and child is born of nature and wholly different than that between man and woman. A child needs its mother. A man does not need a wife. What use does the practice of marriage provide save to limit one's self? A wife must bed only her husband, and a husband only his wife? How dreadfully dull!"

"You cannot fathom being devoted to one?"

"I find devotion to be lacking in most husbands, yet it seems to be expected in the wife."

"It is a requirement unequally placed upon the wife," Sarah conceded. "But if you are Sir Arthur's mistress, he will expect your fidelity as if you were his wife."

"For his wealth, I would happily surrender my desires."

Having reached a part of the river that was particularly foul-smelling, they turned back and talked no more of love.

Chapter 14

I wonder that Sir Arthur has not returned yet if he takes a keen interest in what happens in this election?" the senior Gallant asked.

Charles sat in the drawing room with his mother and father at their home in Porter's Hill.

"He does not require much time," Charles replied. "His voters merely await his word."

"I have arranged baskets of wine and bread for our event this Friday," said Mrs. Gallant. "It does not compare to the twenty shillings Mr. Laurel is offering, but Mrs. Richardson and I did dress the baskets in lovely fashion. I think they will be quite memorable."

Charles kissed his mother's hand. "You are a dear."

"Mrs. Richardson is quite excited for you. Her second daughter, Emma, assisted with the baskets as well. You may not have met her, as she had her come out last year. Quite the lovely child. A bit of a bluestocking, I'm told, but I thought that might appeal to you."

William Gallant chortled. "Your mother can turn any topic of conversation into one of marriage."

She turned her sharp eyes upon her husband. "Does it not concern you, sir, that neither of your sons have married?"

"Not at all. They are particular."

"I begin to think they are fastidious."

"As was I, and thankfully so, or I would not have been a bachelor when I met you."

Her gaze softened, and she could not resist smiling.

"If our son has no interest in marriage, leave him be," he said with a yawn. "He has only to meet the right woman, and it will be off with the banns as fast as you please."

"Meeting the right woman is the challenge. He lost several years in the Orient." She turned back to Charles. "I understand why you may not be taken with Miss Dempsey, but I think Emma possesses the intellect you seek."

"I do not recall voicing the qualities I seek," Charles countered.

His mother pursed her lips while his father rose from his chair after another yawn.

"You mean to leave me to defend myself alone, sir?" Charles asked.

"I require a nap, but I will leave you this advice: never engage in battle with your mother to begin with," his father replied. "It is always better that she wins."

Mrs. Gallant gave her husband a mock scowl. Not engaging with his mother was easier said than done, Charles knew, and prepared his armor as soon as his father was out of the room.

But his mother was a seasoned warrior and came at him with an unexpected blow.

"You have someone," she declared with narrow eyes.

He made a poor parry. "Your pardon?"

"You've a mistress. At the Red Chrysanthemum. It

is why you are in no hurry to marry."

"My dear, I would not be in a hurry to marry whether I had a mistress or no."

"Men who are celibate have a great need to marry. You've no urgency at all because those needs are satisfied for you."

"I am standing for Parliament, and it is no small endeavor," he reminded her.

"Men will move mountains to satisfy desire. Who is she? Who is the lucky jade that has my son's attentions?"

"Jade?" He lifted his brows. "One would think you were not once a member of the Red Chrysanthemum yourself."

"It is possible a decent woman could be had there, but you could do far better."

"I could not do better than you, my dear!"

"Yes, you could. Your father could have done better than me."

"He has no regrets that I know of."

"He might have succeeded in his bid for Parliament if he had married better."

"And you would fault him for choosing love over Parliament?"

She sighed. "I only wish for you to have *both*. But are you in love with this girl?"

He paused. He thought first of Terrell, then of Miss Greta.

"No," he answered.

His mother appeared relieved.

He rose to his feet and paced a little. "But I am in no hurry to give her up."

Her brows went up. "Is it wise to entertain a

dalliance while in the midst of standing for Parliament?"

"I must attend the Red Chrysanthemum every night. It makes little difference if I engage or refrain in its activities."

"And what sort of family does she come from?"

"That concerns you only if I've a mind to marry her, and I am in no haste to marry—much to your consternation."

She wrinkled her nose at him. "Are you so certain you will not fall in love with this skirt?" she challenged.

He was not. But he knew his obligations.

"Do you fear I will disappoint you?" he returned, his first effective attack.

She rose and crossed to him. Though he was quite taller, she clasped her hands about this face. "You could never be a disappointment to me, Charles."

He took one hand in his and pressed it.

"But you understand," she said, "that I only want the best for you. I suppose I must admit that I would be pleased for you to take a woman of superior society to wife, to do better than your father had done. But if she will love you and hold you dear, and if you could do the same with her, then I am satisfied. But it is easy for your sex to be blinded by lust. Lust has no endurance and fades fast. You must, you ought have a woman whom you can respect, whose intelligence matches your own, whose temperament suits yours."

"And you think I cannot find these in a woman at the Red Chrysanthemum?"

"Speak true: this woman you have taken to bed, is

she all these things?"

Charles sat down and contemplated. His mother sat beside him.

"In truth, Miss Terrell is illiterate and vulgar," he said.

His mother stared, agog.

"And absolutely remarkable," he finished.

"No doubt Joan has taught her well."

He shook his head. "Joan did nothing for her, and merely profits from the qualities Miss Terrell already possessed."

"Terrell. That is not a name known to me."

"It was the surname of her last owner. He unwittingly granted her freedom when he took her to England. She was, previously, a slave in Barbados."

He watched his mother's mouth fall farther open.

"A *slave*. She is a—a black?"

"My dear, what she has suffered would have induced an ordinary man to take his own life. Yet, not only did she survive, she managed to pass herself for a courtesan to gentlemen of influence. She may be illiterate but far from brainless. Indeed, she is quite keen and clever."

"And what is she doing at the Red Chrysanthemum?"

"Awaiting her next paramour, I suppose."

"And that is you at present."

"At present," he echoed wryly. "I do not think I am wealthy enough for her."

"If it is riches she seeks, then you will want little of her. I am not such a dolt of a mother as to forbid your continued acquaintance with her. I know that will only make you desire her more, but I pray your infatuation will not last long. I did not know Joan to permit blackamoors as members."

Or that you would take a liking to one, was what was left unsaid. Charles himself had been surprised to discover he could find black flesh as delectable as white.

"I think my infatuation, as you term it, must come to an end when Joan returns," he said, deciding not to divulge the fact that Miss Terrell also entertained the favors of Sir Arthur. Such information would only make his mother fret.

Mrs. Gallant brightened. "And she returns quite soon?"

"I have not heard word yet, but she had anticipated her stay to last a sennight."

"Then I will grant you a reprieve from the subject of marriage till then."

She patted his hand and rose.

"I should have told you of Terrell much earlier," he quipped.

She turned to look at him. "Is it not *Miss* Terrell?"

"Yes and no. Terrell is her only name."

"I see. Does she address you by your given name?"

"She addresses me as 'Master.'"

"Of course." She gazed at him for a length. "I wonder that 'infatuation' will be a fitting term in three days' time?"

"My dear, what can possibly change in three days?"

Even as he spoke, he was aware of how quickly he had succumbed to Terrell—Miss Terrell.

Mrs. Gallant simply replied, "Do not underestimate a mother's intuition."

Chapter 15

As Charles led his horse on a steady trot along the road back to town, he considered what he would do with Terrell that evening. He would have liked to make a show of her before an audience of the Red Chrysanthemum members, but it was better not to draw unnecessary attention to his liaison with Miss Terrell. The servants of the Red Chrysanthemum were loyal. Any instance of indiscretion was punished with immediate dismissal, and its opposite generously rewarded on the Boxing Day after Christmas. Tippy was a newer maid to him, but she did not appear the sort of person inclined to make mischief. He could not say the same of Miss Sophia, however. He had always esteemed Joan's keen judgment of character, but Miss Sophia surprised him. To be sure, she was the most comely of all the women at the Red Chrysanthemum, but her sour disposition marred her beauty.

Hearing hoofbeats behind him, Charles slowed his horse. He had an odd sensation that he knew the traveler. The horse behind slowed as well. Charles drew his horse to a complete stop and waited for the other traveler to overtake him, but the latter did not. Charles looked to the horizon on his right. He was close to town but had limited daylight before darkness attracted highwaymen and the less desirable elements to emerge.

"Mr. Phillips, will you not keep me company more properly?" Charles asked.

The other traveler cleared his throat. Hoofbeats followed. Charles adjusted his gloves as he waited for Mr. Phillips.

"Good evening, sir," Mr. Phillips greeted.

Charles looked over the man, noting his thinner wool coat. In contrast, Charles wore both a thick coat and a cloak. Charles knew journalists did not make a great income but suspected Mr. Phillips had not anticipated he was to be traveling far.

"You take a long journey for a cool day," Charles commented. "Do you often follow me to Porter's Hill?"

"You accuse me wrongly, sir. I did not follow you to Porter's Hill," Mr. Phillips replied.

Charles returned his horse to a trot. This time, Mr. Phillips rode alongside him.

"This, then, is another convenient coincidence betwixt us?" Charles inquired.

"Indeed, it is, sir!"

Despite the man's earnest claim, Charles remained unconvinced.

"You do not believe me," Mr. Phillips observed.

"Would you, if you were in my situation?"

With his silence, Mr. Phillips indicated his concurrence. Not wanting to encourage too much dialogue, Charles said nothing further. He rather liked Mr. Phillips, but the man had interrupted his reverie of Miss Terrell.

"I followed Mr. Chester to Porter's Hill," Mr. Phillips revealed. "It is by coincidence that I saw you take to the road, and I made my decision that I would rather accompany you back to town than Mr. Chester."

"You flatter me, Mr. Phillips."

"Not intentionally," the journalist returned.

Charles smiled. Perhaps it would be good to have the man's company after all.

"Do you not wish to know what Mr. Chester has been about?"

"I am not his keeper."

"You have no curiosity as to his activities?"

"I suspect he was talking to voters."

Mr. Phillips snorted. "He has not talked to a single voter that I have seen or heard. He has not half your industry and prefers the card tables to any other pursuit—when he is not dozing. I heard he once spent two whole days without leaving his bed, all while in good health."

"If you hope to print some derogatory remark from me in an effort to fuel hostilities between me and Mr. Chester, I will grant you no such opening."

"But what he does might affect *your* chances. If I were you, I would wish to know the movements of my rival."

Charles studied the man. "If you wish to tell me something, I will hear it."

"I followed Mr. Chester to the Brentwood home."

"I confess I find your revelation disappointing, Mr. Phillips. I would be surprised if Mr. Chester did *not* pay the Brentwoods a visit."

"Do you still seek the support of the Brentwoods?"

"Their endorsement would be appreciated, yes."

"But they have not yet made a declaration, though

you would seem the obvious choice."

"Mrs. Brentwood was unable to devote much time to consider the election."

"Of course. The unfortunate business with her niece took much of her attention."

Charles started, surprised that Mr. Phillips knew.

"We nearly printed a bit about it," Mr. Phillips said, "but she quite neatly fixed the problem."

"Do you suggest your paper is one of the few above printing rumors and gossip?"

"It is true that we do not eschew scandal—"

"*The Independent* exalts scandal."

"—but we, or I, will report only that which is true. Thus, when we do print a scandal, it cannot be easily dismissed as mere talk."

"And for this you are proud."

"I am. And Mrs. Brentwood has worse troubles than that which concerned her niece. You know she has two sons."

"And two daughters."

"Well, the younger son is a bit of a dandy."

"I am not acquainted with the youngest Brentwood."

Mr. Phillips lowered his voice. "And frequents molly houses."

Charles stopped his horse and stared at Mr. Phillips. "That is a serious accusation. Spreading such rumors ought not be considered."

Mr. Phillips returned an equally stern countenance. "I do not spread rumors, Mr. Gallant."

Charles looked down. For *The Independent* to possess such knowledge, true or not, did not bode well for the Brentwoods. He looked back at Mr.

Phillips. "For what purpose do you tell me this?"

"You said we might be friends."

"I said under other circumstances, we might have been friends. And the sharing of gossip does not constitute friendship. I thought we were talking of Mr. Chester?"

"Yes, we were. I do not think it all unconnected. He was in the Brentwood home for *three hours*."

"And this surprises you?"

"Does it not surprise you?"

"Surely Mr. Chester seeks the endorsement of the Brentwoods as well. That is hardly surprising."

"But three hours is a long time. Can you guess what they might have been doing for such a length?"

"Most likely talking."

"Mrs. Brentwood does not strike me as a garrulous sort."

Charles had the same assessment of Mathilda Brentwood, but said, "Do you wish to distress me with this news?"

"Not at all! As a friend, I thought you would wish to know if your pursuit of the Brentwood endorsement needed to be fortified."

"Mr. Phillips, we are not yet friends, and I liked you better when our conversation was on the matter of slavery."

Charles urged his horse into a faster gait but slowed at what Mr. Phillips said next.

"You may not appreciate my friendship, but I have kept my knowledge of the Red Chrysanthemum in confidence."

Charles kept his gaze ahead of him. "Your pardon?"

"The Inn of the Red Chrysanthemum. I saw you head into the establishment one night."

If Charles were not so vexed, he would have thought Mr. Phillips could rival the talents of Mr. Fields.

"And?"

The reporter faltered a little under Charles' stare, but answered, "I wondered why you would enter such a place and at such a late hour?"

"You must have your own speculations, Mr. Phillips."

"The natural answer would be a woman. But I was not permitted entry, which I find rather odd for an *inn*."

"Clearly the occupants do not wish to be disturbed by snooping scandal chasers," Charles responded as he continued on his way. His tone contained no levity this time.

"Fair enough. I think you regret asking me to join your company. If you wish, I will fall behind and allow you solitude."

Mr. Phillips stopped his horse. Charles took in a long breath. If he eschewed speaking to Phillips altogether, he risked appearing guilty of hiding something.

"You may print what you wish of me, but I will not be accused of rudeness. Come along, Mr. Phillips."

"Shall I confine our *tête-à-tête* to more mundane subjects? The weather, perhaps, or the fashions of Mr. Brummel?"

"Good God, Mr. Phillips, I hope not. You may ride alone if you wish to discuss those."

Mr. Phillips smiled. "What think you of music?

Have you heard the latest composition by that Beethoven fellow?"

Charles agreed to the topic, and by the end of their journey together, they were returned to good terms. He could not consider Mr. Phillips a friend, however. Even if the latter had developed fondness for Charles, he could only prove a dangerous ally, especially as he was now familiar with the Red Chrysanthemum.

Chapter 16

At last she had seen the Chinaman's cock.

Or, she imagined she had. In the quiet of her chambers, curled beneath her bedclothes, Terrell envisioned herself in a room with both Gallant and Wang. She saw the two men naked. Both had chiseled chests, with Wang possessing slightly more profound muscles. Wang had a more consistent width to his silhouette, whereas Gallant's body tapered at the hips. She surveyed them both with much satisfaction, in particular their stiff clocks and the gleam in their eyes as they returned her stare, eying her equal nakedness with hunger.

She lay upon the rug, writhing, arching, caressing herself for them, crossing and uncrossing her legs, moaning as hands passed over belly and fingers curled into the down that graced her mound. Twisting her hips, she gave them a glimpse of her arse and heard one of them grunt.

"May I have cock, Master?" she requested.

When he did not immediately respond, she put two fingers into her mouth and suckled the digits long and hard.

Gallant nodded at Wang, who knelt before her upon the floor and presented her with his protrusion. Turning about, she raised herself on hands and knees. She took his hardness in one hand and licked at its crown. She imagined he tasted faintly of the green tea he always served her. Wanting more, she fit her lips about the head and teased his tip with her tongue. She swirled her tongue about him before sinking his length into her mouth. Her throat knew to relax, and she swallowed all of him, till his cods touched her chin and the scent of his musk filled her nose. Her cunnie, envious of that other orifice, throbbed for attention.

She heard Gallant kneel behind her and thrilled that he might attend her, but instead of spearing her, he gave her rump a resounding smack, shoving her into Wang. She gagged in surprise but recovered herself, relishing the stinging upon her buttock. He spanked her once more. She felt Wang's pelvic hairs in her nose. She depressed her tongue and licked at the base of his shaft. Wang made no sound, nor any motion. Gallant continued slapping her derriere. With each wallop, her face was sent farther into Wang's pelvis, his cock deeper down her throat. After more than a dozen blows to her backside, she thought herself on fire below the waist. Her arse smarted and the area between her legs burned with need.

Her frustration fueled her appetite, and she assailed Wang's cock ravenously. She wanted to hear him grunt or groan with equal fervor. He was quiet but fisted his hand in her hair, setting the pace he desired. She nearly squealed in delight when she felt Gallant's fingers between her thighs. She could spend in such fashion, her mouth stuffed with cock and Gallant fondling her. But she held off and concentrated upon making Wang spend.

And he did. She could taste his seed filling her

mouth. He allowed her to come off his cock to draw a larger breath, and his emission clung to him, forming a bridge between her mouth and his shaft. But then he pressed himself into her mouth once more, his cock still as hard as ever. Her mouth was a little sore at this time, but she was soon distracted by another hardness pressing at her folds. At last! With one swift thrust, Gallant buried himself to the hilt. She now had a cock at either end of her body, filling her with elation.

She clenched the new erection inside her. He responded by pulling out, then shoving himself back inside. The force sent her once again into Wang, but this time, Wang shoved back. They worked in perfect rhythm, alternating thrusts. Trapped between them, she volleyed from one cock to the other. Then they accelerated their motions till they no longer took turns but thrust in unison. It felt as if one cock might touch the other inside of her.

Beneath the bedclothes, Terrell fondled herself to this imagery. She contemplated satisfying just such a scene. Master Gallant had said she could name her pleasure. But she was not certain how Gallant would receive such a request. He had seemed interested but not entirely welcome at her offer to pleasure his valet.

Desire squirming inside of her, she decided to ready herself before she became too tempted to spend. Leaving the coolness of her room, she headed downstairs to the dressing chamber, taking with her *Fanny Hill* and the shirt Gallant had gifted her. It was now her favorite article of clothing.

Tippy, one of the newer maids, was preparing the

room for the members, who would begin to arrive within the hour.

"Evening, Miss Terrell," the maid greeted. "I've not seen Mr. Wang about."

"I do not seek him," Terrell replied as she perused the costumes hanging in the armoire. She fingered the fabric of a sheer gown.

"That be a nice and naughty bit. I seen Mistress Scarlet wear that one. She looked a Grecian nymph in that."

"Mistress Scarlet wore this? It does not seem to fit her tastes."

"Master Gallant ordered her to wear it. I did not think her half-pleased at first, but I saw a side of her I never seen. I heard tell she had not submitted to a man in over two years before Master Gallant come along."

"I knew not she had ever submitted to a man before. It is hard to imagine as she was quite the fierce mistress."

"It does speak to Master Gallant's abilities to *charm*, eh?" Tippy snickered. "He is quite the confident one to have attempted the conquest of Mistress Scarlet. I wonder what challenge he will seek next?"

Terrell was quiet. From what Gallant had said before, his pursuit of Mistress Scarlet did not stem from curiosity, ambition, or a desire for achievement. He had spoken of Mistress Scarlet with a touch of wistfulness. He might have been in love with her.

Fighting back jealousy, Terrell examined the costume of a Roman warrior. Or was it an Amazon? She had seen Mistress Primrose don the outfit once.

"I like this one meself," Tippy said, fingering the collar of an Egyptian gown. "How gay it would be to play the part of Cleopatra."

After reviewing the remainder of the options, Terrell settled on a set of men's attire: breeches, waistcoat, cravat, and a single-breasted coat. She would wear them over her favorite shirt.

"They fit you well, miss," Tippy said with surprise as Terrell studied herself in the looking glass. "I never would've thought the clothes of their sex could look fine on a woman."

With her supple thighs, Terrell filled the small breeches well. The garment clung to the shape of her legs like a second layer of skin. The coat was a little loose in the arms but buttoned tight over her bosom.

"You'll be needing these to complete your attire," Terrell said, presenting her with a tricorn and walking stick.

Terrell rapped the stick into her palm. The implement might come in handy.

"Does Sir Arthur return tonight?" Tippy asked.

Terrell paused. She knew not how many at the Red Chrysanthemum were aware of her and Master Gallant, and decided it was best not to draw too much attention.

"We shall see," Terrell replied.

"And if he does not? No doubt you'll swallow any cock to be had?"

Tippy and Terrell turned their heads to see Sophia leaning against the frame of the door, her arms crossed before her, a disdainful frown gracing her red lips.

"I wonder how Sir Arthur will receive your

inconstancy?" Sophia continued.

"If you hope that he will run into your arms, I fear only disappointment can be had...for him," Terrell replied, turning back to the looking glass and taking up a powdered wig to set over her black curls. She did not see but sensed Sophia's eyes and nostrils flare wide.

No doubt sensing a storm, Tippy went to the far side of the room.

"I would treat him with the respect that a man of his order deserves, and not lift my skirt to any creature with a pair of legs—or two."

"You are free to offer Sir Arthur your veneration," Terrell replied. "We shall see if he prefers your esteem over my cunnie."

"You've a haughty notion of yourself for a Negress. You don't deserve Sir Arthur. And I wonder what Madame will say about your attentions to Master Gallant?"

Terrell stilled before replying, "Are my attentions to him different from *yours*? I've seen the looks you throw his way."

Terrell faced the daggers thrown by Sophia's stare and returned her own boldest gaze.

The page popped his head in at that moment, diverting the tension for the time being.

"Is Mistress Primrose here?"

"No," Sophia spat. "Why do you seek her?"

"Several bouquets 'ave been delivered to her name. Why, there must be hundreds of flowers. I can scarce carry them all to her."

Sophia flushed, and Terrell, too, felt the pull of envy. She was aware that Mistress Primrose entertained the affections of a young gentleman from a family of wealth and breeding. Mostly, Terrell wondered if she would ever meet a man who would regard her with such adoration.

Deciding it best to part with Sophia before she was tempted to do something that would land her in trouble with Master Gallant, Terrell left the dressing chambers. Sophia threw her one last look of loathing.

Behave yourself, Terrell reminded herself. If Gallant discovered she had been otherwise, he would revoke the latitude he had granted her for this evening.

She stopped in the hallway, for Gallant stood in the foyer with a beautiful brunet woman finely dressed and possessed of a regal carriage. Gallant had his back to her, but Terrell had a clear view of the new guest. The woman, whom she had never seen before, was perhaps a few years his senior and beheld him with obvious affection.

"Countess," Gallant greeted and bowed over her hand. "You grace us with your presence."

She smiled at him. "It has been too long. How I've missed this place. And you, Master Gallant."

Terrell hung back from sight. She could feel her heart quicken its palpitation. Who was this woman?

"My condolences—" Gallant began.

"Now that my mourning period has passed, I wish to celebrate my freedom here at the Red Chrysanthemum."

"What is your pleasure, my lady?"

She looked Gallant over. Terrell fought to calm her erratic breath.

"Are you occupied this evening?" the countess

asked.

"I have assumed Joan's responsibilities as she is away attending to her ailing sister."

"Ah, then you are not free to...play."

"I am engaged this evening. But perhaps Master Troy comes tonight. I think he might suit your ladyship."

"Miss Regina. You knew me before I became a countess."

"That was some time ago."

"A mere three years, I think."

"Very well, Miss Regina. Allow me to escort you to the dressing chambers, where you may prepare for the evening."

"I recall where the dressing chambers are and will not stay you from your duties, but if you find you have the time, I should be delighted to hear of your adventures in the Orient."

"As this if your first visit in a long time, I am your humble servant and will endeavor all that I can to make your evening a pleasurable one."

After making her a bow, Gallant proceeded down the hall away from Terrell. Her ladyship went in the opposite direction toward Terrell. Out of habit, Terrell bobbed a curtsy as the woman passed. Up close, the countess was even more striking, with the most perfect oval shape to her face, delicate cheekbones, and a pert little nose. Terrell imagined the woman upon Gallant's arm. The pair made a flawless and elegant couple.

Hanging her head, she pondered the relationship the two could have had till she realized Wang stood before her. Knowing that he had come for her, she followed him upstairs. At the threshold to Madame's chambers, however, Terrell declined to enter.

"I will await Master Gallant in the large room upon the third floor," she told Wang.

He said nothing. She assumed Gallant had given him little or no instruction, for Wang made no objections. He did not follow her but came to the room upon the third floor minutes later with his customary tray of tea, fruit and biscuits.

"Do you think Master Gallant will be long?" she asked after Wang had started a fire and lighted a lamp. "Or will he be some time with the countess?"

"I know not this countess."

She realized from his sympathetic countenance that she must have spoken with more concern in her voice than she had intended.

"Do you wish me to inquire?" he asked.

"No! That will not be necessary. I merely wondered how I might pass the time."

He bowed and prepared to leave.

"*Xie xie,*" she attempted with her best approximation of the proper intonation.

A faint smile seemed to hover upon his lips. He bowed once more. "*Bu xie.*"

After Wang departed, she poured herself another cup of tea and looked about the room. The largest room in the inn housed the greatest number of apparatuses. Canes, floggers, and crops of all types and thickness adorned the walls. A simple four-post bed occupied one side of the room. On the other could be found stocks, a diagonal cross, cages, and a pointed bench. When straddled, the steeple of the bench would press most uncomfortably between the legs. She looked up at the rafters and remembered how, in her first confrontation with Master Gallant, he had tied her to the beam above and left her for a good half an hour before Tippy came and untied her.

Terrell took from the coat pocket the Cleland novel and turned the well-worn pages. She now recognized many a word and phrase: he, threw off the bedclothes, shift he tore open, breasts, he threw...upon me, kiss, wantonness of feeling. She tried to examine another passage, but her thoughts soon returned to Gallant and the countess. How familiar were they? Did they know each other from the Red Chrysanthemum or polite society? Had they ever had congress with one another?

Setting down the book, Terrell took to pacing. She did not like to dwell on such questions. They had no bearing upon her. But she could not turn her mind from the matter. The countess had seemed interested in Gallant. Because Terrell could not see his physiognomy, she knew not if he returned her sentiments. His tone had certainly been friendly. Terrell wondered if she should ask him about the countess. But what would she ask? How would she ask? Would he think her jealous?

She set her walking stick to the floor in the manner of Sir Arthur. He wielded the stick as if it were a third limb—or appendage. Gallant would not have asked her to forsake the MP if he had no significant attachment to her. But would the appearance of the countess change that? Terrell pressed her lips together. Had she missed her opportunity to secure Gallant?

It mattered not. He would always be free to cast

her aside when his infatuation faded. Terrell remembered Sarah once stating that Gallant was sure to find himself a wife, especially if he were successful in his bid for Parliament, and that, once married, he would cease to come to the Red Chrysanthemum. It was a wonder that a bachelor of his qualities had not yet married, but it was believed that his trip to the Orient had interrupted any marital progress.

Or perhaps he hoped for Mistress Scarlet. Sarah had doubted he would marry so far beneath his station. Mistress Scarlet was merely the daughter of an apothecary. But Terrell was less certain. She did not doubt that Gallant had a great sense of duty, but she saw a hint of the rebel in him. If he did not possess this quality, he would not be a member of the Red Chrysanthemum.

The countess, however, would undoubtedly make a fitting wife, though widowed already. She was young enough and more than comely enough. And if she readily participated in the practices of the Red Chrysanthemum, did she have any disposition that Gallant could find fault with?

It mattered not, Terrell reminded herself as an odd sense of despair burrowed deeper into her chest. When Sir Arthur returned, she would be back with him, and Gallant on to his next fancy, be it wife or another submissive one. But the thought of Gallant with another woman wrenched her guts. What if she did not return to Sir Arthur? Could she extend her time with Gallant? But for what purpose? There was no satisfactory end for her.

She stared at the fruit upon the tray. For once, she was not hungry, but when minutes passed and

Gallant still had not come, she took up a slice of the Oriental pear and soon had finished off the entire bowl. She paced again. Why was he taking so long? Was he with the countess?

She would have aroused herself to pass the time and tease herself to intensify what was to come, but she was too distracted to attempt it. Her curiosity burning, she considered going in search of him. But she was still the submissive one. Whatever he might allow her to do tonight, she would not know till he had granted her permission. She sat down upon the edge of the bed and heaved a sigh. She had looked to this night with much anticipation and gladness, but now the specter of disappointment loomed.

Chapter 17

A knock at the door made her jump in anticipation, but it was Wang who entered. He checked the teapot and noted the empty fruit bowl.

"I will bring more tea and fruit."

She eyed him and suspected he had returned to keep her from falling into the depths of boredom. "Will Master Gallant be free soon?"

"I think soon," he replied, taking the tray.

"Is the countess with him?" she blurted just as he reached the door.

"At present," he acknowledged.

She immediately regretted asking. Wang looked as if he meant to speak, but he did not and turned back to the door.

She lay upon the bed and stared at the canopy. A looking glass had been fixed above. Closing her eyes, she imagined seeing the back of Master Gallant in the looking glass and her own writhing body beneath. The imagery helped stir the warmth in her loins and provided a happy distraction from the anxiety and jealousy. The countess may be beautiful, possessed of grace and all the qualities a man may desire, but could she *fuck* better?

Determined to show Gallant that no woman could pleasure him as well as she, Terrell sat up. She crossed to the wall and eyed its adornments. Mistress Brownwen had provided them both with their introduction to the art of pain and pleasure. Terrell wondered which of the many implements Mistress Brownwen had used upon Gallant. She removed a bouquet of nettles.

"Ever felt its sting before?"

Whirling around, she saw Gallant at the threshold. Her heart melted at his dapper appearance. He held a tray of tea and fruit. He looked her over, and, without forethought, she held her breath. Would he approve her choice in attire? His gaze settled upon her thighs with the smolder of desire. She released her breath and returned her attention to the nettles she held.

"I have not," she answered. "Have you?"

He set the tray upon the sideboard and crossed to her. He surveyed the wall. "I have felt the blow of every one of these."

"Truly?"

"A master cannot wield an instrument unfamiliar to him. He must understand the instrument well to properly apply it."

"And how do the nettles feel?"

"They sting like needles applied to the flesh."

"You have submitted to flogging?"

"Yes."

"Caning?"

"Yes."

"Did you enjoy it?"

He thought for a moment. "I did. There was not, I think, any implement Mistress Brownwen introduced that I did not find intriguing in some manner."

She imagined his fine buttocks laid bare to the

cane. Heat flared within her.

"Was Mistress Brownwen gentle with you?" he asked.

"She was."

"I hope you made her aware of your...the back is a common target."

She faced the floggers. Most had flat ends. A few had loops. Only one, like the one Mr. Tremayne had wielded upon her, had knots.

"Not at first," she acknowledged.

Grabbing her by the arms, he whipped her around and stared—nearly glared—into her eyes.

"You made no mention of your condition?" he demanded.

"I did not think it necessary."

"Not necessary?! Mistress Brownwen is an able instructor. She would have asked if there were parts of your body you wished her to avoid."

"I wished to please. Madame had said some members paid well for women who could tolerate high thresholds of pain."

He was mortified. "You allowed Mistress Brownwen to strike your back?"

"I had on my gown and stays. She was gentle with her blows."

Terrell did not reveal that she had had to choke back sobs at the time. The pain from the impact had been tolerable. Being thrown back into the past had been the greater agony.

"You must have been petrified," he remarked. "I wonder that you do not always quake at the sight of a flogger. Had I known—"

She tossed her hair. "I have witnessed others

suffer worse. I have little memory of *that* moment."

He removed the hat, which had fallen over her eyes. Looking down at her, he said, without judgment, "You lie."

The tenderness in his tone made her bottom lip quiver. The concern in his eyes made her heart ache. That he cared for her thrilled her but pained her, too, for it could not endure.

She pulled herself away. She recalled the countess and became vexed, a safer emotion. "I warrant I can bear pain better than anyone, even your sex."

"I would wager it so," he agreed.

She took up her walking stick and donned a mischievous smile. "But perhaps not *you*."

He stepped toward her. "You have something in mind, Miss Terrell?"

"This morning you said I could name my pleasure. Have you reconsidered?"

"I have not."

She could barely speak with calm past the tingles of excitement. "What do you wish for your safety word?"

He had covered the distance between them, and that, too, caused her pulse to skip.

"What mischief do you intend?" he asked, and looked over her dress once more. He pulled her to him by her cravat. "Do you intend to make of me a molly?"

Her breath caught, both at his closeness as well as the thought of Gallant with another man. She blinked several times, her mind filled with the titillating image of his hard naked body rutting against another equally muscular body.

"If such a charade pleases you," she replied with heavy breath.

He discarded the wig from her. "I could not. You look too much the part of a young boy."

"But if I were older? Would you? Have you?"

His fingers, warm and firm, were at the back of neck. For a moment, she entertained the notion of simply tearing off his clothes and taking him.

"You *have*," she said when he had not responded. Her heartbeat leaped. "I should like to have born witness to this."

With his thumb, he tilted her chin up. "Naughty wench, is there nothing that fails to arouse you?"

He was going to kiss her, and if he did, she would succumb to the desire that had gathered inside her. She tore herself away.

"My pleasure this evening is to play the part of Mistress," she declared.

When he said nothing, she worried that he recalled the night she had forced herself upon him, asserting herself in the dominant role because she had thought that his preference. And because she had been angry at words she had overheard him utter to the Viscount Wendlesson.

"It would be for your pleasure as well," she added. "Your *intense* pleasure."

"My safety word is *jyr.*"

She released the breath she had held. "*Jyr.* It is an Oriental word?"

"Yes."

Giddy, she knew not where to begin. There was much she could do to him, wanted to do to him. Her grip about the cane tightened.

"Strip," she decided, "to the buff."

Keeping his smoldering gaze upon her, he stepped out of his shoes, then leisurely unbuttoned his coat. Given the tight fit of his coat, she had to assume the role of his valet and assist him from the garment. She placed it upon the back of a chair as he shed his waistcoat, which he placed upon the same chair. His hands went to his cravat next. Untying it took longer without the benefit of a looking glass. She was aware that his patience seemed to exceed hers. At last his cravat and collar were off. She took a seat upon the bed, that she could cross her legs to stymie the flow of desire.

He slid off the braces and began to unbutton his trousers. She licked her lips in anticipation. He draped the trousers on top of his coat, then removed his stockings. His shirt covered his essential parts.

"Wait," she said when he grasped the shirt hem.

Striding over, she stopped an arm's length from him and ogled his body and where his erection poked at the linen. She knelt down before him and ran her fingers up his calf and the back of his thigh to cup a buttock. There was not a part of Master Gallant that she did not favor. As she rose, her hand caressed the planes of his abdomen and the ridges of his chest. She found a nipple and pinched.

She trailed her hand down to nestle her fingers in the hair at the base of his cock. She avoided touching the rigid shaft. Picking up the shirt hem, she pulled it over his head and let the garment fall to the floor. He now stood in glorious nakedness. She raked her gaze over him. She wanted to throw herself at that stiff rod of his. This was why she could not assume the role of the dominant with constancy. She had not the temperament, the patience, nor the forbearance, especially when presented with such a fine specimen of his sex.

She went to the sideboard and found a cord of rope. She handed him the rope. "Throw it over the beam above."

He did as told. Finding a spreading bar, she cuffed the ends about his ankles. She then affixed a pair of iron shackles about his wrists. Her heart hammered as she eyed the adornments. How far would he let her proceed?

"Raise your hands above your head," she instructed.

She set a stool behind him, climbed atop, and tied the rope about the chain linking the cuffs so that his arms stretched toward the rafters. After climbing back down, she stood before him to assess his position.

Recalling how he had once left her hanging, she remarked, "Should I leave you here to contemplate your solitude till Tippy is free to relieve your bonds?"

"You could," he calmly said, "but do recall your allowance tonight does not last into the morrow, Miss Terrell."

She straightened at the subtle warning. "*Mistress* Terrell."

She cupped his cods and squeezed. Hard. He grunted.

"Mistress Terrell," he corrected.

No longer able to resist the beautiful pole pointed at her, she wrapped her fingers about it. She pulled upon the smoothness of the skin and caressed the ridges of the veins. Kneeling, she eyed his cock ravenously. She glanced up at him to see that lust consumed him as well before taking him into her mouth. He closed his eyes and groaned.

Cradling him upon her curled tongue, she grazed the underside of his shaft as she drew her mouth up its length. She flicked the tip of her tongue at the sensitive spot beneath. He shivered. She tasted a drop of his seed. It ignited her ardor, and she began devouring her prize, swirling her tongue over its head, licking voraciously, making him gasp and grunt. Forcing herself to slow, she reached around his hips to grasp both buttocks as she moved her mouth up and down at a more composed rhythm. She felt his tip graze the back of her throat and went deeper. The muscles in his legs tightened, and his gaze upon her further evidenced the climactic rapture was imminent. But, seasoned as he was, he knew better than to spend without her permission.

Slowly, she came off of him. She wanted to ask if the countess could suck cock as well as she. Instead, she said, "You kept me waiting long tonight."

"Your pardon. It was not my intent. I had to deal with a member whom I advised not to return tonight."

"Is that all?"

"I had to reacquaint a former member to the Red Chrysanthemum."

The countess. Terrell retrieved her walking stick and stood behind Gallant. In what manner did he reacquaint the countess, she wondered. She pulled back the stick and let it smack across his arse. He did not mention the countess by name, offered no more description. Was it because he deemed it none of her affair? She struck his buttocks again.

"Will this new member be a regular patron?"

"I think she will. Why do you ask?"

Terrell felt a slight compression in her chest. "I think Mistress Primrose does not mean to continue here. We will be short of dominant females."

"Alas, this former member is not partial to that role. She prefers men of dominance."

Men like Master Gallant. Terrell whacked his arse once more.

"You could fill such a role," he said through clenched teeth.

She admired the crimson lines crossing his arse cheeks. She had received some instruction from Mistress Brownwen on the dominant role but would much rather submit to the likes of Master Gallant. Nevertheless, she would use all in her power to convince Gallant that he ought prefer her over the likes of the countess. She walloped his arse once more for good measure. His body strained against the rope holding him aloft. Setting down the cane, she kissed his buttocks, then reached between his legs to confirm his cock was still hard.

To reward him for his submission, she knelt in front of him and took his cock once more into her mouth. This time she intended he should spend. She sucked at him rapaciously. With a groan, he began thrusting his hips at her. To add a different sensation, she pulled at his cods and fingered his perineum.

"My God," he breathed. "Permission to spend, Mistress Terrell."

She rather liked the sound of her name spoken

thusly. Most of all, she liked to hear the desperation in his voice. She bore down harder upon his cock.

"Mistress," he pleaded.

Intoxicated by the power, she did not abate. She wanted to prove she could command his arousal as well as he could hers. He tensed, trying to hold off, but she only intensified her fondling while sucking him harder, deeper. Her mouth was sore, but she would enslave his cock and make it do her bidding.

"Terrell..."

And then he bucked his hips quick and strong before unleashing his seed inside her mouth. She had to gulp fast or risk choking, but she gladly swallowed his emission. The quantity suggested he might not have spared any for the countess. Terrell swallowed every last drop and licked his shaft clean. He shuddered. The tension had left his limbs and he allowed his weight to pull upon the rope and shackles.

"Spending without permission, Master Gallant," she admonished playfully as she rose to her feet, triumphant. "I wonder what we shall do for a punishment?"

She did not allow him the chance to answer by crushing her lips to his, that he might taste himself upon her.

"Let me pleasure you, Mistress," he said between kisses. "With my tongue, my hand, or the largest dildo I can find."

What she wanted was his cock, but she would need a little time. She slid her mouth down to his neck and suckled. Aware that she might leave a mark, he tried to pull away, but she held on. He could hide the discoloration beneath his cravat, but if he should appear naked before anyone else, they would know he had been kissed by another.

"Terrell—" he warned.

But it was too late. A crimson oval had appeared where she had bit. Suppressing a smile, she trailed her mouth down to a nipple. She licked and nibbled and sucked. When she had tormented the bud enough, she kissed her way to his belly and his inner thigh. His cock had begun to harden again. She released him from the spreading bar. She sat down upon the floor and rubbed herself between the thighs where the breeches were damp.

"Have you buggered, or been buggered, by a great many men?" she asked.

He stared at the hand moving between her legs. "What do you consider a great many?"

"A half dozen or more."

"Then I have."

His response lit a fire in her mind, and she fondled herself more intensely.

"Two were at the command of Mistress Brownwen," he said.

"Would you bugger me if I were a boy—er, man?"

The burn of his gaze made her churn with arousal. She saw his cock had resumed its prior turgid state.

"I would bugger you if you were sheep or dog, Miss Terrell."

She wanted to fling herself at his cock. Never before had such a statement, so wicked and wrong, been made to her. Never before had she felt more desired. She wanted to believe that he had never spoken such words to any other woman, not to the countess, not to Mistress Scarlet.

She hopped to her feet and slapped him across the face. "*Mistress* Terrell."

She scowled at him, but inside, she glowed with triumph. Grasping his head with both hands, she brought his mouth down to hers and kissed him with a hunger deep and with such ferocity that her lips hurt. She pressed her belly at his erection and ground her hips at him, wanting to mold their bodies into one.

"I think it time you shed your clothes, Miss T— Mistress Terrell," he said when she finally separated to take a much needed breath.

Her body was on fire. She would have taken him without troubling to disrobe, but she would follow the approach he took and use anticipation to heighten his climax. Pushing herself away from him, she began to remove her coat. Discarding it was not as easy as the wearing of it, but she got the garment off by pulling the sleeves through with her arms.

"I should like to bugger you one day," she mused aloud, unbuttoning the waistcoat.

She could not discern from his expression if the prospect found any welcome receipt in him.

"That is a high privilege," he replied.

"But one that can be earned?"

She saw him glance toward the hearth. Above the mantle was a small clock and a painting of a carnal orgy that included, amongst many individuals and couples, a woman wearing a dildo.

"Possibly," he said.

Her mind whirled. How delightful it would have been to take his virgin arse! She wondered who the lucky man or woman was who had that honor. Recalling her task at hand, she kicked off her shoes and undid her breeches.

"Did you enjoy your sodomy?" she asked.

"At first, I found the sensation awkward."

"Were you buggered by Mistress Brownwen?"

"Yes."

"Did she use a cock large and wide?"

"You have a fascination with buggery?"

"With *your* buggery. You seem quite tolerant of it. Most men I know abhor the act."

"Because they fear the unknown or they fear for their manhood."

"Which you do not."

"I own I did not look kindly upon it before my time with the Red Chrysanthemum, but my outlook is much improved. Penetration of the arse can be enjoyed by man or woman."

"Indeed."

After stepping out of her breeches, Terrell pulled the shirt over her head. She stood only in her stockings. His gaze seemed to take in every inch of her exposed body. From a drawer, she found a salve that would sooth the burn of the cane. She applied it to his buttocks, then his cock. The salve lent a sheen to his member. Drawing a footstool before him, she knelt atop and pushed her breasts around his shaft, forming a lush cave for his thrusting. Slickened by the salve, his cock moved easily between her fleshy orbs. She kneaded the pair around his shaft, delighting in its glide. Lowering her head, she licked at the tip whenever it emerged from between the mounds. She could see from his taut muscles and the tightness of his jaw that he was approaching another peak. But her cunnie had been without attention too long. She would have him fuck her long and often.

Venturing back to a chest of drawers, she searched for an item that could cuff his scrotum, delaying release. She found one made of leather and shaped in the manner of a belt. It would suit her purpose well and look quite delicious upon his cods.

But before she could turn around with the cuff, a pair of shackled hands came down over her head. She felt him behind her, his stiffness jabbing at her lower back, his thighs pushing at her rump. Before she could struggle, she was thrown against the wall, curtailing her oath. Too late, she realized that she must not have secured the shackles well, and remembered she had once made a similar mistake.

His heat invaded her, as she stood trapped between twain forms of hardness. Her cheek pressed against the wall, her breasts flattened and her nipples ground uncomfortably into the surface. Wetness dripped between her legs. She heard the clock above the mantle chime the midnight hour.

"It is the morrow," Gallant said. "Your reign is over, Mistress Terrell."

Her lips parted for a protest, but she decided against it. She was happy to have Master Gallant returned. When he pressed his pelvis into her derriere, she sighed in satisfaction. Lowering himself, he positioned his cock beneath her arse. She tried to angle herself to take him in where desire throbbed hot and wet, but his body, pinning hers, stymied movement. His right hand cupped the back of her head through her hair, holding her in place.

"Are you certain you wish it to be over?" she asked in half gasps. "I think you would have enjoyed a longer term."

He moved his hips and his length grazed her folds. "You require more practice in the ways of a dominant one."

"I need your masterful instruction, Master Gallant."

She tried to bear down on the shaft sawing between her thighs, but he did not allow his tip to slip into her wanting slit. Instead, his length dragged along her folds, teasing her need to a desperate pitch.

"Don't patronize me, Miss Terrell."

"I meant no disregard, truly!"

He took the area behind her ear into his mouth. Her knees knocked together as butterflies of ecstasy flew through her.

"Please take me," she begged. "Spear me hard and fast."

He grunted, but his rod continued its rubbing.

"Do you still wish me to forsake Sir Arthur?"

He paused, then growled into her neck, "I do."

"Then *fuck* me."

Chapter 18

How could he resist such a demand, at once insistent and pleading? Bending lower so that his cock could aim properly upward, Charles plunged himself into her. The hardness of his member facilitated the entry despite the awkward angle. Pressed against the wall and impaled upon his cock, she had no escape. She could only submit to his thrusting, which she did with much grunting and groaning. With legs joined tightly to hers, he smacked his pelvis against her arse as he drove himself into her heavenly heat.

Did she mean to say that she would forsake Sir Arthur if he fucked her, as he now did? His mind whirled at the prospect. He needed to be certain. Thus, while he could have continued his delicious pounding, he pulled out before she could ascend her peak. She moaned her disappointment. His own ardor had reached a level from which retreat could not be had without agony, but he refrained from ramming himself back into her. She had equivocated, held back from making any commitment to him. Would she truly forsake Sir Arthur for him?

The shackles still cuffed his wrists but they did not prevent him from lifting and carrying her to a table— it was nearer than the bed. After placing her upon its length, he grabbed from the floor the coat she had worn, folded it and propped it beneath her derrierre. Her molten gaze, the scent of her arousal, her naked body sprawled upon the table, all conspired to make any forethought difficult. His cock wanted only to sink into her depths.

But he would have an answer from her tonight. Climbing atop the table, he knelt between her legs, which she spread for him. For his cock to be level with her cunnie he had to spread his knees wide and sink low into his hindquarters, but the position would allow him to penetrate with all his might. He tossed her left leg over his shoulder. Her leg formed a mast that he could leverage his thrusts against.

"Am I to understand that you will forsake Sir Arthur if I fuck you now?" he inquired, pinning her with his stare.

She nodded. She did not look away.

He searched her gaze for indications of insincerity or doubt. He lowered his voice. "You realize, Miss Terrell, I will fuck you regardless."

"I should hope so, Master Gallant," she replied with a hint of a wry grin, but the earnestness in her eyes touched him.

He wondered what had occasioned this alteration? She had provided no avowals ere now. Why tonight? But it did not matter. She was to be his. All his. Unable to wait any longer, he speared into her. She gave a satisfied cry. Buried in her wet heat, he was tempted to begin thrusting madly into her, but he was no adolescent. He found the motion that elicited the greatest response from her, rolling his hips methodically and without breaking rhythm.

"I want you to state in no uncertain terms that you

forsake Sir Arthur," he said when she began to flex and grasp fervently at his erection.

"If I am to be constant to you, I wish the courtesy returned," she replied, her countenance stern.

"Of course," he responded, surprised at her adamancy. Though some Masters and Mistresses retained the right to take as many lovers as they wished, he knew he had no interest in anyone else. He wanted Terrell all for himself and, admittedly, he derived specific satisfaction from removing her from the arms of Sir Arthur.

"Will you let me spend, Master?"

"Would that provide the necessary enticement for you?"

He half expected a coy answer, and that she would withhold that which he wanted to hear only if he granted her desire first.

But she did not.

"I forsake Sir Arthur," she said, "because I wish *you* for my Master for as long as you would have me."

His pride stroked, he buried himself to the hilt inside of her. She frowned, but the gleam in her eyes told her true reception.

"Harder," she directed.

He received her challenge in the depths of his groin. With every muscle in his buttocks and thighs, he shoved himself into her.

"Harder."

It was nearly a plea. Holding her upright leg to him, he thrust harder than he had ever done before. She cried out, and her hands flew to the edge of the table above her head to keep herself from being pushed over. He knew a part of her enjoyed a rough pounding, and he wanted to demonstrate that no one—certainly not Sir Arthur—could fuck her as well as he. He rammed into her repeatedly, furiously. Her breasts bounded up and down as his pelvis slapped against her flesh. Her cries grew louder and louder.

"Yes! Yes!"

He wanted to see her spend and drove himself into her with abandon. His perspiration fell onto her loins. Her sounds were a garbled mix of cries and groans of delight until they became one as she reached her pinnacle. Her spasms rippled over his cock, and he could no longer hold back his own tide. With heavy grunts, he hammered his way home. His paroxysm, a blinding moment of unconstrained rapture, of pure carnal joy, shook him from head to toe.

When it finally released him from its grasp, he had to prop his arm beneath him to keep from collapsing atop her. But she pulled him down to her nevertheless, wrapping her arms and legs about him.

His heart still drummed with the speed of racing horses. His breathing still heavy, he allowed his weight to settle atop her as his cock continued to throb inside of her. Occasional tremors would assail their bodies. He pressed his forehead to hers, felt the desire to speak, but knew not the words. He was humbled by her invitation to take her with all his might. Cradled in her limbs, he was no longer the Master. He was hers as much as she was his.

Chapter 19

Y ou will want to punish me, Master Gallant," Terrell said after a contented sigh. She relished his weight atop her and would have been satisfied to lie pressed between him and the hard surface of the table but for her appetite that seemed to know no satiation where he was concerned. Recalling how fiercely he had taken her but moments before had aroused her for a reprisal.

"For spending without permission," she finished.

"Indeed," he agreed as he gently withdrew from her, "but first I must see to a member newly returned to the Red Chrysanthemum."

"The countess."

He paused, surprised she knew. She had acquiesced to be his and only his, but as the submissive, she did not dictate the terms. Rather, she could request that he not engage with another woman, but then she would cast herself as self-doubting and jealous. She wanted his devotion to be of his own professing and not of her stipulation.

"I saw the two of you in conversation," she explained. He did not appear chagrined, but still she could not shake the uncertainties.

"Regina and I have been acquainted for the better part of ten years," he said. After alighting from the table, he pulled her upright. She sat with her legs over the table.

It was not what she would have wished to hear. "You are friends, then?"

"We are. It was I who made the Red Chrysanthemum known to her."

"Ah, then you were more than friends." She could not resist but smiled in an attempt to make it seem she found the notion intriguing rather than vexing.

"My interests were engaged elsewhere."

Upon Mistress Scarlet, Terrell elaborated silently, successfully making herself feel worse.

He cupped the back of her head and drew her forehead once more to his. "As they are now."

Her heart skipped—nay, leaped. When his lips grazed hers, she melted.

"But it might be a lark to invite her into a *menage-á-trois*, no?" she tested.

"Would such a thing interest you?"

She could not discern if such a thought interested *him.* She considered the possibility of sharing Master Gallant. Seeing him with another member of the fair sex would make her insanely jealous, but she could also envision herself simultaneously aroused.

"If it would please you, Master," she said, her voice husky. "Is it not the fancy of every male to bed two women at once? The more the merrier."

"I suppose. But, Terrell, while I may hold the position of Master, it is only at your willingness. If there is anything you wish me to refrain from, I would have you speak it to me."

Lest her emotions overwhelm her and shine too brightly in her eyes, she hopped off the table and went to retrieve his garments for him. Returning to him with his shirt, collar and linen, she brushed her fingers over his chest, enjoying the luster of his dampened skin.

"What brings you pleasure brings me pleasure," she said truthfully.

"It is not always so simple."

She kissed at his nipple. "I will envy any man or woman you attend. And be aroused. Is it so inconceivable?"

She saw that his member was no longer soft and was tempted to fall to her knees and claim it. He took the shirt from her and drew it over his head, then cupped her jaw and lifted her gaze to his.

"Not at all," he said, "though I would likely wish to pommel any man who fucked you as envy him."

Her brows went up, but she could not deny that his confession of jealousy delighted her. Even the great Master Gallant was not impervious to less worthy sentiments. She grabbed his shirt and rubbed herself along his hardened length.

"How promising," she murmured. "I should like to be your vestal when these emotions reach the point of boiling. Your cock would surely be harder than iron."

With a grunt, he grasped her buttock and ground himself to her. She did not own that she, too, might be compelled to inflict damage upon a member of her sex in similar circumstances.

Recalling himself, however, he released her. He picked up the collar and linen she had dropped.

"I should make haste," he said, "but rest assured I am not done with you, Terrell."

"How many women have you taken at once?" she

asked as she watched him in a looking glass secure his collar.

"Once, in a Canton brothel, I had five women to myself."

"Five!"

"That is no great number compared to yours, surely," he said grimly as he replaced his stockings and stepped into his trousers.

She tried to imagine the scene of Gallant surrounded by naked women. Warmth percolated through her loins.

"How were you attended by five women?" she inquired.

"I recall one sat upon my face, another licked at a nipple, and a third had my cock, but I rather lost track of the bodies."

Her appetite roused, Terrell placed a finger into her mouth and sucked. He watched her with a smoldering frown before slipping on his waistcoat.

"What of carnal orgies? As a longtime member here, you must have participated in your share. Or perhaps in the brothels of China?"

"I did not frequent brothels in China as often as you may think. It was rather a dangerous venture as foreigners were not permitted outside the factories."

"Then why did you?"

"I had a burning curiosity to see the land and know its people."

"At risk to your own life?"

"It was reckless," he acknowledged. "I suppose, at the time, I wanted to lose myself in another world."

She wondered if Mistress Scarlet had contributed to this desire of his. "It must have been exciting. Was it worth the trouble?"

"As I did not have to pay the ultimate price, yes. I know no place in the world as inspiring as China, nor as revolting. But I wished to see it all for myself and not trust to the descriptions of Englishmen. I remember, as a child, listening to Macartney's admiration of the Great Wall, but he found nothing else remarkable of China. I found it hard to believe that a civilization that could produce the unparalleled grandeur of the Great Wall could offer nothing else."

As he spoke, she assisted in tying his cravat, making sure it covered the bruise from her suckling. When she was done, she stepped to his side so that he could see himself in the looking glass. He stood completely dressed while she remained without a shred of clothing. She adjusted the linen of his cravat, then let her hand fall to his crotch.

"And you found much to admire?"

"I did."

She caressed the bulge beneath her hand. "Such as?"

He watched her motions through the looking glass. "Such as their literature. *Jin Ping Mei* is perhaps akin to *Fanny Hill,* though written over a hundred years earlier. The passages of coitus are quite detailed, offering interesting techniques and the use of objects."

"Perhaps you could read it to me."

"No English translation exists. I had to read it in Chinese, and the written language is exceptionally difficult as their words are not based upon a ready alphabet. Additionally, the prose of *Jin Ping Mei* is quite sophisticated."

"You can read it to me in Chinese. I can imagine what you describe. What is this work about?"

"A lustful merchant and his many wives and concubines."

"What is a 'concubine'?"

"A mistress who lives with a man and his wives."

He caught her hand as she rubbed harder and dragged her to the diagonal cross. He locked her wrists into the restraints. Picking up the neckcloth from her costume, he formed a large knot in the center, which he then fit into her mouth. He tied the rest of the linen behind her head. She thrilled at what he might do next, but a part of her also dreaded what awaited. She would be left, tied to the cross, immobile, unable to address the craving between her legs. She watched him select a long cord of rope, which he wound above and below her breasts. He took a shorter cord and cinched the longer ropes between her breasts. She moaned her pleasure at the tugging of the ropes. He played with her nipples till they were hard peaks, and she hoped he would take them into his mouth. Instead, he found two thin lengths of rope that were more string than rope. These he tied about the nipples and secured them ends to the longer rope circling her bosom.

From his coat pocket, he drew out a small box. She knew the contents to be those silver Chinese balls. Fitting his fingers between her thighs, he ensured she was wet before inserting the balls into her heat. She closed her eyes at the torturous little vibrations of the balls. With another length of rope, he wrapped her waist and passed it between her legs. He had put a knot into the rope and nestled it at her clitoris. She whimpered at the stimulation to her most sensitive bud. He stepped back to admire his handiwork. He had not yet left and already she wanted to squirm with need.

Desire burned in his eyes, but she knew he would leave her. She only hoped he would not be long.

He stepped toward her and leaned into her ear, whispering, "I know you capable of spending without my aid, but you know the rules."

She groaned to indicate she understood. He took teasing bites of her ear before withdrawing. She clenched the balls inside of her and wiggled her hips to feel the rope tight against her crotch. When the door closed behind him, she knew there was naught to do but submit to his wicked and delightful bondage.

Chapter 20

After his conversation with Mr. Phillips, Charles impressed upon the staff that they should be on their guard coming and going, and that no one should leave the inn without accompaniment. Though Baxter and Jones already understood that strangers were not permitted to enter under any circumstances, Charles suggested that Jones take regular walks about the perimeter to guard against lurkers. For himself, Charles decided that he would have Wang attend him from his townhome to the inn. Wang had the eyes of a hawk by day and those of an owl by night. He also had the ears of a bat.

Charles warned the members as well. Only Regina scoffed.

"Do you forget I am a widow now?" she asked.

She sat before a vanity in the dressing chambers as Tippy pinned the final curl in place. Her toilette complete, the countess now appeared in as much order as she had arrived.

"But you may wish to remarry," he replied. "Your youth and beauty have hardly faded."

She brightened. "Do you think so?"

"I should say you are as desirable as any young woman recently come out, my lady."

"Regina," she insisted. "We may not have seen much of one another in recent years, but are we not still good friends?"

"Indeed, but since marrying the earl, you merit a different level of respect."

"Pooh! I do not wish it from the likes of you."

"I hope you enjoyed your evening with Master Troy."

She smiled. "I did indeed, and thank you very much for pairing me with him. He was both gentle and patient with me."

"I can see that he is available at your next visit."

She lowered long curled lashes and pretended to inspect her gloves. "Does your situation here not allow you to engage in any *divertissement*?"

Tippy bobbed a curtsy and discreetly took her leave.

"You never took an interest in me before," he said.

"Because you never took an interest in me! You were more interested in learning the language of Orientals."

"But I was not half as fond of them as I was of you."

She stood and faced him. "I hope we did not miss an opportunity between us?"

He took her hand and kissed it. "We suit best as friends, as brother and sister. Anything else would ruin our friendship."

"Are you so certain?"

"I am. Regina."

She had heaved a sigh but said, "Well, I am not entirely convinced and may decide to persuade you to my opinion."

His mother would like nothing more, Charles had thought. Mrs. Gallant had harbored hopes that the two might form an attachment. Regina was clever and often prevailed whatever she put her mind to. She was, in many ways, a perfect match for him. He could not complain that their preferences in *bed sport* had nothing in common, though she did not venture into the more wicked aspects of the Red Chrysanthemum.

Still, he preferred the likes of Miss Greta. And even Miss Terrell. Regina had great confidence in areas of comfort. She was an extraordinary whist player and could hold a conversation with any bluestocking, but she had a tendency to condescend to the unfamiliar. She had agreed to attend the Red Chrysanthemum out of desperation and concern that her husband might wander if she did not introduce an element of excitement into their bedchamber.

Unlike Regina, Greta would have suited him. She had a daring spirit beneath her vulnerability. And without doubt, Terrell compelled him. She was a rare flame, and one that he wanted to possess, but he was certain to be singed by her fire. She consumed him, and he was uncertain how long he could last before the heat became too much for him to bear.

He had returned to where he had left her tied to the cross. His cock had perked the instant he beheld her magnificent breasts bound in rope, the thinner twine circling her still hardened nipples. Her crotch adorned with rope was another lovely sight, the pale hue of her bindings a fine contrast to her dark skin. His gaze lingered at her belly before traveling down to where the rope cleaved her between the legs.

He had brought up a new tray of tea, which he set down before crossing to her. "How do you fare, Miss

Terrell?"

In response, she pulled against her restraints, arched her back and writhed her hips. Lust burned brightly in her eyes. Her look of hunger, as if she would devour him, made her infinitely more attractive and sent the blood pounding to his groin. He untied the rope from her mouth and gently rubbed her sore jaw.

"Thank you, Master," she said.

He poured her a cup of tea, cooled the jasmine with his breath, and held the cup to her lips

"Was all well with the countess?" she asked after taking a sip.

"Yes."

"Will she return tomorrow night?"

"Perhaps a few nights hence."

"Did she enjoy the arrangements you made for her?"

"You have a great interest in her ladyship?"

She took another sip of the tea before answering. "A simple curiosity. I had never seen her here before."

"Her husband had been ill for some time."

"Ah. How convenient it is that both husband and wife should share the same venereal interests. It must make for a happier union."

He had her finish the tea.

"When you marry, will you seek to introduce your wife to the Red Chrysanthemum, as the viscount did with Miss Katherine?" she asked with lowered lashes. "Or will it be easier to find a woman already familiar with your preferences?"

"Matrimony is not my focus at present," he replied, tugging at the rope between her legs.

She grunted as it cut deeper into her flesh. "The Red Chrysanthemum is surprisingly fertile grounds for the hunting of a spouse. Lady Sarah, for instance—"

"Lady Sarah is not divorced, merely separated, from her husband."

"Even Mistress Primrose might suit you."

"She does not."

"Or the countess..."

She mewed when he pulled the rope harder.

"If I wished to discuss marriage, I would seek the company of my mother," he said, fisting his hand over the crotch rope and twisting to tighten it against her. "You are hardly my mother, Miss Terrell."

She gasped. "Lucky for me! Though I mean no disrespect to the woman who gave birth to you. Only that you would not fuck her...would you?"

"Miss Terrell, that is a vile thought."

"Mistress Brownwen once played with a man who called her 'mother.' Have you no interest in being the father who must discipline his wayward child?"

He stared at her. If she were not yet twenty years, it would not have been impossible for him to have fathered a girl her age. As she still appeared younger than he would have liked, he would rather not engage in any pretenses involving age or incest.

Her eyes sparkled with mischief. "Will you not take me over your knees and spank me, Daddy?"

He frowned. "I will more than spank you, young lady."

First, however, he moved the crotch rope so that the knot grazed her clitoris, eliciting from her a delighted moan. He then proceeded to lock her ankles to the bottom legs of the cross, spreading her limbs wide. He undid his cravat.

She licked her lips. "I have been a bad little girl."

He covered her eyes with the neckcloth.

"How am I to be punished, Daddy?"

"Silence," he ordered.

He untied the rope, sodden where it had cradled her cunnie, from her pelvis. He divested his coat, waistcoat and collar. From the wall of floggers, he selected one with dozens of long tails. Returning to her, he checked that the *ben wa* balls were still inside of her before standing back and lashing the flogger against her left thigh. She jumped in surprise. He slapped the tails against her other thigh. He paced before her, contemplating where to strike next. *The naughty, wanton wench.* She was fortunate he was not her father or she would spend her days locked in her room. Under no circumstances would she be allowed to have contact with any member of the opposite sex. He flicked the tails at her cunnie. She cried out and tensed her body for the next blow. Blindfolded, she could not know where he would strike next. He warmed her entire body with the flogger.

Next, he brushed a bouquet of thistle along her inner thighs. She groaned, low and haggard. Surprisingly, she had yet to drop one of the silver balls. Lowering himself on one knee, he caught the scent of her arousal. He parted the swollen lips between her legs and teased her clitoris with his tongue. She trembled against the cross.

"May I?" she inquired.

"Not so soon," he replied, though he knew her to have been ready for some time.

Softly, he kissed her blushing thigh. The flesh, made tender by the flogging and the abrasion of the thistles, received the gentle caress as if pierced by a sharp needle. Her body bowed off the cross.

"Never address me as 'daddy' without permission," he told her.

"Yes, Master."

He returned to standing. His cock was as hard as stone, and he could wait no longer. He pulled his braces down and unbuttoned his fall. When his tip grazed her wet folds, it took all his restraint not to simply plunge himself in and pound her till the tension burst from his erection. He had to bend his legs considerably and grabbed the back of her thighs to angle her for deeper penetration.

"Spend on my word," he reminded her before sinking his shaft into her, pushing the balls as he entered.

She met his entry with an agonized moan of pleasure. Her cunnie flexed strongly about him, and he released his own groan. The encouragement was too much for him, and he began thrusting. He could not discern if she cried from the burn of her thighs when they touched his or from the bliss of being impaled upon him while the balls shivered inside of her. When he slowed, however, her cunnie grasped him more fervently. He intensified his motions. The cross rattled loudly.

"Spend on my command."

"Yes, Master."

His own climax loomed. He withheld till he sensed her body, desperately restraining the flood of rhapsody, attempting to move away from him.

Holding her tight, he speared into her.

"Spend. Now."

With a high-pitched wail, she released the dam. Her fluids drenched him as tremors waved through her. He shoved his cock into her depths and, after several jabs, unleashed his own emission into her wet heat. He shuddered against her, marveling that the rapture was as divine each and every time.

When the throbbing and the shaking had calmed, he disengaged. The balls followed after him. Her body sagged against the cross. He replaced his buttons and braces, then removed her ankles and wrists from the restraints and carried her to the bed.

Chapter 21

Charles stared up at the canopy of Joan's bed. He would have thought by now he would long for the comfort of his own bed, but he was content to be wherever Terrell was. She lay in the crook of his arm, the even breathing of her slumber a soothing sound to wake to. Morning's light had just begun to overtake the darkness. There was no returning to sleep, for too much occupied his mind.

"Do they have slavery in China?"

Charles started, unaware she had been awake. He replied, "There are states of bondage, though decades ago, the Yongzheng Emperor attempted to free all slaves."

She was quiet before saying, "I think slavery must always exist."

"It need not. Not in our civilization."

Again she was quiet. Her arm, draped across his chest, tightened over him. "Sir Arthur will not be pleased to find I do not await his return."

He said nothing, wondering if she reconsidered her decision to forsake the man.

"I cannot offer compensation as grand as Sir Arthur," he said, "but I can arrange with Joan—"

"I had offered myself gratis to you."

"She will expect you to earn your room and board."

To this, Terrell made no reply. He could, as part of the favor she had promised to return him, request that he have Miss Terrell at no cost. Joan would agree so long as the duration did not last overly long. But he had no qualms of contributing to Terrell's keep.

"What of your election?" she asked. "If it is known that I am with you, Sir Arthur will not likely endorse you."

"He is a man of calculation and understands that politics is its own matter, and that personal events ought not interfere with its business."

"He is governed by his temper."

Charles could not dispute her statement but replied, "Your knowledge of the man is surely limited."

"I have seen enough of him to know."

"Why do you worry of Sir Arthur?"

"Does he not own Porter's Hill?"

"He owns a large part, yes, but it is not yet a borough in anyone's pocket."

"How can you win without his support?"

"There are other people of influence, other landowners, and nonpartisan voters who will take into account the qualities and promises of the candidates and cast their votes according to these merits."

"Do you have the support of these other landowners?"

"I have many pledges of support from them. If I had the endorsement of the Brentwoods, my situation improves greatly."

"But to secure their endorsement you must forfeit your support of slavery's abolition."

He shifted in discomfort. "For the near term."

She raised herself and looked at him. "Then you must."

"I had hoped to discuss it further with Mrs. Brentwood. It is possible she will not require as much time as she currently believes."

Terrell shook her head. "If you do not have the support of Sir Arthur, you must have hers at all cost."

"I am willing to forsake the endorsement of Sir Arthur because I wish to have sovereignty over my own actions, to act according to my conscience. If I barter my vote on abolition with Mrs. Brentwood, have I not curtailed the liberty I seek?"

"It is only on the matter of slavery that she requires your commitment."

"There is perhaps no greater ill upon our nation than slavery."

She straightened, her countenance darkening with solemnity. When she spoke, her words were soft but potent. "I think it the greatest evil of all mankind. Do you think I, though I am no longer a slave, would not wish for abolition as soon as it may come?"

His jaw tightened. "I know you appreciate its evils far better than most."

"You said that many other pressing matters face Parliament, that Parliament is unlikely to take up abolition, especially as they had but banned the slave trade a year ago."

Charles thought back to his conversation with Granville Sharp. To wage a war against all of slavery would require men like Sharp to take arms. The Society for Effecting the Abolition of the Slave Trade had been founded three decades before. It might take another three decades before they saw the complete abolition of slavery.

"But what if it should?" he asked. "My hands would be tied. I would not be free to voice my true thoughts."

"I thought you were inclined to acquiesce to the Brentwoods?"

"Mr. Brentwood had made a similar condition to my father when he sought the burgess. At the time, the Brentwoods were quite involved in the Society for the Suppression of Vice and wished my father to support their proposals. My father refused to constrain himself, for he wanted to be able to act upon his own principles."

"A fine ideal but was he elected?"

"No. He lost thrice."

She took his hand in hers. "I have said before that you are a man who ought be elected to Parliament. It would be better to have you in Parliament, even if you could not always vote your conscience, than not—or someone worse and far less deserving!"

He smiled at the passion with which she spoke. "You are not familiar with the other candidates. There are other capable men."

"None better than you."

Her conviction warmed him.

"And I have known enough men, MPs among them, to make such a claim without pretension."

He refrained from asking who these other MPs were. He knew of Sir Arthur and Sir Fairchild, both of whom he would have to face often if he were successfully elected. "If you were in my position, standing for Parliament, and had the chance to earn

Mrs. Brentwood's support by renouncing abolition, I hazard you would not."

"True."

"Yet you advise me to."

"You have not lived the horror of slavery. *Your* people are not the ones in need of saving. You would not be turning your back on them."

"And for that I am absolved? *My* people are the only ones with the power to set yours free." He paused at the implications of his own statement. "Wherein lies power, lies responsibility."

"But if Parliament is unlikely to take up the matter of abolition, why should you trouble yourself? You are but one man. The abolition of slavery is not your sole responsibility. Rather, your actions ought be grounded in the practical and not accountable to that which will not come to fruition."

"Parliament may not consider abolition, but it ought to."

"As a Member of Parliament, you could write a bill to condemn the mistreatment of slaves."

"*You* know better than anyone that such legislation would do nothing to curb the malice and treachery of slave owners and their overseers. The enforcement of such laws would fall upon the local judiciary, which I suspect would be far too sympathetic to the perpetrators. And even if the guilty could be brought to justice, it would be at what cost to the victim?"

She sat with her arms about her knees, her face turned away from him. Perhaps she remembered, as he did, the dreadful accounts she had told him of how the overseers tortured and punished the slaves, of her own suffering at their hands. He shuddered to think how close to death she might have come in her time in Barbados.

"I said earlier that there were other capable candidates," he said, "but the truth is I believe myself more capable than any of them. The Brentwoods ought to weigh their decision on the qualifications of the candidates."

She turned to him with concern. "You are determined to decline her wishes?"

He had not resolved to do so ere now but was presently inclined in that direction. "I think I shall."

It seemed his breath grew free at the prospect, but Terrell's frown deepened.

"I thought you would be happy," he said. "You advocated for abolition. The atrocities you described—"

"I ought not have."

"Two, three days ago you would have been disappointed if I did not support abolition."

"That was before I considered the entire situation!"

"And now you, a slave girl from a West Indian sugar plantation, presume to give me electoral advice?"

She narrowed her eyes. "By all means, disregard the witless remarks of an ignorant blackamoor!"

"I did not mean—"

But she had looked away from him.

"You are far from witless," he protested. "You must know I regard you. I do not consider your comments merely to humor you."

But her scarred back remained unforgiving.

With a growl, he reached for her. She yelped in surprise as he pulled her beneath him. His cock hardened the instant he straddled her legs. He pinned her wrists above her head, locking her head in place with her arms so that she could not look away. She struggled, but it was not all in anguish. He stared hard into her eyes.

"I know many accomplished women, literate and well-spoken, who have not half your cleverness, your insight, and your perception."

Her bosom swelled. Her hips wriggled against him. He did not need to check if she were wet. Certain that she would adjust, he sank himself into her. There was more moisture there than he expected, but he held himself still, savoring the heat that clenched about his member. Her contented sigh was all he needed to hear. Slowly, he drew himself back, and rolling his hips, buried himself farther into her depths. She met his thrusts with undulations of her own. They reached the summit of elation, together.

Chapter 22

I fear I have erred," Terrell fretted.

Sarah picked up George's ball and tossed it a few feet from the boy, who ambled, much less precariously than before, after it. They stood in a patch of grass behind the inn. The cook maintained a small garden in the corner for her herbs and vegetables, but few others ventured here.

"In what way?" Sarah asked.

"I have forsaken Sir Arthur for Master Gallant."

"That is no error but a triumph of sense!"

"I should have waited till *after* Sir Arthur had returned. I could have persuaded him to cast me off. He would be less cross if the decision had been his."

"Well, let him be cross. I, for one, am delighted that you have chosen Master Gallant. But how did this come about? I thought you would *not* give up Sir Arthur. At least, not his coin."

"Madame Devereux would not approve, though perhaps she can be appeased if Mr. Worthington returns. He might be nearly as wealthy as Sir Arthur."

"If Gallant wishes to have you, I think he can persuade Madame."

Terrell blew out her breath and sat down upon the only bench in the yard. "I half wonder if Ch—Gallant wanted me to forsake Sir Arthur because *he* despises the man."

"Does he?"

"I suspect he does."

"Even so, he would not make such a request of you for purely selfish reasons."

Terrell sighed and rubbed a slipper into the brown grass. George picked up the ball and tossed it for himself, then gleefully went after it. Sarah pulled her shawl tighter and sat beside Terrell.

"I think it quite clear that Gallant is partial to you," she said.

"Yes, but for how long?"

"Is that why you were prompted to forsake Sir Arthur? You fear your time with him to be short?"

Terrell considered Sarah's theory. "What do you know of the countess?"

"Who?"

"The gentlewoman who came last night."

"Ah, I had not known she was a countess. She is not familiar to me."

"I overheard Master Gallant address her. The two are acquainted. Friends. She was quite pretty."

"Dare I suggest you are a little jealous?"

Terrell hopped to her feet. "I acted in haste. And now Gallant stands to lose the endorsement of Sir Arthur for his election."

"How can you be sure?"

"Did you not warn me against Sir Arthur's temperament? His jealousy?"

"But he has other considerations when it comes to supporting a fellow for Parliament."

"Do you think Sir Arthur the forgiving sort?"

"Not at all."

"He will blame Gallant for his loss."

"There are others more than willing to take your place. Sophia. Lydia. Or even Miss Primrose if he prefers a darker complexion."

"I fear Sir Arthur is partial to me as well," Terrell replied with a wry grin. "But you are right. Perhaps I can convince him to consider another, more worthy maiden to bestow his attentions upon. I will explain to Charles—er, Gallant—the wisdom of delaying my decision. We may not wish to be seen together till Sir Arthur is properly installed with another interest, but I think we have the patience."

Sarah raised her brows in question. Terrell scowled.

"You think overly much," Sarah said with a motherly smile. "Follow the dictates of your heart."

"What has the heart to do with anything?" Terrell returned with sincere earnestness. , Sarah, after what she had suffered, should not render such fanciful and impractical advice. "But what if Sir Arthur will not take another? What if Sir Arthur still desires me?"

"What does it matter what Sir Arthur desires? If you are partial to Gallant and he to you—"

"Madame will not approve of my forsaking Sir Arthur. He pays a great surplus for my favors. Of which I stand to lose as well."

She thought of how her savings, which she had painstakingly tucked away a penny at a time into a pouch beneath her bed, had grown in the short time she had known Sir Arthur. Did she truly wish to curtail the flow of coins from such a bountiful fountain? If she tarried with Sir Arthur a while longer, she could make a comfortable amount such that losing her room and board with Madame

Devereux would be a minimal hardship. But could she still see Master Gallant if she was no longer at the Red Chrysanthemum?

Vexed that she had landed herself in such a conundrum, she paced the grounds. She did not like the strain upon her mind. Life before Master Gallant had been far simpler. Before him, she had only to consider how best to pleasure a man. Whether it was Mr. Tremayne, Sir Fairchild, Mr. Worthington, or Sir Arthur, the answer was always fairly plain. The muddle she now found herself in did not suit her.

"There is no benefit to haste," she confirmed aloud. "My forsaking Sir Arthur at this time serves no purpose. Master Gallant will see this."

"Are you quite certain?"

"Yes," she replied without hesitation and with particular emphasis, for she could see Sarah's disappointment.

But her resolution sat no better than her prior uncertainty.

Chapter 23

My goodness!" Mrs. Gallant exclaimed as she parted the stack of books for a place to sit upon the settee in Charles' library. She took up a soft-covered book and read its title. "*An Essay on the Slavery and Commerce of the Human Species, Particularly the African. Translated from a Latin Dissertation, Which Was Honoured With the First Prize in the University of Cambridge.*"

"A gift from Mr. Granville Sharp," Charles replied from behind his writing table as he turned the page of Mr. Sharp's detailed accounts of the *Zong* case.

"Along with those." He gestured to a pile of papers at her feet. They comprised the writings of John Ramsay, William Wilberforce and Hannah More.

"You intend to read them all this morning?" his mother asked after she had sat several minutes in quiet.

He looked up. "Forgive me, my dear. You require my services?"

"I came to see how my son fared. Have you paid your respects to Regina yet?"

"I thought you would not bring up the subject of matrimony till after the election."

"I made no mention of matrimony," she protested. "I was merely making an innocent inquiry."

"Innocent, you say?"

She scowled at him. Charles smiled, for his mother was charming when feigning to be cross.

"Perhaps we could call upon her together. I have not seen her in some time myself. Perhaps this afternoon?"

He shook his head. "I intend to call upon Mrs. Brentwood today."

"Ah," she said, and sighed as she looked upon the poems of William Cowper beside her. "You are determined to reject her condition of support?"

"I cannot accept it. It would feel as if I am sentencing men to their death."

"How can you say such a thing? You are but one man. It is not all your responsibility whether slavery lives or dies."

"How would abolition benefit if each of us defers responsibility?"

"What if Parliament does not consider the matter for years? You will have made a sacrifice for nothing."

"I will have preserved my integrity," he said. "Do you know what the slaves suffer? Do you know what happens to women and children? They labor under conditions no grown man of health could endure. And if they should flee and seek that which no Englishman could live without—liberty—the most horrific and ungodly punishment befalls them."

He looked down at where a print peeked from between books. It was a sketch of an emaciated woman, sitting in a cage in Kingston, starving to death before the eager eyes of vultures.

"I could not describe them to a gentlewoman," he said, his voice turning hoarse. "If you had seen what I—it would turn the stomach."

"But what can you do if you are not elected to Parliament?" his mother returned, undaunted. "You think Mr. Laurel or Mr. Chester would be a better advocate for abolition?"

He shook his head. "You sound very much like Terrell."

"Who? Oh. Your bit of skirt at the Red Chrysanthemum. You were talking of your election with her?"

"She thought I should agree to Mrs. Brentwood's demand to improve my chances."

"Indeed? Was this Miss Terrell not a..."

"A slave, yes. Whilst she was in Barbados. In England, she is free. Is it not a hypocrisy that slavery is against the law here in England but not her colonies?"

His mother was quiet in thought.

"Forgive me if I am short with you," he said. "The situation has weighed upon me. In truth, I wonder that I had not reached a conclusion earlier, but my ambitions ruled me."

"And what rules you now?"

She believed his feelings toward Miss Terrell prompted him. He thought to explain that Miss Terrell had only brought the awfulness of slavery into sharper relief. Instead, he said, "I should not have entertained Mrs. Brentwood's prerequisite for support for as long as I have."

"Well, I hope she has enough sense to see that, even if you cannot agree to her terms, you are a far better candidate than Mr. Chester. When does Sir Arthur return?"

"In a sennight, I think."

She rose and strode over to him. "I do not seek to quarrel with you, Charles. I only wish to see your aspirations fulfilled, and you have desired the burgess, I know for yourself as well as your father. It would not astonish me if you desired it *more* for your father than yourself."

Charles took in a deep breath at the possible truth of her words. Without doubt his victory would be his father's as well. But with his decision to risk the support of Mrs. Brentwood, he might follow in his father's path. A Gallant would lose the election a fourth time.

As if reading his mind, she said, "Do not fear disappointing your father. You have a brighter future than he had at your age. I see the envy in his eyes when you tell him the tales of your travels through the Orient. You must act according to your truth. Your father and I shall always adore you."

She kissed him on top of the head before taking her leave. Charles continued to sit at his writing table in thought. He picked up one of the writings of Mr. Sharp and glanced through it. One sentence in particular caught his attention.

"*A toleration of slavery is, in effect, a toleration of inhumanity.*"

He set the writing down and prepared to call upon Mrs. Brentwood.

Chapter 24

The dreary weather with its dark sky and cold mist could not dampen his disposition. Charles led his horse to the Brentwood residence with the calm of someone who expected the sun would part the clouds at any moment. Terrell had agreed to be his and his alone. The level of his satisfaction surprised him, and he shook his head in near disbelief, for he had not even wanted her attentions when first she threw herself at him.

Or perhaps he only fooled himself in thinking he had never desired her seduction. She certainly filled the emptiness left by Greta in a manner all his campaigning never could, yet Terrell was more than a stopgap. She invigorated him, took him to new heights that exhilarated and startled him, gave him freedom to express his darkest cravings while inspiring a passion to protect and care for her.

And though she persuaded him to withhold his support of abolition, she had made up his mind. He could not look at the scars upon her back without rage. The cruel mistreatment of slaves was not unknown to him, but through Terrell, he could see, he could touch the horror. How could he look her in the eyes and say that he would condemn another to suffer what she had?

He saw his mother's concern, however. She

perhaps knew, at that intuitive level to which her sex seemed exceptionally attuned, his reluctance to accept the support of Sir Arthur. Sir Arthur had not specifically stated but undoubtedly expected that, in exchange for his support, Charles would deliver his vote when needed. Out of deference to his employer and the ability of Sir Arthur to influence the election, Charles, despite his hesitations, had humbly and patiently waited for Sir Arthur to make his endorsement.

But then Terrell had entered his life and, through no intention of her own, had upended his equilibrium. What if her intuition regarding Sir Arthur proved true? How would the high and mighty MP receive the news that Terrell would no longer be his? Charles had not previously been willing to risk the support of Sir Arthur. How quickly his disposition had changed with the advent of Terrell. Would he truly allow a woman to put his election in jeopardy? Without the support of either the Brentwoods or Sir Arthur, his chances of winning the burgess became, perhaps, as difficult to scale as the Great Wall of China.

"Mrs. Brentwood will see you," the Brentwood servant informed Charles and showed him to the drawing room.

"Mr. Gallant, I had been waiting for your visit," Mrs. Brentwood greeted after Charles had made his bow. "Mere weeks remain before the day of election. I should like to give you our endorsement."

"And I should like to receive it, madam, but, alas, I can make no promises concerning the matter of abolition should it come before Parliament, and should I be so fortunate to cast a vote in its favor."

Mrs. Brentwood sat stone-faced. "It is the one condition I requested for our support. Not just for my family but the welfare of all of England's colonies. The livelihood of hundreds of Englishmen would be upset by wholesale abolition."

"And the lives of thousands of slaves would know only misery and death if we allow slavery to prevail. It is not merely humanity that compels slavery's destruction but the principles of liberty. Even the Americans understand that what they fought an entire war for is incongruous with slavery."

"They have not abolished slavery in the United States."

"Several of their states have. Vermont and Massachusetts among them."

"As I have said, I do not oppose abolition, Mr. Gallant. Merely its delay."

"For myself, I feel only an impatience to end what I believe to be a criminal institution at odds with the virtues of every Englishman, every Christian."

"I had not known you harbored such fervency on this subject. I must admit to being disappointed. Mr. Chester did not exhibit such emotion."

"Mr. Chester and I differ in many ways."

"I see."

"I hope that my many other qualities will not cease to compel you, though we may disagree on the solitary matter of slavery."

"You will not be convinced from your current position?"

"I will not."

"Have you anything else to say to me?"

"I should be honored to have your support. At the risk of sounding arrogant, I believe myself the superior candidate. But you must act as you deem fit. Whatever you decide, I will bear your family no hard feelings."

"Thank you, Mr. Gallant. I appreciate your candor."

Knowing their meeting to be at an end, he bowed. He departed feeling as if a weight had been lifted from him, but from the frown that persisted upon her features during the whole of their conversation, he suspected that she had rendered her decision, and it was not in his favor.

Chapter 25

Wang now accompanied Master Gallant to the inn, and Terrell found she missed the preparations of the valet. Before departing for the day, Master Gallant had left her only the simple instruction to await his return. He would decide then how the night would proceed.

But he was late. Members had begun arriving. Gallant had appointed Master Troy steward of the evening in his absence, and Master Troy permitted those members who already had partners to proceed with the evening activities. The unpaired members could then make their selection.

"I know I am not among the most comely of our sex here at the Red Chrysanthemum," said Sarah to Terrell as the women made their way to the gathering chambers, "but I would have thought someone besides Captain Gracechurch would take an interest in me."

"Your beauty can rival that of any woman," Terrell replied, taking George from Sarah, "but you would do better without a babe in your arms. There is little in this world that frightens men more than children."

Sarah looked longingly at her son. "I do enjoy his company beyond any other, but I worry that if I am idle for too long, Madame will not be pleased."

In the hallway, a gentleman from behind brushed

brusquely by, causing Terrell to stumble. Clasping George to her with one arm, she managed to stop her fall with the other arm.

"Watch where you go," the man snapped.

Seeing a golden pocket watch encrusted with emeralds upon the floor, she picked it up. "Your pardon, sir."

Upon seeing what she held, his eyes widened. He snatched it from her. "What are you doing with my watch?"

"I merely saw it upon the floor, sir."

He snorted. "See that you keep your black hands off my effects."

After the man had continued on his way, Terrell turned to Sarah. "Who is that man? I have not seen him before."

"I know him. That is the Bishop Hargrave. It is said he might become an archbishop."

In the gathering chamber, dominant members stood to one side of the room while submissive members stood on the other. Sarah took her place among the latter. Terrell, still with George in her arms, hung back near the door.

"Miss Terrell, do you not join us?" Master Troy inquired. He wore only his breeches, his brawny chest visible for all to see.

"I am spoken for," she answered.

"By whom?"

She hesitated. "By one who is not present."

He turned to the bishop and bowed. "My lord, we welcome your return. Madame Devereux would be disappointed that she was not here to greet you. The baroness is the most senior member present, but perhaps her ladyship would defer the first selection to you."

"I should be honored to grant my place to such an illustrious person," the baroness said.

The bishop was an older man with pockmarks upon his complexion, which he would seem to diminish through the finery of his dress, his pocket watch sparkling above the opal ring adorning one hand. He surveyed the row of submissives. Sarah kept her eyes lowered as he passed before her. Sophia met his gaze above her fan.

"This wench will do," the bishop declared.

Master Troy nodded, and the bishop escorted Sophia from the room. As they passed by Terrell, the bishop brushed once more against her, startling George. Cradling the child closer, Terrell suppressed a desire to glare at His Holiness.

Only two other dominant ones remained, and neither chose Sarah. She reclaimed George from Terrell. "Well, I shall spend the evening once more with my favorite fellow."

Sarah went into the kitchen to find victuals for George, but Terrell remained upstairs to await the arrival of Master Gallant. She wore the corset and skirts she had worn the night she had first set out to seduce him. She recalled how she had stood in his way as he descended the stairs, how he had spurned her advances, how he had swept her and pinned her against the wall. Even his rebuffs had exhilarated her.

Nearly an hour passed, however, and still there were no signs of Master Gallant. He had Wang with him, but she could not keep the apprehensions at bay. Perhaps he had been waylaid by hostile elements. Or perhaps he had an unexpected caller. A *female* caller. The countess. Miss Greta. Or a woman unknown to her. Gallant had a life, a world, apart from the Red Chrysanthemum. It was one that she would never know.

Not wanting to dwell upon such unpleasant thoughts, she considered lying upon Gallant's bed and fondling herself so that she would be more than ready when he arrived. Yes, that was what she would do to occupy her time. She would start a fire in the hearth and discard her clothing. Her corset laced in the front. Thus, she required no assistance. She would prostrate herself naked upon the bed, a proper greeting for her Master. She would have done so already but for her dread in having to tell him that she wished to retreat from her declaration last night. Master Gallant would not be pleased. She had made up her mind to tell him *after* he had spent and was in a better mood.

"There is the Negress!"

Terrell, about to ascend the stairs, stopped and turned to see the bishop, Master Troy and Sophia coming upon her. The bishop drew himself in front of her, eyes blazing.

"Where is my watch, vile creature?"

"My lord?"

"My watch. The one you had set your filthy black hands upon."

"You retrieved it from me," she replied.

"And you pilfered it from me afterwards."

"I am no thief, my lord."

"Bah! Your kind are driven by corrupt impulses."

"I do not seek your watch."

"That watch was made of pure gold, the emeralds mined from Egypt."

She wanted to respond that he should refrain from flaunting such a prized item if he wished not to lose it.

The bishop turned to Master Troy. "I demand this Negro be searched."

"I did not take your lordship's watch!" Terrell protested.

Master Troy, however, reached for her. He searched the pockets in her petticoats.

"It is not on her person," he said to the bishop. "Perhaps the watch fell from your person and we ought survey your prior steps."

"Or search her quarters," Sophia suggested. "She might have hidden it."

"Or search *her* person," Terrell snapped. "*She* was with his lordship the majority of the evening."

"Indeed, I invite you to search all of me so that my innocence will be proven."

"Search the black's quarters," the bishop commanded of Master Troy.

With a vexed sigh, Terrell followed the other three upstairs to her room. She hoped Master Gallant would return soon.

Master Troy lit a lamp and looked about the room. Sophia smirked. Terrell crossed her arms and leaned against the frame of the door. Though confident they would not find what they sought, she worried that they should find the pouch of coins she had hidden deep beneath her bed. They would not believe she had accumulated the money in her time at the Red Chrysanthemum and instead think she had stolen the money. But Master Gallant would believe her. She hoped.

"You've found it!" the bishop exclaimed after Master Troy had pulled back the bedclothes.

Terrell straightened. The bishop whirled around to face her, his gold pocket watch in hand.

"Impossible!" Terrell cried. "I did not take it!"

"Then how is it that we found it in your bed, hiding beneath the linen?"

"If I were to hide such a thing, I should hardly place it haphazardly in my bed linen."

"Liar!" He turned to Master Troy. "Send for the night watchman. I will have this Negress taken to gaol tonight!"

Terrell stared at the man. He was in earnest. She looked past him to Sophia.

"You! You planted the watch in my bed, you wretch!"

"I protest! For what purpose would I do such a thing?" Sophia denied.

"It is clear to me who the culprit is," Bishop Hargrave said. "Master Troy—"

"Perhaps we should wait till Master Gallant is returned," Master Troy said, his brows knit in uncertainty.

"What purpose would that serve? This black must be punished for her crime."

"Yes, but—"

"Justice must be served. Do you not agree, Master Troy?"

"Yes, my lord. I suppose..."

With sinking hopes, Terrell could see that Master Troy would not oppose the imperial bishop. With

Master Gallant absent, she had to rely upon her own wiles. She could not be thrown in gaol this night. Miss Sarah would explain the truth to Master Gallant, but he would have to go through much trouble to set her free. If such a thing were possible if the likes of Bishop Hargrave were fixed upon her incrimination.

"Perhaps I could offer recompense of a different nature," she said, taking a step forward. "I am spoken for by Sir Arthur—perhaps you have heard of him?"

The bishop grunted.

"Sir Arthur is a man of great discrimination. In everything, he tolerates only the finest quality. For good reason, he has chosen me for his own. Would my lord wish to sample that which Sir Arthur pays a formidable price for?"

The bishop turned to Master Troy. "This black is Sir Arthur's doxie?"

"I believe it to be true," Master Troy replied.

The bishop turned back to her. She could see both his disgust and interest.

"I will hardly take the word of a black," he sneered. "Where is Sir Arthur?"

"In Somerset."

"Then I cannot corroborate your claims."

Terrell felt the precariousness of her fate. "You may judge for yourself, my lord."

"Hmph. Indeed. I will render my judgment *after* you have demonstrated the quality of your services."

"I will leave the two of you then," Master Troy said, relieved that the tension had been deferred for the moment.

"I should like to watch if I may," Sophia said.

Terrell drew in a sharp breath and silently cursed

the trollop. But she had to focus her attentions upon the bishop. She had to keep him from having her arrested till Master Gallant arrived.

If he arrived.

Swaying over to the bishop, she slowly sank to her knees. "With your permission, my lord?"

He said nothing, which she took as his assent to unbutton his fall to reveal his limp penis. She cradled it in her hand, caressing it till it began to waken.

"What a masterful weapon is this," she murmured. "I wonder that the maidens do not cry out when you spear them with this instrument."

Though his cock was of barely average length and girth, he grunted in satisfaction. She licked at the head. His shaft perked further.

"I heard tell that one of her talents is arsehole lickin'," Sophia remarked.

"That is most foul," the bishop replied.

"Which is why she is most adept at it, but she has boasted that men enjoy it immensely."

Terrell imagined herself tearing out the jade's hair till not a lock was left.

"Few men wish to be touched there, save for mollies," Terrell said.

"You think yourself too good for his lordship's arsehole?"

Filled with loathing, Terrell could not even glare at the woman. She would promise herself revenge, but the last time she had attacked Miss Sophia, Gallant had punished her soundly for it.

"Have you licked Sir Arthur?" the bishop asked.

"I've not."

"Surely she lies," Sophia said. "You do not think Sir

Arthur pays a hefty coin for the ordinary?"

The bishop looked down at Terrell and nodded. "Lick my arsehole."

He removed his coat and waistcoat that he could access his braces. After pulling down his trousers, he turned around to present his veined and lumpy rump. Terrell suppressed a shudder. She had no wish to upset the bishop or give Sophia the satisfaction of seeing her grimace.

"Have a good whiff," the bishop snarled.

Terrell drew in a loud breath. She caressed a sagging buttock. "What a fine arse you have, my lord."

"Lick it well."

She parted the cheeks and, wedging her tongue between them, rimmed his hole.

"Ah," he gasped. "That is rather pleasant."

Holding her breath, she licked at him again.

"More," he urged. "Ah, ah!"

"It is no mere coincidence that her kind is comfortable with where one shites," Sophia sniggered. "Their complexions be of the same color."

Having committed to the man's arse, Terrell flicked her tongue at his anus over and over. He gasped repeatedly. She reached around to confirm that the man's cock was harder than a birch. She settled herself in front of him, taking his length into her mouth, while she inserted her finger where her tongue had been.

"My God," the bishop groaned, legs quivering.

She took him deep into her mouth and pushed her finger into his arse. She pressed her thumb to the area between his hole and his cods. She sucked his cock as hard as she could. She worked her finger in his rectum.

"God help me," he choked.

"Spill your white seed upon her," Sophia urged. "It would improve her blackness."

With wild grunting, he thrust his hips at her. He yelped and howled like a dog. His sour mettle filled her mouth. She suppressed the desire to spit it out and instead swallowed, then licked her lips and purred as if she had partaken of sweets instead. He wiped his moist prick across her face, muttering, "My God, my God."

"Do you wish for more, my lord?" Terrell asked, withdrawing her finger.

He shuddered. "No, no. That was…"

"Ungodly? Wicked? Divine?"

He had a haggard appearance and seemed too tired to even replace his clothing.

"I should like to present my lord one final vision to remember this night," Terrell said. "A kiss. May I?"

He frowned in revulsion.

"For Miss Sophia."

Terrell triumphed at the look upon her face. The bishop, intrigued, nodded.

Striding over, Terrell grabbed Sophia about the head and crushed her lips to Sophia's mouth, smothering a scream. Sophia pushed desperately, pulling at her hands, but Terrell would not release her, not even when Sophia scratched at her. Bishop Hargrave watched, stunned and mesmerized.

At last, her hands stinging from Sophia's nails, Terrell threw Sophia from her. Too livid for words, Sophia could only quake, wiping furiously at her lips.

"My God," the bishop drawled. He gathered

himself at last to dress.

"I pray my lord is satisfied?" Terrell inquired. At his nod, she continued, "It would not be necessary to comment to Sir Arthur of this. He might not approve of either my part or yours."

He said nothing. He took his coat and departed without another glance at her.

"You bitch!" Sophia shrieked.

Terrell was equally ready to launch herself at her nemesis, but a voice startled them both.

"Miss Terrell," Wang said.

With a cry of anguish, Sophia turned on her heels and fled, no doubt to wash her mouth of the assault.

"I will be but a moment," Terrell said to Wang as calmly as she could, "if you could wait outside the room."

His brows had raised slightly. No doubt he had noticed the drying emission upon her face, but he said nothing as he closed the door behind him.

Once alone, Terrell poured a pitcher of water into the basin above the chest of drawers. With a brush and soap, she attempted to scour and scrape the scent and taste of Bishop Hargrave from her mouth. A strange melancholy filled her. It was not the first time she had been made to suck the cock or lick the arse of one who clearly despised her blackness. Why should this one instance dispirit her? She ought to be relieved that she had avoided gaol. She ought to be filled with fury and plotting her revenge upon Sophia. Instead, she felt wretched and in need of seeing Gallant more than ever.

She splashed the water over her face a dozen times, but it did not wash away the woe.

Chapter 26

"All was well—er, ended well," Master Troy informed Charles.

"I passed Bishop Hargrave's carriage," Charles noted as he sat down at the writing table in Joan's study. "It is unfortunate I was not here to greet him, but I take it he left satisfied with his evening?"

"I believe so."

"Good. I hope there is time enough in the evening for you to enjoy it?"

"I am pleased that I could serve you, sir. That is all I require."

"I do not expect to call upon you in such capacity often."

Rather, Charles hoped he would not. Sir Canning had paid him an unexpected visit at his home, just as he was preparing to leave for the Red Chrysanthemum.

"Have you seen this?" Sir Canning had asked, waving an edition of the *Morning Gazette*, which Charles rarely read, for it printed mostly gossip and made great sport of the personal lives of noted Whigs. "It is an outrage."

Charles received the paper and skimmed the front article, in which Mr. Laurel was mentioned to be seen alone in the company of Mrs. Grimshaw and engaged in *intimate* conversation.

"This will be the talk of town," his employer lamented. "I had it from Henry Faversham, a mutual friend of Mr. Grimshaw, that the husband is furious with the accusations. I fear *The Independent* will take aim at one of ours in retaliation."

Charles said nothing. He could not give Sir Canning warning without revealing the Red Chrysanthemum.

"I cautioned the *Gazette* not to attempt a war with *The Independent*," Canning fumed.

"The *Gazette* feeds on salacious material," Charles replied. "I rather think they delight in making mischief."

"I fear *The Independent* will follow suit. What lies will they print of us? You had best watch your back."

"Alas, I have exposed myself already."

Sir Canning raised his brows.

"I was seen in the company of a Negress, who is employed by a friend of mine. Mr. Phillips saw me purchase a bonnet for her."

"Why were you purchasing a bonnet for a servant?"

"The wind took hers, and I felt quite sorry for the poor creature."

Canning shook his head "Your good deed will not go unpunished."

"Perhaps *The Independent* will find news of the Brentwoods more worthy."

"News of the Brentwoods? What news?"

"I suspect they will be endorsing Mr. Chester."

"Chester?! Surely they know Chester to be an idiot. Mrs. Brentwood had written me inquiring into your qualities. I wrote straightway that you were the obvious choice."

"She had a condition I could not meet. I would not promise to withhold my vote on abolition should it come before Parliament."

"Well, once you have the support of Sir Arthur, the support of the Brentwoods would be meaningless. I will apply myself again to your cause as soon as Sir Arthur returns."

"I pray you would not."

"Sir Arthur is an astute man. He shall not require much convincing."

Charles, sitting in the Red Chrysanthemum, reflected that Sir Canning was wrong. He poured himself a cup of tea, which Wang had arranged to be hot and ready for Charles' arrival at the inn.

Wang entered as Master Troy took his leave. His valet nodded, indicating Miss Terrell was ready and waiting. Having been delayed, Charles looked forward to the sight of her more than ever. He wondered if she would scold him for refusing Mrs. Brentwood and smiled to think that Miss Terrell cared for his success.

Leaving his tea unfinished, he made his way upstairs. He wondered how Terrell might have prepared herself. She seemed fond of the shirt he had gifted her. Perhaps she wore that and nothing else. Or perhaps she would be sans any clothing. His loins warmed at the vision. He would have to teach her some simple rope bondage that she could do on her own.

When he entered the bedchamber, he was a little disappointed to find she was fully clothed, more or less. Her lack of a gown was more than wanton, but the corset, skirts, and shift covered her plenty. Nevertheless, she was a lovely sight, and he would have her out of those garments soon enough.

"Master," she greeted, falling to her knees before him, "may I have your cock?"

Her abruptness surprised him into silence.

"Please," she whispered, her gaze downcast and her hands dutifully clasped behind her. "I have desired it so desperately the whole evening."

Still surprised by the need in her tone, his only reply was, "Have you?"

He lifted her chin and saw that her eyes swam with a vulnerability he had not seen since he had discovered her back against her will.

"Please," she begged. "May I have your cock?"

He could not deny her and nodded. She unbuttoned him in haste and took his cock into her mouth as if starved. It hardened soon enough in her mouth. She sucked upon it with vigor and gently scraped her nail along the skin of his cods, sending shivers through him. He could only wonder for a moment what occasioned such fervor but was soon overtaken by the rapture encasing his shaft.

"You will make me spend," he grunted, then realized that was her intent.

She lapped and suckled, taking him deep into her orifice such that her nose touched his hairs. He refrained from bucking his hips so that his tip would not strike the back of her throat and cause her to gag. But he could not hold back from the force of her assault. His load burst from him, filling her hot, wet mouth. She swallowed the first spurt but seemed to allow the second to linger. When at last she allowed him to slip from her, he stumbled back and shook his head several times to right his mind. No finer greeting could be had.

But she was not done. When the sensitivity had subsided, she licked him clean.

"I wish to pleasure you and ride atop you," she said. "Will you allow me, Master Gallant?"

An odd desperation pervaded in her voice. He wove a hand through her hair, cradling the side of her head.

"Is something amiss?" he asked, then recalled there had been a stiffness to Master Troy's responses this evening.

She shook her head. "Only that you were quite late, Master. I waited and waited, wanting and desiring your person."

"Forgive me. It was not my intention to be this tardy."

"It matters not. You are here now. Come."

Standing, she pulled him over to the bed and pushed him down. She straddled him and began unlacing her corset. He watched as the swell of her bosom relaxed as the stays came undone. She threw aside the garment and pulled her arms through the sleeves of her shift, which she pushed down to her waist. He savored the beauty of her naked orbs with their dark areolas. She pushed her breasts together, fondling them, and tugged at the nipples. He reached for one, plying the wonderful flesh, feeling its weight and curve.

She leaned over him, presenting the breast to his mouth. He took in as much as he could, applying himself with as much zest as she had shown to him.

She gasped and groaned as he teased and sucked. Impatient, she began to pull up, but he caught her head and brought it to his, wanting her lips. He captured her mouth, and the scent of lavender water filled his nose. It was all over her face. She crushed her lips to his, pushing her tongue into his mouth, smothering him. Her exuberance was heady, encouraging his own intensity. Clasping her head in both his hands, he devoured her.

She ground herself atop him. Pushing herself up, she fumbled at the buttons of his coat. She struggled with the last one and decided to rip the coat open, sending the button flying to the floor. He was about to protest but did not wish to disturb her. She made brisk work of his waistcoat and unclasped his braces, then pulling out his shirt and shoving it up his chest, she attacked his nipples. They burned and smarted beneath her licking, sucking, and biting. He grimaced through ground teeth when she bit particularly hard.

"Take care, Terrell," he gasped.

She left his nipples and kissed her way down his midsection to where his cock stood stiff once more. She swirled her tongue over its length and teased the sensitive underside. Fitting his fingers through her hair, he caressed her head as she took him into her mouth, coaxing him to supreme hardness. When she was satisfied, she sat up, collected her skirts and sank herself onto his cock, sheathing him in rapture in one swift motion.

He wished she had removed his coat, for his clothing inhibited his mobility. They, each of them, had far too much attire, but he could see her impatience. She ground herself atop him, her cunnie flexing about him, before rolling her hips. He groaned as her motions stroked his cock.

"Spend for me, Master," she whispered.

Having done so but moments before, he knew he would be slower to spend a second time. Wanting her to achieve her own elation, he replied, "Not before you do."

She tossed her head. "I will make you spend first."

"My dear, you have done it already."

"And I will do it again."

Her eyes flared with determination. He wondered at it. Though she appeared to delay her own pleasure in favor of his, he felt, nonetheless, that she sought to fulfill her own purpose. It seemed she sought a sense of power or control.

She lifted herself up and down his cock till perspiration gleamed upon her bosom. Her thighs had to be sore. He thrust his hips at her to aid in her exertions. Her skirts created a tent that blanketed them and trapped the heat. The sweltering perspiration caused their flesh to slip against one another. He gripped her legs, crushing the skirts to her, to hold her steady and facilitate her pounding.

"Spend," she ordered. "Sp—oh, fuck..."

Her brow furrowed in anguish as she attempted to hold back that divine paroxysm.

He would oblige her wishes. Tightening his grip on her, he hammered himself into her without regard to her pleasure. Her skirts could not muffle the sound of his loins slapping furiously against hers. Rapture pressed upon his cock, his cods, till, at last, the gates were sprung, unleashing spasm after spasm. His body bucked violently beneath hers. She would have toppled over were it not for his hold.

When a little of his control returned, he tugged at her so that her cunnie rubbed against him. It was enough to send her over the edge. Her body trembled and jerked. A wail escaped her throat. Then, with a moan broken by deep gasps, she collapsed on top of him. They lay amidst their dampened garments till their labored breathing had calmed.

"Thank you, Master," she whispered.

He stroked the back of her head. "It is I who should thank you. That was…splendid. You are splendid."

"I would happily perform an encore. As often as you wished."

"You could, no doubt, but I shall require more rest in between."

"A period apart might do us good."

A period apart? That was not what he had meant.

"I have given some thought to what I had said yesterday," she continued, "when I had said that I would forsake Sir Arthur."

An unfavorable premonition filled him. She lay with her breasts pressed against his chest—he could feel her nipples still hard and pointed—and her face turned to the side so that he could not read her countenance.

"I think we might—that is, when we fully consider the matter…" she said.

Bloody hell. Did she wish to retract her avowal? Before he could speak, however, a knock interrupted them.

"You are required downstairs," Wang said from behind the door. "It cannot wait."

Terrell scrambled from him. With a curse, he sat up. His clothing was moist with perspiration, but he would have no time to change.

"What is it that cannot wait?" he asked Wang, not bothering to suppress his irritation. As quickly as he could, he fixed his wardrobe. "Send for Jones if needed."

"Jones has been rendered unconscious."

Charles was startled to think that anything could overcome the imposing blackamoor. He turned to Miss Terrell when he had secured his braces. "Wait here."

Without bothering to button his waistcoat or coat, he hurried from the room. He met Wang, who led him to the gathering chamber.

"I will see her!" a voice cried.

It was Nicholas Edelton.

Charles stepped into the room to see Master Troy and Baxter attempting to restrain the young man. Jones was slumped against the wall, a heavy ivory carving of a naked torso beside him.

"Unhand me! I will see her! I must talk to her!"

"Mr. Edelton, take hold of yourself!" Charles commanded, but he was met with only wild determination. Seeing that Baxter struggled, Charles sought to take the man's place. But in the exchange, Nicholas had a free arm, which he swung at Troy, cuffing the man in the jaw.

Master Troy, whom only Jones could best in fisticuffs, returned the blow, knocking Nicholas to the ground. He lay motionless. Silence followed.

"Is he...?" Baxter murmured.

Bending down, Charles could see Nicholas still

breathed. "No, he is merely in the same state as Jones."

Charles turned to see that the Negro had revived and was rubbing the lump upon his head.

"I lost me footing trying to hold him," Jones explained.

Charles stood and looked about for Mr. Fields. "Where is Mr. Washington?"

"Here, sir," Mr. Fields said upon entering the room.

"Did Mr. Edelton come by carriage?"

"He did."

"Let us return Mr. Edelton home." Charles turned to Wang. "Have my horse saddled. I mean to speak with him when he wakes."

The last thing he wanted was to spend an hour seeing to Nicholas. Charles wanted to return to Miss Terrell and hear what she had to say. But, alas, he would have to wait.

* * * * *

The servants in the Edelton residence were not as surprised as Charles would have expected to see Nicholas carried, still comatose, into the house. Charles and the carriage driver carried Nicholas to his bedchamber.

"Shall I stable your horse?" the driver asked Charles after they had deposited Nicholas onto the bed.

"I shall not be long," Charles replied. "Have a maid bring me smelling salts."

Charles pulled a chair to the side of the bed as he waited. A maid appeared several minutes later, bobbed a curtsy, and handed him the salts.

"And some brandy for Mr. Edelton," he told the maid.

He held the vial beneath Nicholas' nose and watched the young man come to. His eyes fluttered open. As he glimpsed his whereabouts, his countenance twisted in puzzlement.

"You are home, Mr. Edelton," Charles told him.

Nicholas looked at him in greater confusion.

"You made the mistake of taking aim at Master Troy," Charles supplied.

Nicholas groaned, muttered several oaths, and stared up at the canopy of his bed.

"They would not let me see her," he said. "I but wished to speak to her."

"I can see that your desire to do so is strong, but I urge you to restrict your correspondence with her to letters."

Nicholas shook his head. "Letters are insufficient."

"Alas, you have little choice. I cannot allow violence of any order to occur at the Red Chrysanthemum. Your appearance has been too much a disruption at the inn. Regretfully, I am revoking your membership."

Nicholas sat up. "Damn you, you cannot!"

"I can. Madame Devereux may restore your membership upon her return, but whilst I am in charge, you will not set foot in the inn."

"Then have Mistress Primrose meet me outside."

Charles shook his head. "If she wishes. I will not force her attendance."

"I pay bloody good money for my membership!"

The maid returned with a tray. "Your brandy, sir."

Charles stood and poured Nicholas a glass, but the latter swiped it away when Charles offered it.

Charles picked up the glass. "Mr. Edelton, I understand you are pained—"

"You do not! You cannot know the depths of my despair!"

"You are not the only one to have suffered a broken heart, Nicholas. I have learned, through tribulation, that the Red Chrysanthemum is not the place for love."

Nicholas had the consternation of a child.

"I still think of her," Charles said, "but I mourn less what might have been. Your pain, too, shall pass."

Nicholas shook his head. "No, no. She is merely testing me, testing my devotion, teasing me."

"If you believe that her motivation, then do not frighten her with your insistence. Do not smother her with your attentions. Instead, impress her with your patience, your commitment to what she desires."

Nicholas turned silent in thought, then, nodding his head, he said, "Yes, yes! Absence makes the heart grow fonder."

Pitying Nicholas his delusions, Charles said nothing. He was convinced that Miss Primrose wanted nothing more of Nicholas.

"Or you may find your passions toward her to diminish with time," Charles finally said.

"Never! I can scarce breathe without her. I think of her every waking minute. Your love could not have run as deep as mine if you could even think that mine would fade."

"Perhaps your feelings are greater, but women are reflective creatures. They want time and liberty to contemplate their heart's desire. You must not overwhelm them. Nor should you allow your sensibilities to govern too much. Take time to reflect upon the best course of action when your mind and passions have cooled."

Nicholas frowned but offered no opposition. "I will write to her then so that she will not mistake my absence for faithlessness. You will see that she reads my letters?"

"I will ensure she receives them."

"Will you not also speak to her on my behalf? Tell her how I long to see her? A minute of her presence is worth a hundred guineas to me!"

"My responsibility is to keep the peace and order of the inn. Nothing more."

"When does Madame Devereux return? She will restore my membership. I will pay any cost!"

"With what money?" a voice asked.

They turned to see a tall man with long legs, a few years older perhaps than Charles and hair several shades darker. Nicholas shrank as if confronted by his father. The man narrowed his eyes at Charles. "Who are you, sir?"

Charles bowed. "The name is Gallant."

"You are a friend of my brother?"

Charles studied the man, who bore only a faint resemblance to his fair-haired sibling. "I think Mr. Edelton would regard me more as an acquaintance. I had the pleasure of seeing him safely home, but will now take my leave."

"Before you do, Mr. Gallant, I will have a word with you."

Charles raised his brows at the imperious tone. He

recalled the senior Edelton was the Marquess of Carey.

"If you please," his lordship added.

Still anxious to return to Terrell, Charles hesitated. "As the hour is late, I should return."

"I will not be long with you."

Charles considered that he might be able to compel the older Edelton to assist in keeping Nicholas at bay. "Very well."

Hat in hand, he followed the older brother downstairs to the library. The marquess closed the door behind them.

"Where did you find my brother?" Carey asked.

"I shall leave the answer to your brother, my lord," Charles replied. He wondered how much of the conversation with Nicholas the marquess had heard, or if he had merely walked in at Nicholas' last statement.

"Was it the Inn of the Red Chrysanthemum?"

"As I say, you may ask your brother."

"He will tell me he was at some gaming hell, but Nicholas is a very poor liar. Tell me, are you also acquainted with Miss Primrose?"

The man seemed to force her name.

"You have an interest in Miss Primrose?" Charles returned, feeling the need to protect her. He wondered if it was the marquess who had hired Mr. Fields.

"She has an interest in my brother."

"Your brother is fixed upon her."

The countenance of the marquess darkened. "Yes, he is."

"It is not my place to interfere, but I did advise Mr.

Edelton to take the time to cool his passions."

"That is sound advice, Mr. Gallant. I should also thank you for seeing my brother safely home."

"None is needed, my lord." Charles replaced his hat. "Now I must bid a good evening to you both."

The marquess clearly wished to continue their dialogue but allowed Charles to take his leave.

Given the dark conditions, Charles could not ride his horse as quickly as he would have liked. The Red Chrysanthemum was quiet upon his arrival. He made straightway for the bedchamber. Opening the door, he found only the light of embers from the hearth. He discerned Miss Terrell lying in the bed.

"She has been asleep this past half hour," Wang whispered from behind him.

He would not wake her then. With a disappointed sigh, he allowed Wang to assist in his undressing, then slid into bed beside her. She turned toward him in her sleep, her head coming to rest against his shoulder. He put an arm about her and closed his eyes to join her in slumber.

Chapter 27

"When I awoke, he had already left," Terrell said to Sarah. "Wang said he had an early meeting at a coffeehouse."

They walked through the market, shopping for sugar and flour for the cook. Sarah had left George in the care of Lydia and pushed an empty pram into which she would place the groceries.

"You could just as easily speak to him tonight," Sarah said. "And you most certainly should tell him of Bishop Hargrave. What Sophia did was unforgivable!"

Terrell looked up at the midday sky. "I gave the bitch—your pardon, Lady Sarah—I gave her a bit of reckoning."

"Is that why she turned livid and quaked when you passed her by?"

Terrell smiled. "Did she indeed?"

"Why not tell Master Gallant? He might send her from the Red Chrysanthemum."

"I've no wish to trouble him. He has much on his plate and had to attend to Mr. Edelton last night. Jones said the man was as mad as all Bedlam."

Sarah stopped before a stand selling flour by the pound. "Cook wants three pounds' worth."

"Fourteen pence for three pounds," said the vendor.

"Fourteen pence! I should think a better price in

order for the purchase of three pounds' worth."

"Fourteen be a price fairer than most."

"But surely you can do better?"

The vendor shook his head. "Fourteen is as low as I go, miss."

"Perhaps I will see what other options I have."

She and Terrell strolled on and found another vendor.

"Allow me," Terrell said. "I think your demeanor and speech suggest you to be a woman above your means."

Turning to the vendor, Terrell assumed a diffident air. "How much for a pound, sir?"

"Five pence," a man replied.

"Oh no! My mistress said I was not to pay above three pence."

"Three pence? Are you blasted mad? I might as well give the flour away for free."

"My mistress insists. Last time I paid a price not to her liking, she beat me soundly. I simply cannot pay more than three pence."

"Four and a half pence. That is the best I can do."

"What if I were to purchase three pounds? Could you do three pence per pound then? It is more flour than my mistress desired, but she would get the price she wanted."

The vendor scrunched his face in contemplation. "Four pence if you purchase three pounds' worth."

"No, no. I cannot pay more *and* return with too much flour."

The man huffed several times but relented. "Three and a half for three pounds then, but tell your mistress she'll not get that price often."

"Thank you, kind sir. You spared me a beating, you did."

Terrell fished the coins from the purse cook had given and paid the man. She placed the bags of flour in the pram. They then found a vendor for sugar. As Terrell bargained with the vendor, Sarah spoke to a man, who handed her his newspaper.

"Who was he?" Terrell asked.

"No one I knew," Sarah replied, "but I was interested in his paper, for I saw the name of Brentwood upon it. It is *The Independent*, which I have never read. Sir Rowan detests the paper."

"What does it say of the Brentwoods? Is it the Brentwoods of Porter's Hill?" Terrell scanned the paper though she could not recognize above a handful of words.

"It is the Brentwoods of Porter's Hill. They have elected to endorse Mr. Chester."

Terrell said nothing.

"That is unfortunate news," Sarah remarked.

"Why? Why did they endorse Mr. Chester?"

"It does not say. I am rather surprised. I do not know the Brentwoods, but Mr. Chester is not well regarded, though his family have been Tories for generations."

"It is because Charles would not accede to her demands on the matter of abolition. Is the Brentwood endorsement so very significant?"

"I have heard their support carries great weight and that Mrs. Brentwood is exceedingly active on behalf of their chosen candidates."

"Can Charles win without their support?"

"If he has the support of Sir Arthur."

"And if he does not?"

"Mr. Laurel is the only Whig in the race, so he will shore up all the orange votes. I think Gallant must have either the Brentwood support or Sir Arthur's support to prevail."

"But he has not the Brentwood support. Is it most certain that the Brentwoods will support Chester?"

Sarah read the paper once more. "It is claimed that Mrs. Brentwood herself confirmed the endorsement."

"Could they be wrong? Can it be a falsehood?"

"I suppose it were possible. *The Independent* bears no fondness for Tories, though this article is not as critical. It is interesting that it alludes to Mr. Gallant as the more qualified candidate. I suppose they mean to mock the soundness of an influential blue family like the Brentwoods."

They headed back to the inn. Terrell was quiet most of the way, her mind turning. It was her custom to brace for the worst. Though Charles had not declared yester morning that he would forsake the Brentwood endorsement, his words and tone had suggested such an action. Terrell suspicioned *The Independent* to be correct. That left Charles with the necessity of Sir Arthur's support.

"It is a shame," Sarah sighed. "There could be no man better than Master Gallant, no man more honorable or deserving of a seat in Parliament."

"The Brentwoods are a relation of Viscount Wendlesson, are they not?" Terrell asked.

"I believe they are."

"Perhaps the viscount could persuade them?"

"Perhaps. You know the Wendlessons better than I."

"Do you know where they reside?"

"I cannot recall. I think Berkeley Square. Or perhaps it was Grosvenor Square."

They were a few blocks from the inn, and Terrell came to a stop.

"You mean to call upon them?" Sarah asked.

Terrell nodded. "I do not think Charles would. He did not appear to be on the best of terms with the viscount."

"No?"

"They are men of different temperaments. I should not tarry if I wish to return before dark."

"But we are not supposed to know the members outside the Red Chrysanthemum."

"I am willing to risk Madame's displeasure. While I have the favors of Sir Arthur, she cannot be too vexed with me."

"Here, take my cloak. It will be colder when you return."

Terrell hesitated, remembering how the last item she had borrowed from Sarah had ended in ruins.

"I dare Sophia to attempt her mischief," Sarah declared. "If you will not complain of her, *I* shall. I welcome her to give me a reason."

Terrell accepted the cloak, bid her thanks, and hurried off in the direction of Grosvenor Square. It was a fair walk of nearly two hours, but, during her time working the sugar fields in Barbados, she had spent more time than that upon her feet. Upon arriving at Grosvenor Square, she asked for the Wendlesson residence, but those who would reply to her did not know it. After several dozen inquiries, she decided to try Berkeley Square. By then, her feet were sore, but she forged on. At first, she met with the same sort of responses, but just as she was about to despair, Terrell spotted a young blackamoor boy.

"You work hereabouts?" she asked him.

"Aye. For Mrs. Hopkins in Number 13," the boy replied.

"Do you know the Wendlesson residence?"

The boy shook his head.

"I'll give you a penny if you can find me the answer to whether the Viscount Wendlesson resides in Berkeley Square."

"I shall indeed!"

She followed him to Number 13. He skipped inside and was several minutes before emerging with a victorious grin.

"Wendlesson, you say? His lordship lives on the north side, second unit from the left."

Terrell happily gave the boy his penny and hurried across the square. In front of the Wendlesson residence, she nearly considered approaching the front door. There had been a time when she used the front door. But she was not now situated to do so. Instead, she sought the servants' door.

A maid opened the door and looked her over with skepticism.

"Begging your pardon, madam," Terrell said. "Is his lordship at home?"

The woman narrowed her eyes. "There be no open positions at this time."

She prepared to close the doors, but Terrell placed herself in the way. "It is not employment I seek but a word with his lordship."

The woman's eyes widened to saucers. "*You* wish

to speak with *his lordship*? Are you daft? Out with you!"

"I come on behalf of my master," Terrell lied. "He wished to send word of a private nature to the viscount."

"And why does your master not *write* to his lordship?"

"He had not the time."

"Then you may deliver the message to me."

"It is of a confidential nature."

But the maid was not convinced.

"The viscount will regret not hearing it himself," Terrell said.

"Then you must find another means of reaching him, for he and milady have left town and will be gone a fortnight."

Terrell stared at the maid but saw no evidence that the woman was lying.

"Tell your master that if his matter is of such urgency and importance, he ought to call upon the viscount himself. A funny thing, sending a servant to speak to his lordship!"

Terrell allowed the woman to slam the door before her. It was a disappointing end given the effort she had put forth, but if the viscount returned within a fortnight, there was still time before the election to speak with him. He had little reason to intervene simply because she wished it so, but perhaps he would remember his act of infidelity and oblige her because he would rather forget the moment when he, frustrated that he could not complete the act of congress with his wife, had pounded her instead.

Wearied, she took twice as long to walk the

distance back to the Red Chrysanthemum. Night had already shrouded the town when she came upon the inn. She took the service entry but paused. She thought she saw a carriage down the block and remembered that Charles had warned of possible snoops. But no one would pay much attention to a black woman.

Having missed dinner, she searched about the kitchen for what might have been left over. She found some potatoes and helped herself to an apple. Kicking off her shoes, she decided she would change her dusty attire before returning to the kitchen for more food. She also wanted to return the cloak to Sarah as soon as possible lest she should come upon Sophia armed with a glass of wine. After removing the cloak and her bonnet, she picked up her shoes and headed upstairs.

"Your gentleman be here," Jones informed her.

Charles was early? she wondered. But the voice she heard coming from down the hall was not Master Gallant's. Turning the corner, she saw first the form of Sophia, who, sensing her presence, turned around. Sophia smirked, her eyes glimmering with triumph. But Terrell's attention was drawn past her.

Sir Arthur had returned.

Chapter 28

Her pulse quickened, but Terrell continued down the hallway as if nothing were amiss, as if she had not observed the intense frown upon Sir Arthur. He had narrow eyes, but she could see the constriction of the pupils.

Sophia bid him good evening, curtsied, and took her leave of him. She passed Terrell, a malicious smile spread across her face. Terrell felt the weight of a brick settle into her gut, for she suspicioned what Sophia might have been talking to Sir Arthur about.

Sir Arthur stood before the room he and Terrell always used. Aside from Madame's bedchamber, the room was the nicest in the inn, for the furnishings were newer, and silk paper and sconces adorned the walls. He was still in his traveling clothes, but had removed his hat and gloves. A sapphire ring sparkled on one hand. His other clasped his ivory-handled walking stick.

"What a pleasure to find you are here, Sir Arthur," she greeted him.

He said nothing but stood aside to indicate she should enter the room. Her nerves balked, but she sauntered past him. He followed and closed the door behind him.

"I take it you were successful in your mission or you would not be returned early?" she asked with a gay tone.

He stared at her, and she had to rally herself not to cower before the intimidation.

"Lord Beggington is still undecided as to whether or not he will sell me the properties," Sir Arthur replied. The chill in his tone would have frosted the Thames. He took several steps toward her. "I returned because I could not rid you from my mind."

She swallowed with difficulty. "I have thought often of you as well, Sir Arthur."

"Did you?" he snarled. "Did you think of me when you were rutting with Mr. Gallant?"

She wanted to back away from him but stood her ground. Retreating would make her seem guilty. She lifted her chin. "Is that what Sophia would have you believe—"

He cuffed her on the side of the head, sending her sprawling to the sofa.

"Don't you dare lie to me!"

Her head ringing, she turned to see his eyes blazing with anger. His pale features had taken on a violet hue. He grabbed her by the arm in a fierce grip and yanked her up.

"I paid a grand sum for your fidelity," he scowled, "for your constancy during my absence, but you could not wait for my return before spreading your legs beneath another."

He flung her to the side, and she struck the sideboard before falling to the ground.

"I should have known your kind could not be trusted," he spat, "and would be, instead, governed by all that is lowly, ignoble and fetid."

Her mind whirled, though she found it hard to

settle upon a stratagem. She did know, however, that protests were useless and would only provoke his ire further. Whatever Sophia had told him, he believed it. He knew the truth of her and Gallant.

"I have erred," she said. "Forgive me."

His nostrils flared. "Forgive you? Forgive you! I will see you turned out of here—and Gallant as well! The two of you shall rue—"

"No! It is as you say, I am a lowly creature incapable of resisting the baser callings of my nature. Without your presence to guide and hold me steadfast, I became restless, bored. Master Gallant is a victim of my wanton cravings. Do not censure him for my faults."

"Gallant has a mind of his own, and he should have thought better than to cross me. I had thought him more sensible than that, but he shall pay, and pay dearly for his mistake."

Lord, no. If she had time to pray, she would have done so, though she had not prayed in years. She could not let this happen.

"The rules of membership—what occurs here is separate from—" she began to remind.

"Hang your rules! If I mean to crush Gallant beneath my heel, I need no reason. Have you no concept of my influence, you poor simpleton? I hold the burgess of Porter's Hill in my hand. Without my endorsement, Gallant stands a fraction of a chance to win. But withholding my support is insufficient. He will never be elected to Parliament. I will see his entire career ruined."

He turned toward the door, but she scrambled to him and caught his leg. "Pray have Christian mercy,

Sir Arthur! I have few morals or principles. I know only the carnal. I seek only to fulfill the cravings of flesh over soul. I have been cursed with the deepest desire for cock. But when I have it, yet am I insatiable. But I see in you, Sir Arthur, much greatness, much power. And I am drawn to you. I hunger for you in every form."

Her words gave him pause, and she continued to stroke his vanity. "If you would condescend to grant me another occasion to prove my worth—"

"Worth? The worth of a shameful whore?"

"You inspire me, Sir Arthur! I promise I can be constant. In your absence, my lack of continence prevailed. But if you do not leave me, I would be yours and yours alone. To do as you wish. Discipline me. Teach me how I can be a better whore for you. Only give of yourself to me, for I must have you. All of you. Fill me with your greatness, Sir Arthur."

She stared in hunger at his crotch and knew that lust and anger dueled for prominence within him.

"Fuck me, Sir Arthur," she said in her most husky tone. "Fuck me with your enormity."

When he said nothing, she moved her hand over his fall and felt the hardness there. With trembling hands, she unbuttoned him and freed his erection. She took his cock with the appetite of a babe starved for its mother's tit and had the satisfaction of hearing him groan. She had to remind him of her talents, remind him that no whore could best her.

"What delectable cockmeat," she murmured. "How I have starved for this!"

She encased him fully, taking him as deep as she could. She cradled his scrotum, gentling tugging at the stones within. He grunted and, grabbing the hair at the back of her head, pumped her up and down his shaft. She could not have come up for air if she tried, but she wanted only to pleasure his member in all the ways that she could. He growled his impending climax and soon she tasted the seed of him. She swallowed every drop, then with her gaze, indicated she wanted more.

He stumbled from her and leaned against the wall. But she was not done.

"I would have more of you, Sir Arthur. I would you had three cocks that you could fill all of me at once."

He stared at her, mouth agape. While he was still in a half-stupor, she led him to the bed. By accident, he stepped upon her bonnet, but there was no time to mourn the damage. He sat on the edge of the bed. She took his hand and put it to her bosom, moaning as he groped a breast. Glancing down at his crotch, she saw that he was still soft. She pulled his coat halfway down, locking his arms in place, then pushed him down onto the bed.

"What do you intend?" he demanded.

"I intend to fuck you, Sir Arthur."

His brows shot up. "But I have just spent."

"And you will spend again."

Pinning him with a devouring gaze, she straddled him and fondled her breasts through her gown and stays. She pinched her nipples through the fabric. She rolled her hips above his crotch, then slid down to assess his status. His prick was less soft but still needed coaxing. She licked at him, sucked upon his cods, and teased his perineum. When his shaft began to show more promise, she sat astride him once more. This time she ensured her skirts and petticoats did not interfere between them. Without taking him in, she pressed herself atop him and ground her quim along his length. He groaned and attempted to divest his coat, but became distracted when she began to whimper and pant, quickening her hips. When he was sufficiently hard, she moved to encase him.

"Ohhhhh," she cooed.

Laying herself atop him, she kissed at his neck and scraped her teeth over his earlobe. She bucked against him, keeping her motions contained, for he was shorter there than one might expect.

"How wondrously you fill me, Sir Arthur," she whispered, grunting as she pushed herself down on him. She squeezed her cunnie over his cock, making him gasp. His hips moved to meet her thrusts.

"Yes," she cried. "Oh, fuck me. Fuck your little black whore."

Her words must have enflamed him, for he bucked against her more rapidly. She kissed and sucked and bit the area above his cravat, crying words of encouragement between her own gasps and groans. With a roar, he shoved himself at her with such violence that she came off him. She felt a squirt of fluid upon her thigh. He lay, shuddering, his eyes closed, his breath fast. She remained in place, planting gentle kisses along his jaw.

"Have you a desire to spend thrice?" she asked when he had recovered some.

"No, no," he said.

After several minutes in which he seemed to battle sleep, he finally roused himself. He shrugged his coat back into place.

She fingered his lapel, and though she hoped he was very much done, asked, "Are you certain you do not wish to fuck me a third time?"

He caught her by the throat, his penetrating gaze gleaming. "Not tonight. But I will have you at my disposal whenever I wish. You, my wanton doxie, will be mine and mine alone."

"Indeed, Sir Arthur," she replied, ignoring the discomfort of his fingers curled into her.

"But too many temptations lurk here, especially in the absence of Madame Devereux, but I do not trust your proprietress any more than I trust you."

"I promise—"

"The promise of a black is worthless. But your kind possesses a hardiness, your bodies less delicate. I have an apartment in town that could be readied..."

Her breath stalled. "You wish me to be your mistress?"

His hand still wrapped about her throat, he pulled her closer. "I wish you to be mine. You have cast some black sorcery upon me, but I will overcome your devilry through satiation."

She pulled at his hand. Seeing her distress, he released her. She slid from him and the bed onto the floor.

"I should like nothing more than to be yours alone," she said carefully, "but I wonder that Madame will permit it?"

He stood and replaced his fall. "She will give you to me at the right price."

She balked at being handed over like chattel once more. "Madame provides me a stipend."

"If you are good, I may entertain the provision of

pin money. I can assure you the accommodations I provide will be better than your current quarters."

"Shall I have servants, too?"

He snorted. "I can make you the envy of London— shower you with riches that no other courtesan dare dream of. But first you must prove your worth. You may start with a maid."

She looked down in thought. It was what she had hoped for when first she sensed his desire for her. This was her opportunity to resume a life she had briefly known, a life of luxury. She looked up at him.

"I will be your mistress, Sir Arthur, without price, for I do not belong to Madame Devereux. But I have one condition."

He looked for where he had dropped his walking stick. "You have a condition?"

"I will be faithful to you, and you may have all of my devotion. My body will be yours to do as you please as often and at such times as you dictate. For as long as you please. Provided you give your endorsement, free and clear, to Master Gallant— without provision or expectation of any kind."

He picked up his stick, his eyes beading at her. "You wish to barter yourself for his victory at the polls?"

"But you must decide now, Sir Arthur, that I may inform Master Gallant that I cannot attend him this evening."

His lips curled in a smile that was merely a warped frown. "Very well, Miss Terrell, as I had intended to give him my support from the outset."

"Your unrestricted support, that he may be free to act as he sees fit in Parliament."

"My unrestricted support," he echoed. He looked upon her crushed bonnet and planted his walking stick on it. "But if you fail me again, Miss Terrell, you will wish yourself back in the chains of slavery."

He ground his stick into the bonnet before turning to leave. "I will send word. Be ready."

He opened the door and departed without a last glance. Though a part of her wanted to crumble to the floor, she instead rose to her feet. She did not know the hour, but what if Charles were to arrive early? She picked up her articles from the floor and hurried from the room. She could not tarry.

Chapter 29

I wish you found me much less intriguing."

Charles watched as Mr. Phillips took a seat at his table in the tavern where Charles had been talking to voters but a moment ago.

"I as well," Mr. Phillips replied with a broad smile. He looked over at Charles' near empty mug. "May I buy you another pint?"

The hour being late, Charles declined. He intended to return home, where Wang awaited him, before proceeding to the Red Chrysanthemum.

"In truth, you cannot claim my whole attention, for I had sought Mr. Chester earlier," Mr. Phillips confessed.

"You wound me, Mr. Phillips."

"Forgive me, but I think the greater injury to be caused by the Brentwoods?"

Not wanting to encourage a *tête-à-tête*, Charles said nothing. He wanted to be in the company of Miss Terrell, not Mr. Phillips.

"I'm sorry to hear it," Mr. Phillips continued. "I had thought the obvious choice to be you, Mr. Gallant."

Charles finished his drink.

"As I do not think Mrs. Brentwood whimsical, I wonder that her endorsement did not involve some consideration other than the qualities of the candidates? What could Mr. Chester offer her that you could not?"

Still met with silence, Mr. Phillips rambled on. "You are certainly deserving of their support. I have not seen a more hardworking candidate. That you would seek voters who must necessarily be persuaded by their landlords to favor another is quite commendable."

"Or a foolish waste of time."

Mr. Phillips shook his head. "You speak to voters as if you cared for their opinions, as if their thoughts might be rational, sound, and worthy of consideration."

"All men are deserving of respect till proven otherwise."

"You have even spoken to a number of Whigs."

"I am not so prejudiced as to confine my attention to one color."

"The Prince Regent was once a Whig."

"As was my employer."

"Ah, yes, Sir Canning. But you do not seem the sort of man to tilt where the wind blows."

"I hope not, but do not place me on a pedestal. I am mortal and imperfect."

"Have no fear of pedestals, Mr. Gallant, lest you turn a Whig!"

Charles chuckled and pushed his chair from the table. Rising, he asked, "Do you intend to follow me home tonight?"

"Not tonight, for it is too cold. Perhaps another night."

Charles shook his head as he prepared to take his leave. If Mr. Phillips could be trusted at his word, he could make straight for the Red Chrysanthemum.

He had taken his curricle to Porter's Hill and decided to take the reins from his driver despite the cold. The elements would stay his ardor if he should think too much of Miss Terrell and what he might do with her this evening. Strange, but he had as much a wish to make love to her as take a crop to her.

When they approached town and Charles was assured that no one followed, he turned toward the inn. After alighting, he told his driver to return home to inform Wang of the change in plans.

"Evening, Master Gallant," Baxter greeted at the door. "A gentleman awaits you in Madame's parlor."

Charles removed his hat and gloves. "A gentleman? Who?"

"I know not."

"I gave instruction not to permit entry to anyone who was not a member."

"Your pardon, Master Gallant. He was most insistent. Said his wife was here."

Charles paused. He had thought he could send the man on his way forthwith, but this was not to be the case. He gave Baxter his cloak. "Did he give his name?"

"No. He wears a mask, though I am quite familiar with all the faces of the members such that I can discern them if but half their face is revealed. He is not a man I know."

"Send Jones to the parlor."

Charles made his way to the parlor. Miss Terrell would have to wait.

The masked gentleman stood in the middle of the room. He had flaxen hair and a similar but leaner build than Charles'. His attire, dull and inferior, did not appear to be his own, for the shoulder seams of his coat sat far too close to his collar, and the hem of his trousers covered his shoes. He turned upon hearing Charles enter and appeared surprised.

"How may I assist you, sir?" Charles asked. "If it is a room you seek, we have not one to let tonight."

The man looked Charles over from head to toe. "You are a gentleman and familiar to me somehow."

"If you state your name, perhaps I can place where we might have met."

"No, no. I—I merely wished to see this place."

Charles raised his brows and waited for further elucidation.

"What is this place?" the man asked.

"An inn."

"I can see that. I meant—I had heard that nefarious activities occurred here."

"And you take an interest in such doings?"

"I take an interest in my wife."

"Your wife, sir?"

"I am told she resides here."

Charles looked the man over and noted the gold signet he wore upon his hand. That ring, and the man's speech and carriage, were at odds with his costuming.

"Your wife does not reside with you?" Charles inquired.

The man flushed and grew even more uncomfortable. "We are separated."

"I see. Who is your wife?"

"If I reveal her, then you will know *my* identity."

Charles was tempted to reveal he already knew. There could only be one woman in the Red

Chrysanthemum married to a gentleman wealthy enough to possess a gold signet.

"But you wish to speak to her?"

"No! I was merely curious as to why she resides here. I mean only to observe that she is well."

"Are you so very certain your wife is here?"

"I was told by S—by someone that she was here."

"Indeed? Whom?"

"By someone whose word I would not doubt. A man of significance, but I wished to confirm his claim for myself."

"Sir, I know you not. I cannot permit peeping Toms to wander the premises."

"I mean no harm."

"Perhaps you could leave your wife a note?'

"No! I've no wish for her to know I am here."

"And why is that, sir?"

The man bristled. "I have my reasons."

The two men stood staring at one another. The masked man took out his coin purse.

"Perhaps I can offer an incentive."

"As you know me not, I will not consider your bribe an insult. But nothing short of the truth will make me consider your request."

The gentleman squared his shoulders. "I am not at ease with this establishment to trust it with the truth."

"Then I fear we are at an impasse."

He looked Charles over. "You do not fear recognition?"

"Why should I fear it?"

"Because you are here—in this place."

"This is an inn, a place of business. You have heard

otherwise, it seems. For the sake of our guests, most of whom desire privacy, I must ask you to leave." Charles looked to the doorway where Jones stood. "Jones, will you escort the gentleman?"

The man whipped around. As with most who beheld the tall and strong Negro, he did not resist.

"Are you certain you will not leave word for your wife?" Charles asked before the man walked through the door.

"I am certain," the man mumbled.

Left alone, Charles went to sit behind the writing table and rubbed his temples. He was fairly certain the man behind the mask was Sir Rowan. What was the man's motivation, aside from curiosity, for coming? Charles wondered if he should inform Miss Sarah of the possible appearance of her husband but did not want to alarm her needlessly if he should be wrong.

Seeing the papers upon the table, Charles was reminded that he needed to review the status of membership dues. He would have preferred to delay the task till after he had seen Terrell, and decided that he would call upon Master Troy once more to oversee the arrival and pairing of members while he tended to the bookkeeping. He would then see Terrell soon enough.

Chapter 30

S he could not face him. Not tonight. Perhaps not ever.

Terrell hurried up the flights of stairs before Baxter could allow Master Gallant entry into the inn. In the sanctuary of her room, she quickly closed the door and leaned her brow against it, her heart pounding. But she could not hide in her room all night. He would expect to see her.

She nearly laughed at the cruel irony. She had made every effort to seek his company, had employed her every wile to seduce the man. Now that she had finally triumphed, she could not bear to see him.

Perhaps she could leave. Tonight. Having vowed to save every penny she had earned whoring at the Inn of the Red Chrysanthemum, she possessed few belongings. She had the garments she wore, a shift, corset, petticoats, stockings, and garter. Beyond these, she owned a muslin, another shift, corset, a shawl, and a pair of slippers. She looked down at the rumpled bonnet she held. There was, too, the shirt. The finest shirt. The one Charles had gifted her. But she would take neither with her. The sight of them would only bring her pain.

"My dear, are you ill?"

Terrell turned to see that she had disturbed Sarah from her nap. The latter appeared bleary in the eyes, but when her gaze came into sharper focus, her brow furrowed.

"Terrell, you look...pale."

Pale. The word, applied to a blackamoor, seemed incongruous, but Terrell certainly *felt* pale. She did not immediately answer. Surely Sarah could not discern too much with only a candle lighting the small room. Despite the constrained quarters—two beds fit into a space more properly designed for one—it was far better than the room in the attic they had once occupied. Madame had awarded Terrell the better room for her contributions toward the education of the Viscountess Wendlesson in the ways of the Red Chrysanthemum. Terrell had felt then that she was on the path to securing a better life for herself, a return to her former glory, when she had tasted the finer things. Now that she was on the precipice of her objective, her sole purpose, she could not have felt more despondent. Emptiness wrenched at her inside. She told herself it was because she had not partaken enough of supper and that the pangs were not manifestations of a hollowed spirit.

"What has happened?"

Recalled by the concern in Sarah's tone, Terrell forced herself to smile and said in a soft voice, for George still lay asleep beside Sarah, "It is nothing. I am merely in some astonishment. Sir Arthur has asked me to be his mistress."

Sarah knit her brows. "But I thought—Sir Arthur is returned?"

"I know you disapprove of the man," Terrell said as she knelt before her bed and reached beneath the mattress for the pouch that contained all that she had saved during her time at the inn. She might need to spend the night elsewhere, at another inn, perhaps for several nights, till Sir Arthur readied the apartment for her. She had no doubt he would.

I can make you the envy of London—shower you with riches that no other courtesan dare dream of.

"He is certainly a wealthy one," Sarah conceded, "and, as a Director with the East India Company, his fortune only seems to grow with each passing year."

"And influential, would you not say?" Terrell added quietly. "A man who could make or mar the careers of others."

"He is quite ingratiated with the current administration and certainly one of the most esteemed—rather, I should say feared—Members of Parliament."

He will never be elected to Parliament. I will see his entire career ruined.

Terrell inhaled deeply and said as cheerfully as she could, "Then I could not hope for better."

Sarah sat up and watched with furrowed brow as Terrell gathered her other possessions. "I have remarked before on his precarious temper."

Terrell stopped. Turned away from Sarah, she pulled at the sleeve of her gown to ensure it covered the bruise just above her left elbow where Sir Arthur had grabbed her before flinging her toward the wall. He had warned her that she was not to entertain the attentions of another man, but she had disregarded his directive. She should be grateful that he still desired her enough to want to make her his mistress.

"I am aware that he is a man of great passion," she replied, dropping her bonnet behind the bed before returning the cloak to Sarah. She spread a square of linen upon her bed to serve as her knapsack. "He does not frighten me. Perhaps you have forgotten that I have suffered far worse."

"But will Sir Arthur treat you better than the men in Barbados?"

Terrell folded her spare shift and placed it upon the linen. "England is not Barbados. I am a free woman here. If Sir Arthur mistreats me, I am free to choose another, but, given my circumstances, men like Sir Arthur are my only means to a life of comfort."

"What of Gallant?"

The slippers tumbled from her hands, and Terrell was glad that her back faced Sarah. She mustered indifference, as much to convince herself as her roommate. "What of Master Gallant?"

"I doubt he would be pleased."

"It is none of his affair," Terrell said more harshly than she intended.

Undaunted, Sarah responded, "But he cares for you."

Terrell closed her eyes. She did not wish to hear such statements. They only worsened her misery. A small part of her desired, very much, to bear her soul to Sarah, whom she might have called a friend were she in the practice of having any. She knew Sarah to be different than those who had called themselves friends but spurned her quick when she no longer had drink and merriment to offer them. Nevertheless, she had made her decision to accept Sir Arthur and the sooner it was settled, the better.

"I suppose," Terrell said, "as he is the interim

proprietor of the Red Chrysanthemum whilst Madame is away, he must care for all of us."

Sarah shook her head. "I have seen the tender manner in which he looks at you. Madame does not look upon you in such fashion."

"Because I've not lifted my skirts to Madame," Terrell replied wryly. "Perhaps she would if she were of the Sapphic persuasion."

"Will you not wait till Madame has returned? She, too, will not be pleased."

"Madame is not my keeper."

"Surely you can find someone better than Sir Arthur," Sarah persisted. "You are young yet, beautiful, and have never wanted for admirers."

"Youth and beauty will pass. I mean to build my savings so that when I am old and homely, I will have funds at my disposal."

Terrell finished packing.

"You are not leaving *now*?" Sarah asked, dismayed.

Terrell turned to face Sarah. She would miss her. Though the two women could not have been more different, one fair and born into gentle society, the other dark and born into slavery, they shared a bond in the Red Chrysanthemum. Terrell had always admired the grace and forbearance Sarah displayed despite her tribulations.

"I am. I've no wish to cross paths with Ch—with Master Gallant. He will only attempt to convince me to stay, as you do. It is the interest of the Red Chrysanthemum that I stay. But it is not mine."

Nor his.

"When I am set up in my own residence, I will send word so that you and Georgie may visit," Terrell said. Feeling a strange rush of sentiment that threatened to water her eyes, she hastened to prattle, "I don't suppose I'll have an address as fancy as Grosvenor Square, but Sir Arthur might provide me a carriage for mine own. I shall buy some new clothes for Georgie, shall I? How quickly he does grow!"

Still bewildered, Sarah sat in silence.

Terrell continued with a flippancy that belied her melancholy. "When next we meet, I think you shall hardly recognize me. I shall be dressed in gold muslin, and my hair will be done *à la mode*. Sophia would seethe with envy if she could see me!"

She gave Sarah a broad smile before departing. After shutting the door behind her, she dropped the falsehood. Closing her eyes, she gathered her nerves. Only when she had put the Red Chrysanthemum behind her could she know relief. The pangs in her belly stirred anew, and she considered that some sustenance would ease the discomfort. She would go to the kitchen and depart through the servants' quarters. Charles would likely be in Madame's study or the room that served as his temporary chambers whilst Madame was away.

When Madame had first asked Charles to oversee the Red Chrysanthemum in her absence, Terrell had been elated to have his increased presence. She had always found him handsome despite his contrast to her, with his soft golden locks and chiseled features. She recalled how tenderly he had held her in his arms not two nights before, how blissfully she had gazed upon him while he slept, how beautiful the morning, waking to his smile and the glimmer of his eyes of crystal blue and grey.

She thrust away the memory, for it now only twisted at her heart. Charles was not her destiny. She suspected his partiality for Miss Greta had not expired, and as a man who aspired to greater political office, he could not afford to have a Negress for a mistress. Barely thirty years of age and fine in form and countenance, Charles was certain to marry a woman of polite society. Sir Arthur, widowed and with no need to remarry, for he had his heir, his position in life assured, was her destiny, one that she had vowed she would achieve.

At last, she had accomplished the goal she had set for herself. Perhaps, in time, she would celebrate her triumph. For now, it was sufficient to know that Charles would see his own ambitions fulfilled.

With cautious steps, she descended the stairs toward her new and long-awaited future.

Chapter 31

Sitting at the writing table in Madame's study, Charles reviewed the membership rolls. A few of the patrons needed to renew their memberships, and he intended to speak with them before the activities of the night began. He only hoped the discussions would not take long. His mind kept turning to Terrell.

The pages before him faded from focus as he wondered what he would do to Miss Terrell tonight. Her appetite for the erotic knew no bounds, and her fervor thrilled him. Her nubile body seemed capable of withstanding anything he might attempt. The challenge invigorated him in ways he had not expected. She was exceptional. He knew no woman like her. In her days as a submissive, Greta had come close in her ability to accept and enjoy the duality of pain and pleasure. Greta, however, received whereas Miss Terrell instigated.

"Enter," Charles responded to the knock at the door.

Hoping it was Miss Terrell come to disrupt his work—it would be just as the minx would do, for he had provided her no advanced instruction this day—he could not help his disappointment at seeing Miss Sarah. George, half asleep, was at her hip, his little head resting against her bosom. He was reminded of the time he had come across Miss Terrell pushing the boy in a pram. It was the day he had bought the bonnet for her. He had seen the yearning in her eyes as she held George. It was a tragedy that her days working the plantations in Barbados had taken away her ability to conceive.

Recalling his manners, he stood up and bowed.

Miss Sarah colored. "You forget I am no longer Lady Sarah."

"It matters not."

He pulled a chair for her but noticed the disquiet in her demeanor.

"I do not mean to tarry," she replied. "I come only to inform you that Miss Terrell has left...to be with Sir Arthur."

He stared at her without word as the news sank in. He should have anticipated this to happen, but the last few nights had changed his expectations. After all, she had agreed to forsake Sir Arthur, though she had seemed less resolved last night. Nevertheless, he had been certain she favored *him.* He had even thought Miss Terrell to be, quite frankly, in love.

"She has left tonight?" he asked, trying to comprehend the urgency of the events.

"Mere minutes ago. Sir Arthur is apparently returned from his trip. I came to find you as quick as I could. I know she aspires to be a courtesan to a wealthy man, but I cannot deny that I have much misgiving where Sir Arthur is concerned."

"As do I," he said grimly.

"I pleaded for her to reconsider, but I think, perhaps, you might be better able to persuade her."

Miss Sarah blushed, and he realized her ladyship

knew his feelings for Miss Terrell. How did her sex sniff out such things?

"Perhaps. I know no one more obstinate than she. But we must find her."

He went straightway to Baxter. The man denied having seen Miss Terrell. The only other egress was through the kitchen and the servants' quarters. Charles left Baxter with instructions to stop Miss Terrell at all cost and added the incentive of a perquisite, for, unarmed with a superior motive, the man might succumb to the ploys of the temptress.

Just as he had done.

Anger suddenly flared inside him. Was there no one the woman could not seduce—would not seduce? He believed her attraction to him to be genuine, but it was clearly insufficient to stay her from the appeal of Sir Arthur. Charles let out an oath as he made his way down to the lower level. Of all men to choose, she had to select the one he liked the least. If Madame did not favor Sir Arthur so, if his own career did not depend so greatly upon the man, he would not tolerate the bloody bastard. He would not permit Sir Arthur to set foot in the Red Chrysanthemum.

But he could not. He could not keep Sir Arthur from Miss Terrell, and the impotence only further fueled his anger.

At the entry of the kitchen, he stopped. Her back was to him, but it was Miss Terrell. She had on her gown and slippers, a clear indication she intended to set off, for she usually went barefoot inside the inn. Even the back of her, clothed, was a feast for the eyes. She had pinned her tight black curls into a chignon, exposing her beautiful neck, which he had adorned with kisses last night. He watched as she set down the apple she had just bitten and sliced a loaf of bread. She put one half into a knapsack.

"Sir Arthur does not keep his kitchen well stocked?" He could not resist while attempting to temper his agitation.

She whirled around, the alarm in her eyes betraying her. She had clearly hoped to avoid him. He crossed his arms. She intended to depart without a by-your-leave, did she? The rational side of him understood that she had no wish to hear him attempt to convince her to decline Sir Arthur. Nevertheless, he felt he merited better from her.

As if reading his mind, she swallowed and said, "I-I intended to send word to you in the morning."

"Indeed?"

She lowered her gaze. At least she had the decency to feel some semblance of shame, he thought, but found no comfort in it. He crossed the threshold, and she immediately looked up, tensing. She had always reminded him of a panther, which, even in a menagerie, lost none of its grace and prowess. At the moment, however, she looked more like a cornered mouse.

"Sir Arthur could not have sent for you at this hour," he said. "He favors the card tables at his club this time of night."

"I could not wait."

His jaw tightened. "Why the urgency? Are you in need of funds? I could assist you."

She shook her head. "You've not a tenth of Sir Arthur's wealth."

"I grant his affluence is vast, but for what pressing

purpose do you require it?"

She faltered a little before answering, "Gowns, baubles, pin money."

"I could afford you these," he said, and realized he had erred. He had made no offer to her before. He had, in truth, not considered it. And now Sir Arthur had beaten him to the punch.

"And carriages, a townhouse, horses—"

"Horses!"

She pursed thick, supple lips. "Any courtesan worth her salt must have her own stable. And servants. Plenty of servants. I will require them for my parties. I once hosted the most impressive parties."

"You are certain Sir Arthur will provide you all this? As a Director of the East India Company, he is most known for his parsimony."

She frowned but then lifted her chin, her gaze unblinking. "The Company cannot fuck him as well as I can, can it?"

Her words stabbed him in the groin. He stared at her. The jade. The hussy. Granted, she had asked nothing in exchange for lifting her skirts beneath him, but neither did she hesitate to trade her favors for riches.

A muscle along his jaw rippled. "And does Sir Arthur fuck *you* well?"

Her lower lip dropped. It was nearly his undoing. He wanted nothing more than to capture those lips with his.

"That matters not," she said, regaining her composure. "He is endowed where it counts."

Her statement stunned him with its boldness. He

crossed the distance between them. "You lie, Terrell. Your body craves punishment by pleasure. You cannot persuade me that Sir Arthur can satisfy you as much as I."

She would have backed away from him but the table prevented her. She could only lean away. "Take care, Master Gallant, your words ring of arrogance. I do not deny that our time together has been amusing—"

Amusing? Is that all she thought of the times he had made her spend? Had she counterfeited her cries of ecstasy? And how dare she accuse him of arrogance? An odd whisper from the past called to him, but he was too enraged to pay it any attention. He grabbed her arm and yanked her body to his.

"Pray do not be modest on my account."

Noticing that she grimaced, he released her arm and saw a bruise where he had held her. It had not been there last night. Wishing he could unearth the truth from her with his piercing stare, he demanded, "Did Sir Arthur hurt you?"

She said nothing, only gripped the table behind her with both hands.

"Did he?" he barked.

Her eyes flared with defiance. "We had a bit of a rough play earlier today, but, as you know, I am partial to a forceful fucking."

Bloody hell. Her words were driving him mad. She had lifted her skirts to Sir Arthur this night? But she was *his.* His submissive. Just as she had requested.

The vision of Sir Arthur pounding into Miss Terrell made him ill. He had born it before because he had had no choice in the matter. Madame had been more than delighted when Sir Arthur approached the Red Chrysanthemum for membership, asking specifically for Miss Terrell, and Charles understood that she depended upon Madame for room and board. Her submission to Sir Arthur, therefore, was a transaction prompted by necessity. For Miss Terrell to imply that she actually *enjoyed* fucking Sir Arthur—*that* Charles could not stomach.

He stepped into her, pressing her against the table. "Do you mean to tell me you prefer his bed to mine?"

Her thick lashes lowered, drawing his attention to her physiognomy, her unblemished skin—dark though it was—the glow in her cheeks, those plush lips, so much fuller than the mouths of other women, enticing him, like ripened fruit, to taste of her. His gaze fell lower, to her bosom. She was breathing deeply. The blood churned in him, desire looming alongside anger. He lifted his gaze back to her eyes. He would see them while she answered.

But she kept her eyes averted. "I do."

He grasped her by the jaw, forcing her to meet his gaze. "Do not lie to me, Terrell."

"I do not lie. I prefer his bed...and his..."

He knew what she would say but would not have her finish. Either it was the blaze in his eyes or the tightening of his grasp that stayed her, for she allowed her sentence to trail into nothing. The blood was pounding in his head, in his groin, obliterating his ability to think. He only knew that he would not suffer yet another woman to leave him for another man. Not when it was plain that his touch was the superior one in both instances.

"I do not tolerate dishonesty, Miss Terrell," he tried again. A vein in his neck throbbed.

She pulled at his arm with both hands, trying to free herself. When she could not, she glared at him with an intensity he had never seen. He nearly released her because of it. "You desire the truth, Master Gallant? Then I will speak plain. I prefer Sir Arthur because I *tire* of you."

Stunned, he stood motionless, wordless, as she continued to struggle from his hold. There was a desperation in her voice he did not comprehend, but she had spat his name with contempt. He allowed that she might prefer Sir Arthur for his purse, the riches he could bestow upon her, but Charles could not abide her preference for the man in any other capacity.

I tire of you.

No woman had ever accused him of being dull. After all that he had done for her, and done to her, she dared to say she found him wearisome? *She* had sought *his* company, forcing herself upon him at every turn, ignoring his objections, seducing him and putting them both at risk if Sir Arthur or Madame should discover them. Now she would choose Sir Arthur over him? The duplicitous doxy. The false harlot. She had played him for a fool.

"Prove it."

She stopped struggling. "Wh-What?"

"Prove it."

Whirling her around, he pushed her over the table and pinned her in place with his body, his hardened cock pressing against her derriere. He leaned over her and spoke into her ear, "You say you tire of my attentions. You profess to speak the truth. But I will prove your falsehood."

Chapter 32

The edge of the thick wooden table dug uncomfortably into her hipbones. Trapped between the table and the weight of him, her heart beat madly. Had she erred? She had thought her remarks would have convinced him to leave her be. *You damned idiot*, she wanted to yell at him. Did she have to explain to him what was at stake? That he would have no chance of winning his election if they did not do as Sir Arthur wished?

No. She could not. She knew what Charles thought of the man, knew his sense of honor would not allow Sir Arthur to intimidate her into submission. Charles might act rashly and forever ruin his career. And it would all be her fault. This was, after all, her doing. If only she had never seduced Master Gallant to begin with, he would not risk losing Sir Arthur's support. If only she had not been so selfish. If only she did not desire him as much as she did.

She felt his pelvis press against her and nearly groaned, her body responding in an instant to his presence.

Prove it.

Panicking, she tried to push herself from the table but could not throw him off. Dear God, what could she say, what could she do? She ought not to have stopped in the kitchen or she might have been on her way by now.

Lacking anything better to say, she cried, "Get off of me!"

She struggled harder. When she reached behind herself to club his ears or yank his hair, he grabbed her wrists and pinioned them in front of her upon the table.

"Sir Arthur awaits me," she lied, gasping.

"Let him wait," he growled, holding her wrists in one hand.

"You've no wish to risk his ire."

With his free hand, he pushed the curls off her neck. "A little late to worry of that, Miss Terrell."

She moaned, both at the truth and the feel of his lips searing her nape. But she would set things right. Charles deserved to attain his life's ambition.

She renewed her struggle. "He is expecting me at his—"

As if ignoring her, he continued to kiss her, softly behind an ear and between the shoulder blades. She resisted melting into the kisses and attempted to kick him, but he only pressed her harder into the table.

"If I am not arrived, he may seek me here," she added.

Reaching between them, he grabbed her arse and dug his fingers into a buttock. "I ought to contrive a unique punishment for each and every fib."

A shiver shot through her. Once upon a time—yesterday—she would have greeted such words with glee. But she could not now.

His hand snaked around her hip toward her mound. She attempted to clamp her thighs together though one of his legs cleaved hers, but his fingers managed to insinuate themselves against her.

No—no—no. He must not touch her there. She did not trust her body. It was certain to betray her. She cursed and felt the heat of her breath bounce off the table and back into her face. Feeling his tongue beneath her ear, she shuddered. Distracted, she relaxed her lower body. Taking advantage, he sank his hand farther between her thighs and rubbed the most vulnerable part of her. She groaned. In an instant, her mind lost ground—lost *further* ground, for the mere weight of him upon her, his chest upon her back, his hardened desire against her derriere, threatened to weaken her resistance. How could his touch ignite her with such potency?

Desperate, she aimed a heel at his shins. It glanced off him.

He slapped her rump. "Behave yourself, Miss Terrell."

She stopped. Master Gallant made his presence known. An excited flutter went through her. She had always thrilled to the tone of his voice when he assumed the role of her dominant. Simply hearing it made her warm and wet. How often had she relished misbehaving with him on purpose so that she could merit one of his delicious punishments? How hard had she worked to convince him, to seduce him, to agree to dominate her? But now her accomplishment worked against her.

Summoning what remained of her resolve, she said, "I am no longer yours, Charles. I mean to have a new Master."

He stiffened against her. She meant to add Sir Arthur's name as the final nail in the coffin but had not the courage. He flipped her around. Being bent backwards over the table was far more uncomfortable but not as distressing as seeing the pained fury in his eyes. He had released her wrists and she pressed her hands against his chest as if to stay him from crushing her into the table.

"I might have known you were no more than a grasping whore," he choked.

Her mouth fell open, and she thought her heart might shatter. She wanted to accuse him, accuse him of ingratitude, of conceit, of arrogance. She acted so that *he* might know happiness.

Were she able to reflect upon their situation with calm, she would forgive him his hasty denunciation of her. He knew not her sacrifice, and she could not reveal it to him. In truth, her choice of Sir Arthur was the only appropriate end. Charles had never indicated he had an interest in retaining her as his mistress. Even if he had, he could not afford her the affluence Sir Arthur could. Indeed, she would have felt reluctant to take more than Charles was willing or able to give. She had no such compulsions with Sir Arthur.

At present, however, still wedged uncomfortably between Charles and the table, she considered how easily his kind devalued her kind. She had, of course, deliberately given him the impression that she wanted no better than material trappings, but it hurt that he so easily accepted the worst in her. He did not hesitate now to call her a whore and to treat her as one. But even lowly hedge whores deserved some consideration. Alas, his kind was given to superiority, to entitlement. His kind thought they had a right to her, thought they could impose their will upon her because she could never be more than an inferior being, incapable of grander thought or emotion, barely better than property or cattle, at best a...whore. She had thought Charles to be different, but at some deeper level where instinct dwelled, he was perhaps little different from his fellow countrymen, his kind.

"Damn you," she seethed. *Damn your whole bloody lot to hell.*

She tried to throw him off, but when he did not budge, she clawed and cuffed at him. Her fingernails caught the left side of his face, scratching him along the cheek and jaw. Stunned at her own doing, she paused in her struggles. She had no wish to hurt him.

"Disobedient harlot."

He grabbed her wrists and, jerking her from the table, threw her upon the floor. He planted a knee upon her back to hold her down. Various items clattered to the floor—apples, the bread, her possessions. She realized he had the linen she had used as a knapsack. Her arms were jerked behind her and wrapped together above the elbows. For a brief moment, when she glimpsed one of the maids in the doorway, she thought she might be rescued, but the astonished maid quickly turned upon her heels and fled. There was no one here who could help her escape. Not when her assailant was the interim proprietor.

But she could make a scene. If she attracted enough of the servants or members to gawk upon them, Master Gallant might recall his senses. She began to call for help, hoping that others might be near enough to hear her.

"Silence!" Charles barked at her. "You've no wish to amass more punishment than you already have."

Ignoring him, she screamed as loudly as she could till her mouth was stuffed with his handkerchief. He held the plentiful fabric in place with one hand while he thrust the other beneath her skirts. She had a pair of spring garters, gifted to her by a former paramour. He unclipped one with ease and tied it about her mouth to secure the handkerchief.

Though she knew the odds to be against her, she continued to resist, especially when he reached beneath her hem once more. She still had the use of her legs and tried to raise herself up on her knees. When she could not, she kicked at him, but her efforts were in vain. She had lost her slippers in the scuffle, and he grabbed a leg, peeled down one of her stockings and bound her ankles together. He finally took his knee off her, but she could only wriggle or inch her body across the floor in the manner of a caterpillar. He hoisted her into her feet by the collar of her gown.

He yanked her to his chest and growled into her ear, "You'll not fool me, Miss Terrell. I know what it is you desire."

She trembled. In fear. Or anticipation. Or both.

In a swift motion, he threw her over his shoulder. She attempted to squirm off him, though a part of her wondered that she should bother. She would only succeed in falling to the floor if he did not drop her first.

"You've seen what I am capable of with Mistress Scarlet," he warned. "I promise you I will not be as merciful."

As he exited the kitchen, she ceased her writhing to contemplate another stratagem. What if she were to submit to him and fuck him one last time? Fuck him into a stupor. Then, while he rested, she could make her escape. That was more viable than fighting him.

"Oh!" gasped Tippy, whom they crossed in the hallway.

Charles paused at the bottom of a staircase and turned to Tippy. "I will be indisposed for an hour, but Master Troy can facilitate the start of the evening."

"Yes, Master Gallant."

Though such a scene as what Tippy had encountered was not extraordinary at the Red Chrysanthemum, Terrell felt her cheeks burn because she had not agreed to be trussed and carried by force up the stairs as if she were a child being put to bed. She grunted, her mouth parched from the handkerchief.

He headed up the stairs to the second floor, to the chambers at the very end of the hall. It was the room he had favored during his sennight with Mistress Scarlet, who had also favored the room for her submissive maidens. It contained the wickedest implements, instruments that evoked medieval torture chambers. Charles kicked the door open. The room had not yet been prepared for the evening, but he knew the layout. Finding the bed, he deposited her upon it. While he lit a candle and went to kindle a flame in the fireplace, she struggled against her bonds. The bleeder had pinioned her arms uncommonly tight. With her shoulders pulled back, her bosom was thrust forward. The bindings held, as she expected they would, for Charles had a mastery of bondage unmatched by any other.

Reminded of her plans, she told herself to be patient. With patience and persistence, she had finally claimed victory over the Master. Tonight need be no different.

Lit by the fire from the hearth, the apparatus in the room cast eerie shadows upon the walls. The bed, in contrast to the opulent bedclothes she had lain upon yesterday, was sparsely clothed. Everything about the room was austere. The adornments were whips, crops, canes, and other implements of pain. The handkerchief in her mouth seemed to soak up all hydration and she cast a thirsty eye toward the decanter of wine upon the sideboard. The fire started, Charles went to the sideboard. He seemed to know her gaze—he always did—for he poured a glass.

"Yours if you behave," he said, setting the glass down.

She could do nothing but lay upon the bed and stare, as helpless as a fish out of water. She watched him open a drawer and pull out long, thick strands of jute. Her heart skipped a beat. At any other time, she would have greeted the ropes with delight, but not tonight. Ropes took time, and tonight she only wanted to quit the Red Chrysanthemum as soon as possible. If she could take his cock into her mouth, she improved her chances of an earlier departure. No man could resist her ability to suckle cock. Not even Master Gallant.

Something else in the drawer caught his eye and he pulled out a small leather belt with a metal ring in its center. The straps were far too short to fit about the waist, and the ring had four metal spokes protruding at diagonals, reminding her of a spider.

"I've not used one of these before," he murmured. His stare at her was unrelenting. "But as you have always disclaimed the need for a safety word, I see no harm in this accessory."

She faltered, wondering if she had been foolish in her past bravado. The ring gag in hand, he sauntered over to the bed. He pulled her to a sitting position by the back of her hair, undid the garter wrapped about her and removed the handkerchief. She tried to coax the moisture back to her mouth.

"If it be a fuck you want," she said, attempting as much sultriness as she could against the dryness, "you had but to ask, Master Gallant. No need to tie me up. I would happily fuck you, for old times' sake."

He only stared at her, and she could not discern what he thought. She hoped he would untie her so that she could employ her hands to hasten his arousal.

"A farewell fucking," he replied wryly as his gaze dropped to her lips.

The hint of sorrow in his voice did not escape her, and her heart ached to know that he did not wish her to leave. She almost assured him that she might visit the Red Chrysanthemum from time to time, but that would never do. As the mistress of Sir Arthur, she would be further bound to the man. No good could come of a liaison with Master Gallant.

"It would be a proper *adieu* for us," she said.

But he did not appear placated. He cupped her chin. "Open wide."

She licked her lips and looked down at his crotch. "I could taste of your c—"

He jerked her chin higher. "Open, Miss Terrell."

"Would you not first wish for me to—"

Releasing her chin, he reached into her décolletage and pinched a nipple. Hard. When she parted her lips to gasp, he slid the ring into her mouth, then buckled the straps behind her head. The ring sat behind her teeth and prevented her mouth from closing. The metal spokes held her lips aloft. The contraption made the act of swallowing quite awkward. She recalled the scold's bridle one of the slaves had been made to wear after refusing to eat.

Gallant took a step back to admire the effect before yanking her back down onto the bed. Her head hung off the edge.

"You were saying you wished to taste of cock, Miss Terrell?" he asked, unbuttoning his fall.

She had, but not in this manner. The infernal ring gag prevented her from taking his cock the way she desired, from sucking him till he thought he might explode if he did not spend. He unleashed his stiff and ready shaft, and for a moment, she forgot herself as she stared at the beautiful length of hardness. The sight of it never failed to arouse, and hunger of a different sort made itself known.

She had seen and known many a cock in her lifetime and none were as perfect as his. Others might have been longer, thicker, curved, straight, but she adored Master Gallant's cock. She adored every part of it: the flare of the crown, the veins along the shaft when his cock was hard as steel, and the soft, sensitive sac dangling beneath. Most of all, she adored what his cock did to her. She would have licked her lips if she could and taken his erection into her mouth with an eager appetite.

He presented the tip of his cock into the ring. She licked at it, tasting a drop of his clear seed. She had never before cared for the flavor of a man's mettle, it being far too salty or too piquant, but she did not mind the taste of Master Gallant. Her zest had surprised him, and it had pleased her to know that she could astonish the veteran Master.

With a groan, he pushed his cock farther into her mouth. Though the angle ought to have facilitated his entry, she, unaccustomed to wearing the ring, began to gag. She expected him to withdraw. He did, but only briefly. She felt his cock sliding down her throat. She had wanted his cock inside her but struggled for control as if she had never eaten cockmeat before. Her body convulsed as she choked upon his member. The blood had been draining into her head, making it harder to focus.

He fucked her mouth slowly before giving her a reprieve. Grabbing the linen binding her arms, he dragged her off the bed. She stumbled onto her knees. He replaced his cock before she could fully recover. Fisting his hand in her hair, he moved her head down his length. She fought the urge to gag. When at last she had mastery of her reflexes, he thrust himself into her as he brought her head down till her nose tickled the hairs at his pelvis. He pulled out abruptly and the tip of his cock grazed her cheek. She felt a spot of dampness there. Salivation dribbled from the corner of her mouth because she could not close her lips. The choking did not vex her as much as the fact that he retained control. She could not impose upon him while he could use her mouth as he wished, when he wished.

"Do you require your safety word?" he asked through his heavy arousal.

She did not respond. She had told him numerous times that she required no safety word, had not even wanted one with Master Gallant, till he had insisted upon it. She ignored the current courtesy he extended, for she would not contravene her earlier avowal. Anger swirled within her, anger at her own helplessness, at his forbearance, and that he had found a way to dominate her when she had no desire for his domination. Or did she?

When he replaced his cock and the fall of his trousers, the disappointment in her was palpable. That she would, after tonight, never again feel his touch made her relish each and every deed. That his actions bore an uncharacteristic harshness worried her even while it *titillated.* The heat pregnant in her loins was undeniable. Her body craved this man, and would take him in any form and any manner.

Returning to his ropes, he threw them at the rafters till they dangled from the beams abovehead. She groaned in both expectation and dread, her hopes for a short duration to her predicament dashed. Master Gallant had a thorough, unhurried quality that both frustrated and impressed. And she had no choice but to submit to his will.

Sweeping her into his arms, he set her on her feet below the ropes. Her breath grew uneven as he wound one of the dangling ropes behind her and below her bosom. She relished the caress of the ropes about her and considered that she ought to cherish what was likely to be her last experience in such bondage.

Stepping around, he looked her full in the face. "I will untie your ankles, and you shall behave."

The look in his eyes dared her to defy him. She had never before seen such severity in him. Before, she would have had few qualms, and her impish nature would have gaily taunted him, enticing him to discipline her. At present, she knew better than to risk his ire. When he bent down to loosen the stocking binding her ankles, she remained perfectly still and allowed him to take her right ankle and bend her leg behind her, forcing her to balance upon one leg, though the ropes would have held her up. He reached beneath her skirts and bound her ankle to her thigh. Her chest bumped against him, and the nearness of him flooded her senses. He paused, as if he, too, were affected by the proximity.

After grabbing another rope hanging from the rafters, he bent down, pulled up her left ankle, and hoisted it behind her at an angle. She was now fully suspended in the air. Though her weight pulled upon the ropes, they served as a cradle that she could relax into but for the asymmetry and the slight forward tilt of her body because her left leg was suspended behind her. Gallant stepped back to study his handiwork. Her skirts had slid down to expose her calves and ankles, her left leg still bearing a stocking and garter. Stepping back toward her, he fingered her décolletage, grazing her breasts. She suddenly wished he would maul her.

As if reading her mind, he tucked his fingers

beneath the décolletage and found the ribbons of her stays, which laced in front, but the tight fit of her gown's bodice did not permit him easy access. Her breasts strained against their confines, wishing to be free for him. He grabbed the center of the neckline and tore the bodice open.

Her gag prevented her exclamation. *The bloody bastard.* He had torn her best gown. How was she supposed to leave the Red Chrysanthemum now?

She thrashed against her bonds as if she could keep him from doing further damage, but he easily loosened the ribbons and wrenched apart the top of the stays. He had not unlaced the garment far enough for her breasts to spill free, but there was room enough for him to thrust a hand down and cup an orb. She ceased moving when he groped her. Her nipple hardened against his palm. He kneaded the flesh, sending shivers into her cunnie. His fingers forked the sides of her nipple, making her toes curl. He rolled the nipple between his thumb and forefinger, and the sensation tugged at another bud beneath her pelvis.

She was supposed to be plying *him* with her touch, provoking *his* lust, and driving *him* to distraction. *He* was supposed to be the one writhing in desire, succumbing to *her* caresses. Instead, she could only submit to his fondling, unable to resist, unable to stem the delight her body derived from his ministrations. Seeing the ardor in his penetrating gaze only made her cunnie throb more. She craved his touch there.

Once again, he seemed to know her thoughts. He reached beneath her skirts and slid his hand up the length of her left thigh. She moaned at the soft caress, but she jerked when his hand came up to her mons. The ropes, however, held her in place. His other hand stilled her from swinging. Soon his fingers were combing through the patch of down between her thighs. Her cunnie throbbed at his nearness. His thumb found the bud nestled between her folds and swirled it. She closed her eyes. It was useless to resist. His touch felt too marvelous. It would be simpler, wiser to surrender and have done with it all.

He found the wetness beneath and coated her clitoris with it. His fondling caused the most delicious agitation to wave through her. She forgot the discomfort of the ring gag holding her mouth open while prying apart her lips. She wanted only to fulfill the promise of his stroking, wanted that lovely paroxysm to roll through her. Master Gallant remained unhurried, requiring no time to put her body into a state of blissful tension, coaxing the heat inside of her into a vibrant flame. When he ceased his ministrations, her whole body groaned at the loss. She would know no peace till she had spent at his hand.

When she opened her eyes, she saw that he held another cord of knotted rope, which he pulled between her thighs. He secured the ends to the rope circling the bottom of her chest. The rope cleaved her folds and pressed sharply against her flesh where her skirts had not bunched. One of the knots pushed against the bud he had caressed to engorgement. The other rested near her rectum. She knew struggling to be fruitless. She could not escape the pressure between her legs. She might not have minded the knot if it did not fit so forcefully against her, if she could rub herself against it, for her clit still radiated pleasure. His knuckles brushed her labia, his soft touch a contrast to the hard, unyielding rope.

At last he unbuckled the gag from her. Her lips were sore, her jaw was sore, her cheeks were sore. But the discomfort did not compare to the carnal tension coiled inside of her, wanting release, needing release. Remembering the wine, he retrieved it for her and brought the glass to her lips. She drank readily.

"Thank you, Master," she uttered, hoping her good behavior would merit her more caresses—or possibly his cock.

But if she had thought the tide to have turned, she was wrong. He cupped the side of her face with one hand, his fingers pressing into the back of her head.

"When I am through, Miss Terrell," he said, "you'll never again think to prefer Sir Arthur's bed to mine."

Chapter 33

Never again.

The past pounded in his mind as much as the present. Greta had fled, but not, to his knowledge, into the waiting arms of another. If she had, in her heart, chosen Damien over him, she had not had the effrontery to say it to his face. Terrell, however, had no end to her impudence. She had the gall to say she tired of him, to lie to him as if he had no sensitivities and was impervious to her biting words. He had misjudged her. He had not thought her to be the heartless greedy creature she had revealed herself to be.

"I will return to address your punishment," he informed her.

As he looked upon her, dangling in the ropes, her lower legs revealed, her bodice torn, a pulse shot through his still hardened cock. The pressure in his groin threatened to explode, fueled in part by a jealousy that ached down the length of his legs. He had not thought himself the kind of man given to envy or covetousness, but how was it he could be bested yet again? After all the pleasure he had given, first to Mistress Scarlet, then to Miss Terrell, the heights to which he had taken these women, they would yet prefer men who always put their own interests first, who would mistreat them and care for them only so far as *their* sense of ownership allowed.

It was unfair for Terrell to bear the brunt of his vehemence on behalf of both women, but he knew not where one anger ended and another began.

"Return? Where do you go?" she asked with widened eyes.

"I have duties to perform for the Red Chrysanthemum," he replied.

He tugged at the rope cleaving her mons. She grunted. Satisfied, he headed for the door.

"Rest a while, Miss Terrell," he advised. "You will require stamina to endure your punishment."

He saw both anger and concern flash in her eyes before he closed the door behind him. He took in a deep breath, then cursed, his body continuing in turmoil. The sight of her still filled his mind's eye. The gag with the metal ring and spokes was a rather ghastly item, yet it had looked devilishly fine upon Terrell, holding aloft her plump lips to reveal even, white teeth and providing him access to that hot, wanton mouth of hers. He wanted nothing more than to return to her and pound his cock into her. He wanted to fuck her senseless, fuck all thought of Sir Arthur from her.

It seemed little time had passed since he had first tied her to the rafters from which she currently hung. He had known then that succumbing to her would lead to no good, and now that inevitability had come home to nest. He had warned her, but she had refused to listen. Now she had damned them both. The seductress deserved to rue her actions.

Of course, he knew he was as much to blame. Was he not the older and wiser one? Perhaps if he had offered for her in some way, provided her more, she might have been less eager to become Sir Arthur's mistress. He would have to provide her a new gown now. He would have to find her a shawl or fichu in the meantime, but he realized he wanted to buy her a gown. He wanted to buy a good many things for her, as he had done with the bonnet. The delight that shone from her face that day he had taken her to the millinery had satisfied him with surprising warmth. If the election had not taken so much of his time, he might have attended to such things. Hers had been a harsh life, and she deserved better.

But as she had distinguished, he could not offer what Sir Arthur could, and it was clear she valued the opulence of the latter over any *sentiments* she might have held for him. He had thought her to harbor feelings of a tender sort for him, but he was mistaken, and perhaps that was what hurt the most.

The charitable part of him would reason that she knew no better. Her life was one of survival. The cruelty she had suffered barred munificence and higher emotions. Alas, the voice of compassion could not be heard above the tumult of the other passions raging inside of him. What good had compassion done him? He had an abundance of the quality, but it only brought him torment. The women in his life still preferred selfish, hardhearted men.

They deserved each other then: Greta her Damien and Terrell her Arthur.

He adjusted himself. His cock had not completely softened, but the business of the inn needed tending to. The faster he dispensed with his responsibilities, the faster he could return to Miss Terrell. With quick, angry steps, he descended the stairs.

"Master Gallant!" Miss Sarah called to him as he reached the first floor. "Have you spoken to Terrell?"

"She means to have Sir Arthur," he replied brusquely.

"Truly? And you mean to let her go?"

He narrowed his eyes at her, but had no desire to affirm what she insinuated by her query. Instead, he replied, "Miss Terrell is not in leading strings. She is free to make her own decisions."

"But…her decision is a terrible one."

"That is merely our opinion. Tell me, was she happy when she told you of her news?"

Sarah thought for a moment. "I suppose she was, although—"

"You have known Terrell longer than I. You must know her to be stubborn and headstrong. She will accept no counsel from us. Perhaps the best we can do is wish her well."

It was not what Sarah had hoped to hear, and he did not add that he intended a parting gift for Miss Terrell: a night of all the pain and pleasure she could ever wish for so that she might rue her decision. It satisfied him to think that she might pine for him while she lay beside Sir Arthur in his bed.

Noticing that Sarah did not have George with her, he asked, "Who watches your son?"

"Lydia."

"I have a new member who has expressed a preference for women of dark hair."

"I will prepare myself then."

"If you prefer, I can pair him with Lydia."

She nodded. He could see that she wanted to talk

further of Miss Terrell, but he did not. After returning to the study, he kept his appointments brief and declined a member's request to use the far room on the second floor. During his meetings, his cock had returned to a softened state, but as he climbed the stairs and made his way down the hall, it began to harden once more. The temptress had cast a potent spell upon him. He had heard more than one West Indiaman remark upon the dark arts that the blackamoors employed. He had dismissed such mysticism, but it did seem his body was not his own when it came to Miss Terrell.

Suspended from the rafters, she presented a lovely vision, more provocative than the erotic paintings of Titian or Romano. When she met his gaze, he found it difficult to look away. The whites of her eyes were so bright, and the blackness of her pupils contained such depth that he found himself like a ship pulled into an eddy.

"You tore my only dress," she accused.

"Sir Arthur can afford you many more," he replied placidly.

She frowned, and he was finally able to tear himself from her stare. He approached her and untied the rope that bound her bent leg. She groaned through gritted teeth as the circulation there returned. He encouraged the flow of blood by rubbing the poor limb. When the soreness had subsided, he retied the rope about the ankle and pulled the leg behind her in similar fashion to the other. He adjusted the suspension ropes so that she was no longer upright but nearly faced the floor, her torso at a slight angle to the floor below. With her legs stretched behind her, she looked ready to take flight. He stood beside her and pushed her skirts to the waist, baring her arse. His cock twitched. Unable to resist, he palmed a buttock. She had a bottom as smooth and unblemished as that of a babe. He kneaded the supple flesh, then gave it a sharp slap. It quivered only a little before returning to tautness.

He wiggled the knot at her clitoris. She moaned with a shiver. Her moisture had soaked the rope between her thighs. As he suspected, he could still arouse her. She had not tired of him. She had merely lied in her haste to run to Sir Arthur. His cock lengthened as he inhaled her arousal.

She eyed his crotch and said, "Shall I attend you, Master? You gave me but a mere taste of your cock tonight."

He gave her a hard stare. "You wish for *my* cock, do you?"

"Have you not determined by now that I am a whore for cock?"

He frowned and considered replacing her gag. Though he often marveled at her brazen wantonness, tonight she could say nothing that did not vex or sicken him.

"Thus far, I have permitted your colloquy," he said, "but tonight you will speak only when addressed or have been granted permission to speak. Do you understand, Miss Terrell?"

Taken aback, she said nothing. He had been lenient in the area of speech, with her and with Greta. But it would seem he would fare better with a more exacting approach. He fisted his hand in her hair and pulled her head back.

"Do you understand?" he repeated.

"Yes, Master."

Releasing her, he stepped back to unbutton and remove his coat, which he hung over a chair.

"You will have a chance to earn cock," he informed her as he undid his cravat and placed the linen over his coat.

She pursed her lips in thought. "If I behave, I earn cock. If I don't, you will discipline me. It would seem I win either way. But why should *your* pleasure be dependent upon my conduct? Why not dispense with the contingency and take your pleasure now?"

He kept his face down as he unbuttoned the cuffs of his shirt sleeves. With Terrell, he was always tempted to dispense with contingencies. That was how the trouble began. His forbearance could not best his body's desire for her. And she knew it. Tonight, however, he was determined. He rolled his shirt sleeves to his elbows.

"Miss Terrell, you were not granted permission to speak."

"Your pardon, Master Gallant," she said with lowered lashes, but he did not trust her demure demeanor. Though he was the dominant one, he did nothing that she did not desire or prompt. She was as often in control as he and frequently the initiator. He went to the sideboard and retrieved two small clamps joined by a length of chain.

"Perhaps these will remind you not to speak out of turn," he said upon returning to her. Reaching down her décolletage, he cupped a breast, found the nipple, and pried it to a hardened peak before clipping one of the clamps to it. She grunted, for he had affixed the clamp to the tip rather than the less sensitive base of the areola. He did the same to the other breast. Taking her by the jaw, he opened her mouth and presented the chain.

"Bite down," he instructed.

With a groan, she secured the chain between her teeth. The chain pulled upon the clamps pinching her nipples.

"Well done," he said as he stroked her cheek. She could not look lovelier than she did then, with her hair mussed and her garments in disarray, the metal chain in her mouth more beautiful than any necklace Sir Arthur might gift her. His cock throbbed.

He passed his thumb over her top lip and recalled how the ring gag had forced her mouth open, providing him unfettered access to the delightful orifice. No one took cock as well as she. She had admitted to perfecting the art of cock sucking to hasten men to spend. It pleased his vanity to know that she took her time with him. His cock yearned toward her, remembering the times she had brought him near to spending but did not permit him to pass into ecstasy because she wanted his cock for her cunnie.

Deciding he would allow her to look upon what she stood to lose if she went to Sir Arthur, Charles undid his fall and pulled out his stately erection. She looked as if she might have licked her lips but for the chain in her mouth. He caressed his length. It was hard and ready for her. He considered masturbating himself till he spent his seed upon her. He would send her to Sir Arthur *after* he had marked her.

But that was something Damien would have done,

and try as he might, he could not be Damien. He could not be Sir Arthur.

He replaced his cock and the fall of his trousers. Terrell emitted a low moan of disappointment. He could see her mind working. At what, he knew not. To distract her from her thoughts, he wriggled the knot at her clitoris once more. She strained against her bonds but did not drop the chain. Satisfied, he walked over to the wall adorned with the implements of pain. He eyed the crops of varying lengths. Canes light and heavy. Paddles of different shapes, some with holes to allow swifter passage through the air, some with studs to inflict welts, and others fleeced to prevent them.

And then there were the floggers.

There was little Terrell shied away from, and her daring spirit had aroused and inspired him. She had no match at the Red Chrysanthemum. She satisfied every wicked lust, every lascivious urge of his. But floggers sometimes daunted her. She had suffered too much from that instrument during her years in Barbados, and her back might forever bear the scars of her former torture.

Passing the floggers, he chose a two-forked leather tawse and tested its stiffness against the palm of his hand. The sharp slap drew her attention, but she could not turn her head without pulling further upon her nipples.

He walked back and stood behind her. "Here is your chance to earn cock, Miss Terrell, by keeping the chain in your mouth. Drop it and I'll double your punishment."

He caressed her left buttock, a most perfect cheek

with a high arch, supple and shapely. His blood boiled. His cock wanted to be buried in her arse, but he was not in the habit of seeing to his own pleasure before hers. And that was his folly. The likes of Greta and Terrell took his generosity for granted. Perhaps he would not be so gallant tonight.

Taking a step back, he whacked the buttock with the tawse. Her body jumped.

"Once, when I was barely ten," he recounted as he fingered the leather, "the headmaster of the school must have applied a tawse to my backside three, four dozen times."

He whipped her once more. She groaned into the chain. The blush upon her arse was almost instantaneous.

"I was told my arse was red with welts," he continued, letting the tawse fall twice upon her derriere. "My offense? Letting his daughter steal a kiss from me."

He walloped her across both cheeks. She cried out but did not drop the chain. He stilled her body from swaying in the bonds and delivered half a dozen blows. He had to take care, for the streaks of red produced by the leather thong did not appear as visibly upon her dark skin, but the furrow of her brow when he glanced at her face confirmed the spanking was of sufficient impact. He slapped the tawse against the bottom of her foot and heard her shriek. Still, she did not release the chain. Returning his attention to her arse, he smacked her good and hard. A dozen times. She thrashed against her bonds as if wanting him to strike a part of her that did not already fiercely smart.

He paused to see if she might employ a safety word. The impudent wench had once dared suggest his given name serve as her safety word. If she had not memorized the word he had assigned her, she had only herself to blame.

But in order to utter any safety word, she would have to let fall the chain, and if she did that, she would fail to receive her reward. How desperately did she want his cock? Or how badly did she wish to avoid further punishment? He whacked her rump with the tawse and watched her squeeze her eyes shut. Last night he had held her in tenderness, worshipped her with gentle caresses. And she had done the same with him. He thought she had looked upon him with affection, with *love*. But it must have been an illusion.

His jaw tightened as he applied the tawse several more times. Had he merely hoped that her sighs last night were those of contentment? He slapped her arse. Had he merely cast his own sense of serenity and gratification upon her? He delivered another whack. Because, as he cradled her in his arms, he had recognized the depths of his own feelings for her. He rained several more blows. Once again, he had fallen for a woman who would not, did not return his affection.

As he struck the vaults of her feet, she screamed and bit down harder upon the chain. Her fortitude made the blood course hot and strong through him. He wanted to untie her and make love to her with mad desperation. Yesterday he might have indulged doing so. But the world had changed since then.

Still, she had performed admirably. Realizing he

was breathing heavily, he cast aside the tawse. He stood before her and removed the clamps from her nipples. She dropped the chain and glared at him. Her eyes glistened with moisture but she looked ready to kill him.

"Permission to speak, Master," she said.

"Granted."

"Have I earned my cock?"

He wondered if she would bite him if he offered it to her mouth. Reaching for her nipples, he gently rolled them. She whimpered, for they must have been quite sore from the pinching of the clamps and the tugging from the chain.

"You have," he informed her.

That seemed to mollify her in part. "Then present my prize."

"In due time."

He undid the knotted rope cleaving her between the legs and rubbed her folds, still slick with her wetness. She groaned in relief. He spread her nectar to her clitoris and fondled her there, enjoying her sounds of pleasure.

"The hour grows late," she protested.

"It is hardly midnight," he replied, wanting to remind her how they had once spent an entire night fucking, sleeping no more than an hour or two at a time.

"Nonetheless…"

She moaned and trembled as he quickened his ministrations. Why was she in such a bloody hurry to leave him?

"You wish to be done?" he inquired.

"Does a quick, hard fucking not appeal to you?"

The blood pounded in his ears, and his cock pressed against his fall. A quick, hard fucking. He knew of no woman who would truly desire such a thing, let alone request it. But Terrell differed from other women. He considered her motivations for such a request, and his chest tightened with a discomfort worse than what the tawse or cane or crop could inflict.

As if sensing his turmoil, she urged him, "Come. Fuck me hard. I have earned your cock, have I not? Then fuck me. Fuck me hard and fast."

He pressed his lips into a grim line and went to stand behind her. "Very well. If that is what you desire."

Did he not always oblige her in the end? He freed his cock from his trousers and, gripping her thighs, he plunged into her without ceremony.

Holy hell.

No matter how many times he claimed her, the wet heat encasing his shaft lost none of its magnificence. His cods boiled in anticipation, and he groaned low and long when her cunnie clenched his member. He had buried himself to the hilt. He stared at the hairs of his pubis curled at her still blushing arse.

She flexed her cunnie about him. He needed no further invitation. After withdrawing his cock till only the crown remained inside, he rammed himself back in. She cried out in surprise, but he pulled out and thrust into her once more. Quick and hard. Hard and fast. That was what she had requested. The beautiful tension in his loins swirled and beckoned. He could unleash himself into the glory of her hot, wet cunnie.

But he wanted her capitulation. He wanted her to surrender to the pleasure he invoked.

He pulled his cock out slowly and pushed it back in at an angle he knew she favored. She moaned. Her cunnie pulsed of its own accord. He rolled his hips in deliberation, her suspension facilitating his motions and the glide of her cunnie up and down his shaft. He knew her body well enough to discern that she had reached the point when cessation would bring torment. She would wish to spend. And he would have her spend. To prove his point. To prove to her that she wanted him.

To his surprise, however, she resisted.

"You can fuck harder than that," she grumbled.

Her cunnie clasped him, and he responded instinctively by driving himself farther into her womanhood.

"Harder," she urged.

In disbelief, he paused. He had only ever fucked harder with a molly. A man he had no qualms drilling into, but as sturdy as Miss Terrell was, he could not bring himself to use the full force of his strength.

"Harder," she repeated.

Loosening some of his reserve, he slammed himself into her.

"Harder!"

Despite the bliss of burying his cock deep inside of her, he could not. He reached around her hip for her clitoris and stroked the swollen bud.

"Come on then!" she exclaimed with frustration. "I would expect, as you are younger, that you would be more virile than Sir Arthur, yet he—"

He did not permit her to finish. He shoved himself

into her as hard as he could, ignoring her cries as he pounded into her, his cods swinging furiously. *Damn her tongue. Damn her ability to drive me mad. Damn her...*

The pressure coiled in his groin, ready to spring, but he held off as best he could. Through it all, he still wanted her to spend. His grip dug into her thighs, and he did his best to position his thrusts for her pleasure. But she felt too exquisite. The tightness wrapping his cock, the liquid heat of her desire, all conspired against him. His reserve gone, he sank himself into her as far as he could, as if he could sink all of him into her. He pounded his cock into her with perilous ferocity, the slapping of his pelvis against her arse overwhelming his grunts and the loud drumming of his heart.

Her body erupted into paroxysm just as he surged into her. He had not thought to spend quite yet, but he was no match against her rapture. He could feel the spasms of her cunnie along his entire length. With a roar, he bucked himself at her, unleashing all that had been dammed inside. His legs quaked as he pumped his seed into her, proclaiming her his. For a moment, he thought he might go blind from the relief and elation.

When at last the furious beating of his heart receded from his ears and he discerned that her cries had softened into moans, his cock had not burst but lay pulsing inside her, and he had not lost his sight, he gently disengaged from her. Her wetness and some of his mettle were warm and pleasant upon his cock still. A final shudder went through him. Quickly, he wiped himself and began to untie the ropes. Having spent a while suspended in bondage, she collapsed into his arms. He carried her to the bed and lay her down. His wrath diminished, he hoped he had not been too brutal with her.

Her lashes rested against her cheeks. Flushed, she was a beautiful sight to behold. He would be damned if he allowed Sir Arthur to claim her.

As he watched the rise and fall of her bosom return to an even pace, he tried to place his thoughts into order. He knew he was not done with her. She belonged to him. And he would make that known to her by night's end.

Chapter 34

Terrell had no wish to move, could want to be nowhere else but in his arms. Her body still warm from the rapture, the area between her legs wet, she wanted to savor the sensations of their congress. Surely she could stay a while longer? But the longer she stayed, the harder it would be to part. And what if Sir Arthur were to discover them? She had pledged her fidelity to him.

She could not stay.

His breathing sounded even. He might have fallen asleep. Many men did after spending, but she had come to know Master Gallant did not tire as easily as other men, nor did he require much in the way of time before his cock was at the ready for a second or third attempt. As swiftly and as lightly as she could, she attempted to slide off the bed. But his hand was in her hair, yanking her to him.

"We are not yet done, Miss Terrell."

Getting out of bed, he dragged her to where the ropes lay upon the floor. He pulled her onto her knees, but then pushed her face down to the ground, folding her body with her rump in the air. He grabbed her arms behind her and, with the rope, pinioned them loosely behind her knees. He threw her skirts over her waist, baring her arse, then tightened the bonds around her wrists. Bent with her arms wrapped about her own thighs, she could not move most of her body. She wanted to fall to the side to ease the discomfort of the position, but he retrieved several clusters of nettle and set them on either side of her to dissuade her from lying on her side. And to enlighten her on the potency of the plant, he broke off a leaf and, reaching beneath her, stuffed it into her stays. It stung her breast on contact.

"Please, Master Gallant," she tried, turning her head to look at him. "I am wearied. If you wish, I will suck your cock, and then let us be done."

"Not till you have spent yourself into oblivion."

Damnation. By the hard set of his features, she knew he intended no hyperbole.

"Surely you have no wish to cross Sir Arthur," she reasoned.

"Damn Sir Arthur," he grumbled as he went to the sideboard and wrenched a drawer open.

"Charles, please! You are a gentleman of sense. Do not attempt what you will regret in the morning! You will bring his wrath upon the both of us!"

He turned around sharply. "You have no right to use my given name when you intend to open your legs to another—or have done so already."

She could not respond. Why was it so damned hard to lie to the man? Even if she told him a falsehood, however, he could ascertain the truth easily enough. He had only to speak to Sophia, after all.

His lips formed a grim line. "You did. You offered your cunnie to him, did you not?"

She could make him hate her, detest her so much that he would throw her aside and want nothing more to do with her.

"Did you not?" he growled.

"Of course I did!" she snapped. "Why else would he have come? I did not wish him to leave unsatisfied."

A muscle rippled along his jaw.

"He fucked me well," she continued, "and filled me with his seed. Before you did."

Revulsion was writ across his features. "If he fucks you so well, why did you agree to forsake him?"

She would have shrugged if her shoulders were not pressed into the floor.

"I had forgotten how much I enjoyed his cock," she replied.

"You were attempting my seduction before he had even left."

"I am an insatiable whore. But, now, Sir Arthur has made me an offer I cannot refuse."

In disgust, he whipped around and rummaged through the drawer once more. When he turned around again, he held what appeared to be a collar with a short wide dildo attached to it.

"I mean to honor my accord with him," she said. "He will take me as his mistress, and I will forsake all men but him. I own I have enjoyed our time together. I will look upon the memories with some fondness, but now I—"

He had knelt beside her head and pushed the dildo into her mouth. He fastened the collar upon her. "That will keep you from uttering another word of Sir Arthur."

Rising, he went to the wall and removed a flogger. She groaned into her new gag. Her pulse quickened for the flogger always gave her pause. He snapped the tails against her rump. Her arse, still sore from the tawse, received the sting with exception. He landed the flogger on the tender folds beneath her buttocks. She yelped. Over and over the tails landed on her derriere and the back of her thighs. When he applied the tips of the flogger to her cunnie, she rapped her feet against the floor. A fire consumed the lower half of her body.

But her predicament worsened. She felt his hand between her thighs, stroking. She could not contain her moan. Her body sought relief in his sweet caress. The pleasure made the pain bearable, enjoyable. She wondered if he would take her now and hoped he would.

He did not, but went to the sideboard once more. He returned with seven or eight metal beads attached in a row and in increasing size upon a string. With a silent oath, she closed her eyes. How was she to escape?

She felt a hand upon her arse, and then the beads were in her cunnie. She shivered, knowing where they would head next. Once coated with the moistness from her cunnie, the beads were inserted, starting with the smallest, into her other orifice. She moaned in pleasure as the balls passed through her narrow sphincter, filling that cavity.

When all the beads were inside her, he took up the flogger and lashed her several more times till she was a quivering mess of arousal. If the dildo had not incapacitated her speech, she would have begged him to add his cock. He seemed to contemplate it, for he set down the flogger.He knelt behind her, and to her delight, sank his length into her. She adored the sensation of being filled fully and instinctively pushed her arse at him. He groaned and, grabbing her hips, began a rhythmic thrusting. She made all manner of strange sounds into her gag as her orgasm mounted. Waves of pleasure fanned through her body, foretelling the coming elation. However, she had already spent without his permission. If she failed him a second time, what would he do? But, as livid as he was, would he ever give her his assent?

She could not hold back the tide. She tried. She bit the dildo. She sucked it. Nothing could keep the tension welling deep inside of her at bay. It burst through her in shudders and screams. Through it all, he continued his pounding, his pelvis slapping viciously against her backside, drilling his cock deep into her. His fingers dug into her hips as he pulled her back to meet his every thrust, stoking the waves of pleasure once more. A part of her wanted a moment to catch her breath, to attain a calm before the next ascension. But he had a way of making her body greedy, and soon, she could no longer resist. The waves built toward another peak.

Just as she was about to reach the pinnacle, he pulled the beads from her. Her body fell into a vortex of rhapsody, wringing every nerve in her body. And in that moment, she cared not for the consequences, cared not for Sir Arthur. There was only the greatest bliss her body could know.

Chapter 35

Charles wanted nothing more than to unleash the pressure in his groin and pour himself into her hot, pulsing wetness, but for what he intended to do to, he could not afford to tire himself too soon. He withdrew, wiped his cock with his hand, and replaced his fall. She gasped for breath through her gag, and he considered removing it but he dared not. She had said enough. Any more might extinct the last ounce of gentleman in him.

He pushed the nettles away and allowed her to collapse onto her side. He grabbed the ropes and tested the cord still hanging from the rafters. His heartbeat was still at a quick pace from his exertions, but he pressed on. He had said he would show no mercy. When he was done, she would be fortunate to walk out of the room on her own two feet.

He untied her wrists so that she could uncurl her body. Spent, she turned onto her back. Her lashes fluttered as she attempted to right her gaze. Grasping the sleeves of her gown, he yanked them down her shoulders, sending pins scattering. This awakened her, and she started to fight him, cuffing him on the side of the head hard enough to make his ears ring, but he straddled her and grabbed her wrists, pulled them above her head and quickly bound them again.

He got off her to pull the gown and petticoats

down. Since her hands were joined, he decided to leave the stays in place and admired the length and shape of her legs, the black curls that adorned the mons, and the swell of her belly. He had not feasted of such delights enough. If only she would let him worship her body with hands and lips. Instead, she tried to scramble from him. With his foot, he pushed her arse back down to the ground. Lucky for her, she had a sturdy body, and he could permit himself more forceful actions with her than he would with others of her sex.

"Do not tire yourself too early, m'dear," he advised. "The night has barely begun."

Tire. Had she truly said she tired of him? He had but shown her a fraction of what he was capable of. Tonight, she would bear more than many members of the Red Chrysanthemum would know in a lifetime.

He kept his foot on her arse, still blushing from the tawse and flogger, as he bent her right leg and tied the foot to her left knee. He bent her left leg and, attaching another cord about that ankle, affixed it to her bound wrists. About her hips he wrapped a rope loosely. He took the rope from the rafters, secured it about the rope cradling her hips, and hoisted her into the air.

She was a sight to behold.

Dangling upside down from the rafters, her left knee pointed to the ceiling, her right leg pulled toward her wrists, her body was a work of art as fine as any sculpture. He pried her stays farther to free her breasts. He could bind the magnificent orbs till they darkened in color and protruded as odd shapes. He could crush them between two planks of wood.

For now, he simply rolled the pliant flesh in his hands. She moaned. It thrilled him to know she responded to his every touch. He knew no body more wanton, more lascivious than hers.

Reaching for her mons, he curled his fingers into the hair there, then caressed the bud of flesh below, gently rubbing and tugging. His digits forked the clitoris, stroking both sides till it swelled. She twitched. He sank a finger into her cunnie. It had never felt so wet. Perhaps he should have spent inside her a second time and flooded Sir Arthur's seed from her. But there would be plenty of time for that. He curled two fingers inside of her. Plump and wet, her cunnie was ready for his attentions. He easily found the spot that made her body thrash. She grunted. Her body began to sway. He continued his ministrations. The walls of her cunnie flexed about his digits. He could feel her arousal. Smell it. Hear it.

He withdrew his fingers. She emitted a haggard moan at the loss. He ought to make her lick his fingers clean, especially if she had such an affinity for Sir Arthur's mettle. Wiping his fingers across her belly, he went for the flogger. He gave her leg a push, and she began to slowly rotate through the air. As she spun, he whipped the flogger at her breasts, snapped the tips at her belly and thighs, and flicked it across the arch of a foot. She yelped several times, but he did not relent. She had seduced him against his wishes, misled him, and lied to him. Now she would pay the price.

A knock at the door interrupted him.

"Master Gallant," said Master Troy through the door, "there is a matter requiring your attention."

"I will be there shortly," Charles replied.

He gave her breasts a final flogging, then pressed two fingers into her cunnie once more. He did not want her arousal to diminish in his absence. He frigged her till he sensed her climax looming but left her incomplete. She had the nerve to glare at him. He bent down and gave her cheek a light slap.

"Worry not. I shall return, though you may wish I had not."

What he wanted was to hear her begging him to stay, begging him to stay forever.

Chapter 36

She already wished he would not return.

Terrell tried the bonds. Her head was heavy from the flow of blood downwards, but that did not stop her cunnie from aching, from wanting his touch and wanting to spend, though she had endured the most exquisite rhapsody but moments before. She had erred. She should not have vexed him as much as she had. But could she bring herself to beg for his mercy? Would that induce his reason to return and overcome his jealousy?

She knew not. Her head ached to think. She knew only the discomfort of her bondage and the unmet yearning between her legs. *Damn him.* When would he return? The rope cradling her hips now dug harshly into her. She worried that if she remained in her current position much longer, she might lose consciousness.

The door opened, but it was not Gallant. She glimpsed the familiar form and attire of Wang. No doubt he had been set to relieve her from her suspension. As she guessed, Wang unfastened an end of the rope and lowered her to the ground. She contemplated how she might make her escape when he untied her. However, instead of attending to the remainder of the ropes, he picked her up and brought her to a low pillory that came to about the height of the knees. He laid her head face up in the center and closed the frame and locked it over her neck. She could not escape.

He quickly undid the ropes about her so that she could rest the weight of her body on her knees, but it was hardly comfortable. She would have preferred to face the floor than the ceiling. And she had hoped he would remove the gag from her mouth, sore from having to remain open. Pressed down by the dildo, her tongue wanted freedom of movement. Her hands could not reach far enough over the frame of the pillory to access the gag herself. She gestured to it, but Wang paid her no heed.

She jumped when she felt his hand between her thighs. Had Gallant given him permission to touch her or was the Oriental taking liberties for himself since she could not speak or flee? She was unsure how she ought to receive the situation. True, she had dreamed of the Chinaman and would not have eschewed his attentions, but that was when she had desired it, not when she was helpless to stop it.

His fingers, however, melted all resistance. He had a different touch from Charles but no less effective. She grabbed the top of the pillory as he pressed down upon an area that sent shocks through her body. She was going to spend in mere seconds. But as with Gallant, he ceased before she could reach the summit. She felt her forbearance slipping away. She only wanted to spend once more. It was as if she had not already spent thrice, and gloriously. Her lust had been made hungry again.

The door opened and this time it was Gallant. He looked to Wang, who nodded. Gallant strode over and looked down at her.

"I take it you wish to have the gag removed?" he asked.

She nodded as best she could.

"I will do so, but if you dare utter one word, I will leave you locked in the pillory the whole night. If you oblige and behave that saucy mouth of yours, you may be rewarded with the chance to spend."

He did not appear to be jesting. She nodded. She had no choice but to obey. Thus, she could not beg nor appeal to his reason. With sinking hopes, she began to think she had no recourse but to submit and endure what he would do to her. The gag removed, she worked her tender mouth and jaw.

"I will gift you a real cock instead," he told her.

He and Wang switched places. The valet undid the buttons of his fall. Dear God, she was to have the Oriental's cock? But why? Why did Gallant do this?

Wang braced himself on the frame and lowered his cock, a narrow length with a dramatic curve. She hesitated.

"Take it," Gallant commanded as he pushed her knees apart and knelt between them.

But doing so might fuel his jealousy, she considered. Was this a test? Or was it simply part of her punishment?

She cried out, for he had seized and twisted her clitoris. Wang shoved his cock into her mouth. She gagged at the angle and curvature. She tried to relax her throat, but Gallant's digits were at her cunnie, distracting her, percolating the pleasure there. His thumb was on her clitoris, his forefinger in her cunnie, and his middle finger in her rectum. Her body soared in delight. Wang began thrusting, and every time she gagged, Gallant would slap her breast.

"You will make him spend," Gallant said.

She barely heard him for she had begun to scale her own summit. She sucked on Wang as Gallant fucked her with his fingers. Would he let her spend? Perhaps he would if Wang did. She sucked harder. Gallant increased the ferocity of his frigging. She plowed into her summit, fluid gushing from her. Her body bucked and shook the pillory. Her hands had slipped from the wooden boards and flailed for something to grasp. Before she began her descent, Gallant spread her thighs wider and speared her with his cock. His hands dug into her breasts. He shoved himself hard and deep into her. At times, the men alternated in rhythm, pushing her body in one direction, then another. At others, they rammed into her in unison.

Despite the discomfort of the pillory, she found it too wanton, too titillating. Yet another orgasm began to build. Gallant grasped the back of her thighs, lifting her to better meet his thrusts. He ground and hammered into her. Perspiration dripped from him, and this time, he spent. She felt a flare of warmth inside of her. And then Wang spent, filling her mouth with his seed. The volume surprised her and she began to choke. He quickly released the latch and Gallant pulled her upright.

The coughing subsided, and she crumpled to the floor. The heat between her thighs still simmered, but she was tired and sore. Various parts of her body ached, and she felt her shoulders might develop bruises from hitting the frame of the pillory. They allowed her to lie for a few minutes before Gallant sat her up. Wang held a cup of tea before her. The beverage was no longer hot, but she welcomed it.

"Fetch her another cup," Gallant told Wang. "She will require greater stamina."

Stamina? They were not yet done? She wanted to lie back upon the floor. Wang returned with another cup, and it was then that she noticed his cock had not softened in the slightest.

She would indeed require stamina.

Chapter 37

C harles could see she was tired. He, too, felt weary. Only Wang, whose cock could spend three, four times and still remain hard, seemed no less worn.

After she finished the second cup, he laid her back down upon the floor. She was not going to Sir Arthur. Not tonight. Perhaps, in the morning, she would reconsider her decision. And Charles would give her several reasons not to.

Hot and sweating, he divested all of his garments. He went to a bookshelf and surveyed the items there, including an iron collar. He would have liked to fix one upon her, a symbol that she belonged to him. But he was mindful that such collars were often used upon actual slaves. Noting that she had recovered some from her weariness and had sat up, he selected the iron cuffs from the shelf. He needed to restrain the hellcat or she might scratch their eyes out.

Wang stood in front of her, but Charles could see her mind turning, assessing how she might overcome the two of them. She did not relent easily. As he suspected, the instant he grabbed her arm, she began resisting.

"You wish to be locked in the pillory once more?" he asked.

The threat stopped her and she yielded to having

her wrists cuffed behind her. He stood and held his cock before her.

"You proclaim an insatiable appetite for cock," he said, "and I believe it true."

He presented his cock. She frowned. When she looked up, he saw daggers in her eyes. She would likely hate him by morning, but he knew he would not earn her respect till he had obliterated her resistance with his domination. Yes, he was, in all likelihood, headed for hell, but she had drawn him in first, and they would go there together.

She took his cock into her mouth, and he groaned. That he might never again feel her exquisite orifice wrapping his shaft—it was enough to make a man weep. She spared nothing and coaxed him to hardness with her magic. She murmured as if she had never tasted anything finer. When he realized she intended to make him spend, he pushed her away.

Wang had decided to remove his clothing as well. Gallant knelt behind her and held her against his lap. Wang settled between her legs and rubbed the tip of his cock along her folds. With the crown, he fondled her nub. He pushed himself into her slit, pulled out, and spread the moisture onto her clitoris. He repeated this many times till her breath was quite uneven. He agitated his cock harder and faster against her. She began to quiver. When Wang withdrew, she moaned. Her body sagged in disappointment.

"You have spent many times without permission this night," Charles said to her.

She was about to make a retort but recalled herself in time.

"You must work for your next one," he finished.

Wang lay with his back against the floor and stroked himself. Gallant lifted her and placed her atop Wang. Understanding their intent, she sheathed herself on Wang's cock. At first, she merely ground herself against his pelvis.

Charles stopped her. "You must make him spend first."

For her mischief, he retrieved two clamps with dangling weights. He affixed them to her nipples. She could not become accustomed to the tug of the weighted clamps, for when she moved, they would move. She began slowly, lifting herself up Wang's erection, then settling back down. She did for several minutes.

"Faster," Charles encouraged, stroking himself as he watched her bounding up and down, "or I will add more weight to your nipples."

She obeyed and increased her exertion. The weights flew erratically about her nipples. Her bosom gleamed with perspiration. She groaned and gasped, grunted and panted. Wang grabbed her hips to aid her motions. His pelvis smacked against her loudly, and then he found his release. The veins protruded from his neck as he drove himself as rapidly and as deep as he could.

Charles nearly spent at the scene before him but refrained. Jealousy flamed through him as he considered that she now had the seed of three different men inside of her. Oddly, even as it emasculated, the jealousy also titillated. No woman had ever vexed him to this extent, nor aroused him beyond reason.

He held her aloft by her hair as he removed the clamps from her doubtlessly aching nipples. He allowed her to collapse atop Wang. Finding a vial of oil, he coated his shaft. If it was cock she cherished, then she would have it as often as they could give it. His cock dripping with oil, he went to pick her up and bent her over the back of a chair. He remembered the first time he had done so, throwing her skirts over to bare her arse. God, what a beautiful arse she had.

But his cock had waited long enough. He pried open her buttocks and aimed himself at her anus. He popped the head in and groaned at the delicious tightness. What a beautiful, delicious arse. His for the fucking. He wanted to shove his whole length in but, as she was not fully wet there, he forced himself to take his time. He sank himself in one exhilarating inch at a time. She managed a moan between heavy breaths.

Nothing in the world could compare to the perfection of being buried in her arse. Resisting the desire to begin pounding, he withdrew to pour more oil upon himself. He reentered her, pressing farther till the hairs of his pelvis tickled her arse. He stilled himself, relishing the contractions about his cock, before starting a leisurely thrust. The oil slickened her tract, and he thrust in growing earnest. Her groans, low and long, shortened and increased in pitch.

From the corner of his eye, he saw that Wang stood near. While still inside of her, Charles picked her up by her legs and turned to Wang, who penetrated her from the front. Wang took her legs, and Charles wrapped an arm about her midsection.

He let Wang guide the motions. Between them, she was tossed about like a ragdoll. Forgetting his directive not to talk, she murmured something, but as it was incomprehensible, he let it pass. Her head fell against his shoulder as Wang propelled himself long and hard into her.

Overcome, she wailed as she achieved her paroxysm. Her legs jerked uncontrollably. She strained against them and might have slid from them, but they kept a firm grip on her. Wang closed his eyes and, seconds later, he spent, hips bucking wildly. When done, he staggered back. Charles disengaged and caught her before she crumpled to the floor. He placed her on the bed and spread her thighs. Lowering himself between her legs, he caught the scent of the various fluids collected there. He licked at her engorged clitoris.

She whispered words that sounded of, "Please...enough."

But he continued to lick her, burrowing his tongue at the plump pearl. She arched her back as if to escape the direct pressure on the sensitive area. He held her folds apart and continued his assault. The blood pounded in his head and throbbed in his cock. He would see her spend once more upon him, by him. Did she truly think a wanton creature such as herself could ever be satisfied by the likes of Sir Arthur and his bloody wealth?

She emitted a soft wail that sounded like a sob. Her body shuddered and reared with every lick. He knew she had spent but did not relent until she begged him to stop. He did, but only to flip her onto her stomach. He released the shackles from her wrists and laid the length of his body atop hers. He angled his cock and sank back into the glory of her arse. This time, impatience won out. He drilled himself into her. For once, he could not tell if her groans were of pleasure or not. Insinuating a hand beneath her, he reached to fondle her clitoris as his pelvis slapped into her rump. She tried to wriggle from him, but his body pinned hers.

He briefly wondered if Sir Arthur had sown this field as well and bucked himself harder against her. Having spent already, he was able to hold off till her arousal began anew. He pommeled her into the bed, giving her an intermittent reprieve so that he could better ply her clitoris. She ceased to struggle and succumbed. Spasms rippled through her, caressing his shaft. His own glory burst forth. His every muscle coiled and released with such fury that it took his strength. He let his full weight sink onto her. His heart beat as if he had sprinted miles. He could do no more. She had drained him. Exhausted, he rolled off her and was overcome with sleep.

When he awoke, she was gone.

Chapter 38

L ook at all the letters of support that have come in since you received Sir Arthur's endorsement!" Mrs. Gallant remarked as she placed another letter upon Charles' writing table.

Charles spared only a second's glance at the letters before returning to the speech he was writing.

His mother opened another letter. "And here is an invitation to a dinner from Lady North! You will attend that one, I am sure. You can have no excuse, now that your services are no longer required at the Red Chrysanthemum."

Joan had returned several nights ago, and Charles was not as relieved to relinquish his command as he would have thought because he had entertained the hope that Terrell might return. But, like Miss Greta, she did not.

"What! Miss Terrell left with Sir Arthur?" Joan had exclaimed when he had told her the news. "And without a by-your-leave, without waiting for my return?"

"Sir Arthur is far too rich a prize to delay even a day, I suppose," Charles had said, trying to keep his chagrin at bay.

"I hope Sir Arthur intends to compensate me my loss. Without Miss Terrell, I may lose the membership of Mr. Worthington. He should offer at least a hundred guineas for taking Miss Terrell."

"But Miss Terrell is neither property nor commodity. She is free to choose whom she pleases."

And she had chosen Sir Arthur. Nothing Charles could do had persuaded her. He did not doubt but that he held dominion over her body more than Sir Arthur, but Terrell, despite her passions and her deepest desires, was a woman of practicality. In the end, wealth spoke strongest to her sense of survival. When he considered this, he allowed that she had made the better arithmetic choice.

Still, a sense of betrayal pervaded. She had agreed to forsake Sir Arthur. How could she have changed her mind with so little time in between? He had not thought her a fickle woman. But perhaps she had merely pretended to agree, to humor him or refrain from wounding his pride.

"Well, I doubt it to last," Joan had said. "I should not be surprised if Miss Terrell returned, begging me to accept her once more to the Red Chrysanthemum, and I shall not be so quick to take her back."

"*Au contraire*," Charles had replied. "You will. For Miss Terrell is an uncommon woman."

"That is praise indeed coming from you. Pray, what has she done to merit such a compliment?"

"Anyone who can survive the hardships of slavery and tolerate the nature of activities that happen here must be uncommon."

"I had forgotten she was once a slave, but I would think her past bondage to have prepared her well for what occurs here."

"Have you seen her back?"

"Her back? Have you?"

"If you had seen its mutilation, you would be astounded that she does not flinch at the very sight of a flogger, cane or crop."

"You wish to paint Miss Terrell as some brave soul?"

"Little seems to daunt her. She possesses an intrepid determination."

"Hmm. I had thought her clever and ambitious, certainly, and self-seeking. But how is it you have glimpsed Miss Terrell's back?"

He had considered a lie and did not immediately respond. At the Red Chrysanthemum, there were any number of ways he could have come across Miss Terrell naked, but he saw no need for pretense now that she was gone.

He had no need to respond, however. Joan was perceptive enough.

"Ah, she had made of you a target," Joan had said. "I had wondered what she might be capable of in my absence, though I had not thought Sir Arthur was so besotted with her that he would take her for his mistress. What a greedy wench to want both you and Sir Arthur!"

Greed. That was what had compelled Terrell.

"But I do not fault her for wanting the best of all worlds—a handsome man to fuck her in bed and another to shower her with riches beyond compare."

No longer wishing to talk of Terrell, Charles had proceeded to apprise Madame of other developments concerning Nicholas Edelton and the possible appearance of Sir Rowan.

"Miss Sarah's husband?" Joan had wondered aloud. "Now that is interesting. I wonder how he knew? I had suspected she was here as much in hiding as for want of room and board."

Charles had also warned Joan of Miss Sophia and how she might have ruined Miss Sarah's shawl on purpose, thinking it to have been Miss Terrell's. Upon discovery of the shawl, Terrell had engaged Miss Sophia in a brawl that ended in the latter losing a fistful of hair. Miss Sophia did not regard Miss Terrell highly, but she underestimated the blackamoor at her peril.

"Regina called upon me at the Jeffers residence," his mother said, pulling Charles from his recollection. "But I sent her a note suggesting that she call upon me at *your* residence. She would be merely returning my visit."

Charles saw through his mother but said nothing. He looked at his half-written speech. As with the departure of Miss Greta, he had sought to plunge himself into work and his election. At the least, it should have been easier this time. His heart was not as taken with Terrell as it had been with Miss Greta.

But his body was another matter. It craved Terrell. He could relieve the tension—and he had done it often—but the attainment was trifling compared to the rapture he experienced with Terrell. He could know no higher heights, no rhapsody more divine. He doubted a man like Sir Arthur could fully appreciate what Miss Terrell offered, and, selfishly, he was glad. It satisfied his vanity to think that he alone could unearth the ecstasy within her.

"Will this Friday serve?" Mrs. Gallant asked.

"I have a meeting with Sir Canning and Mr. Morton."

"Mr. Morton, the banker? Regarding your election?"

"Yes."

"How splendid! That will be much needed to counter what Mr. Laurel is offering voters. It is grand to have the endorsement of Sir Arthur! But I see you are not entirely happy. What does the man expect in return, did he say?"

"He expects nothing."

Taken aback by his answer, she stared at him agape. "Nothing?"

"Nothing," Charles affirmed.

"Oh. How pleasantly surprising!"

Charles had indeed been surprised when Sir Arthur informed him of his unencumbered endorsement in the office of his employer and in Sir Canning's presence.

"You have my support, Gallant, free and clear," Sir Arthur had confirmed when Charles had asked what Sir Arthur desired in exchange for the endorsement.

"Free and clear?" Charles had questioned.

Sir Arthur had stretched his legs, his walking stick between them. "You sound surprised, Gallant."

"It is customary to expect something, perhaps a vote to be named in the future?"

Sir Arthur had given him a smug smile. "I have all that I could want. A certain membership has paid unexpected dividends, and I mean to reap the rewards on a daily basis."

The hairs on the back of Charles' neck had stood on end, but he could make no response. Sir Canning had congratulated Charles on the good news and praised Sir Arthur for his wise decision and dedication to Parliament and the governance of England.

"Well, he is more accommodating and munificent than we gave him credit for," Mrs. Gallant remarked happily.

Charles rubbed his eyes He did not agree. He wondered if Miss Terrell had somehow coaxed Sir Arthur into such an action. Undoubtedly, having his cock sucked by her put the man in a better, more generous mood.

He had thought of paying Terrell a visit. He could find her easily enough, but there was no purpose to chasing after her. It was clear to him that she preferred Sir Arthur. In truth, who would not? The man possessed influence and wealth to a degree Charles could only imagine. In his lifetime, he could achieve only a fraction of what Sir Arthur already possessed.

If Terrell should have a change of heart, she knew where to reach him.

Chapter 39

The footman cleared his throat. "Miss Sarah is here to see you, madam."

Terrell raised her head from the settee where she had been drifting to sleep. The midday sun shone brightly into the drawing room.

"Show her in," she replied. The visit from Sarah and George was a favorite occurrence.

"Lady Sarah!" she greeted with pure delight at the sight of a familiar face.

The two women embraced.

"And look at you!" Terrell knelt to embrace George, who stood unwavering beside his mother. "You seem taller with each passing day!"

"I would have come Tuesday, but Georgie had such a bad cough and fever," Sarah said. "I feared it more than influenza."

Seeing a wooden boat upon the low table, George made straight for the object.

"And how well he walks," Terrell marveled.

"Georgie, be careful," Sarah said when he grabbed the boat.

"Oh, it is his to do as he pleases. When it is spring, he might take it to the park and see if it floats upon the water. Pray, sit, Lady Sarah. I will have the cook prepare a lunch."

Terrell gestured to the footman.

"You have added quite the number of new servants," Sarah observed, taking a seat opposite Terrell on the settee. "

"Sir Arthur has been pleased to give me a footman and another maid."

"And that is a new gown you wear? It is very lovely."

Terrell looked down at the soft muslin of pale blue with ruffles. "I think I have plumped since leaving the Red Chrysanthemum, for my prior gowns no longer fit me well. The cook is much better than what we had before."

Sarah bit her bottom lip.

"But I do not mean to boast," Terrell added. "Or perhaps I do. Sir Arthur hires the servants and has much higher standards than Sir Fairchild ever did. But he did permit me to select the wallpaper for this room, for I had found the prior color rather dark and gloomy."

Sarah examined the striped silk upon the walls. "It is a nice choice."

Still fatigued, Terrell arranged a pile of pillows to lean upon.

"You are happy here?" Sarah asked.

"How could I not be? I have servants, gowns, an apartment of my own."

"And Sir Arthur has been good to you?"

"Do not worry yourself, Lady Sarah. I could not wish for better. But how do you fare? Is Captain Gracechurch returned and as enamored of you as before?"

"He is. He says he made for the Red Chrysanthemum the day his ship pulled into port."

"He must make a decent income as captain. Do you think he would wish to marry you?"

"I am still married as far as I know, though I suppose if Sir Rowan were successful in securing a divorce, I would not know it."

They both looked at Georgie, now rolling the ship across the floor.

"Even if I were free, I am not partial to Captain Gracechurch in that way," Sarah said.

"And what way would that be? You get on in the bedchamber, do you not? That is more than what many a husband and wife enjoy."

"Captain Gracechurch is a bit of a rough man. I prefer men a little more refined, like..."

Silence fell between them. Over a fortnight had passed since Terrell had left the Red Chrysanthemum. She would have thought the heartache significantly dissipated by now. She had done what she could to forget about *him.* Fortunately, she seemed to require more sleep these days, and when she slept, the slumber was often dreamless.

The first few days, she had passed no hour without thoughts of him. Even when Sir Arthur bucked against her, attempting to bury himself as deep as he could, he could not drive Gallant from her mind. Sir Arthur's presence only reminded her of whom she had not chosen. Her heart ached for what could not be. The pain, being more recent, seemed as terrible as the yearning for freedom in her time in Barbados. She recalled that she had once promised herself, if she should be free, that she would want for nothing more. But it is the nature of man to desire more than he has. She had her freedom, but that did not stop her from wanting more, wanting a life of comfort, of extravagance even. Most of all, she wanted Gallant.

As if reading her thoughts, Sarah said, "I've not seen him since Madame returned."

Terrell lowered her voice. "Do you hear of his election? Will he win? I would pick up a paper and have the footman read it to me, but I suspect he tells Sir Arthur all my doings. The maids as well."

At that, a housemaid entered with a tray of toasted cheese, peas soup and tea.

"And some biscuits for the boy," Terrell said to her.

With a nod, the housemaid left. Terrell looked at the food and grimaced.

"This smells wonderful," Sarah said, handing Georgie a slice of the toasted cheese.

"You and Georgie may have it all," Terrell said. Her stomach turned. "I can bear to eat little these days. The very smell of food can make me retch."

"The last time I was here, you complained of being sick for hours each day."

Terrell stifled a yawn and settled deeper into the pillows. "Yes. I think I had some orange wine that did not agree with me."

"Still? Or did you partake of more?"

"I have not since first my stomach took ill."

Sarah helped herself to the soup, but she made no comment on its taste for she seemed distracted in thought. A new silence fell. Terrell searched her mind for another topic but was too tired to settle on one.

"When were your menses?" Sarah blurted.

"My menses?"

"When did you last have the flux?"

Terrell shrugged. "Sometimes it is months in between. It is rare for me to see any consistency."

"You were quite fatigued the last time I called. Are you still?"

"I rest often that I might be up to task whenever Sir Arthur visits."

"You suspect nothing?"

Terrell stared at Sarah. "Why do you ask such a question?"

"Because I had much fatigue and nausea when I was with child."

Another spell of silence ensued till Terrell said, "That is not possible. I cannot conceive."

"I was once close to a cousin of Sir Rowan. She and her husband tried to have a child for *seven* years. She believed herself incapable of bearing children. After seven years, lo and behold, they had a boy. It is possible."

Terrell did not know how to receive such news. While she would have been overjoyed to think she might have a little one as adorable as Georgie, she could not think of a worse time to be with a child. And *whose* child would it be?

"No, no, it is far too unlikely," Terrell insisted. "Do you know how many men I have f...how many times I have had congress—without French letters—and had nothing come of it?"

"I hope you may be right, but I think your symptoms suspect."

Terrell considered that she had slept for eleven hours last night, woke at eight in the morning, only to be tired a mere four hours later. And after a sedentary morning of perusing sketches in *The Lady's Magazine* and half-heartedly attempting to learn how to knit a purse, no less.

"Perhaps you should seek the counsel of a doctor," Sarah suggested.

"Perhaps. I shall see how I fair in a few days."

She did *not* wish to see a doctor. If she should somehow be with child, how would Sir Arthur receive such a development? Would he throw her out, especially if he thought there to be a chance that the child was Gallant's?

Her breath caught in her throat at the thought. A child. Perhaps Charles' child. She did not dare consider it joyous or she might succumb to sentiment.

"What if you are with a child?" Sarah asked. "What if it is *his*?"

"I doubt Sir Arthur would be pleased to father a bastard."

"I meant *him*."

Of course she had. Terrell looked away. "What of it? He need not know. He shall not know."

"But why? What if he should want to know?"

Terrell gave Sarah a sharp look. "That is neither here nor there. It serves no purpose."

"If it is his, he has a right to know."

"We shall never know if Gallant or Sir Arthur be the father—if I am indeed with child."

"I saw Sir Rowan in Georgie the day he was born."

"Because you knew your husband to be the father. For me, it is just as likely that the Viscount Wendlesson is the father."

Sarah started.

"Though it is doubtful," Terrell hastened to add. "It was but a one-time occurrence."

"You have no intention of telling Gallant?"

Terrell sighed in exasperation. "I do not. There is nothing he could do, perhaps nothing he *would* do."

"I doubt he would shirk his responsibility."

"What if he is not the father? I would make him fret needlessly. He has enough to concern him at present." Seeing Sarah's discontent, she added, "But I will take your advice and see a doctor."

She would see a doctor, but would have to do so without the knowledge of Sir Arthur. If she was with child, she would have to contemplate what must follow next, and what was the obvious solution to her was not one she was willing to reveal to Lady Sarah, who would undoubtedly protest. They would have a heated argument, after which they might cease to be friends.

Sarah would not understand. She would appeal to Terrell's desire for a child and the joys of motherhood. But Terrell was of a more practical persuasion. She relied upon Sir Arthur and could not at present support a child on her own. While she might be able to convince Madame Devereux to take her back, Terrell did not wish to raise a child in the Red Chrysanthemum. Her child would not only be a bastard, it would be a black bastard. She could not bring a child into such a life for her own selfish reasons. Because she would have liked a babe to cradle to her bosom. Because she would have liked to have a living memory of *him.*

From her stare, Sarah seemed to discern Terrell's contemplation, and Terrell was glad when the maid returned with a plate of biscuits for George, who did not hesitate to partake of one for each hand.

"One will do, Georgie," Sarah said.

Terrell laughed. "Let him have them. His enjoyment of the biscuits will be my finest amusement."

To her relief, they talked no more of uneasy matters, and Terrell was quite sad when they had to leave.

Chapter 40

I had said I would not take visitors today," Charles told Wang from where he sat in the library, without halting his pen. "I mean to finish my work for Sir Canning before heading to Porter's Hill."

He had taken to canvassing every day this week, and he was seeing a return for his efforts.

"Shall I tell her to return tomorrow?" Wang asked.

Charles looked up from his papers. "Her?"

His first thought was of Terrell, but Wang would not have omitted her name.

"She has a boy with her," Wang elucidated.

"A boy? Miss Sarah?"

"Yes, that is the one."

If Miss Sarah had come all this way, and with her son in tow, he would not turn her away. He put down his pen. "Show her in."

When she entered, he rose to his feet and made her a bow.

"You and Terrell are much alike in your treatment of me," she remarked. "I feel as if I am still Lady Sarah."

"You are," he replied, showing her to a chair. He smiled at the boy, who reached for the jade figure on the table beside them. "He has grown significantly since I saw him last."

"Children grow in sudden bursts, I think."

"Shall I have some biscuits and milk brought for the boy?"

"That is kind of you, but I will not take much of your time. I know you must be busy, with the day of election drawing near. Georgie, no!"

She stopped him from grabbing the jade figurine. Charles went to his writing table and picked up a rattle drum. On the sides of the drum were pellets attached by strings. He rubbed the stick between his palms, causing the pellets to twirl back and forth, striking the drum. He handed it to George, who examined the item with great interest.

"What a darling little instrument," Sarah said.

"It is from Xian, China."

"Then it is precious. Georgie ought not have it. He might break it."

George shook the stick. One of the pellets struck the drum, and his eyes lit up.

"He is welcome to keep it," Charles said. "I bought it off a street vendor."

"How kind you are, Master Gallant."

"Mr. Gallant," he reminded her.

"Yes, Mr. Gallant," she echoed, then lowered her voice. "Your presence is much missed at the Red Chrysanthemum. Shall we have the pleasure of your company there?"

He looked out the window. Half the leaves had fallen off the sycamore trees. The weather had grown much colder.

"I think not for some time," he replied.

She seemed to have expected this answer but was silent.

"May I be of service to you, Miss Sarah?" he asked.

She shook her head and placed George upon the adjacent armchair. "I came with news that I thought you might wish to hear."

She looked down and appeared uneasy, clasping and unclasping her hands. He waited patiently. He had thought at first that she had come to seek his assistance in some monetary way, and he had been ready to give it. But what news she could have for him, he could not guess.

"I believe Terrell with child," she blurted.

The blood drained from him. She had lifted her head to observe his reaction, and her gaze wanted to unearth something from him.

"You have seen Terrell?" he asked. The calmness in his tone belied the churning of his mind.

"I have called upon her thrice."

"And she told you…"

She shook her head. "I discerned it for myself. The indications are unmistakable."

"I thought her incapable of conceiving."

"The ways of the Lord are mysterious."

He put a hand to his temples. "But you cannot be certain."

"I fear I am. As a woman, as one who has suffered the same: fatigue, biliousness, a missed flux. And I can see the difference in her form."

Dear God. He considered pouring himself a drink, though there were still hours in the morning to be had.

"I think she refuses to believe me," Sarah continued, "but she cannot deny the truth for too long."

"And you come to tell me this because you believe

me the father of this unborn child?"

She blinked several times. He did not mean to speak as brusquely as he did, but she could not have come with more devastating intelligence than if he had been informed that he had been discharged from his employment.

"It is possible, is it not?"

Turning from her to hide his anguish, he gripped the writing table. Hell and damnation.

"She resides in an apartment in—"

But he turned around. "You intend I should go to her?"

Sarah furrowed her brow. "Would you not?"

"You said she refuses to acknowledge that she is with child. You want I should try to convince her? If *you* failed, my chances of success are even less."

"I thought…"

"In truth, I expect she would not even receive me. She has chosen her bed."

"Then you mean to—"

She frowned, no doubt disappointed with his response, though how could she expect any other from him?

"—to permit Sir Arthur to take responsibility?"

"It is just as likely to be his child."

"I doubt Sir Arthur would be pleased to assume such a charge."

"Ha!" His laugh sounded harsh even to his own ears. "I think you put it mildly, Miss Sarah."

She rose and picked up George. He regretted his retort, but he was too overcome to ask her pardon at the moment.

"Well, I do not think Terrell will impose upon Sir

Arthur. She is not yet on such footing with him that she could do so with confidence. She will fix the problem. Only I shudder to think what solution she will seek."

He paled.

"Good day to you, Mr. Gallant," she said, and left the room before he could see her out.

When she was gone, he sank into a chair. His head pounded, and a pit had opened in his bowels.

Miss Sarah was right. Terrell was too practical to bear a child whilst she relied upon the favors of Sir Arthur. What would Sir Arthur want with a bastard? The solution Miss Sarah alluded to was a frightful one. A questionable elixir as likely to cause death as stem the courses. In a brothel in Canton, he had witnessed the aftermath of a woman who had partaken of such a *cure*. How the poor woman had screamed and writhed! As if her insides were being torn from her. Nothing had relieved her agony. He had learned she later died.

He could not let such a fate befall Terrell, but what could he do? She was no longer his concern. It seemed she had never truly been his to start with.

Chapter 41

Having arrived home, Terrell handed the basket of lace and notions to her maid, Peggy, at the threshold. The wind blew at her dark green cloak, whipping it around her. She untied her bonnet before it took flight on its own. Despite the weather, she had insisted on going out. She had spent several days indoors due to fatigue and the rains. Today, she had finally felt rested and found the thought of staying inside stifling. Peggy had not appeared pleased to have to take a walk with her, but she had mollified the maid by promising her some new lace for them both.

"That gentleman appears to take an interest in you, miss," Peggy said.

Turning about, she beheld a man standing not twenty feet away with his horse behind him. He was of fine form and dress, his garrick resting upon broad shoulders, his trousers encasing the most well-formed legs, his riding boots buffed and gleaming, locks of dark golden hair blowing beneath his columned hat.

It was Charles.

Her heart stopped. When at last she found her breath, she said as archly as she could, "I think he has never seen a blackamoor so finely dressed."

She happened to have on a new gown, one of pale

canary, with long sleeves and a wide embroidered hem.

"I will have a word with this impertinent fellow," she said with lifted chin. Inside, she quaked.

She wished Peggy would step inside the house but expected the maid would remain at the door instead. With her heart in her throat, Terrell walked over to Charles. A part of her thrilled to see him, to think that he might have come all this way for her, but fear and dread overcame all other sentiment.

She could not place his expression. Was he taken aback to see her so fashionably dressed? With her hair, unruly and unkempt in her days at the Red Chrysanthemum, in a perfect coiffure; pearl earrings adorning her ears; a wide-brimmed bonnet with satin ribbon and ostrich plumes, she must have appeared a different woman entirely.

Was he glad to see her? Vexed? Disappointed?

"Master Gallant, what do you do here?" she asked.

He looked past her, taking in the modest but appealing facade of her residence. When his gaze returned to her, settling on her countenance, it was all she could do not to lose herself into the depths of his crystalline eyes. Unsure of her strength, she wanted to sink to the ground.

"You look well, Miss Terrell," he said, his eyes searching hers. It was a simple and sincere observation on his part, yet the words wrung her heart. She would have preferred his petulance, would that he called her a bitch rather than pay her a compliment.

From the side of her eye, she saw that Peggy still stood at the door. She had to make quick the conversation.

"You happened to be near?" she asked.

His eyes hardened at the annoyance in her tone. "I came to see you. I had sent my card but received no answer."

Her heart struggled to continue beating. She had torn his card into several pieces as soon as she had received it, hoping none of the servants had taken note of it.

"I cannot see you," she said, unable to keep the quiver from her voice. "I have no wish to see you. My life now is quite different from what it was before. I wish to cast off all memory of those inferior days."

A muscle rippled along his jaw. He glanced over at the maid and kept his voice low. "You left without the slightest fare-thee-well."

"I was eager to begin my new life as the courtesan of a very rich, very influential man. I would you take your leave, Master Gallant, for I expect Sir Arthur for supper and mean to prepare myself for his arrival."

She batted her lashes to signify how she looked forward to her preparations. Picking up her skirts, she turned to leave him, but he grasped her by the arm.

"Miss Sarah came to see me."

Her fortitude withered. Sarah. Why did she have to invite his interference?

"Are you?" he growled.

Rousing her courage, she faced him with flashing eyes. This time her words had the edge of a knife. "Am I what?"

"Are you with child?"

Her bosom heaved as breathing became difficult

once more. "Lady Sarah is deluded. I am not."

"You lie, Terrell."

"If I was, it is none of your affair," she replied hotly.

"No? What if the child is mine?"

"I assure you it is not!"

"How can you be certain? I wager my seed is buried as deep in your womb as any other."

She tore herself from his grasp. She spoke through clenched teeth. "The child would be Sir Arthur's. Of that I am certain. A woman knows such things. As for you, I urge you to plow a different field, Master Gallant, for I will see no more of you."

"What do you intend?"

But she had whirled about and hurried back to Peggy. She stepped inside and closed the door behind her. Her cheeks burned.

I wager my seed is buried as deep in your womb as any other.

What insolence! How dare he come round asking such indelicate questions and demanding to know? She was not his concern!

"The gentleman has upset you, miss?" Peggy asked.

Realizing that she trembled, Terrell gathered herself.

"Who was he?"

Though Peggy was unlikely to have heard their conversation, she had seen the heat of their exchange.

"A man who claims I owe him money," Terrell replied, "but I do not, and I will not entertain his demands. Is he gone?"

Peggy looked out the window. "He leaves now."

Terrell let out a shaky breath. "I will take no callers other than Miss Sarah from this day forth."

"Yes, miss."

Terrell looked in the mirror to assess her composure. She smoothed back a curl. Tonight she would seek the midwife that Madame Devereux had once recommended to a tenant of the Red Chrysanthemum. The midwife was known to make an elixir that would induce a miscarriage. She would take it whether she was with child or no. Then she could state with certainty to Sarah that she was not. And Charles would have no reason to attempt to call upon her ever again.

Chapter 42

Wang stood aside as Charles entered, cursing heavily, but not because he had slipped off his horse and fallen to the ground—that had simply been aggravating. Charles took off his hat and gloves and cast them roughly onto a table in the foyer. Wang caught the garrick before it fell to the floor. Charles had intended to spend the day at Porter's Hill. Sir Canning had advised him to retard his efforts now that Sir Arthur's support had made it all unnecessary, but Charles preferred to continue as before.

Instead of taking himself to Porter's Hill, however, he had opted to see Terrell. And for what? To be told that she wanted nothing more of him, though she might be carrying his child. But his very appearance seemed to sicken her. Her face was fuller, and despite the thicker gown and her heavy cloak, he could see a slight difference in her body, suggesting that Miss Sarah was right in her assessment. More than the obvious evidence, that which confirmed the truth was the look in Terrell's eyes and her responses to him. She was, without doubt, with child. And she knew it.

Charles realized he had not moved, for Wang cleared his throat.

"You have a caller."

Charles was in no mood to see anyone. "Who is it?"

"Mr. Washington."

"Washington? I know no Washington." He stopped. "Ah. Mr. Fields."

With a sigh through his nose, he made his way to the parlor where Mr. Fields stood. Wang closed the doors behind him.

"Mr. Fields," Charles greeted. "This is unexpected."

"Your pardon. I tried the Red Chrysanthemum, but they were unsure when you would return."

Perhaps never, Charles could not resist thinking. He had the worst fortune there. His mother was right. He needed to turn his attentions to the women of proper society. Feeding his wicked carnal penchants had only led to disaster, first with Miss Greta, then with Miss Terrell.

"I fear my time is limited, but how is Mr. Nicholas?"

"In truth, he remains devastated. I have never before seen a man in the grips of such melancholy."

"I am sorry to hear it."

Mr. Fields nodded. "But I came to report on your business, sir."

Collecting his manners, Charles bid Mr. Fields take a seat and offered him a drink.

"I will sit but forego the Madeira."

"Then I will help myself." Charles went to the sideboard and considered which of the drinks would burn the most. He reached for a small ceramic bottle containing *baiju*, a strong distilled spirit. When Charles had first partaken of the clear liquid Wang had offered to him, tears had poured from his eyes. Over his time in the Orient, he had built a small tolerance for the beverage.

"What have you discovered?" Charles asked, his voice slightly hoarse after throwing down a small cup of the *baiju*.

Mr. Fields eyed the drink and the ceramic cup curiously but answered, "Am I free to speak here?"

"Yes." Charles poured himself another cup.

"You may recall in my last appraisal that I was able to review the records of the Justice of the Peace and that Lady Arthur's maid, Miss Adams, had first attested that she saw Sir Arthur push his wife down the stairs, but under interrogation, became uncertain. It was only clear, for even Sir Arthur acknowledged, that he and his wife had quarreled."

Charles grimaced after swallowing the second cup. "Yes, I recall."

"I was able to find Miss Adams and inquired after the incident. Her fondness for her mistress is still evident, and she spoke to me without reservation. She recalls the incident as she had first testified, that Sir Arthur was angry at his wife and pushed her down the stairs. She said it was not the first and only time Sir Arthur had put a hand to his wife in a rough manner."

"And why did she, then, change her account?"

"She said she was much intimidated by the men asking her questions, especially the man who was Sir Arthur's counsel. And Sir Arthur himself. The counsel warned her that she might never again find employment if she intended to accuse a man as highly regarded as Sir Arthur. She said she feared she would be thrown in gaol for perjury, even if what she said was the truth, for she was but a lowly servant girl."

Charles sat down with his third cup of the brutal

beverage. "And do you believe her?"

"She seemed to me without artifice. But what convinces me of her truth is the corroboration I received from the housekeeper, Mrs. Franklin."

"The housekeeper? I thought it was the word of Miss Adams versus the word of Sir Arthur. Clearly, the word of an MP wins over that of a maid."

"Yes, well, Mrs. Franklin was not as eager to speak with me as Miss Adams. I was able to offer her a satisfactory bribe—she said her son had a poor habit of gambling. Once she started talking, however, it seemed she was relieved to reveal that which she had locked away for years. You see, she happened to be standing beneath the stairs when the quarrel started and heard every word. She said she dared not move for she had had no wish for her presence to discomfit Sir Arthur or her ladyship. She had been with the family for thirty years and had witnessed Sir Arthur's temper, according to her, a hundred times. And as she discerned him to be in a fair rage, she wanted to call no attention to herself."

"'I remember the quarrel as if it were printed upon my mind by fire,' the housekeeper told me. Sir Arthur had said to his wife that he would be damned if he had to raise another man's bastard as his own. Lady Arthur had laughed and said he had no choice, that the bastard would inherit everything. Sir Arthur responded that he would see to it that the bastard was never born. Mrs. Franklin then heard a scuffle, and Lady Arthur begging Sir Arthur to unhand her, pleading with him not to harm her or the unborn babe. Sir Arthur replied that she should have considered the matter before becoming another man's whore."

Charles felt sick, though he could not tell if his revulsion was from the *baiju* or Mr. Fields' account. "Did she see what happened?"

"She said she did glance up then. It looked to her that Sir Arthur pushed his wife. She said she was convinced of his intent when, later, the doctor informed him that the babe would survive. She said the look of disappointment upon Sir Arthur's face sent chills through her. She did not alert anyone to the fact that she had witnessed the scene but quietly left her employment. She recalled that Sir Arthur, before he married, had once taken a mistress and broken the poor girl's arm—because he suspected she had been unfaithful."

Charles was staring into the space. He could readily envision Sir Arthur pushing his wife to her death—or that of the child.

"Do you have reason to doubt the word of the housekeeper?" he asked.

"The woman shed many tears with me. I think she has carried much guilt over the matter. She said she would testify in a court of law if needed. She said Lady Arthur was a kind and gentle woman, though perhaps too young when she had wed Sir Arthur."

"Where is the child now?"

"He resides with Lady Arthur's family. Sir Arthur has disowned the boy but agreed to entail the income from certain properties for his care. Lady Arthur's family is satisfied with the arrangement."

"The mistress he had. The housekeeper witnessed the breaking of her arm?"

"She heard from behind closed doors. She heard

them quarrel, and then the young woman screamed. I found the woman—she is a Covent Garden lady—and, for the price of a shilling, she let me know quite bitterly how Sir Arthur had not only broken her arm, he had ruined her life. The man did not even send for a doctor, she said, but she was too terrified of him to ask for anything."

"Mother of God," Charles whispered. The man was a monster. A murderer. For certain Terrell was in jeopardy while in his company.

Rising from his chair, Charles started pacing.

Mr. Fields watched him move to and fro across the rug. "Do you wish for me to provide a written report of my findings?"

Charles stopped and gazed at the floor in thought as he replied, "Yes, but I will have you submit the details of your findings to Lady Arthur's family. They may wish to seek redress on her behalf. You have done an extraordinary job, Mr. Fields. I commend you. Do you require payment now?"

"I will send a receipt for my services."

"You have been worth every penny."

"Thank you, sir. May I ask what you intend with the information?"

"At present, nothing, though the man ought to be brought to justice. He should be held to account by his peers, though his soul will be tried by God."

When Mr. Fields was gone, Charles sank into the nearest chair and rested his head in his hands. He had suspected Sir Arthur capable of violence, but to hear it confirmed was distressing.

For certain Terrell could not remain with Sir Arthur. She was capable of daring and its cousin, recklessness. It would likely not take her long to upset Sir Arthur, and he was not a man to be crossed.

Chapter 43

Sir Arthur looked across the table at her plate and frowned.

"The supper does not agree with you?" he asked Terrell.

"It is delectable!" she responded. "I've not had pheasant more pleasingly prepared."

"But you have partaken little of it."

"I think I have eaten more here than I did in twice my time at the Red Chrysanthemum, but a woman must mind her figure."

Satisfied with her answer, he finished his meal with a glass of wine.

"I understand you had a visitor today."

She kept her gaze upon her plate of food while her heartbeat quickened. "I would hardly call it a visit."

"Who was he?"

She looked up to meet his stare. "A man I had once taken to bed. He fancies I owe him money."

"He had the appearance of a gentleman."

"At a cost he can ill afford. He is deeply in debt." Her heart palpitated at the lies, and she prayed she showed no outward appearance of apprehension.

"How did he know where to find you?"

"I know not. I thought for certain he would not discover me at the Red Chrysanthemum, but he did. You might have crossed his path and not known it."

"Did you pay him?"

"I did not."

"Then he will likely come again till you do. How much does he think you owe him?"

"Twenty guineas."

Sir Arthur sniffed at what was to him a paltry amount. "Why does he make this claim of you?"

"Because we shared quarters. The residence was his, but when we parted ways, he said I owed him rent."

The falsehood slid off her tongue easily enough, and she hoped it would fit neatly in with the rest of her tale.

"We must put an end to this man's visits."

"I should like nothing more, but I will not pay him."

"I could advance you twenty guineas."

"No, Sir Arthur, I will not trespass upon your generosity for a false claim."

Sir Arthur thought for a moment before saying, "I will pen this gentleman a letter. If he should call again, you will give him the letter, which will direct him to me. After meeting with me, I doubt he will ever trouble you again."

"You are too kind!" she extolled and, rising from her chair, crossed to his end of the table. She gave him a small, allusive smile. "I think my appetite tilts toward a different sort of meal, and I would feast upon it long into the night."

She sat upon his lap.

"I cannot humor you tonight," he said, "for I am to meet with friends at White's."

"But you could return when you are done?"

"That is unlikely. I foresee a late night at the club."

It was as she had hoped. She knew Sir Arthur could spend hours at the card tables, and it had been some time since he had enjoyed White's into the late hours.

"Then I must take my fill now," she said, hiking up her skirts and straddling him in the chair. She clasped her hands at the back of his neck and pulled herself to his crotch.

"Do not soil my clothes," he warned.

She dropped a hand to his fall and began undoing the buttons. "Then spend quick, Sir Arthur, before I am too wet."

She saw it was what he wanted to hear. When she had freed his cock, she angled her hips and guided his shaft into her slit. Once he had spent, he would not tarry. She would have the rest of the evening to herself and pretend to go to sleep early. Once the servants had gone to bed, she would sneak out the balcony of her bedchamber. By great fortune, an oak tree stood within reach. She could climb down and make her way back to the midwife for the elixir. If she had the courage, she would take it tonight, and hoped it might even help her to sleep.

The sight of Gallant had woken memories in her body. She had not dared to recall her final night with him for fear she could not quell the demons if they stirred, though she had not always been able to stifle the pining, the longing for his touch, the heights he would take her to. That last night, when he had devastated her body, tormented it with rapture and the most exquisite pain—she would never know its equal. She marveled that she had survived, though there was no finer way to perish than in such elation.

She ground her cunnie at Sir Arthur, wishing he would pound her harder that the discomfort might banish all thoughts of Charles from her mind.

Sir Arthur did not require long. He rarely did. He was done before she felt even the first spark of desire. He sank into his chair, his eyes closed as he recovered. His softened cock slid easily out of her. She set her legs back down and softly kissed him about the jaw.

"Are you certain you have no wish to return?" she asked before tugging his lower lip between her teeth.

He looked down at her. "Patience, my wench. I will return on the morrow."

"May I satisfy myself then?"

"As often as you wish."

The clock above the mantle chimed the hour, and he shifted to indicate that she should take herself off his lap. She did so and watched as he replaced his fall and straightened his clothes.

After Sir Arthur had departed, she told the servants she wished to retire early. They were accustomed to her early bedtimes. Peggy assisted her into her night rail. Terrell waited several hours till it seemed the servants had gone to bed as well. Then she quietly took off the night rail and dressed herself. She kept the layers of petticoats to a minimum, for it would be no easy task to climb down the tree in them, though more would have kept her warmer in the cold night. She shoved her hair into a cap, donned a spencer, and put on half-boots.

Once outside on the balcony in the cold, she reconsidered her plan to venture out into the night.

She missed the balmy nights of Barbados. The weather was the only thing she longed for from her past. But despite the hour and the cold, she wanted to be done with Charles. Memories of him still pained her, and the fewer memories she had, the better.

Resolved, she climbed onto the railing and reached for the tree branch. The moon, near full and unobstructed by the rainclouds looming in the distance, lit her way. Nonetheless, she nearly slipped on the first footing, and she worried that she might harm the nascent life inside of her. Then she reminded herself that the whole purpose of her visit to the midwife was to terminate her current condition. She moved more carefully and gently lowered herself to another branch below. From there, she managed to drop to the ground below. She scurried at a quick pace to keep herself warm.

An hour later, she had a bottle of the elixir in hand. The midwife said the ingredients consisted of tansy oil, pennyroyal, rue, ergot, and other fairly harmless-sounding substances. Terrell was to take it daily for a sennight. The midwife had said five days would do, but if she wished to be certain of the desired outcome, then she would want the additional days. The woman had also warned her of the foul taste and that she might experience fevers and cramping. These afflictions were to be expected.

She was fortunate that her excursion was without event. Her only mishap was in climbing up the tree outside her bedchambers, for rain had begun to fall minutes before her return, the clouds shrouding the night. A branch she had gasped to pull herself up snapped. She struck and scraped her knee against the tree, but she worried more that the sound of the breaking branch might stir the servants. She remained still and quiet where she was. When only the patter of the rain greeted her, she proceeded. She felt her way back to the balcony and into her bedchamber.

Carefully, she opened the doors. Once inside, she fumbled about for a candle. She removed her wet spencer and took out the elixir. Her hands trembled, and it was not all from the cold of the rain, but she braced herself. There was no sense in wasting time. She was to take four spoonfuls, but she had not thought to procure a spoon. Perhaps she could simply estimate four spoonfuls and pour the elixir into a cup.

She looked about the room for a cup and considered lighting another candle when a breeze blew across her neck. She must not have closed the balcony door securely.

Before she could turn around to check, she felt an arm about her and points of pressure at her neck. She gasped. The elixir slid from her hand. She tried to struggle free from her assailant, but she could not even muster a scream. Moments later, she felt herself sinking into complete blackness.

Chapter 44

Charles stood beneath the balcony, waiting in the cold rain. If he were seen, he would be hard-pressed to explain himself. The hour being exceedingly late, however, it was unlikely anyone would discover him.

They had wondered at the light emanating from the room. Charles knew Sir Arthur did not often ride, but they had seen no signs of the man's carriage. They had agreed that if Sir Arthur were present, they would abort their plans. Wang had ascended the tree and looked into the balcony. When Charles no longer saw Wang, he assumed his valet had gained access into Terrell's bedchamber. The Chinaman moved with the silence and agility of a feline predator stalking its prey. How he might then pick the lock of a door or window, Charles knew not, but if it could be done, Wang would prevail.

A shadow appeared on the balcony. It was Wang with Terrell prone in his arms. Charles signaled, and Wang lowered her over the railing of the balcony. After catching her, Charles hoisted her over his shoulder and went to stand beneath the balcony, away from the rain. With one hand, he untied his cloak and threw it over Terrell. Instead of descending down the tree, Wang had leaped from the balcony, landing softly on the ground below. Together, they made their way around the corner, where they had left Charles' curricle.

Wang climbed into the vehicle, and Charles handed Terrell to him. Charles then lit a lamp, alighted, and took the reins. Because of the rains, he did not urge the horses into a faster gait. By the time they had arrived back at his townhome, the rain had soaked through his clothes. He took Terrell from Wang, who grabbed the lantern and opened the doors. Charles carried her upstairs to his bedchamber and laid her upon a sofa.

Wang stoked the fire, which had greatly diminished in their time away. Charles prepared two warming pans, placed them between the bed linen, then, with Wang's help, stripped the damp clothing from Terrell. She emitted a soft moan but did not waken. Charles glimpsed a greater suppleness about her belly and thighs as well as an abrasion upon her knee. His first thought was of Sir Arthur. Had he harmed her already? He looked over her body for other signs of injury but found none. Wang pulled back the warmed bedclothes, and Charles laid her naked body upon the bed.

With Terrell settled, Charles addressed his own state. Wang assisted him from his sodden garments. Charles slipped into a banyan and went to the sideboard to pour himself and Wang cups of *baiju*. He downed his cup and started coughing. Wang drank his as easily as consuming honeyed milk.

"I will see to the curricle," Wang said, setting his cup down and heading for the door.

"Wang," Charles called when his coughing had subsided. "*Xie xie*. I could not have done it without your able assistance."

Wang made no reply. He merely glanced toward Terrell.

"When you entered her room, was she asleep?" Charles asked.

"No," Wang answered, and took from his coat pocket a small glass bottle, which he handed to Charles. "She had this."

Charles examined the contents but could not guess what they were. The bottle was still full. He removed the cork and caught a harsh scent. He handed Wang the bottle for inspection. Wang took a sniff, stopped the bottle with his finger before turning it over, then tasted the liquid from his finger. He grimaced then shook his head. He could not name the tonic, but Charles had his suspicions.

After Wang left, Charles poured himself a brandy, a much easier drink, and sat down in a chair before the fire. From where he sat, he could look to the bed where Terrell lay in warmth and comfort. Here, with him, she was safe. He could not protect her otherwise, either from Sir Arthur or what she might do to herself. He hoped he had taken her in time.

Recalling the scrape upon her knee, he went back to the sideboard and poured a little of the brandy onto a small towel. Lifting the bedclothes over her legs, he pressed the towel to her knees, then bound it with his handkerchief. He gazed upon her legs, tempted to run his hand over their smoothness, before replacing the bedclothes. The sight of her body warmed his blood more than the brandy. The selfish prurient part of him wanted to shed his banyan, climb into bed beside her, touch her, fondle her awake, cover her body with his, and sink into her glorious eternity.

But he took himself back into his chair to finish his brandy.

How had it come to this? If she had been Sir Arthur's wife, he would be guilty of kidnapping, though he would not put it past Sir Arthur to charge him with a crime if he knew. Charles looked over at Terrell. She had never voiced any aspirations of marrying Sir Arthur. Such a thing would be unimaginable. No gentleman of his standing would sink so low as to marry a blackamoor, not when he had his choice of women to pluck. If only the world could know the man's crimes, his villainy. If only Terrell knew.

She would know now.

In their last encounter, she had dismissed him, wanted nothing of him or his words. It seemed the mere sight of him sickened her. How quickly she had turned her coat and changed her colors! It had not been so long ago that he had possessed her most intimately, had thrilled her body and commanded her willing submission. And she had wanted all this, making every effort to seduce him. In the end, he had given her all that she had wanted and more.

Perhaps he was not so different. He had not waited long after Greta had left him before he had succumbed to Terrell. He could attempt to place the blame squarely upon her, but that would suppose he had no will of his own, had no command of himself. At times, when in her presence, it felt as if he did not. His body reacted to hers as consistently as it would to drink or opiates.

He let his head fall back against the chair and closed his eyes. This time she would listen to reason when he disclosed the findings of Mr. Fields to her. She would, surely, then not return to Sir Arthur.

Chapter 45

Terrell nestled into the bedding and wrapped her arms about the pillow beneath her head. The casing felt soft and silken. Finer than the one she owned—or, rather, Sir Arthur owned. Blinking, she pried her eyes open to see the room filled with the grey light of early morning. Her eyes flew wide as she realized it was not her room. Of a sudden, she realized she wore nothing—not a shred of clothing, though there was something about her knee. She thought back to last night. Had she somehow traveled to Sir Arthur's residence? No, that could not be. She remembered...venturing into the night to see the midwife, returning to her bedchambers with the elixir, and...

With a jolt, she sat up. To her astonishment, she beheld Charles, half dressed in shirt and dark nankin blue trousers, sitting in a chair facing the foot of the bed. Aware of her nakedness, she pulled the bedclothes to her. How had she come here? Had he come to visit her, ply her with wine and she yielded to his charms? No, he would not deliberately intoxicate her. She recalled the vise about her before she lost consciousness. Had he brought her here? Was she dreaming all this?

"You were not harmed," Charles assured her.

Not harmed? What had happened? She glanced at

the mahogany tester bed upon which she sat and about the room, furnished in the way of a gentleman.

"Are these your chambers?" she asked. "Did you bring me here?"

"I had assistance, but yes. This is my bedchamber."

She gathered his assistance comprised of an Oriental valet. But why did they remove her from her residence without her knowledge or consent? Was he mad? Inebriated? Whatever the reason, she had to return to her own domicile. Though Sir Arthur did not usually arrive till supper, and mostly later, the servants would soon find her missing.

"Where are my clothes?" she demanded. She noticed he had faint half-circles beneath his eyes, but they did nothing to diminish his handsomeness. She tried to ignore how delicious he appeared in minimal garments, his golden hair slightly tousled. If she had spent the night in his bed, had he slept alongside her or in the chair?

"Drying. I shall have a breakfast prepared for you."

She stopped him in his tracks. "No! I know not why I am here, but I will take my leave."

She looked about the room but did not see her garments. Now that she was fully awake, her perturbation grew.

"I will have my clothes, if you please," she huffed.

He stood, crossing his arms over his chest. His stance troubled her, as did the hard set of his jaw. She felt as if she were about to be punished, only there was not the sparkle of delight or playfulness in his eyes.

"You do not require them at the moment."

What the bloody hell did he mean by such a

response? Her fingers curled tightly into the bedclothes that she held to her bosom.

"I will have my gown, sir, for I wish to depart at once," she told him between agitated breaths.

He narrowed his eyes. "Why such haste? Does Sir Arthur expect you so early in the morning?"

"He will not be pleased to discover me missing."

"Do you fear his displeasure?"

She made no dispute, for he would know her lie. Instead, she replied, "I will not incur it."

"That is wise, for you might acquire a broken arm if you did."

His statement perplexed her, but she did not want to delay her departure with questions. She looked about the room once more for where her garments might have been placed and spotted her bottle on the sideboard. Her breath stopped.

He followed her gaze. "Do you realize that causing a deliberate miscarriage, whether before or after quickening, is punishable by death or transportation for life?"

Her lower lip trembled. "Nothing can be proved."

"Where did you obtain that concoction?"

"From a midwife."

"And you trust this woman would not testify against you? You think the courts would trust the word of a blackamoor—provided you are still alive to stand trial?"

"Madame Devereux herself once recommended this midwife to Mary, a former member."

"And how did Mary fare?"

"I know not. She did not return to the Red Chrysanthemum. Madame insisted upon the use of condoms thereafter."

He pressed his lips into a grim line and his arms remained crossed. "Taking any substance designed to induce a miscarriage is dangerous to the health of the mother and as likely to cause her own death."

She scowled at him. "What choice have I? You think Sir Arthur would permit me to raise a bastard that may not be his?"

Charles raised his brows. "I thought it for certain his."

She faltered, but rallied her anger to her defense. "I will have my clothes!"

Wrapping a sheet about herself, she clambered out of bed and searched the room for her clothes.

"Wang took your garments," he informed her.

She wanted to scream—and wring his neck. "Then ring for him!"

"Not till you have promised me that you will do yourself no harm."

Her breaths came short and shallow. She was seething. Through gritted teeth, she muttered, "I promise."

He rolled his eyes and gave an exasperated sigh. "Is the promise of a blackamoor so lightly given?"

She could no longer contain a cry of rage. If he were nearer, she would have launched herself at him, with good desire to pommel the man.

"If you will not give me my gown, I will wear what clothing I can!" She threw open the door to an armoire and began rummaging through the contents. A simple shirt and trousers would do.

He crossed the room and grabbed her arm. "Terrell! Terrell! I have no wish to see you harmed."

She turned to him, shaking from infuriation. How dare he attempt to advise her? But of course he dared. Because his kind was superior to hers. "You wish to see no harm done to me but would impose upon me a bastard? A bastard I can ill support, for I doubt Sir Arthur would keep me!"

"Terrell, I would support the child. And you."

Stunned, she stared at him. Her voice came near a whisper. "You know not that it is yours."

"It matters not. It may well be Sir Arthur's." He frowned. "Or that of another. But it may also be mine, and I would bear the consequences of my actions."

Lowering her gaze, she felt the tremors of a different emotion. Did he mean for her to be his mistress or that he simply would provide her funds? Or did it matter? With either, if word got out that he had a blackamoor for a mistress or might have fathered a black bastard, he must surely be ruined. This was England. It was not Barbados. And he could not afford to provide for her as well as she might do for herself with the likes of Sir Arthur or Sir Fairchild or Mr. Worthington.

She shook her head. She could not allow him to be so burdened, especially if the child was not his. "You may speak liberally now, but you will feel differently when you see that the child is not yours."

"I vow I will not. I would support the child, even if it were Sir Arthur's, so that I might support you."

Her heart ached at his words, the pain a chasm ready to swallow her whole. She yanked her arm from his grasp and turned back to the armoire. She pulled from it a coat. "I do not care to have your charity, Mr. Gallant."

He slammed the door of the armoire shut in front of her. Undaunted, she stalked over to a dresser, opened a drawer and found a shirt. "I told you that I have no wish to see you again. That you would take me forcibly from my home—if Sir Arthur knew, he would see you thrown in gaol, for I do not doubt but he can find a means to do anything he wishes. There is no man more influential, more powerful, more formidable—"

He grabbed both her arms. "Nor more dangerous! He is far more treacherous than you know!"

The linen had slid from her, exposing her body. Trapped in his gaze, she could not tear away. She felt herself pulled into the depths of eyes, and they would undo her. She wanted to tell him to unhand her but could not form the words. His gaze upon her body, calling to something deep in her womanhood, lit a fire.

His mouth descended upon hers as he crushed her to him. There would be no struggle, no opposition. She had craved his caress for too long. The touch of his lips had instantly obliterated her defenses, and she melted into his brusque embrace. His dominant hand clasped the back of her head, holding her still so that the voraciousness of his kiss would not bend her head backwards. She twisted her fingers into his shirt, holding on to him with desperation and anguish.

How she hated this man.

She hated that he had taken her to his residence without her knowing—for which she most certainly would earn Sir Arthur's ire—hated that his kindness should cause her so much pain, and hated that she could and would so easily succumb to him. She devoured his mouth with as much hunger as he did hers. Her nipples dug uncomfortably into his chest, but she could not press enough of her body to his. She relished his hardness pushing against her belly and would not be satisfied till their bodies had melded into one.

Impatiently, she shoved her hips at him, lust screaming inside of her. He grabbed the back of her thigh and hoisted her up. She wrapped her legs about him and braced her arms upon his shoulders. Their lips, still joined, did not stop for a second. To be so close to him, to feel his desire matching hers, brought her to a frenzy.

She ground her crotch at him. He responded by carrying her back to the bed. He sat her on the edge, then leaned her down. She clung to him, not wanting to part from him in the slightest. His hands caressed her ribs, her thighs, a breast. She arched herself into him. He tightened his grasp on the orb, kneading the flesh, rolling and tugging its peak. The fondling shot shivers to her crotch, stoking the need between her legs. She tried reaching for his fall. When she could not access it, she bit down on his lips. He reeled back in surprise. Now she had space to attempt the buttons on his trousers. Her hands, however, shook. She managed only two buttons. He resumed kissing her, suckling and licking her neck. But the fire within her demanded one thing. In exasperation, she yanked at the fabric, ripping the buttons, to reveal the piece she yearned for most. She grabbed his cock and guided its ready hardness to her cunnie. He needed no further encouragement and sank himself into her.

Her head fell back at the exquisiteness, the rapture. He fisted a hand through her hair and kissed her throat as he pushed himself farther into her. She cried out in relief, in joy. His cock, perfect in size and shape, was meant for her cunnie, and she embraced his shaft with such fervor that he moaned and had to stop and brace himself. He pressed her back down into the bed, trapping her beneath his upper body. Her hands roamed his back, grasped his neck, and pulled his hair. Lust had reduced her to an animal state.

She moved her hips to induce more action. He grabbed her legs and pulled her arse over the edge of the bed so that he could penetrate deeper. She clutched at him till he could no longer resist and began a fierce thrusting. She did not care how hard he pounded—the harder the better. She did not even care if she should spend. She wanted only to claim him and be claimed.

The intensity of his motions reminded her of how angrily and relentlessly he had driven himself into her their last night at the Red Chrysanthemum. But she adored his savagery as much as his tenderness. With his cock, he touched the deepest part of her, filling her to the brim, her softness made to be plumbed by his rigid staff. He drove himself into her with large, strong motions, urging the tidal wave to build inside of her. She neared its crest with surprising swiftness and dug her fingers into his back, wanting and fearing the magnificence threatening to crush her.

She cried and groaned, clawing him as her body scaled the wave. He accelerated into a rapid thrusting. Seconds later, pleasure, pure and full, rolled through her body. She knew neither time nor place, nor heaven from earth. She could only wail and shudder as her body lurched against his. With a roar, he slammed into her, and she felt an increase of heat and wetness inside her. All other sensation had faded, save the pulsing of her cunnie echoing to her toes.

Chapter 46

There was no place more marvelous than the heat of her cunnie. All her qualities—her strength, her roguishness, her passions—wrapped his cock, infusing him with her essence and enlarging his life. He had poured his emotions, penned and bolted for over a fortnight now, into his thrusting. With any other woman, the pommeling would be too much. With Terrell, he could unleash his full vigor.

Charles started, remembering that she was not the same. Leastways, not in the same condition. He raised himself off her body. She lay upon the bed, relaxed, but, like him, still breathing heavily, her legs resting about him.

"Do you think I harmed the..." he began, wishing he had restrained himself.

Her eyes widened and, shoving him away, she scrambled off the bed. She went to the clothes she had pulled from the armoire and dresser and stepped into the trousers. They were ridiculously large upon her, and she had to hold them up with one hand.

"Terrell..."

He could see her frantic thoughts: how was she going to explain her absence? No doubt her mind was bouncing from one possible alibi to another. But what could be the reason for her returning in men's garments?

She whirled about to face him. "My gown. Give me my gown."

"You are not returning to Sir Arthur," he replied, vexed that he had not even had the chance to hold her. Why was she in such a damned hurry to return to that man?

Anger flashed in her eyes. "You fancy yourself my guardian? Or my owner?"

He protested, "I would never presume to think you were my property. My submissive, yes, but not my chattel."

"Then I bid you stay away from me."

Stay away? Minutes before, she had launched herself at his cock. Now she wanted nothing to do with him again?

"Not till you have disavowed Sir Arthur. He is a menace."

"Who is the menace? He is not the one taking women from their bedchambers in the middle of the night!"

She threw on one of his coats and made to stalk out of the room. He grabbed her arm once more.

"Sir Arthur killed a woman."

That statement stayed her. Finally. He took a calming breath.

"He murdered his wife," he explained.

She looked down at his grip. "Then how is it he walks a free man? Has he even been tried?"

"There were two witnesses to the crime. One recanted her account under duress. The other, a housekeeper who had been with the family three decades, never came forth."

She stared at him. "How do you know all this?"

"I hired a former Bow Street Runner. He managed to find and speak with the two witnesses. The housekeeper has declared she will unburden her guilt and speak the truth. She will testify against Sir Arthur if need be. Sir Arthur believed his wife an adulteress, and she was, according to her own maid. The child Lady Arthur carried was not her husband's. Sir Arthur meant to kill the unborn child and pushed his wife down the stairs."

Terrell was quiet, then said, "I am not his wife. I am but his lowly black mistress."

"It matters not. The housekeeper said he once broke the arm of one of his mistresses."

"You forget I have known men capable of much worse."

He stared at her, taken aback at her swift dismissal. "Surely, you have seen his temper. He is a violent man."

"Worry not of me. I know how to handle such men."

His grip tightened on her arm. She would yet choose Sir Arthur over him? She could not be in love with the man—though he now had his doubts—but could she be so blindly enamored with his wealth?

"I have seen the apartment he provides you. I could afford you such a dwelling and pin money for clothes and baubles."

She sighed with impatience. "Not as well as Sir Arthur! Now, you will kindly return me my clothes or I shall make such a fuss that all your servants will come running."

There was no convincing her. It was true that he

could not offer her half what Sir Arthur could. He did know that Sir Arthur could not fuck her as well as he, or she would not have succumbed so willingly, would not have shuddered in his arms with such ecstasy. But still she would go to that monster.

Over his dead body.

Charles dragged her over to the bed. She resisted and tried to free herself from his grasp.

"Unhand me!" she cried.

Unlike their last scuffle, she resorted to more extreme measures faster. She sank her teeth into his hand. He roared but refused to release her. At the bed, he reached below and fished out a pair of shackles he had procured from the Red Chrysanthemum. She kicked at him. He released her suddenly, and she fell to the floor on her rump. Before she could scramble to her feet, he secured one shackle to her ankle and closed the padlock. She tried to crawl away, but he locked the other end to the foot of the bed.

"This is outrageous!" she exclaimed, then changed her tactic. "If you wish no harm to come to me, then you will set me free. If Sir Arthur discovers I am missing, he will think the worst of me. He will suspect—you yourself have stated the possible consequences. He could well give me a beating."

"And that is the sort of man you prefer?" he returned, flabbergasted.

She yanked the chain of the shackles. "Damn you!"

He wrapped a banyan about himself. "Curse and scream all you like. I mean to instruct the servants not to enter my bedchamber. Only Wang will be excepted."

Recalling the elixir, he retrieved it and stuffed it into his pocket. He slammed the door behind him and indulged his own oaths. After spending, he had felt at peace, ready to cradle her safely in his arms, but she had riled him all over.

She now knew the truth of Sir Arthur and *still* she would go to him. To a murderer. Had the harshness of her life in Barbados rendered her impervious to the threat of peril? Charles was at a loss. He could not keep her prisoner in his bedchamber forever, but how else could he keep her away from Sir Arthur?

Chapter 47

When tugging at the lock and yanking at the chain yielded nothing, Terrell let loose a string of oaths. She looked at the mahogany bed. It was too heavy, of course, to lift. She looked about herself for an item to pick the lock, but nothing but the bed itself was within reach, and all she had on herself was his coat and his trousers.

Assessing the morning brightness, she believed her servants to be awake. They did not often disturb her, but what if Peggy chose today to look in on her? She could say that she had woken early and did not wish to wake any of the servants, but that would only serve if she returned at a credible hour. What if she did not appear till noon or later?

With a frustrated cry, she tried the shackles once more. The damn bleeder. He would ruin everything, especially his chances to win the burgess. If he knew what was at stake for him...but he would not permit her to return to Sir Arthur, especially now that he believed the man to be a murderer. She ought pleased that Charles cared enough for her to intervene, but she had not asked to be his concern! She would not dwell on his motivations, however generous or tender, for if she did, she might fall into tears.

Instead, she considered his faults. His arrogance.

His meddling and imposition. His self-righteousness. Did he think her incapable of fending for herself? Did he think her a child? If he truly cared for her, he would let her be, free to be the mistress of one of the wealthiest men in England. But he wanted her for himself. Selfish, selfish man! And he would compel her to bear a child she did not want—rather, that she could not have. She would have loved to have a child of her own. How cruel the fates could be! She had conceived—perhaps with Charles—but she could not keep the babe. Charles might afford her and her bastard a comfortable living, but for how long? And what if Charles should tire of her one day or feel compelled to cast her aside in favor of his future wife?

But her attempts to cast him a complete and utter scoundrel rang weak. Stirring her anger at him would not prove useful. She needed to figure out how she was going to free herself from these shackles. What could she say to Charles to gain her release? He was impervious to bribing or cajoling. She could beg, but he believed himself in the right. She could…seduce him. He was as drawn to her in the venereal way as before. She had seen and felt his ardor. She would entice him to undo the shackles. As soon as he unlocked them, she would flee.

Provided she did not yield to *her* ardor for *him*. Time had not dulled her passions. His caress upon her body was as potent as ever. The tacky moisture between her legs reminded her of where he had been, how he had unleashed his seed deep inside of her.

What if she did carry his child?

She scolded herself for the worthless question.

She needed to fix upon how to escape and how to obtain her own garments.

The door opened. She thrust her hand down the trousers, which had fallen past her hips. She would pretend to pleasure herself. She had seen the gleam in his eyes whenever he watched her fondle herself.

It was not Charles but Wang who entered. The valet carried a tray with tea and breakfast. To her relief, she saw her garments draped over his arm. That she was wearing Charles' coat and trousers and was shackled to the bed did not seem to surprise him in the least. He set the tray down on a table, placed her articles over the back of a chair, and poured a cup of tea.

Perhaps she could seduce the Chinaman into setting her free?

"Where is Master Gallant?" she asked. "I had forgotten to mention something important to him."

Wang set the tray with the tea and food upon the floor beside her. She tried to ignore how inviting the toast, eggs, and ham smelled. Her hand still in the trousers, she stroked herself and moaned low and soft.

He appeared not to notice and went to the dresser and armoire, removing a coat, waistcoat and other articles of dress.

"It is of some urgency," she added.

"He has business to attend and wishes to depart forthwith," Wang replied. "I will relay your message."

If Charles was to be gone for some time, her only hope was the valet.

"I need a fuck," she said.

In reaching for the boots, he dropped half the

items he held. He retrieved them and his composure.

"You will tell him?" she asked. "In those very words. And if he cannot attend me, I hope he will grant you permission to do so."

He said nothing and, taking the clothing with him, departed. Terrell looked at the food. She might as well partake of some sustenance while she waited. To her surprise, her appetite had returned with a vengeance. She ate heartily of everything on the tray. Not a crumb was spared. When Wang returned, she nearly asked him for more.

"What did Master Gallant say?" she asked, situating herself so that the coat front parted to reveal a breast.

Wang picked up her tray. "He warned me against your wiles."

She frowned. Was that all?

"And said he would oblige your need when he returns," Wang finished and retrieved her clothes for her.

"Does he fear to come and tell me himself?" she huffed, receiving her garments.

"He prepares to leave."

"When will he return?"

"I know not."

"Did he give you leave to attend me then?"

Wang gave her a look that told her she should not attempt to seduce him.

"And I am to be shackled to this bed till then? What if I need to heed nature's call?"

He did not seem to understand.

"What if I need to piss?" she rephrased.

Comprehending, he went toward the bed, reached

beneath it, and pulled out a chamber pot for her. She groaned. This did not bode well.

"Wait," she called to him when he opened the door. She had no further tactics to employ save the truth.

He turned and waited for her to speak.

"You are devoted to Charles—to Master Gallant," she said.

He said nothing.

"You would wish to see him succeed, to see his wishes fulfilled."

Still he said nothing. She took a fortifying breath.

"As I do," she continued. "Then you will let me go. I *must* return to Sir Arthur. I must keep him in good cheer so that he will continue to support Charles in his bid for Parliament."

Wang waited for additional explication.

"I made an arrangement with Sir Arthur. I would be his mistress and forsake Charles. In exchange, Sir Arthur will give his endorsement to Charles without condition. You understand that Charles values the freedom to honor his integrity, and he cannot win the election without Sir Arthur's support. But I cannot tell Charles this—and you must not either. I think he won't let me return to Sir Arthur no matter the reason, but I *must*. I *must*."

Wang stared at the floor in thought.

"Set me free," she pleaded. "I beg of you, Wang. Sir Arthur can ruin Charles, all his hopes, his efforts—all that he has worked for will be for naught. But we, you and I, can ensure the fulfillment of his dreams. Please, Wang. Please."

She had started shaking. If she could not convince

him, she knew not what she would do. She held her breath as Wang gazed upon her. He seemed to weigh what she had said, but he showed no signs of how he might proceed.

Without word, he took his leave, closing the door behind him.

She stared at the back of the door, then crumbled to the floor, her clothes clutched to her bosom. What was she to do? What was she to do?

Chapter 48

I *need a fuck.*

Bloody hell, Charles thought to himself as he surveyed his reflection in the looking glass of his study. The damnable doxy. She knew just how to rile and rouse him. All at once. And what the hell did she mean by asking if Wang could attend her? He had allowed it once, but, by God, he wasn't about to let any other man have her again. He had been tempted to return upstairs and give her a proper admonishing. But that might lead to actions that would greatly delay what he was to do.

She had looked far too inviting wearing nothing save his coat and trousers. She could wear the rags of a scarecrow or a burlap potato sack and still be alluring. He pictured her in the latter and thought perhaps he should find himself a burlap sack. Sensations stirred about his groin, and he forced his mind to fix on the matter at hand. If Terrell would not relinquish Sir Arthur, he would see that Sir Arthur relinquished Terrell. She had endured too much in her life to end it with Sir Arthur.

It astounded Charles that she wanted the murderer. Wanted the man over *him*. Did a life of luxury truly call to her with such influence? What else of that man could possibly appeal to her? With an oath, Charles slammed his fist upon the mantle of the fireplace.

"How long will you be gone?"

Charles turned to see Wang with his hat and gloves.

"I know not," Charles replied. "I hope to find Sir Arthur at his home."

Wang blinked several times. It was a near imperceptible reaction to most, but having spent every waking hour with the man for months during his time in China, Charles took note of it. Nevertheless, he put on his hat, determined to see his plans through. "Your one task is to ensure Miss Terrell does not leave the premises."

Charles expected the man to give a curt nod of acknowledgment, as was his custom. Instead, Wang glanced at the floor.

"Do you worry that you will fall for her charms?" Charles asked, his voice stern. He had never had an adverse feeling toward the man till now.

Wang stared, and Charles imagined him to say, *It is not I whom you need worry of most.*

Reproved, Charles cleared his throat. After all, he had invited Wang into the *ménage-á-trois.*

"She cannot return to Sir Arthur," Charles said. "It astounds me that she values his wealth enough to risk her life."

"You are not her keeper."

"I bloody well should be! It would be a tragedy for her to have survived all that she has only to perish at the hands of Sir Arthur or some treacherous brew."

"She has made her choice."

"Yes," Charles acknowledged with bitterness. "I can only think that, in addition to being partial to his money, she is fond of the man as well. Love blinds us to the faults in others."

"She is determined. I do not think you can stop her."

Charles was rattled by Wang's response. The man rarely argued with him. He could not help but think Wang audacious to refute him in this matter.

"I fully intend to," Charles replied. He finished putting on his gloves and made for the door.

"At what cost?"

Though impatient to leave, Charles paused. "I see that she has cast her spell upon you."

"She is not a child."

Charles, now thoroughly vexed, turned to face Wang. Though he had wondered at her youth and suspected her years in slavery had made her seem older than she was, it was not his valet's place to take him to task. But Wang was more than a valet, and at times Charles had felt the one honored by the Oriental's service.

"You think I should allow Terrell to return to a murderer or imbibe some concoction that will bring her harm or even death, as surely as Sir Arthur would?" Charles returned hotly. "Granted, I cannot give her all that Sir Arthur can in the way of money and gowns and baubles, but I can offer her a comfortable and secure living. My God, I am even offering to see to the care of a child that may be, according to her, Sir Arthur's bastard! What more can I do? In time, I hope, she will see the wisdom of what I propose. She may, at present, fancy the trappings of a greater wealth; she may fancy Sir Arthur will not harm her; she may fancy that her affection for him will—"

"Love. It is love that compels her."

The muscle along Charles' jaw rippled. Too livid to converse further, and not wishing to curse Wang to his face, Charles turned and flung open the door.

"For you."

Charles stopped.

"She is in love, as you say," Wang said, "but not with Sir Arthur."

His anger suspended for the moment, Charles turned. How could Wang be certain?

"Have you not wondered how it came to be that this man gave you his endorsement, expecting nothing in return?" Wang inquired.

"Sir Canning knew my reservations regarding Sir Arthur. I suspect he persuaded Sir Arthur. I am clearly the better Tory candidate. Sir Arthur would wish me to prevail over Mr. Laurel, and I have a better chance than Mr. Chester."

"I have heard you say that Sir Arthur has one primary concern: to further the interests of Sir Arthur."

"It is true. He would do so above country and king, I believe. He does nothing that does not advance his own desires."

"And he is a man who derives satisfaction from his influence and position in society."

"*Much* satisfaction."

"Then why would he give you his unfettered support, even if your employer had requested it? Would you not think Sir Canning more likely to convince you to accept Sir Arthur, than Sir Arthur to acquiesce to you?"

Charles was silent as he considered Wang's statements. It was true Sir Canning had urged him, quite keenly, to seek the endorsement of Sir Arthur. In truth, Charles had been too upset over Miss Terrell to pay much attention to his fortunate support from Sir Arthur.

"What has this to do with Terrell? With love?" Charles asked.

"Sir Arthur is a man accustomed to attaining that which he desires."

Charles felt his impatience return. "Yes. And he does. Have everything. Including Terrell. Though I will see to it that he never again lays a hand on her."

"If he does not have her, you will no longer have his support. That is the arrangement they made."

"Arrangement? What arrangement?"

"One between Sir Arthur and Miss Terrell."

Charles stood stunned. Sir Arthur and Miss Terrell had agreed to some compact?

"How do you know this?" he asked.

"It is why she so desperately wishes to return to Sir Arthur, so that he will not withdraw his support of you."

"She told you this?"

"She believes it true."

"But she made no mention of any of this to me."

Wang said nothing, allowing Charles to resolve the explanations for himself.

Of course Terrell would have told him nothing, for she knew he would never have allowed it. He would not see her make such a sacrifice for him—and partly because he could not bear the thought of her in Sir Arthur's arms.

But this account made sense. It would explain why, the day after Terrell left him, Sir Arthur had come to him to make his endorsement, free and clear, known. Charles had thought Sir Arthur rather smug that day, but he had been in too much surprise, and some relief, to contemplate what lay behind the man's complacency.

Terrell, knowing how much the burgess meant to him, had given herself so that he could know success. Because she loved him. Loved him. Wang would not have made an assertion he did not deem true.

Charles shook his head at how Terrell might have ended up making the ultimate sacrifice. The fool. The wonderful and magnificent fool.

"I have betrayed her trust in telling you this," Wang said. "I think she would kill me if she knew."

"Yes, she might well try," Charles said, feeling a dark and heavy cloud had lifted from his heart. He turned back to depart.

"You go to Sir Arthur still?"

"I do," Charles answered over his shoulder, "but first I mean to stop at Doctors' Commons."

"To seek a civil lawyer?"

"No. I mean to seek the Archbishop of Canterbury. About a special license. I mean to make her an offer Sir Arthur never could."

Chapter 49

"Sir Arthur expects no callers," the butler informed him when Charles arrived at the impressive great house in Kensington.

"He will see me," Charles replied confidently.

While he waited, Charles took in the foyer, from the ornate molding and painting upon the ceiling to the grandiose chandelier. Upon the walls, painted in azurite, hung tapestries, the largest depicting Sir James Lancaster, commander of the first East India Company voyage, meeting with a maharaja.

The butler returned. "Sir Arthur will see you in his study, Mr. Gallant."

Charles followed the man to a large room filled with bookshelves and Persian carpets. All manner of ornaments—figurines, clocks, pottery, music boxes—adorned the room. Sir Arthur sat at a gilded writing table near the center of the room.

"Mr. Gallant, to what do I owe this unexpected pleasure?" Sir Arthur asked, his solemn features expressing not the slightest *pleasure*, and he had emphasized the word *unexpected* above all others. He was reviewing a letter and kept his gaze there, suggesting that, and not Charles, was his priority. "If you have come seeking supplementary support, I do not think it necessary. You are expected to have a commanding lead when the votes are cast."

Charles straightened. "I came in regards not to the election but to Miss Terrell."

Sir Arthur frowned. "What of Miss Terrell?"

"As you are my largest supporter, I owe you my candor on the matter, though you may wish to withdraw your support after you have heard what I will say."

Sir Arthur's body tightened. He said nothing.

"I mean to marry Terrell," Charles declared.

Sir Arthur did not lift his gaze, but Charles saw the area about his mouth whiten. When Sir Arthur did look up, it was to say, "Is this some absurd jest?"

"I do not engage in such pranks. It is my true and sincere intent to marry Miss Terrell."

Sir Arthur leaped to his feet. "Are you mad?"

"Perhaps."

"You mean to marry a *blackamoor*? A *Negress*?"

"I would not be the first."

"But you're a gentleman, not a sailor or a convict."

"Neither are you, but you enjoy her charms all the same."

The white expanded throughout the man's face. "But I am not so ridiculous as to marry the wench! And I could afford to bear the consequences better than you. Have you considered how such a marriage would affect your election? With how society will consider you after this? Who, in their right mind, would take you seriously?"

"I would do right by her."

"Bah!" Sir Arthur reacted with disgust. "And what makes you certain she will marry you? She is well situated as *my* mistress. As *my* mistress, she will enjoy what you could never afford."

"I can offer her my hand, which you, I dare say, would never do."

Sir Arthur narrowed his eyes. "I see what this is about. You are overcome with jealousy, Mr. Gallant. You envy all that I have, all that is mine. Since you cannot come near what I am, even if you spent the rest of your life trying, you mean to take Miss Terrell from me. Well! You do so at your own peril. Do not think for a moment that I would not support Mr. Chester if you dared trifle with me."

"That is your privilege, sir, but I remain steadfast in my commitment to Terrell."

Sir Arthur glared. His face twitched in fury. "I will not only see you fail your election, I will *bury* you. You will be fortunate to wake employed on the morrow!"

"I expected as much from a man like you."

"You, sir, are impertinent!"

"I would sooner be impertinent than be a murderer."

Sir Arthur's eyes bulged. He was too enraged to speak, so Charles continued. He leaned in.

"You may have been exculpated for any part in the death of your wife, but I wonder that you can sleep at night."

The man looked ready to reach across his writing table and throttle Charles, and Charles would not have eschewed a fight.

"You may do what you will to me," Charles said, "but you will not harm Terrell. She is mine."

Without a bow, Charles took his leave. Still in a silent rage, Sir Arthur did not move from where he stood.

Charles brushed by the butler and saw himself out. He had, in all likelihood, sounded the death knell of his career, but he was surprisingly reconciled to his fate. He might regret his swift actions in the morning, but for now, all that concerned him was convincing Terrell to marry him.

Chapter 50

Charles opened the door to his bedchamber to discover Terrell no longer had the shackle about her ankle. Instead, she was tied to his bed, one arm stretched to the left bedpost and the other to the right. Wang had told him that, in trying to escape from the shackle, she might injure herself. Because her screams had alarmed the other servants, Wang had also gagged her with handkerchiefs. One, dampened so as not dry her mouth, was stuffed into her and another tied about her head to secure the first in place. Charles imagined she must have put up a struggle, for she half-sat, half-lay upon the bed, slouched against the headboard.

Setting down the license he had obtained, Charles went to the bed and picked up her foot, which Wang had already bandaged. She kicked at him, but he peeked beneath the bandage to see the skin about her ankle was bloodied. He regretted having used the shackle. He took in the sight of her, now wearing nothing but his coat. Though fury lit her eyes, she looked absolutely delectable. His gaze traversed the valleys and swells of her body with awe. She was suppler than ever before. He even admired the darkness of her flesh.

All this, at last, was to be his.

Unable to resist her state of limited immobility, he

sought appropriate substitutes for rope. He pulled the sash from one of his robes and selected his longest neckcloth. He grabbed the unharmed ankle first and tied the sash about it. She kicked him several times with her other foot, but he welcomed what corporal pain she would give him. He tied the other end to the same bedpost that her arm was bound to. He did the same with her other leg. The bindings spread her legs, exposing her cunnie. He put his hand there, and she jerked as if his touch might burn her. He caressed her softly.

She tossed her head angrily at him. It would seem their earlier congress meant nothing to her, though he had tasted her longing and felt her passion, but he understood now her motives. And though she had put him through excruciating distress, he was now filled with gratitude. The marvelous, intrepid, and wayward African beauty.

The gag had done nothing to diminish the plumpness of her lips, and her eyes appeared especially large and bright. She spoke, but he could not understand her muffled words. He suspected that she cursed him. Unruffled, he sauntered over to the sideboard and opened a drawer. He had a few items from the Orient that he had not taken to the Red Chrysanthemum yet. After selecting a small, narrow glass tube, he went and lit a candle.

Thinking that he meant to drop hot wax upon her, she yanked at her bonds. He approached with the glass tube and candle. He slid the opening of the tube over her folds, wet with either prior moisture or new arousal, then held the tube over the candle flame. Swiftly, he moved the tube to cup her clitoris. As the air inside cooled, it contracted, creating a suction upon the bud and drawing it into the tube. She gasped. They both stared at the glass tube to see her clitoris pulled long and hard inside.

Setting aside the candle, he inserted two digits into her slit. He frigged her till she realized there was nothing she could do but submit to the pleasure he wrought upon her body. Wanting her to spend upon his cock, he retracted his fingers. Slowly, he began to undress. His coat fit tightly and was the hardest to remove. His boots were the next hardest. By the time he had gotten himself completely naked, his cock was stiff and throbbing with impatience.

Climbing onto the bed, he pulled a pillow beneath her arse and braced one arm against the headboard before sinking his cock into her. The glory of her cunnie did not diminish with wear. It was heavenly each and every time. He pulled his cock out and delved back in. She whimpered. Her eyes no longer sparkled with anger but with lust. He drew his cock as close to her clitoris as possible, knowing the area to be sensitive from the cupping, an ancient Chinese tradition intended mostly to advance the circulation of the blood to improve one's health.

Her breath quickened with his every thrust, but she remained still in her bonds. He could feel her eminent paroxysm and buried himself deep inside of her with long strokes. With a grunt, she spent with a geyser of clear liquid. He pulled out of her and slapped his cock against her flesh before pushing back in. He pounded himself into her several more times. When his cock popped out, he was met with another spray. The glass tube lost its suction and fell to the side. While pressing down on her left thigh, he rubbed his shaft along her swollen bud. Her groans quivered through the gag. He pushed in, he pulled out. Each turn was met with a stream of her wetness. It was mesmerizing. And titillating beyond belief.

She grunted, her brow furrowing, as his every thrust produced more and more of the curious fluid. Her thighs, belly, and even her bosom were fairly covered and glistened from the amorous shower. He pulled aside the coat to bare her breasts, then pumped his cock back into her cunnie. Her gag softened her wail as more of her moisture streamed over them.

Aroused out of his mind, he hammered into her at a furious pace until he founds his own release.

His heartbeat drummed in his ears with the rhythm of horse hoofs beating on the race track. All the bliss boiling in his cods and heating his loins had erupted, burst, exploded in the most extraordinary fashion. If such rapture were to render him blind, in that moment, he would not have complained.

Emerging from the sea of rhapsody, he reached over and pulled down her gag. She spit out the handkerchief and gasped the cool, free air. His gaze took in the faint blush upon her cheeks, the thickness of her lashes, the curve of her brows. The child would be as beautiful as its mother. No matter who the father might be.

She did not meet his gaze but stared into the distance. "Please let me go."

Her voice bore the faintest hint of despondency, and he realized that he had heard it the night she had left him for Sir Arthur but had been too furious to pay it much heed.

What a wretched creature he was! Had he known her reasons for leaving, he would never have treated her in the manner he had. Would never have held her against her will and attempted to devastate her with corporal pleasure. Would never have invited Wang to take her. Now he would pay the price of it and always wonder if the Chinaman was the better of the two.

"You still wish to return to Sir Arthur?" he asked. He would untie her, but he did not trust what she might do.

She looked at him, but the anger was gone. "I do. Your offer is a generous one, but I prefer Sir Arthur still. And if you do not release me and let me be on my way, I fear my disappearance will vex him. He is a mistrustful man, and for good reason. Truly, I do not wish to incur his wrath"

"Because he might hurt you."

"Yes."

"Knowing this, knowing his temper and that he would not refrain from raising a hand against one of the gentle sex, you yet prefer him?"

"He is no worse than the men of Barbados."

Charles shook his head and ran a hand through his hair. "And what of Sir Arthur compels you so much that you would risk your life to be with him?"

Her impatience returned. "His wealth. I have said it before."

"And nothing else? Only his wealth?"

She hesitated before answering, "His person. His power and influence. Men fear and respect him. And...and his abilities in the bedchamber."

Satisfied that she had made no mention of

affection or love, he cupped her breast and passed his thumb over a nipple. He would use the glass tube on this bud next. "You said you tired of me, but your body suggests otherwise."

"I am a carnal creature."

"Indeed you are."

He leaned over and took the nipple into his mouth. She let out a groan of aggravation. He swirled his tongue about her and murmured, "I could protect you from Sir Arthur."

"You could not! He is a man for whom nothing is out of reach. Even if you made me your mistress, he would come for me. He would—"

"But not if you were my wife."

"—not be stopped...what?"

"My wife. He could not take you from me then."

She turned pale—or as pale as a Negress could become. He would have thought she would receive the prospect of matrimony in a happier light. She looked absolutely petrified.

"I thought you intended me for your mistress?" she asked, her voice shaking.

"I did. But as my mistress, your child would still be born a bastard. I have resisted taking such a step because...because I had not the courage to do what is right. But I have found inspiration in *your* courage, your sacrifice."

"My sacrifice?" she cried, baffled or worried.

"You gave several reasons for why you preferred Sir Arthur, but you made no mention of love."

"Love is irrelevant!"

"I think not. Wang told me—"

She drew in a sharp breath. "What I told him was a

fabrication! In the hopes that he would set me free!"

Planting his hands in the space between her arms and legs on either side of her, he hovered above and pinned her with his stare. "Terrell. I dare you to tell me you do not love me."

She looked panic-stricken. Her bosom heaved in difficult breaths.

"Terrell, look at me." When she did not, he pressed his forehead to hers. "Terrell, I want you for my own. I'll be damned to hell if I let Sir Arthur have you."

"But—but you're mad! You'll ruin your chances for Parliament. You'll be miserable."

"I'll be more miserable without you."

She tried to shake her head. "You think so now, but you will rue your decision. It is best that I return to Sir Arthur."

"It's too late."

She met his gaze squarely this time.

"I told him we were getting married," he told her.

"You—what?!"

She strained against her bonds. He reached over and untied her legs only. Though it was fruitless to attempt slipping from the ropes, she yanked and pulled.

"You're a *fool*," she exclaimed.

"I've already procured the marriage license. It's a special license and permits the couple to wed without calling banns or marrying in the parish church. We can wed at any place and at any time."

He untied her arms, freeing her. But she did not attempt to flee.

"Do you not understand?" she cried. "You will ruin yourself. You will have no career to speak of! Sir

Arthur will make it so! I wonder that you will even be permitted into polite society?"

He caught her arms. "I know what it is I risk. It is not necessarily as dire as you would think. The nephew of Lord Mansfield had a child by a black woman. The child was raised by the Earl himself as a gentlewoman."

"But do you not wish to win election to Parliament? Do you not wish to fulfill your desires?"

"I do. And I desire you, Terrell."

He pulled her, trembling, into his embrace and kissed her brow. "I know what I do. Pray, do not demean my offer as charity but say you will take my hand and be my wife."

She groaned.

He had never seen the fierce and defiant Terrell look so vulnerable. He tilted her chin up and covered her mouth with his. Through the kiss, tender and sweet, he hoped to give evidence of his feelings for her. Cupping her face, he deepened the kiss. She grasped his hands with her own, clinging to him as if for dear life.

When at last he disengaged his lips for hers, for there was always the threat that the kiss could lead to more, he, sensing she was melancholy, tried to lighten the mood. "Hang Parliament. They can't fuck me as well as you can, eh?"

She gave a shaky laugh.

"I know 'tis the custom for brides to prepare a wedding trousseau," he said, "but I think it best that we marry without delay. The special license requires only a clergyman and two witnesses. I know a minister who was once a member of the Red

Chrysanthemum, and I mean to fetch him. You will remain here, in my chambers. Wang will attend you. I will leave you free, but I expect you to behave or Wang will secure you in ropes again. Do you understand?"

She lowered her lashes. "Yes, Master Gallant."

Her words shot straight to his cock. Suppressing the desire to launch himself at her, he rang for his valet, then poured a glass of port for her. After expending so much wetness, her body needed replenishing. He retrieved his clothes. She was quiet but helped him in his dress.

"I hope you do not doubt that we will be happy?" he asked after he had put on his shirt and trousers.

"I do not doubt that *I* could be happy as your wife," she replied. "I wonder that you will be happy as my husband?"

He sat down to pull on his boots, then pulled her onto his lap. "Terrell, I have never known a woman like you. It is true I could marry a woman of superior birth and situation, but I would find myself comparing her qualities with yours, and she would be found lacking."

She tossed her head. "I am a selfish, wanton creature. And, as you say, wayward."

He cupped her cheek. "I grant you have your selfish moments, but I have had my share as well. I adore your wantonness, and as for your waywardness, I will enjoy curbing that quality."

Her eyes gleamed, and, to his relief, she smiled. "I hope you will curb it often."

He growled and had to set her off his lap before he was tempted to undo all the garments he had put on.

Wang arrived and assisted with the rest of the clothing. Charles left instructions regarding Terrell. He was not going to take any chances till they were wed. He would not even stop to inform his parents. He regretted not telling his mother—she would be devastated—but she would surely attempt to talk him out of his intentions.

But he felt he had much to atone for with Terrell, and he would start as soon as they were man and wife.

Chapter 51

Kneeling beside the prone body of the Chinaman, Terrell confirmed he still breathed. He would likely have a terrible bump from the vase she had dropped on his head when he entered. But she had to escape. She could not let Charles marry her.

She ought to be overjoyed by his offer—a part of her heart did swell at the thought that he would go to such lengths to possess her—but she felt mostly wretched. If she had not seduced him, this fine, upstanding gentleman would undoubtedly fulfill the promise of an illustrious career.

But she had ruined it all for him. The fool had even gone and told Sir Arthur! She could imagine precisely how the man would have reacted. It was unlikely now, even if she returned to Sir Arthur, that she would have a chance of saving his support for Charles. What tale could she weave that he would believe? He would believe Charles over her. If she protested that she wanted none of Charles and had no wish in the least to marry him, and provided Sir Arthur believed her, he would still be furious at Charles. Neither man liked the other, and they would take satisfaction in crossing each other.

Stepping over Wang, she hurried down the hallway toward a set of stairs and eventually out of the house, passing only one startled servant along the way. She had dressed herself back in her own clothes, but with her hair in disarray and sans a bonnet, she must have presented quite the wild vision. Outside, she did not recognize the lawn and square before her, but if she kept walking, she would come across a street she knew. She guessed she was somewhere in or near Mayfair.

The sun shone unusually bright after the storm of the prior evening, but the air was still cool, and she began to wish she had pilfered a coat. Returning to Sir Arthur now seemed to hold little promise and would make Charles miserable. She could leave London. Go to Liverpool, perhaps. She had heard there were many blackamoors there. Charles would be hard-pressed to find her.

She had no money upon her, but all she would require was enough to travel by post, and the one person likely to give her money was Lady Sarah.

"Miss! Miss!"

She had made it to a street large enough to support traffic and was about to make inquiries with a passerby when an unfamiliar voice called to her. Terrell had not thought the voice directed at her till she heard footsteps closing in on her. It was a young man of average build, a wide brow and discerning eyes. His clothing was ordinary but tidy. He looked upon her as if he knew her, but she could not place him.

"Your pardon," the man said, "but you were the young woman with Mr. Gallant, outside the millinery shop."

Terrell stiffened. "Who are you, sir?"

"The name is Phillips."

"I know you not."

She continued walking.

"Mr. Gallant knows me."

She slowed but resumed her prior pace soon enough.

"Does that name not give you pause?" he asked, following her.

"Why should it?"

"He seemed on rather intimate terms with you."

This time she stopped. She turned and narrowed her eyes at him. "Are you some manner of spy?"

"Spy? You insult me, miss. I am a reporter for *The Independent.*"

The Independent. Had Sarah said it was an oppositionist paper?

"Are reporters much different from spies?" Terrell returned.

The man colored.

"Have you been following me?" she challenged. "With the intention of spreading vicious rumors of a fine gentleman?"

"No. I was on my way to see Mr. Gallant with news regarding the burgess of Porter's Hill."

"You are not a friend of Mr. Gallant?"

"He would not likely regard me as a friend, but he will thank me for the word I bring him."

Her pulse quickened. She wondered what news the man had. "And you are to be trusted?"

"It will be in the paper, but I thought he might wish to know sooner."

"Know what, Mr. Phillips?"

"That Mr. Chester means to quit the race. He will

not stand for Parliament."

"Mr. Chester? But why should he quit? He has the support of the Brentwoods."

"It cannot compare to the support of Sir Arthur."

"True, but much can change before the final vote is tallied, and his odds, though low, are not impossible.

"He is quitting for personal reasons."

Her mind churned. If Mr. Chester was no longer in the race, then Charles might be able to pick up the support of the Brentwoods. He might stand a chance.

"Are you certain?" she asked.

"I spoke to the man myself, for I happened to be standing outside the m...well, he saw me and we conversed. You have an interest in the election, miss?"

Since Mr. Phillips had seen her with Charles, she could not deny she knew him. "I am acquainted with Mr. Gallant and wish him all the success he deserves. If ever a man could serve in Parliament with honor and integrity, it is Mr. Gallant."

Her voice quivered with more emotion than she intended. The reporter was intrigued, and she wished she had not spoken.

"You admire him."

"How can anyone not? He is a gracious gentleman and most charitable. You see, when you had spotted us, Mr. Phillips, he had taken great pity upon me, for he knew I had once been a slave in Barbados and was treated most poorly. Mr. Gallant was kind to me, as an uncle might be kind to her niece. I think I fell in love with him that day, but, alas, he could never return my affection. I can only pine for him and wish I had not been born a blackamoor."

Her words made Mr. Phillips visibly uncomfortable, which was what she had hoped. She did not think it wise to converse much with the man.

"How were the two of you acquainted?" Mr. Phillips asked.

"You are very prying."

"It is the nature of my occupation."

"I would indulge your questions, but I am in some haste to reach my destination."

She turned from him and spotted a sedan chair. What luck! She did not often see sedans, but as it was chilly and she supposed she was some distance from the Red Chrysanthemum, it was the perfect mode of transportation. She turned back to Mr. Phillips. "By chance, would you be willing to spare a sixpence?"

He looked her over, not knowing what to make of her odd appearance. She was without bonnet or even a shawl, but her gown was of quality.

"I will," Mr. Phillips said, "if you answer my questions."

"I will answer three of your questions and no more."

"Fair enough."

She hurried over to the sedan and asked if the carriers were free to take a passenger. They were and asked her destination.

"Eight pence," one of the carriers said of the price.

She looked to Mr. Phillips, who pulled out his purse.

"I will remember your kindness, sir," she said.

"What is your name?"

Deciding that providing her name could not do more harm, she answered, "I have but one name.

Terrell."

"How did you come to know Mr. Gallant?"

"We have friends in common."

"Indeed? Such as?"

She thought for a moment. "Sir Arthur Reginald."

"Sir Arthur? Of the East India Company?"

She smiled as she entered the sedan. "I have answered your three questions, Mr. Phillips."

The carriers lifted the chair and went on their way. It was near dusk when they passed near Mayfair, and she had a sudden inspiration and called to the carriers.

"I wish to stop at Berkeley Square first," she told them.

She directed them to the Wendlesson residence. Once there, she prayed that the viscount was home. This time she did not go by the servants' quarters and went up the front steps, surprising the footman who answered the door.

"His lordship, please," she informed the man with her most imperial air.

He hesitated.

"Or perhaps I should ask for her ladyship?" Terrell mused aloud. "The viscountess has such a sweet nature, I know she would not turn a visitor away."

Suspecting that Terrell might be trouble, the footman undoubtedly decided that the viscount was better equipped to deal with the situation.

He returned to show her the way to the library, where Lord Wendlesson stood waiting.

"This is most unorthodox, Miss Terrell," the viscount said after the footman had closed the doors behind him. The man did not often look of cheer, and today was no exception. He had square features, broad shoulders, and generally looked quite imposing, but Terrell was not afraid. She was here on behalf of Charles, and that gave her courage.

"It is the policy of the Red Chrysanthemum," he continued, "that members not engage with one another outside the inn."

"Save where it is mutually necessary."

He raised his brows.

"Your cousins, the Brentwoods, had endorsed Mr. Chester for the burgess of Porter's Hill," she began.

"Yes, I am aware of that. It quite surprised me. I had written a letter recommending Gallant for the burgess."

"You, too, see that he is the better, the best, candidate for Parliament."

"Yes, but why do you come to me regarding this?"

"Mr. Chester has quit the race. Your cousins are free to lend their support to Gallant, and I think they might do so at your urging."

"Gallant does not need their support. He has the endorsement of Sir Arthur."

She drew in a difficult breath. "He may not after this day."

"Why? What has happened?"

She looked down and closed her eyes momentarily to gather herself. "Because they disagree...about me."

Wendlesson crossed his arms. "Not enough cunnie to go around, eh?"

"I made a terrible mistake, but I fear Gallant will pay the price, through no fault of his own."

"I will speak to my cousins because Gallant is a

good man and because I bear no fondness for Sir Arthur. He thinks far too well of himself."

"But the support of the Brentwoods may not be enough. I understand the only Whig in the race is paying voters twenty shillings."

His jaw tightened. "Are you asking me for money?"

"Gallant will require much to overcome the deficit of Sir Arthur."

"But twenty shillings a voter?" Wendlesson boomed.

"That is the amount, yes."

"You are audacious, Miss Terrell."

She thought for a moment. She turned her large bright eyes up at him. "If there is anything I can do to persuade you…"

He stared at her, but she saw no repugnance. "You exaggerate your value, Miss Terrell."

"Perhaps something with her ladyship?" she suggested, recalling her own pivotal participation in the introduction of the viscountess into the ways of the Red Chrysanthemum. "I do recall her ladyship tasted quite delicious."

Wendlesson cleared his throat and placed his hands at his hips. "I will consider it."

She sauntered over to him, swaying her hips. "I hope you will more than consider it, my lord. I will not be long in town, and I think on the memories of you and Miss Katherine with fondness."

"You are quite insistent on Gallant's behalf."

She lowered herself to her knees. "I would do anything you ask, my lord. I know your predilections, and I can satisfy them all."

His lower lip dropped, but he quickly straightened

himself and pulled her to her feet. "No. Katherine is here. I could not." He took in a calming breath. "I will make a contribution to Gallant. Of what amount, I am yet undecided."

"Thank you, my lord. If I am able to exceed your expectations of me, would you consider as much as twenty shillings a voter?"

"Perhaps. Mr. Laurel will not be paying *every* voter twenty shillings."

She nodded. "Will you and Miss Katherine be at the Red Chrysanthemum tonight?"

"I had not intended to make a visit, but you make an enticing proposal, Miss Terrell."

Leaving the Wendlesson residence, Terrell felt much better. She had cost Gallant Sir Arthur's support, but she had done what she could to compensate for the loss.

* * * * *

"Well, well, look who's come crawling back," Sophia sneered. "I knew Sir Arthur would tire of you soon enough."

Too intent on what she needed to accomplish, Terrell brushed by Sophia and made her way upstairs to her old room, astonishing Sarah, who lay beside George while he napped.

"What are you doing here?" Sarah whispered. She got out of bed and placed another blanket over him. "What has happened? Did you attempt to—"

"Charles has asked me to marry him," Terrell blurted.

Sarah was rendered speechless, confirming to

Terrell that such a thing was shocking, preposterous.

"He has?" Sarah responded.

"Because you told him. You told him I was with child. He could not have known otherwise."

Sarah's face fell. "I thought he should know. I thought I acted as your friend, truly I did, Terrell! I admit I had not thought he would resort to—"

"I'll not let him do it," Terrell insisted. "I need to borrow money, for I mean to leave London. For Bath. Or Liverpool. I will repay you when I can."

"You are leaving Sir Arthur then?"

And Charles, Terrell added.

"What of the...child?" Sarah continued.

"I will think on what to do after I have settled."

Still flummoxed, Sarah became silent again.

"You will help me, will you not?" Terrell pressed.

"Why will you not marry Charles if he would have you? Do you know how many women would not hesitate to take his hand and celebrate their fortune?"

Sarah did not say it, but Terrell knew she also implied, not unkindly, that such a prospect was the best a woman such as herself could hope to receive.

"I would, but think what marriage to me, a Negress, must do to his standing in society?"

Sarah could not refute such reasoning. "It is a shame! He ought not suffer for what is a most noble gesture!"

"No doubt he has already lost the support of Sir Arthur, for he went and told the man that we were to marry."

"Oh my!"

"But I have hopes that all is not lost. I went to see—"

A knock at the door interrupted them. Apprehension seized Terrell. What if Wang or Charles came after her? It would be too soon. Charles could not have returned with the clergyman yet, but it would only be a matter of time before they looked for her here.

"Madame wishes to speak with Miss Terrell," Jones said through the door.

"There must be some other way," Sarah said as Terrell opened the door.

"This is the best way," Terrell assured her. "And you must promise me this time that you will not betray my intentions should Charles come to inquire. Will you promise me, Lady Sarah?"

"But—"

Terrell grabbed Sarah by the shoulders and pleaded, "I've not asked you for much, but you are as near a friend as any I could ever have. Please. Promise me."

Sarah looked tortured but relented. "I promise."

Satisfied, Terrell followed Jones into the anteroom of Madame's bedchamber.

Madame was seated on a lounge chair reading the writings of some fellow named the comte de Mirabeau.

"Miss Terrell," she greeted. "It is a pleasure to see you again. Your presence has been missed."

Terrell tried not to recall all that she and Charles had done in Madame's bedchamber.

"I came to bid farewell," Terrell said. "I tire of London and mean to settle in a new place."

"Really? You tire of Sir Arthur?"

Madame did not delay in seeking the heart of the

matter.

"I do," Terrell answered.

"But he has such wealth." Madame peered over her spectacles at Terrell's gown. "You'll not come by better."

"He frightens me."

"You poor dear. But why not come back here? I have treated you well, have I not?"

"Perhaps, for this night at least, if I may."

"But of course. You can stay with Miss Sarah. And perhaps we can discuss how you might become a member again."

"I will consider it. Only…" She looked down, wondering how to tell Madame that she might need to *hide* in the inn.

"Master Gallant has not visited in some time."

Terrell looked up sharply.

Madame smiled. "You think I did not know?"

Terrell flushed.

"It is *du passé.* Water under the bridge."

"He is the reason I do not wish to stay," Terrell admitted.

This surprised Madame some. She arched a thinning brow. "We have much to talk about, *ma cheri.*"

Terrell hesitated. She had always felt Madame held her own interests in priority first.

"Come, sit," Madame urged with motherly gentleness, patting her chair.

Terrell decided she had to tell Madame something, for if Charles should come to the inn, she might need the assistance of the proprietress to hide from him, especially if Charles should arrive at the same time as

Wendlesson.

Yes, she needed to enlist the aid of the proprietress. Thus resolved, she took a seat beside Madame.

Chapter 52

Given what, according to Mr. Phillips, Terrell had told the sedan carriers, she could only be headed to the Inn of the Red Chrysanthemum. At least she was not fool enough to return to Sir Arthur.

Charles glanced out his parlor window to see night falling. At least darkness would prevent her from traveling much farther. He turned to Mr. Phillips, who had graciously waited for his return.

"I thank you, sir. It is most fortuitous that you came to call when you did."

Charles cursed himself for not having trussed Terrell to a chair or the bed. He should not have underestimated her, though he had been surprised to arrive home and find Wang nursing a wound to the head.

"You are in some haste to catch Miss Terrell?" Mr. Phillips inquired.

"I am."

Charles gestured to the clergyman, a Mr. Collingsworth, who had been sitting quietly in the corner.

"You see," Charles said to Mr. Phillips and he pulled his gloves back on. "I mean to make her my wife."

The surprise gave Mr. Phillips whiplash.

"When you have the time and if you have the inclination, I will relate to you why I wish to honor the sacrifice she has made for me," Charles continued, "but if I do not make haste now, she might forever be out of my reach."

Charles thought of Greta. Never again, he had told himself.

The carriage, which had conveyed Mr. Collingsworth and himself, remained at the ready. Though Wang had sustained a blow to the head, he offered to come along. The men rode in mostly silence. Mr. Collingsworth was an occasional member of the Red Chrysanthemum and had much admired a young Italian who frequented the inn, but the latter, after marrying the daughter of a baron, came no more.

To Charles, the carriage took an interminably long time to reach the inn. The light in the lantern had gone out and needed to be relit. They had to slow through one of the narrow cobbled streets. And once they had to stop because a drunkard had stumbled before them and would not rise. When the carriage finally pulled up in front of the inn, Charles was out of his seat before the vehicle came to a complete stop.

"Master Gallant! Mr. Collingsworth!" Baxter greeted. "What a pleasant—"

"Where is Terrell?" Charles asked.

"Terrell? I know not that she is still here."

Charles paled at the prospect that she might have come and gone. He turned to Wang, who knew his orders before Charles would speak, and took up a position outside the inn so that he could see anyone entering or leaving.

"If you would wait in one of the parlors," Charles said to Collingsworth, "I will be as swift as I can and return you to your home once the service has been performed."

He reached into his coat to ensure that the special license was still there, then made his way upstairs. If Terrell had come to the Red Chrysanthemum, she would have spoken to Sarah. He knocked at the door to the room Sarah and Terrell had shared.

"Master Gallant," Sarah greeted with less surprise than one would expect if Terrell had not already been here. "Your pardon. Georgie is still asleep. He woke up at an ungodly early hour."

"May I come in?" he asked.

She seemed to hesitate but opened the door farther. He stepped in and scanned the room. Terrell was not there.

He turned on Sarah. "Where is she?"

"Gone, I suspect. I gave her money to travel by post to Bath."

He closed the distance between them and gazed down into her doe-like eyes. "You lie worse than Terrell, Miss Sarah."

She flushed and lowered her eyes. "She made me promise. I have betrayed her once already—"

"It would be in her best interest that I find her.".

"I think what you attempt to be most valiant, Master Gallant."

As she appeared on the verge of breaking into sobs, he decided not to press her. Someone else in the inn would tell him. Jones or Tippy. Maybe even Sophia.

"*Mon cherí*, what a delight to have you grace us

with your presence tonight," Joan said as their paths crossed in the hallway. "Will you join us for dinner?"

"Terrell is—or was—here," Charles said. "Where is she now?"

"She spoke of leaving London."

"Then she has left? Already?"

"I would try the nearest posting inn if I were you."

"No coach would leave at such an hour."

Joan shrugged. "Why not join us for dinner then? You can resume your search of her later."

He found it curious she had not asked *why* he sought Terrell. He grasped both her shoulders. "When I agreed to oversee the Red Chrysanthemum in your absence, you said that I could ask of you any favor. I ask it of you now. I require your assistance in making Terrell my wife."

Her shoulders sagged. She pursed her lips. "Very well. But only for you, Charles. Truly, I never would have guessed *you* of all people to fall for the blackamoor. Are you quite certain you wish to marry her? Is it truly necessary?"

"Yes and yes. Now where is she?"

"She is still here in the inn, but where exactly, I do not know."

"I will search for her room by room, and I will have the assistance of Jones. I will not leave till I have found her."

She nodded.

Charles started with the attic and told Jones to begin searching the rooms on the third floor. Finding no sign of Terrell, Charles proceeded to the second floor. He began with the room at the back, the scene of much anguish and tortured pleasure. He set his lantern down on the table where they had fornicated. He passed by the pillory in which she had been taken by Wang on one side and he at the other. Heat stirred in his groin. Though it had not been one of his proudest moments, he took consolation in the fact that she had wanted the punishment at some level for she had spent several times that night.

He looked behind the curtains and under the bed but found nothing. He went through the other rooms on the floor and saw Jones come down the stairs, shaking his head. They checked all the rooms on the first floor, then checked the servants' quarters. No Terrell.

Then he realized there was one place he and certainly Jones would not think to try: Joan's chambers.

Charles went back upstairs and threw open the door to the anteroom.

But he sensed her presence.

He sauntered into the room. He walked around the furniture and even glanced into the fireplace. Perhaps she was in the bedroom. The door being opened, he went to stand at the threshold and scanned the room. Hearing a faint rustle behind him, he whipped around and saw her. She must have been hiding behind the door. With long, quick strides, he crossed the room and yanked her back in by the collar of her gown. He shut the door so she couldn't escape.

"Enough of this!" he growled. How many times did he have to wrestle her down? She was like a lamb knowing it was being brought to slaughter.

Whirling her around, he pinned her to the door with his body. Her attempts to kick him became fruitless. He held her wrists above her head and tried to gaze into her eyes, but she would not look at him.

"Terrell. Terrell!"

She shook her head violently, as if doing so could plug her ears. Unable to secure her attention with words, he kissed her, clamping his mouth down full and hard upon hers. She resisted, and breathed hotly through her nose. But he only pressed down harder, devouring her lips until hers parted, allowing him entry, allowing him into the depths of her mouth and perhaps her soul. She quivered, making the blood pound in his head, threatening to disperse all thought. Fiercely and unrelenting, he probed her mouth with lips and tongue, and little by little, her resistance began to ebb.

His hips pressed into her of their own accord. He moved his mouth off hers and kissed her throat. Breathless, she said nothing. He could sense her trying to gather her forbearance, attempting to ignore the effect his mouth was having upon her. But it was too late. He, too, was tempted to give in to the lust flaring through his veins.

"We could do this the hard way," he murmured against her neck. "I could arouse you, then deny you, over and over, all night long, if necessary. I would ravage your body with pleasure, torment it with all manner of wicked delights. Our last time would pale in comparison to what I would do tonight, but we shall be married, Terrell, you and I. You may choose to do so without defiance and struggle. Or you may choose to beg for my hand."

She groaned. "Please let me be."

"Why? So you can find yourself another man like

Sir Arthur? Or die in an alley after drinking some dubious brew? I know you love me, Terrell. You can no longer fool me into thinking otherwise."

She stared at him, a touch of wildness in her eyes. "It is because I love you that I will not permit you to ruin yourself."

"You would ruin me if you leave,"

She furrowed her brow.

"I would search for you," he explained. "As far as Liverpool or Scotland or farther. I would not be able to tend to the election, and polling begins in barely a sennight. I would miss being proposed at the husting and addressing the voters. Because I could think on nothing but you. Because my mind, my body could know no rest till I have found you and made you mine. Thus, it is far, far better that you marry me, Terrell."

Moisture glistened in her eyes. "Oh, Charles, I am sorry. I am truly sorry. I should never have desired you—or I should not have been so selfish—"

"Shh. It is not like you to lament the past, to regret and dwell upon what might have been. Your resolve to press *forward* is a quality I both admire and hope to emulate." He dropped her wrists and ran his thumb along her trembling bottom lip. "There is much in you I adore, Terrell, and I should be more than happy to call you my wife."

At last she yielded, surrendering into his embrace. He held her close till her shivering quieted.

"Are you cold, my dear?" he asked, feeling her hands.

"A little, though my heart is warm and in danger of bursting. I worry that I shall wake and find this all to have been a dream."

He smiled and kissed her.

"Or that you shall wake and find it a nightmare when you are not...when you are not elected."

"All may not be lost. Mr. Phillips—he's a reporter—came to tell me that Mr. Chester has decided not to stand for Parliament."

She nodded. "Yes."

"Come. I have a clergyman waiting downstairs. Joan and Baxter will bear witness to the ceremony, and then, we shall return home, as husband and wife." His eyes glimmered rakishly. "And consummate the marriage, of course."

She hesitated. "We cannot."

"We will marry or do nothing else."

"No, no. I cannot return with you straightway. I expect the Viscount Wendlesson here tonight."

He could hardly believe his ears. *Bloody hell.* She expected Lord Wendlesson? After abandoning himself and Sir Arthur, it had not taken her long to set her sights on another. He felt like driving his fist into the door behind her.

"Why are you expecting Lord Wendlesson?" he demanded.

"I—I made him an offer. He will likely bring Miss Katherine."

Not mollified, Charles asked through gritted teeth, "And what is this offer? Do you intend to lift your skirts to him?"

"Anything he wished."

"*Damnation.* There is no way in hell I am going to let my wife fuck another man!"

"It would be in your interest to allow it."

"How? How is it in my interest?"

"Because he might consider a significant contribution so that you could match Mr. Laurel."

Charles looked upward and let out a haggard sigh of relief. His jealousy returned to a simmer. He tightened his grip on her arms.

"You must stop making these arrangements, Terrell, and bartering your body for my benefit."

"It is the only currency I know."

He stared into her eyes, luminescent with emotion, with a love that truly humbled him.

"Please let me do this," she pleaded. "It would do much to relieve my distress, my regret."

His frown remained, for he was still uncertain how he felt about spending his wedding night with the Wendlessons, though the Wendlessons had unwittingly thrown him and Terrell each on a course that could not avoid collision.

"I think his lordship might consent to have your presence as well," she said, playfully adjusting his cravat.

"I will consider it—after we are married." He wrapped his arm around her waist and yanked her closer to him. "And after I have administered your punishment."

"My punishment?"

"I told you, when I went to fetch the clergyman, to behave yourself. And what do you do? You shatter one of my vases—a rare porcelain from the Yuan dynasty—over my valet's head."

"How is he?"

"It would take more than a vase to destroy Wang."

She blew out her breath, then looked up at him

with a grin. Her hips slid subtly along him. "Are you certain you wish to wait until we are married first before rendering my punishment?"

He grabbed her arse tight. "Yes, but worry not. I will ravage you soon enough. Mrs. Gallant."

Chapter 53

As they walked down the hall from Madame's room, Terrell began to tremble. Her legs felt uncertain. Sensing her unease, Charles clasped her hands in his.

"I mean to make you happy, Terrell," he said.

Her eyes brimmed with moisture as she looked upon him. "It is not my happiness that concerns me. I am in greater danger of being far too happy than not. But you—"

"Do not presume to know more than I what comprises my happiness."

"What of Mistress Scarlet?" she persisted.

"What of her?"

"Do you not love her? What if she were to return?"

He released her hands and took hold of her shoulders, his gaze penetrating deep into hers. "Terrell, it is of no consequence if she returns. While it is true that my affections for Greta may not have vanished—I do not think we ever cease to care for those we have loved—it is you I wish to marry and you I *will* marry. If I have to tie you to a chair, I will. Do not tempt me to gag you as well."

She scowled at him. "If you did, I would not be able to speak the vows."

The corner of his lips curved upward, and she thought she might melt at the sight of his smile. To have such a man for her own—to *marry* such a man—who was she to have merited such incredible fortune? And she had thought, when first she became mistress to a man of means in England, that she could know no better life.

She looked down at her torn and dust-stained dress. "I fear I present a poor bride for you."

"That matters not."

"Let me at least make myself as presentable as possible. And let Sarah know. After all, she had hand in this."

She could see that he was not pleased to delay, but he relented with a warning. "I have Wang standing guard outside the inn, should you attempt to flee. And if I have to chase after you, I promise that after I have caught you, your arse will receive such a tending to that you will not be able to sit for days."

Her backside tingled at his words. She retorted, "Do not entice me with such threats."

She turned to leave, but he caught her wrist, yanked her to him, and kissed her with a passion that knocked all breath, all thought from her. When at last his lips released hers, her head continued to spin. Her body hummed.

It was a parting reminder of what awaited her.

"Be quick," he told her.

Not to be outdone by him, she grabbed the lapel of his coat with one hand and wrapped the other about his neck, bringing his mouth back down to hers. She ground her hips at him till she felt his length pressing into her belly. Heat flared through her from head to toe. She was, most certainly, damned by her desire for him. She could put a thousand miles between them, and it would not diminish her yearning.

"Be *very* quick," he reiterated when they had separated.

As she hurried upstairs, she glimpsed Charles leaning against the wall. He put his head back and drew in a deep breath. She had to admit that undoing a Master of such poise and forbearance was most exciting. And arousing.

Sarah knew it all the instant she saw Terrell. Her eyes lit up with glee.

"Thank God!" she cried as she stepped into the hallway so as not to disturb her slumbering son. "You have come to your senses!"

"And he may come to his and realize the grave error he has made," Terrell returned.

"Hush! Is it not plain the man is in love with you?"

Terrell paused. "He did not express it in words."

"He need not! His actions speak for themselves. But how marvelous for you both!"

Unable to contain herself, Sarah threw her arms about Terrell, surprising her with the exuberance of the embrace.

"And when is the wedding to be?" Sarah asked.

"Tonight. Here."

"Tonight? How is that possible?"

"He obtained a special license."

"My goodness! Well, he is a man prepared."

"But I, no doubt, look far too wretched a bride."

They heard a cry from behind the door. George was awake. Sarah looked Terrell over. "I have a thought. Wait for me downstairs in the dressing chambers."

"Charles told me to be quick."

"For goodness' sake, this is a *wedding*. You have not even had the benefit of preparing a trousseau or exchanging gifts. I will be down shortly. Now, go."

Sarah had taken on the air of a general before his army. Terrell obeyed and went downstairs to the dressing chambers. The last time she had been in the room, she had selected a costume of breeches and a man's coat. Sitting down at a vanity, she examined herself in the looking glass. She looked a little tired, but she could not use the white powders to conceal the shadows beneath her eyes. Still, there was a luminescence, perhaps the glow of happiness, to her countenance.

Tippy burst into the room. "Miss Sarah told me to come assist for there is to be a *wedding* here!"

Terrell said nothing. She did not want to call attention. A part of her still did not believe the moment more than a dream from which she would wake.

Sarah appeared shortly after and, setting down George, immediately went to assess Terrell.

"I wish I had one of my prior gowns to lend you!" she sighed. "Alas, all my belongings belong to Sir Rowan. I do not think anyone here to possess one fine enough for our purposes."

"I had only intended to fix my hair," Terrell said.

"We've no proper wedding gowns," Tippy said, eager to participate in the excitement, "but we've costumes fit for a princess."

Intrigued, Sarah followed Tippy to the wardrobe. Tippy pulled out a sheer linen fabric.

"An Egyptian princess," Tippy supplied.

"What a marvelous idea!" Sarah replied. "You will

be a bride to remember, Terrell!"

Sarah would brook no protest from Terrell. She and Tippy divested Terrell of her garments and put her into a sheath held up by two wide straps. The neckline of the dress came naturally below the breasts, but Sarah thought some propriety in order, despite their being in the Red Chrysanthemum, and moved the straps to cover the nipples. Tippy draped the sheer linen on top, then found a crimson and gold turban. A gloss of rouge to the lips was the final touch. Sarah and Tippy stood back to admire their efforts.

"Oh, Miss Terrell!" Tippy gasped, clasping her hands together.

Terrell looked at her own reflection. The costume did suit her more than a white gown of silk and organza. She even decided against footwear, as was her custom in her days at the inn.

"I have kept Master Gallant waiting long enough," Terrell said when she had found her breath.

Tippy held the train of the drape as they proceeded down the hall to the parlor, where Charles waited with the clergyman.

"What is this?" asked Sophia as she came upon them in the hall.

Terrell stiffened. She felt she still owed the woman retribution, though, faced with the prospect of having more happiness than she had ever thought possible for herself, she could be more forgiving. Or not.

Sarah positioned herself in front of Sophia. "Take care you do not sully the bride with your person."

"The *what?*"

"Did you not know, Miss Sophia?" Tippy said,

giddy, and plainly forgetting the animosity between Sophia and Terrell. "Miss Terrell and Master Gallant are to be married! And 'tis no farce!"

"Come, let us be on our way," Sarah said.

They passed Sophia, who was bereft of words and could only gape in stupendous disbelief.

Sarah leaned in toward Terrell. "The best revenge is a life lived in happiness."

"I suppose," Terrell replied, wickedly thinking another fistful of Sophia's golden locks would satisfy as well.

They stopped before the parlor doors, and Terrell felt the thumping of her heart.

"Well, you are bent on taking one of my most valued members from me," Madame was lamenting from inside. "Nevertheless, I wish you all the happiness you deserve, my dear Charles, but I do hope others will not follow in your steps."

Sarah entered to announce the bride.

"That was hardly quick. I told her—" a disgruntled Charles began, but his words dissipated on beholding Terrell's entry. His jaw fell open as he took her in from head to toe.

There was silence as they all looked to her. A few of the servants, including the cook, Baxter, and Jones, had assembled to witness the only wedding to take or have taken place in the Red Chrysanthemum.

"Why was no one at the door?" a deep and commanding voice boomed. "I thought—What the devil is this?"

The Viscount Wendlesson, his wife behind him, came upon them. For a moment, Terrell worried that the man might not wish to honor their arrangement if she was a married woman.

Madame began to explain how the Inn of the Red Chrysanthemum was a place where the extraordinary could happen.

"For now we may even claim a wedding to our credit," she said.

Lord Wendlesson looked from Charles to Terrell, and it seemed his frown deepened.

As Madame continued, Charles said something to Baxter, who took his leave briefly and returned with Wang. Terrell took a sharp inhalation. She owed the man an apology for the bump on his head. Wang met her gaze and bowed. He was a man of little emotion, but he seemed rather satisfied and had perhaps forgiven her already.

"Well, Gallant," said Wendlesson, "you are a man of surprises, I must say, and great brazenness."

"Courage," Sarah objected.

"I suppose." He looked at Charles keenly. "You never struck me as the whimsical sort and must understand what it is you do."

Terrell felt her chest tighten. Here was where Charles would come to his senses. A man such as Lord Wendlesson would know how to impress reason upon him.

But Charles crossed to her and took her hand. "I hope you will stay to wish us felicitations, my lord."

"Most certainly!" the viscountess exclaimed, then glanced at her husband, fearing she had spoken out of turn.

"You have a proper license, I take it?" Wendlesson inquired.

"Bearing the seal of the Archbishop of

Canterbury," Charles replied.

"You will need witnesses."

"Indeed."

Wendlesson looked to Mr. Collingsworth. "Then let us proceed."

The trembling returned for Terrell as the clergyman began. She barely heard the words he spoke, but she heard each and every word of Charles'. His gaze did not leave her as he made his vow.

"I, Charles Gallant, take thee, Terrell, to be my wedded Wife, to have and to hold from this day forward, for better for worse, for richer for poorer, in sickness and in health, to love and to cherish, till death us do part, according to God's holy ordinance; and thereto I plight thee my troth."

Hers was not as perfectly delivered, and her voice shook as she echoed his prompts. "I, Terrell, take thee, Charles Gallant, to be my wedded Husband, to hold—er, to have from this day forward..."

He pressed her hands. "Breathe."

She took a deep breath. "To have and to hold from this day forward..."

"For better for worse, for richer for poorer."

She imagined if he should be as poor as she one day. Was it possible such a thing could befall him? If he should lose his position with Sir Canning? If he should be cast out of polite society?

All of a sudden, she was clear that all the things she had thought she desired, that life of luxury she had known as a courtesan, were nothing next to Charles. She would want him even if he had not a penny to his name. She could support the two of them.

She thought of her belly. Nay, the *three* of them.

"For better for worse, for richer for poorer," she said firmly.

"In sickness and in health."

"In sickness and in health."

"To love, cherish and obey."

She smiled as she spoke, for it did not escape her that the word "obey" was not in the groom's vows. "To love, cherish and obey."

"Till death us do part, according to God's holy ordinance; and thereto I give thee my troth."

"Till death us do part, according to God's holy ordinance; and thereto I give thee my troth."

She exhaled the breath she could not release earlier. His smile set her heart aglow.

"Now with the ring," said Mr. Collingsworth.

Charles stiffened. "The ring. Damnation."

He and the others looked about for what might serve until Wang handed Charles a circle of green jade.

Charles sighed in relief and looked at Wang in awe. "How did you...?"

But knowing the Chinaman would unlikely answer, he turned back to Terrell and took her hand.

"With this ring I thee wed, with my body I thee worship, and with all my worldly goods I thee endow: In the name of the Father, and of the Son, and of the Holy Ghost. Amen."

Everyone echoed an "amen" as Charles slid the ring in place. He cupped her face and brought her lips to his. She quivered still upon the inside, but there was, too, a rapture as engulfing as the most poignant lust. How far she had come from the fields of

Barbados! She had thought nothing could taste sweeter than freedom, but in that moment, she was wrong.

She had herself the best possible Master, and doubted she would ever want to be free from her present bondage.

Epilogue

Charles stroked the back of her head, which she had dropped to the writing table before her. They had just returned from the husting, where, the polling having ended, the returning officer declared Mr. Laurel the victor. Charles looked at Terrell with sympathy. His new wife was more disconsolate over the results than he.

"It was close," the senior Gallant said, taking a seat in the drawing room. "Perhaps close enough to warrant calling for scrutiny."

Charles shook his head. "It would only give Sir Arthur more time to marshal his votes and witnesses."

Mrs. Gallant turned to Terrell. "My dear, I will have tea and a bite to eat brought to you. You must be quite tired."

Terrell had stood before the husting daily for six days while the polling took place.

Charles was glad to see his mother's kind treatment of Terrell, whom he had never seen so terrified as the day she met her mother-in-law. Informing his mother of his nuptials had not been easy. He had sat his mother down, without his father, for the elder Gallant was not as strong as his wife. A state, Charles thought wryly, not too dissimilar from his own.

In the drawing room where they now congregated, Charles had delivered the news to his mother.

"You will not, hereafter, need to prompt me with regards to matrimony," he had said after he had ensured she had taken a seat, though he thought he should have had some smelling salts on hand.

Mrs. Gallant was intrigued and sat at the edge of the sofa. "Indeed? Who is she?"

"Before I give you her name, I will first tell you how much I admire her: her strength, her courage, her...passion. She has gone to such lengths for my happiness, or what she deemed would make me happy, that I would not have done myself. I have wronged her, in several ways, but she forgives my faults."

"Wronged? What wrong could you have done?"

He took her hands in his. "My dear, I wish for you to understand how much I wish to make her happy, and in so doing, assure my own happiness. She would trade her life for me, and I would do the same."

"Goodness! Who is she? Why have you told me none of this before? You have been keeping me in the dark!"

"I admit I have because I knew not how you would receive her. She is far from our place in society, but it would bring me great joy if you could take her into your heart as you would a daughter."

"I would gladly if my son loves her to such depths, and if she loves you."

"Her love could rival yours."

She tightened her hands about his. "Tell me who she is, Charles! I cannot wait to meet her!"

"You will not till you have heard the whole of what I wish to convey. It is no quaint romance, but you were wrong to think I could not find love at the Red Chrysanthemum, as you had found father."

He had spared his mother all the details and instead spoke of how he and Sir Arthur had become enamored of the same woman while at the Red Chrysanthemum. His mother had frowned a little when she realized the woman who had captured his heart was certainly a member there, but she, a former member herself, could not cast stones. Charles had told her of Terrell's arrangement with Sir Arthur, how devastated he had been when it seemed he had lost her to another man, and how the discovery by Mr. Fields made him realize that he had to take action.

"If Sir Arthur's support was contingent upon her," his mother had worried, "then will you not have it if she leaves him?"

"I bid you set aside your concerns for my election," he had urged, "and consider the matter of my heart."

He had told her how Terrell refused to leave Sir Arthur, even after Charles had told her of Sir Arthur's horrid past.

"I felt I had little choice but to kidnap her," Charles had said.

Mrs. Gallant's lower lip had dropped to the floor. "Charles! What madness!"

"I wanted—I did propose to her then. But she, still believing that I should benefit from Sir Arthur's support, refused me."

This had had his mother dumbfounded.

"Yes, it wounded my pride greatly," Charles had

acknowledged, "especially as I had gone to great lengths to procure a special license."

"A special license!"

"But when I went to find a clergyman, she bolted. She had intended to leave London without money, without support, and with only the clothes on her back."

Mrs. Gallant, flabbergasted, had also become vexed with him. "Were you not going to invite your own family to your wedding?"

"I was not going to let her slip through my hands, my dear."

He had divulged then that he was married. The service had taken place at the Red Chrysanthemum with Joan and the Viscount and Viscountess Wendlesson as witnesses. Charles had not been particularly pleased to see the Viscount enter at that critical moment, but the witness of his lordship would lend further credibility to the marriage.

Charles had omitted the part of Terrell being with child. He had provided enough for his mother to fret about. She had been beside herself when he revealed that it was Terrell whom he had married. Mrs. Gallant had seemed to vacillate between disbelief and disquiet. However, she had eventually rallied herself and vowed she would support her son to the ends of the earth and that anyone who turned upon them be damned!

"This is not a paper I read," the senior Gallant said, holding up *The Independent*, which had arrived with his letters.

The only other person Charles had informed of his marriage, besides his parents, was Mr. Phillips.

Charles had half expected to find news of his marriage to a former slave in the paper, but Mr. Phillips had refrained from writing any of it.

"Why, it says here," said Mr. Gallant of the newspaper, "that the family of Sir Arthur's former wife wishes to reexamine the elements of her death, including the suspicion that Sir Arthur might have *caused* her death!"

Terrell raised her head. "An investigation might keep him too busy to—"

Charles shook his head subtly at her. He had not yet told his parents how Sir Arthur had vowed to see Charles ruined. Thus far, he had not felt the full weight of Sir Arthur's wrath, but he expected it would come.

The maid arrived with a tray of tea and refreshments. His father finished reading the paper, then declared himself ready for a nap. His wife offered to assist him into bed. Charles stood admiring how well Terrell looked in her spencer and stylish headdress, though he rather missed her costuming in the Red Chrysanthemum and liked it when she dressed in nothing but one of his shirts. Of course, he liked her best stripped to the buff. If they were not in his parents' drawing room…

"I should have sought more contributions for you," she bemoaned. "We could have appealed to Madame. I'm sure there is an arrangement I could have offered. Or perhaps I should have approached Sir Fairchild…"

Charles gave her a sharp look. "It is enough that I permitted your arrangement with Lord Wendlesson."

He had not wanted to consent to spending their wedding night with the Wendlessons, but Terrell had begged and pleaded such that he agreed for *her* sake. He had insisted, however, he be present. In the beginning, he struggled with what he might do if he had to watch Terrell take the viscount's cock into her mouth or, worse, elsewhere. If Wendlesson should land too heavy a hand upon her, Charles would be hard pressed not to pommel the man.

But soon enough, arousal overcame all other sentiments as he and Wendlesson watched Terrell caressing the viscountess, worshiping her body with hands and lips and tongue. Terrell had shown Miss Katherine how to take cockmeat orally. Charles had then had the idea of tying the two women together. Wendlesson had been particularly impressed. In the end, the night had not been as devastating as Charles had feared.

"When will the next elections take place?" Terrell asked.

"We will talk of that another time," Charles replied, taking the copy of *The Independent* his father had been reading. "It surprises me that Mr. Phillips did not report on our marriage."

Terrell smiled. "I think Mr. Phillips a little enamored with you."

Charles looked at her half-eaten plate of cheese and cold meats. "You ought to eat more, Terrell."

"I have eaten plenty! If I eat more—I look as fat as a sow already!"

He shook his head. The first time she had accosted him, she had reminded him of a panther. He would always liken her to a panther.

"Eat," he commanded. "The sustenance is not for you alone."

"I will not. And if I had known being married to you entitled you to order me about, I would not have let you cajole me into marriage."

"I am not instructing you as your husband...but as your Master."

He heard her sharp intake of breath, and his cock hardened in an instant. She feigned vexation, but he saw the corners of her mouth curl. He cupped her chin and all he could think of was how much he wanted to ravish her then and there.

"You would not dare," she murmured. Or taunted.

"I would not underestimate me if I were you. After all, I now have your submission—for life."

Even as he spoke, however, he had the feeling that it was he who would render the final submission.

THE END

ABOUT THE AUTHOR

EM BROWN is an award-winning multi-published author of contemporary and historical erotic romance. She found the kinky side to her writing after reading stories at Literotica.com. She likes to find inspiration from anywhere and everywhere, be it classical movies, porn, embarrassing high school photos, her favorite Sara Lee dessert, and the time she accidently flashed an audience with her knickers.

For more wicked wantonness, visit
www.EroticHistoricals.com.

www.ingramcontent.com/pod-product-compliance
Lightning Source LLC
Chambersburg PA
CBHW071633260626
47170CB00001B/81